4

Delayed
Rays
of a Star

Delayed Rays of a Star

A NOVEL

Amanda Lee Koe

NAN A. TALESE

DOUBLEDAY *New York*

Copyright © 2019 by Amanda Lee Koe

All rights reserved. Published in the United States by Nan A. Talese/Doubleday,
a division of Penguin Random House LLC, New York, and distributed in Canada
by Penguin Random House Canada Limited, Toronto.

www.nanatalese.com

DOUBLEDAY is a registered trademark of Penguin Random House LLC.
Nan A. Talese and the colophon are trademarks of Penguin Random House LLC.

Poetry on pages 32–33: "Klage" by Rainer Maria Rilke; on page 47: "Lebenslauf II" by Friedrich
Hölderlin; on page 226: "Der Panther" by Rainer Maria Rilke. All translations from the
German by the author.

Text on pages 90–93 adapted from Walter Benjamin's "Gespräch mit Anne May Wong. Eine
Chinoiserie aus dem alten Westen," in: ders., Gesammelte Schriften, Bd. IV/1, S. 523–27.
Translated from the German by Pauline Fan.

Book design by Maria Carella
Interior images (pp. viii, 385): Alfred Eisenstaedt / The LIFE Picture Collection / Getty Images
Jacket images: Women, left to right—Eugene Robert Richee / John Kobal Foundation;
    John Kobal Foundation; Frederic Lewis / Archive Photos; all Getty Images. Camera—
    Bettmann; fan—John Kobal Foundation; both Getty Images. Flowers and geometric
    pattern—Shutterstock
Jacket design by Michael J. Windsor

Library of Congress Cataloging-in-Publication Data
Names: Lee, Amanda Koe, 1987– author.
Title: Delayed rays of a star : a novel / Amanda Lee Koe.
Description: First edition. | New York : Nan A. Talese, Doubleday, 2019.
Identifiers: LCCN 2019004675 (print) | LCCN 2019013510 (ebook) | ISBN 9780385544344
    (hardcover) | 9780385544351 (ebook)
Subjects: LCSH: Dietrich, Marlene—Fiction. | Wong, Anna May, 1905–1961—Fiction. |
    Riefenstahl, Leni—Fiction. | BISAC: FICTION / Literary. | FICTION / Biographical. |
    FICTION / Contemporary Women. | GSAFD: Biographical fiction. | Historical fiction.
Classification: LCC PR9570.S53 (ebook) | LCC PR9570.S53 L393 2019 (print) | DDC 823/.92—dc23
LC record available at https://lccn.loc.gov/2019004675

MANUFACTURED IN THE UNITED STATES OF AMERICA

10 9 8 7 6 5 4 3 2 1

First Edition

To Kirsten

Either the puppet or the god.

—Heinrich von Kleist,
"On the Marionette Theater," *On Dolls*

Contents

1

efore she crossed the ballroom to ask the Chinese woman for a dance, Marlene unloosed a curl from the crown of her finger wave, letting it fall across her forehead. It was a habit, now mostly unmindful, that she had acquired for herself as a schoolgirl, every time she wanted the attention of a classmate or the teacher.

Even from where she had been standing, Marlene could smell the fresh magnolia tucked behind the Chinese woman's left ear whenever she moved, which was often. This woman was cutting up the foxtrot, polka, and waltz, even as gouty gents swathed in silky cummerbunds trod on her toes, shod not in shoes but dance slippers, and so providing a winsome view of the high arch of her foot. To be sure, Marlene did not know if it was more that she wanted to dance with the woman, or to be together with her at the center of attention. The most satisfying thing about going with the moment was not having to wait to find out, but a pomaded, middle-aged man had stuck his cane out just as Marlene was about to reach her.

Ahem, he coughed.

Marlene raised an eyebrow. She'd crashed the ball on a producer's last-minute extra invite, and while it would be disappointing to be thrown out so soon, she would not have been sorry for dropping by. But the stranger had not meant to chase her away. She saw him point now, crooked thumb perched over thick fist, to the line of men waiting their turn behind him.

Ah, she said.

He dismissed her with an imperious nod, flashing Marlene a close-range view of the snot-clotted snuff flecking the nose hair extending unevenly from both his nostrils. Unkempt daddies in expensive suits were disgusting. She joined the queue to dance with the Chinese woman. After waiting for a quarter of an hour she grew bored and stepped out of line. Slouching against the wall, she wedged a fresh cigarette into her pipe-shaped cigarette holder, appraising the violin-ists' playing. The only legitimate job she'd known before her current gig with the cabaret-theater and her bit parts in a string of abysmal movies—which, combined, barely defrayed her rent—was second vio-linist in a movie palace, scoring silent images as part of a live orchestra.

Stepping out of the music pit's anonymity to try and catch the light on the stage or screen sounded dreamy, but Marlene was realistic about her prospects. After watching her latest film cameo, where she entered a room for less than five seconds to set down a teacup for the leading lady, Marlene exclaimed to her friends: I look like a potato with hair!

Everyone breathed a sigh of relief that they would not have to cod-dle her and pretend otherwise, although they remained encouraging: Your big break is bound to come!

Better sooner than later, Marlene said darkly. I'm almost thirty, these pups aren't going to stand at attention forever. With that she weighed her left breast in her right palm, like a savvy hausfrau sizing up sweet oranges at a fruit stall. Anyway, she went on in a loud voice, why must a woman always have beautiful breasts? Accustomed to her skylarking even in a quiet café by day, Marlene's friends did not blink as she joggled her own flesh up and down, attracting affronted looks from the nearest patrons. They can afford to sag a little, can't they?

Not even so long ago, Marlene was committed to the impression that she would be an accomplished concert violinist in the near future. How sobering to have circled up to the realization that while she was adept at the violin, past a certain proficiency, technical competence meant little to nothing. Skill was predictable. The movie palace paid, but it was not the concert hall. What was her magic, and where did it live? She was afraid, too, of giving up the violin to chase down an aspect of herself that might be absent rather than dormant, and then having to disingenuously explain away the embarrassment of failure as a lack of fair opportunity. Midway through the score for a roman-tic dramedy one evening, Marlene saw with limpid clarity how seam-lessly the path of the movie-palace second violinist segued into that of the middle-of-the-road music teacher in an all-girls school, the private violin tutor for provincial children and their cornball parents.

The next morning, she tendered her resignation. The manager took her aside.

You're one of our better players, he said. I want you to know that.

Thank you kindly, Marlene said. Tell me, do you believe in God above? She scooted closer to him. Involuntarily, he squirmed from the unexpected proximity. Yes, she prompted as she blinked up at him, or no?

Why yes, he stammered. Of course I trust in Him. Don't you?

Alas for me, Marlene said, no. So you see, she added as if for his benefit, if there is neither savior nor paradise in my world, it would be best to be singular in this life.

She pretended not to notice the manager shuffling a half step away to reinstate between them that more respectable distance. All the best, he pronounced gingerly, as she prepared to take her leave. A bead of sweat traversed, with comic timing, the side of his forehead. Marlene dropped her hat, and then her coat, as she burst out laughing.

Now the ballroom violins were inching on to a flimsy and polite Strauss waltz.

Marlene scowled down an oversimplified glissando till it tailed off. Looking up, she saw the Chinese woman curtsy away from the man with the snuffed-up nose hair at the front of the line. Throwing his hands up in disbelief, he refused to let her pass but was elbowed aside by a bushy-haired brunette in a long-sleeved dress. A short way behind them was a photographer with his camera. A waiter capered about the coterie of shiny people in motion, offering up flutes of champagne. What a circus!

Tipping back her drink, Marlene went over.

As if dancing with no pause was not enough of a challenge, Anna May had to beat her gums and keep up light conversation with every white chump who wanted to know her name, what was it like in China, how long would she be in Berlin, was she really a Hollywood actress, maybe they could show her around, all while making excuses for those who went off rhythm and stepped on her feet. She was perspiring steadily under the arms. Her dress was sleeveless and black, so there was no worry about sweat stains, but she wanted to catch her breath, and her mouth had tired of smiling.

The last heeler spun her in and threw her out with such smug gusto, as if she were a newly purchased hand-loomed carpet he was unfurling in his sitting room for all and sundry to admire. As the tune petered out, he leaned in. She thought he was bowing his thanks.

Just so you know, he whispered right by her ear, I'm a high roller on this continent.

Unsure of what she was supposed to do with this information, she went with: That's neat.

Well, he said. Have you decided with whom you'll spend the night?

Anna May bit down on the inside of her cheek to cover up her wince. Three men ago she told herself to turn the next dance down. Each time, as the following guest stepped up, she found herself unable to say no, and she saw that in any case everyone was more than happy to misread her hesitation for shyness, even anticipation, as they took her hand. What she found repellent here was her unvarying incapacity, at times like these, to react in immediate accordance with her own feelings. She found it easier to fleece herself than to leave someone else less room to stand. Things had to hit the skids before she insisted on her terms. As the music changed, finally, she curtsied politely away from the next man in line.

He, middle-aged and greasy-haired, was not amused by her rejection.

After all, he said in German-edged English, refusing to budge as he waved his cane at the queue and his place in it. Who must you think you are? She, too, might have liked to know the answer to his question, but to help them both out of it, she said: My apologies, but I am afraid I am much in need of a glass of water.

All the waiter had was Moët & Chandon.

He promised to come back with some water.

Sparkling, he said, just for you.

Still is fine, she called out after him, still water is better for me if you wouldn't mind, but he had already left to fetch up the seltzer. When Anna May turned back, a flour-faced brunette in a long-sleeved metallic knit dress was standing rather too close, introducing herself as "just like you—also an actress—but here in Berlin." She was well dressed, if in the self-conscious way of a freshly clipped poodle, and she had quick, darting eyes. With no small talk, she wanted practical tips for transitioning into Hollywood. Already I have appeared in several Berg-films, the brunette said. Are there mountain movies in America? Do I need an agent?

I'm not sure about mountains, Anna May said, but as long as it has a love story—

It's true, isn't it? A blonde stepped in, interrupting their conversation apropos of nothing. Only pansies know how to dress like a sexy woman.

Anna May did not know what she was talking about, but the woman had a charmingly nasal voice. A wavy lock of hair came loose across the blonde's forehead as she took a short drag on her cigarette, tucked vertically into a holder shaped like a pipe. She nodded approvingly toward a gamine man in a red dress. The man's dress was cut down to his coccyx, and he was on the arm of a man in a velvet smoking jacket, with a matching wine-red rose for a boutonnière in his lapel.

Personally I find such aberrations troubling, the mountain-movie actress said, after the couple had passed. The world might as well be topsy-turvy.

The blonde exhaled smoke into their faces without blowing it upward.

What's not to like about a topsy-turvy world, the blonde said, pushing back the curl from her forehead. Women would be kings, and I'd wear pants all the time.

Anna May saw the brunette clutching for a rejoinder, but before she could open her mouth, a dignified-looking man with a camera (or was it just a man with a dignified-looking camera?) approached them. The brunette surged forward to exchange a social embrace with him.

He wanted to take their picture.

All three of us, the brunette hesitated, together?

Yes, the photographer said, if they found themselves suitably inclined?

As the three shuffled together, the blonde met Anna May's eye. Her gaze was sportive and insolent. Did this woman go through life looking at everyone this way, and how did that pan out for her? Before Anna May could look away, she was wet down the front of her dress.

The flute of champagne had slipped from the blonde's hand.

I am so sorry, the blonde said, holding up Anna May's string of pearls, dabbing the damp with a scented silk handkerchief. I ought to be spanked thoroughly!

At this, the brunette gave a scandalized snort. Though he tried to hide his amusement, the photographer was clearly enjoying the frivolous spectacle. The wet fabric clung to her skin, and Anna May tried to hunch her ribs and breasts away from the surface of the dress. Far from home for the first time, she had already been nervous enough—worrying that she was embarrassing herself even as she enjoyed herself—even without an infelicitous wardrobe hiccup.

Prior to the voyage, she'd prepared an annotated list of questions and answers.

Can you tell us about the films you have acted in, what projects are you working on in Europe, who are your favorite directors, how did you know you wanted to be an actress? She'd made phonetic annotations in her notebook on how best to pronounce Robert Wiene (VEEN) and Fritz Lang (LAHNG), but thus far the question most often put to her was: How do you mean you aren't from China? Having been born

and bred in L.A., Anna May had to admit that she well and truly had
not thought to prepare for that. When she was little, her father told
her China was on the opposite side of the world from California. Later
she asked him if that meant people walked upside down in China. Her
father laughed, patted her head. The conclusive answer never came,
and she did not dare ask again.

It was something the boy who sat behind her in class had said.

His father was an anthropological craniometrist.

People in China walk upside down, the boy explained matter-of-
factly, that's why your brains are less developed. Having long learned
to hold her tongue with him, she said nothing. Why don't you give up
already? the craniometrist's son had asked her before, when she'd chal-
lenged him in an argument. It doesn't matter if you're right or wrong,
he said with a meaningful smile beyond his years. You're never going
to win at anything. Right before Anna May asked just what he meant,
he pulled slit eyes at her, and she understood perfectly. Dressing for this
party, she'd teeter-tottered between wanting to look her glamorous
best and fearing she would stand out too much. At the last moment,
she'd eschewed ornamentation for the simple black dress with sheer
paneling at the shoulders, and pearls worn long. Going with black was
a stroke of luck, there would have been nowhere to hide her face here,
in a roomful of fashionable strangers, had she sustained a wine spill on
a light-colored gown.

A waiter was kneeling by her feet to pick up the broken glass with
his white-gloved hands. Don't worry, she thought she heard the blonde
say, I'll make it up to you. Anna May was distracted by the heady fragrance of the blonde's handkerchief. There was nothing sweet about
it. It reminded her of leather-bound books and the jute gunnysacks of
Chinatown spice merchants.

The blonde winked.

Taken aback, Anna May tried to recall if she had ever been winked
at by a woman. No, she believed this might be the first time. There was
nothing spiteful in the blonde's eyes, but why else would one woman
spill her drink on another at a fancy party?

I

All evening Leni attempted to put herself in the photographer's line of sight so he would take her picture. She knew him to be one Alfred Eisenstaedt, up and coming with the fashionable magazines, in good standing with the noteworthy papers.

Of all moments for him to choose to notice her, it had to be this: regrettably sandwiched between an Oriental visitor, who would surely snatch the focus of the photograph by way of those foreign looks, and the chintzy wannabe, whom Leni had spotted playing bit parts in recent movies. What an odd picture it would make, and how lucky for the blonde to be included in it at all, when she was not even a real actress, just another eager skirt trying to break into the industry! Leni could sniff out that skunky optimism from a mile off, and it took substantial effort to keep herself from wrinkling her nose at the woman.

Mentally distance yourself from mediocrity if you want to look good in the picture—

Teeth or no teeth?

No teeth—eyes carrying smile, chin tucked gently, elbow articulated just so as it fell against side of body. Leni had tested out enough self-portraits from different angles, with varying expressions, to discern that in general she photographed most enigmatically when she pressed her lips together and inclined her head. The first pneumatic temporized action device she bought as a self-timer for her shutter was spring powered. It offered a delay of one and a half to three seconds. When a cable-release model appeared on the market with a nine-second upgrade, she ordered it immediately.

Leni wished she could check her appearance first in a mirror, but there was no time. Men like these, who favored a lightweight Leica over an imposing Hasselblad, were drawn to the putative authenticity of spontaneity.

First she stood in the middle of the two women, then she moved to the left. It would make a better portrait if the Chinese woman stood in the middle, and besides, if Leni stood at an angle, it would balance out her irregular gaze. When Leni was born, her mother cried bitterly upon seeing that her baby's eyes were slightly crossed. For nine months her mother prayed as she carried her to term: Dear God, give me a beautiful daughter who will become a famous actress! The ardor of her mother's prayer came from the ambition she'd stowed away in her own heart, one so secret yet so routine, so hallowed yet so trite, among girls across every epoch of time: she, too, had wanted to be an actress. Anything could be achieved, as long as you applied your will to it. All through her teenage years in suburban Berlin, Leni tried to coach her lazy eye into balance with a hand mirror, till it was barely noticeable in person. She only had to be careful in photos, wherein the defect was occasionally apparent.

Leni was anxious about her future, that is, she believed it was bright and would like for it to come faster. She'd given her first public modern dance recital, at twenty-one, to a sold-out audience. A wealthy admirer had sponsored the concert hall, and was chivalrous enough to buy up a whole chunk of unsold tickets. Nothing was so difficult if you got to know the right people. When Leni broke her knee, it was far from the end: she began to carve out her transition into acting while still on crutches and managed to attract the attention of a director before her bones healed. Not yet twenty-six, but already with a varied body of work to call her own, Leni wanted to be the reason for things, to have her name known, and she was pleased to consider herself immaculately on track.

Quite unlike second-rate nobodies like the blonde, who in their last-ditch desperation resorted to making a scene in public. Nothing pained Leni more than having to put up with a woman who did not know how to act like a woman. Some people should be barred from parties; just look at what the blonde was wearing. She needed an urgent referral to a good couturier—if she could only afford one! Garish sashes with busy prints crisscrossed her body, and had she really thought to tie a white swan's feather to her purse? Her style alone was enough to give Leni a headache. This was the Berlin Press Ball 1928, not the Bavarian Yuletide Fair 1890. The blonde had tried to steal everyone's thunder with her idiotic pipe-shaped cigarette holder, and when no one paid any attention to that, she had the cheek to spill her drink on the Chinese actress visiting all the way from Hollywood. What would she think of Berlin now?

To Leni's surprise, they were sharing a laugh, and the Chinese actress had not kicked up a fuss. She was even game enough to relight the blonde's half-smoked cigarette. The blonde had to inhale with all her might because the cigarette holder was so thin and long. She started coughing from inhaling too deeply. The Chinese actress patted her on the back. The cigarette went out again.

The photographer had a smile on his face: Ah, *women*.

Leni pictured what he saw. She could perceive with ease the audience or camera's viewpoint, reversing how things appeared to herself. She had an instinct for mise-en-scène, and would later apply a dancer's understanding—that beauty was *line*—without reserve to every canvas. Floating her arm in a deconstructed arabesque, capturing the grace of gravity in an acrobatic high dive, counterpointing the stark swastika of a Party flag with a twenty-thousand-strong marching contingent— she had a singular talent for visual harmony, and she never passed up a chance to show it. What is my crime? Leni turned around and asked the press after the war. Don't let's be unsporting after the fact. If the films I made were really propaganda, would they have toured film festivals and won prizes? I was good at what I did. He saw that in me, nothing more. Naturally, none of this discouraged the papers from churning ever more lurid and pulpy headlines: RIEFENSTAHL'S NAKED DANCES FOR THE THIRD REICH; NAZI SLUT WITH A MOVIE CAMERA.

Eisenstein made movies for Stalin, Leni said to the papers, and nobody calls him a slut. Was it that I made movies for the NSDAP, or is it that I am a woman?

But retrospection is a ripe-looking fruit a few sly boughs out of reach. We are not given to know if its flesh is tart or sweet until everything is too late. To be fair, as of this moment that whole scrum of set pieces was still up in the air, and things could have gone any which way. The Great Depression was still a year off, the re-formed Nazi Party had garnered a pitiful 2.6 percent of the popular vote in the latest federal elections, Hitler was just another rabble-rouser slapped with a public-speech ban who'd recently renounced his Austrian citizenship for fear of being deported back to Linz, and Leni had yet to pick up a movie camera. She was simply an actress posing for a photographer alongside two young women at a party, sliding her left foot up so the dress would fall around her calf and flatter the line of her body, imagining how the picture would turn out as she heard the shutter click: in the foreground their three bodies of proximate height—all three were tall, the Chinese woman ever so slightly taller than the other two—in the background, a gilded mirror framed by banded wallpaper.

The photographer turned the knob swiftly with his thumb to advance the film, sounding a ratchety zip, the amorous call of a lonesome cicada on a quiet summer night, half a second of blinding flash lapsing into the white heat of the party, as the likenesses of these three women were registered scrupulously together by the evenhanded and all-seeing eye of his camera.

The Sole Purveyor
of *Madame Bovary*
in Beijing

2

Marlene had fashioned for herself the dainty idea that if she put her face on and made everything in her room perfect, the boy would call again. But there was hardly enough lip color left to paint her mouth with, the lilies reeked, and the once-a-week maid was late.

Fiddling for her mother-of-pearl opera binoculars on the bedside table, she trained its sights on the crystal vase across the room. Lily watching: an indoor sport she'd grown marvelously good at, aside from that crick in her neck. She watched the lilies for what she would have approximated, at maximum, to be ten minutes, but it turned out, at least according to the bejeweled hands of the wristwatch she kept bedside, that an entire hour had gone by. For an eighty-eight-year-old woman who lived alone, this was some dubious and frightful business, but Marlene shrugged it off and turned back to her binoculars, just as a flaccid lily head nodded right off its wilted stalk onto the white carpet.

She zoomed in.

Dead rat, she would have cried out loud, were there someone in her apartment to hear it. Kaput penis! But she was quite sure that she was on her own in here. She went back to excavating pigment out of the burnished tube with her pinkie finger. When she had scraped up a nub of color, she applied it carefully, searching for the impressionist blear of her mouth in the back of a silver spoon.

IT HAD BEEN some time since Marlene had looked into a mirror, and even longer since she had last seen natural light. She had not left the house in more than a decade. Aside from the beaded glass lamp and the TV near the foot of her bed, it was dark in her apartment.

Her ruined legs had disqualified her from standing by the fifth-floor window and enjoying its view onto the rooftops of Paris, but propped up in bed, all-purpose slouch supported by goose-feather pillows and a sheepskin rug, that snippet of sky she could still glimpse had been adequate consolation. The solace it afforded came to the rudest end several years ago, when a tabloid photographer hired a forklift and planted it on 12 avenue Montaigne.

Impersonating a maintenance worker, he floated the platform right outside her window and pointed a telephoto zoom lens in. When she squinted at the cocked head and raised elbows, Marlene thought he was an assassin with a punt gun. Much obliged, she shut her eyes and arranged her hands in a chaste clasp under her breasts, for a star of Marlene's amplitude was compelled to go in one of two ways: loud or early. Not adroit enough to die young, she was uneasy about her octogenarian obit, had frittered away many a sleepless night worrying over the building superintendent discovering her body deliquescing gently into a bedpan. Homicide was more chic than cancer, and it wasted neither time nor money. Was he the fan who couriered homemade brownies frosted lightly with his semen this Christmas past? Baby let me melt in your mouth, the card ended. Or the one who sent a photograph of his shaved calf, on which an oversized, startlingly photo-realistic tattoo of her much younger self had been inked?

Son, she wrote back soberly. Start saving up for the laser.

Still alive, Marlene opened her eyes. Pointing her binoculars at the window, she saw, too late, that it was the enemy: a photographer. Elbows first, she thrust her way out of bed. When she pushed some weight on one leg, her knees protested right away. As she fell, she threw her sheepskin over her face to hide it.

THE PICTURES APPEARED exclusively in a gossip magazine called *Oops!*

Glamour was far from effortless, and she'd been willing to work hard for that illusion, but the part no one talked about was how the fallout grew harder and harder to manage. Her image was an enormous strain as she aged. Holding the fort as long as she could, she'd gone into hiding once it was impossible to keep up. It was too late to stop, then or now, when she had built an entire life around a half truth. Marlene paid the super a small fortune to install blackout drapes in her apartment. The one last thin leak of light, straight-edged between drape and window, was eliminated with heavy-duty tape. In the darkness, she'd tried to cheer herself up: It's just like being in a womb. For some reason, this thought felt hideous. She shelved it quickly and tried again: It's like being in a movie theater before the movie begins!

Every so often, Marlene pictured distinctly the morning sun heating up the muggy waters of the Seine, Notre Dame's rose windows, and that newfangled pair of fiberglass pyramids poking up outside the Louvre that everyone had bemoaned as monstrous. She loved it all. Her favorite Italian butcher, whose half-chewed leathery cigars she smoked while he tenderized her veal cutlets, the Russian hole in the wall she patronized in a copper wig and dark glasses, where the resident musician, a hulking man with hands like baseball mitts, made her sob with the light-footed hymns he performed on his violin.

None of it belonged to her anymore, and it had been years since she had applied foundation to skin and rouge to lip, but now that she wanted something from the universe again, Marlene was prepared to make some effort, for surely her physical energy conducted itself irresistibly into the invisible forces governing this planet and its abstruse connections. This was hardly the enfeebled nonsense of a woman a year or two shy of ninety; she characterized her convictions as metaphysical rather than spiritual. Since pubescence, she, a Capricorn circa January 1901, had been a steadfast believer in astrology. Her audacity she attributed away to her birth chart. Before she stained her best skirt with her first period, she'd already sacked her name to make it her own: Marie Magdalene. That was much cleaner and clearer, trimmed of the pretty hypocrisy of ecclesiastical gilding.

As for her surname, that could stay: she liked everything about it.

Dietrich was the word for *a skeleton key that opens all locks.*

To incubate the boy's phone call, she had been for the past week dressed in a nude chemise slip and her signature swansdown coat, custom made from the lithesome feathers of three hundred white swans— PETA had written an impassioned letter to say that a trendsetter like Marlene was under obligation to dress far more responsibly—for her Vegas cabaret premiere in 1957. She had two identical coats fitted out for a queen. They trailed such long tails she had hardly been able to move around onstage in them. One of the coats had gone to a museum, and the other she'd tailored down into a less cumbersome piece. Three phone calls came since she'd made it a point to dress up, but none had been the one she wanted, so today she was breaking out her lucky diamond bracelet and the makeup.

Every third stone studding the diamond bracelet was paste.

Marlene had begged it off her favorite aunt for a violin recital back in boarding school. As long as you wear them like they're all diamonds, Aunt Jolie had said, I promise you no one will be able to tell the difference!

Finishing up with lipstick, Marlene moved on to mascara, but the mascara wand she soon dispensed with, because this rheumatic hand could not apply mascara to eyelash without intermittently stabbing eyeball. No matter, when the maid arrived with her flowers and newspapers, she could help. Her hands were small but they were steady.

THE SLOW-FESTERING LILIES smelled alarmingly as if they were not on the mantel, but right next to her. It was a sick, wet blond smell that made Marlene swimmy in the head and clammy under the arms—to think that fresh flowers in showy bouquets used to precede her person!

Privately, her favorite flower was the modest tuberose, but ever since she'd played Shanghai Lily in *Shanghai Express*, no one thought to gift her anything else. Press conferences, studio trailers, and hotel rooms brimmed with her signature bloom. She never stopped to admire them; anything in great quantity soon becomes a small nuisance. When traveling, Marlene used to request two bathtubs. One to soak in, the other to jettison all the cut flowers. She should not have been so flippant back then. Now that she was bedridden, the flowers were out to get their revenge. Steeling herself, Marlene raised an armpit to chance a sniff. Just as she feared, her smell was indistinguishable from the weeklong wilt of the lilies.

Peeling her pillowcase back, she reached in for her YSL flacon and misted the air around her liberally, masking with eau de parfum the odor of floral decay diffused evenly with oxidizing piss. That came from the Limoges pitcher under her bed. The current maid was good about cleaning out the pitcher and the casserole dish, but the previous help, a middle-aged Iberian woman, had the nerve to make a face.

Everyone should be glad I can still pee, Marlene had said to her crisply.

The maid had to go when the landlord came around demanding the rent Marlene had owed for three months. Hernia, don't listen, Marlene said, but the woman had thrown off her apron and exclaimed in Spanish. Marlene didn't understand her, but the landlord did: She would like you to know, once and for all, that her name is Hermínia, not hernia. Marlene stated that it was extremely rude for someone to come into your house, tell you what to call your maid, and throw around fanciful words like *arrears*. She'd run out for the moment. These things happened.

She was informed that they were about to begin seizing her personal effects.

Lay off, Marlene bellowed, shaking an already shaky fist at him from the bed. I'm not quite dead yet, and if natural causes aren't quick enough for you, you are most welcome to plot my demise! Let me tell you upfront what would please me, she added. A knife in the neck, just make sure it's sharp. You could be famous.

For a week Marlene cowered in her bed, picturing herself as a crippled hobo plying the boulevard Saint-Germain. At least let me take my sheepskin, she thought, a sheepskin makes everything nice. Then someone from the French culture ministry stepped in and quietly began paying her rent check, *"en continuant à apprécier votre rectitude et votre intégrité pendant la guerre."* They even agreed to throw in a new once-a-week maid.

To have old morals pay new bills! Marlene felt royale.

She wrote back, signing off with Bisous rather than Cordialement, and pinned her Legion of Honor medal above the bed like a crucifix to ward off the cold, keen blood of rentiers.

3

Bébé ran down the Champs-Élysées in her pastel-pink maid uniform, outsized bouquet of lilies in hand. In a certain mood she held the lilies in the crook of her elbow like an infant, and in another she held them by her side, the flowers upside down, facing the pavement.

Today she was late, so she hugged them to her chest, the better to run faster.

At 12 avenue Montaigne she whirled through the front entrance, catching her breath to thank the doorman. Entering the fifth-floor apartment with the key she had been given, she made her way toward the bedroom. The old woman was snoring gently as she approached. At first Bébé thought Madame's face had been injured. Then she saw that it was badly applied blush and eye shadow. Lipstick missed her mouth widely, and she had spittle on her chin.

Bébé took a tissue to the spit without waking Madame.

Only a few low-wattage lamps lit corners of the apartment, but by now she knew the place well enough to navigate without bumping into anything. Bébé prepared a fresh pot of black tea and set it down on the table with the telephone. Madame had three tables positioned around the perimeter of her bed. The one with the telephone had a Rolodex on it. Another carried an assortment of hard liquor, shot glasses, and cutlery. The last was full of stamps, envelopes, and picture postcards of Madame as a young woman. She sent these back to fans who wrote her. Every week Bébé brought a pile down to the concierge, who would take them to the post office.

Madame was stirring.

Good morning, Bébé said as she lifted the duvet with care, folding it down around the hips. Madame preferred having her legs covered. You're late, the old woman said drowsily. Look at the flowers! She pointed at the offending lily head on the carpet. I'd planned on screaming at you, Madame continued, but I don't feel up to it right now. I'm sorry, Madame, Bébé said. The trains having delayed. She served up the hot tea, blowing on the surface to cool it down. For god sakes I've told you I'll pay for your cab, Madame said. How can anyone expect to get anywhere on public transportation, and who knows what germs you'd catch and bring to me in here. Come, help me put on my face.

The old woman put down the teacup and raised a mascara wand.

Bébé cupped Madame's face and applied mascara steadily. She averted her eyes from the filmy translucence of the chemise, under which Madame's breasts hung low and loose. When Bébé was done, Madame peered into the unpolished back of a soupspoon, where hardly anything could be seen. Wonderful, Madame said. We'll see if he doesn't call now. Then she reached over to catch Bébé's chin in her hand, turning it this way and that in the sparse light.

Are you wearing any makeup? Madame demanded.

Bébé shook her head, no.

What nice skin you have, Madame said, and the blush in your cheeks! Most of us need our war paint to get by, she added as she ran a dry, knobby finger down the side of Bébé's face. You know, the makeup man is an actress's closest accomplice, in more ways than one. On any set, he alone knows the right number to call when the producer needs to awaken an actress who has overslept—which means he knows what numbers *not* to call. Do you get my drift, choupette? Or perhaps you are a virgin?

Bébé felt herself blushing. The old woman laughed and let go of her chin.

SETTLING MADAME DOWN with the papers, Bébé placed the giant magnifying glass into her hand. Madame should have had reading glasses, but protested vehemently that glasses were for ne'er-do-well grandmothers. She waited for Madame to open up the papers before ducking down to reach the waste receptacles under the bed. For her bathroom needs, Madame insisted on a two-quart casserole dish and a porcelain pitcher with hand-painted roses. The smell of fresh news-print masked momentarily the stench of overnight urea as Bébé con-veyed dish and pitcher from the room. When she first started clearing

Madame's waste, Bébé was startled by how old-people piss smelled nothing like her own. Theirs was rich and mineral. Back in her village in Taishan, they had an outhouse with no plumbing. Heaped together, it had not been possible to isolate whose smelled like what.

In the summer they buried it over and started a new hole.

One evening after her shift on a Sunday with Madame, she made her way to the 13th arrondissement, where Chinatown was said to be. Walking under the red decorative arch with 唐人街 emblazoned across it and into the stink of wholesale vegetables and two-day-old uncollected garbage, an old man shuffling past her in broken rubber sandals worn over thickly socked feet, singing under his breath in Cantonese, the apartments crowded like bad teeth, a garish floral bedspread hanging out the window alongside an enormous faded bra, Bébé felt a revulsion that was far more tender than she might have guessed it to be. How was it that when her people traversed the world and disembarked in a port of call so far from China, they could still make their part of Paris so recognizable, so homely?

Sometimes, cleaning bathroom floors in the cavernous office building she worked at on weekdays, or flushing down loose stools at Madame's on Sundays, she found it hard to see what being here was worth. But walking out of the subway to avenue Montaigne never failed to remind her that it was Paris, she'd made it to *Paris*, she was the first child on both sides of her family to have even left Guangdong province. Falling in step with well-dressed Parisians in muted colors on cobbled passages, browsing fashion magazines she could not read at street-side newsstands, stopping short at the next roundabout as a rush of pigeons landed on the outstretched arms of a limestone sculpture, Bébé felt better, then worse, then better again.

TODAY MADAME'S STOOL was shaped just like a petit-croissant.

She flushed it down, the petit-croissant shape coming apart with the force of the water. Bébé was fascinated by the different breads available in Paris. Bread for her meant something very different from rice. She made an effort to remember the names of all the breads, practicing their pronunciations so she would not make a fool of herself at the bakery: baguettes, boules, croissants, fougasses.

She washed out the pitcher and the pan with the bidet, scrubbing them down with pine-fresh cleaning liquid. This she'd bought for Madame with her own money. The old cleaning liquid smelled like a hospital ward, not a home. When Bébé brought the pitcher and pan back into the room and stowed them under the bed, she turned the handles outward for Madame's easy access. Madame did not even seem to notice she was back with the emptied receptacles. She was busy reading the papers, making conspiratorial asides. Magnifying glass in hand, she looked amusingly bug-eyed to Bébé on the other side. Sometimes Madame read out headlines that caught her attention. Today she was stabbing at a picture of the newly unearthed remains of an Egyptian mummy. Be careful of archaeologists, Madame warned her without looking up from the papers, they are the worst. Them, murderous surgeons, and tabloid photographers! Why should a queen of the Nile be woken from her slumber, just because a few thousand years later some riffraff wants to have a poke at her face under all those bandages?

Bébé listened as she discarded last week's lilies.

Replacing them with sprightly ones and refilling the water, she shook the blooms lightly so they would spread themselves out in the vase. She did not always know what Madame was talking about, but Bébé liked that Madame talked to her anyway. Did Madame talk aloud to herself this way when she was alone, or did Madame do it only in her company on Sunday? The oven dinged and she stepped out to retrieve the cotton towels and flannel bath blankets. She'd popped them in to warm them up on low heat. Draping them on her forearms, she approached Madame's bedside with a basin of warm water. Madame went en garde as soon as she noticed the offending objects, pushing aside the newspapers as she wielded a tassled decanter. Fool, she called out, when will you understand? Bathing is for people like you! People like me have perfume.

Madame spritzed the air aggressively with her bottle.

Bébé waited for the fragrant mist to settle before approaching the bed. Before she grew accustomed to Madame's ways, she'd walked headfirst into the cloud of perfume. It stung her eyes terribly, and as she flushed them out with water, Madame could not stop laughing: Blinded by Yves Saint Laurent, serves you right! Do you know he said he would make me a perfume?

Now Bébé knew better.

Having put up her fight in principle, Madame would surrender peaceably in practice. If you started at her shoulders and worked downward Madame would screech, but if you massaged her feet through the bath blanket, folding the bed linen back bit by bit, she would let you get through with it. Reaching Madame's face, Bébé had learned to provide her with a small towel. She'd noticed that Madame liked to clean her face herself.

Today, Bébé put the towel aside, since Madame had just put all that makeup on.

After drying Madame off, Bébé slicked some moisturizing cream onto Madame's papery skin. Although she was bedridden, Madame had no bedsores. Only itchy skin, soothed by the seasonal aloe Bébé procured from the Turkish supermarket near her guest workers' dormitory. After moisturizing, Bébé trimmed Madame's fingernails and toenails, and finally, she bicycled Madame's legs forward and backward to exercise them. If Madame appeared to be in a fairly good mood, Bébé would encourage her to get up and walk across the room. Her flesh was atrophying from the bone with lack of use.

Try, Bébé said. Bed to TV.

Why should I try?

Bed to TV. Bébé hold Madame.

Stop skiving on the edge of my bed, the old woman said. Don't come so close to me. Have you washed your hands? You'd best get on with the housework before I lodge a complaint with that uppity-tuppity lawyer lady.

BÉBÉ'S MONDAY-THROUGH-FRIDAY cleaning job, in one of the administrative buildings of the city's tax department, had been arranged for by a pro bono human-rights lawyer. The lawyer's father was an old bird in the cabinet, a minister's aide. It wasn't difficult to pull some strings on a topical problem, sold smoothly as a pilot program her fledgling organization was looking to implement with selected female refugees: Bébé, two Tunisian sisters, an Iranian, a Vietnamese child. A private donor had given a substantial sum through the UN, and a bite-sized trial would help them build up a prototype for meaningful refugee integration, skill training, and job matching in the future on a much wider scale.

Bébé had asked the pro bono human-rights lawyer if she could take on an extra weekend job since there was nothing to do on weekends.

You should take yourself out, the lawyer said.

Nowhere to go, Bébé said.

It's Paris, the lawyer said encouragingly, there's lots to do.

For you everywhere, Bébé said, for me—

She shrugged and smiled.

Sensing her class-insensitive faux pas, the lawyer stammered: The parks, they are free!

SOCIAL ENTERPRISE WAS new to the lawyer.

It was deeply invigorating every time she was asked what she did now, and she got to say "nonprofit," "female refugees," and "at risk" in the same sentence. Having quit her high-flying corporate finance job in mergers and acquisitions, she was raring to go humanitarian and vegetarian at the same time to stave off an incipient menopausal midlife crisis. Founding Secondes Chances pour le Deuxième Sexe (SCDS) was more challenging than she'd anticipated. She was impatient to roll out her plans for PTSD counseling and art therapy, but of course the basic logistics like gainful employment and shared housing had to be put in place first. Her father advised her to cut it down to Secondes Chances when she was registering the charity, but the lawyer was unwilling to lose the Beauvoir reference.

Second Chances for The Second Sex, Papan. I thought you would get it right away.

I did, her father said dryly. Over dinner he told her about how the

Ministry of Culture supported Legion of Honor awardees who had
fallen into various states of disrepair, like Malraux and Sagan. The lawyer rolled her eyes. Men, she said. Her father wagged a finger. Not so
fast, he said, Piaf before she passed, how do you think she maintained
the Riviera villa? And Dietrich now, too.

She's French now, the lawyer said, is she?

Does it matter, when you are Marlene Dietrich? All the old fogies in
the cabinet are still dying to drop their trousers for her. She even wrote
a postcard addressed to Mitterrand directly, asking if he could send her
the new cordless telephone she had seen advertised on the TV—and a
maid. I miss the General very much, she wrote, he was a personification of my code of conduct. A great man. You know we have de Gaulle's
portrait in the office. Mitterrand looked up at it, muttered, "Politics of
grandeur, indeed," and told me I'd best look into Miss Dietrich's needs.
What am I now, a personal shopper for some ancient who still knows
how to milk what's left?

An invaluable skill for any woman, the lawyer joked. Actually, she
said in a serious tone now, why not use one of my refugees? They're
being trained as seamstresses, cleaners, janitors. There'll be a fair
remuneration, yes?

But, my dear, can they be trusted?

Papan!

Oh, I didn't mean it *that way*!

BÉBÉ HAD BEEN briefed by the lawyer—the woman she would be
working for on Sundays was about ninety years old, and she was once
a very famous actress. She was to be treated with utmost discretion and
addressed as Madame at all times.

Bébé did not know who Madame was, but dusting the cabinets and
shelves and looking at all the pictures, she saw that Madame was the
center of the picture even when she wasn't in the center of the picture.

The old woman had a sweet tooth.

She was always asking for dessert and pastries, and Bébé was by
now familiar with the short walk from avenue Montaigne to various

pâtisseries in the huitième. Bébé kept receipts for everything, although Madame considered herself above such things. Spare me the trouble, she would say, keep the damned change! What am I going to do with a pocketful of coins, go to the arcade?

Once Madame had craved gelato, and Bébé, afraid it would melt, sprinted back from the ice-cream parlor an avenue away, cone in hand, tripping and twisting her ankle on a curb. Disguising her limp when she reentered the apartment, she handed the cone to Madame, who licked it and declared unhappily: This is *banane*. I said *vanille*!

IT WAS MACARONS Madame wanted today.

When Madame wanted macarons, she wanted only Ladurée macarons from Rue Royale, but Bébé could pick the flavors. A trip to Ladurée was a treat. The display, which changed regularly, could be counted on to mesmerize: lilac meringue, caramelized puff pastry, Morello cherries, rose petals. Looking into the shop window Bébé felt like the sort of girl for whom the world was precious and everything was possible. Back home in Taishan she encountered a cake just once. White cream frosted over sponge with white icing, it was ensconced in an icebox and transported from the city to her village for someone's wedding, where it stood out amid steamed chicken and roasted pig, both fowl and beast with heads still on, eyes hollowed out.

Bébé snuck into the compound, watched as bride and groom bowed to sky and soil. Some adults disapproved of the white cake. Untraditional, funereal, inauspicious! Freely they dispensed negative comments, though that did not stop them from clamoring for a piece or two when the cake was cut. Bébé received a slice. How the cream tasted: like it was from a better, faraway place. She let it melt slowly on her tongue. On her next birthday, as she sat with her parents over the longevity flour noodles her mother had prepared, the same as she did every year, Bébé said: I would so like a cake next year.

She received from her father a little slap.

Though it did not hurt, she flinched as soon as she recognized the condescension in its lightness. She sat outside the house in disgrace.

Her mother came to her. Without asking, she began combing and braiding Bébé's hair, affixing a big red ribbon to the end of her plaits. For luck, her mother said tenderly, make a wish.

I wish I were someplace else, Bébé said.

Taken aback, her mother looked at her vacantly.

With an uncertain smile her mother wanted to know: Where?

Bébé ran to the creek on the edge of the village. Upon catching her murky reflection, she pulled off the hair ribbon and threw it into the water. Then she was afraid it would be spotted by her mother, so she squatted to retrieve it with a broken branch. Digging a hole with her hands, she buried the ribbon. As she washed the mud off, she pressed her palms together and whispered: Better off dead than to remain here. With the end of a twig she traced the characters in the sand: 给我留在这 我死了算了. Before she left she dribbled river water over them, so nobody but the earth could know.

Now, standing in line at Ladurée, sunlight streaming through tall windows under the champagne glow of crystal chandeliers, pointing out rose, lychee, and pistachio bonbons to fill a celadon-green gift box finished with a powder-pink ribbon, nodding while saying to the shop-girl, *Une boîte de douze*: it all made her feel so—fine. You could let yourself go in an ugly little town. A beautiful place made silent demands on your person in no uncertain terms, even as it gave nothing of itself back to you. What Bébé was enthralled by wasn't Paris. It was only the person she liked to think she could have been here.

NUMEROLOGICALLY, 1988 HAD been an outstanding year for Bébé to undertake a new venture in a foreign land. It was imperative to set out before the year was over. She was eighteen in a double-prosperity year, eighty-eight, falling under the sign of the dragon, and she had been guaranteed a job in a Nike factory in Marseilles.

For the job matching, Bébé paid a hefty brokerage commission to a subsidiary agent of the Corsican-Chinese Friendship & Trade Association in Shanghai. She'd been out of the village for three years, saving up the scant wage she made in one of the city's new textile export factories.

When she wrote her mother in Taishan to say she was leaving Shanghai for Paris, her mother asked where that was. Bébé enclosed in her reply a world map most rudimentary, hewn from hearsay and her imagination. Her mother wrote back: Shanghai is far enough. Her mother wrote back: Explain to your long-suffering parents. What is the difference between working at a factory in China and a factory in France? Her mother wrote back: Why does our daughter have a comet for a heart? The restrained and impersonal calligraphy of her mother's letters belonged to the village scribe (three yuan a page), who also read to her the letters she received in a reedy tenor (free of charge). How embarrassing for her mother to have dictated while wringing her thick knuckles on those scraps of fabric she had the gall to call handkerchiefs: 为何咱家的女儿有颗流浪的心?

Alongside three other girls from Shanghai, in the cargo hold of a ship, Bébé subsisted for two weeks on a stash of flour buns filled with preserved vegetables, and tangerine peel to stave off the seasickness. It was so hot and stuffy one of the girls fainted. They stripped her down to her underwear to cool her body, not realizing the floor had traces of ship diesel, leaving her with faint chemical burns on the backs of her calves when she woke. Upon docking, Bébé thought they'd reached Marseilles, but a tall African man appeared belowdecks and told them, in perfect Mandarin, that they were in Nairobi. Knocked out by his language skills, the girls dissolved into nervous giggles. They had to switch ships to avoid detection, he explained. The transit could take two hours, two days, or two weeks, depending. Depending on what? they asked. Your fortune, he said, as he brought them their first hot meal in a long time, a simple but delicious cornmeal paste with green peas. When he stretched over to refill their drinking water, he smiled kindly. The salty-sour edge of his perspiration reminded Bébé of five-spice powder, and she wanted to touch the kinks in his hair.

All Bébé saw of Nairobi was a crane moving a container.

They were given clearance to depart in a few hours.

Safe travels and smooth winds, the tall man said, as he chirruped like a starling and locked the hatch.

· · ·

AS SOON AS they reached Marseilles, the girls were transferred from a container in a shipyard to the back of a van with tinted windows. Welcome to the Corsican-Chinese Friendship & Trade Association, a middle-aged Chinese woman said in Cantonese-inflected Mandarin. She had a bad perm and was flanked by two stocky white men who had collected their passports upon arrival. I am gravely sorry to inform you that the Nike factory has been shut down, the woman continued. Fortunately we have for you *options*. There was a management fee for the business contacts, transactional logistics, round-the-clock protection, communal housing, but not to worry, automatic installments would allow for ongoing repayment. Things don't always go according to plan, it's hard to be on one's own in a foreign land. Ahyi understands— she referred to herself in the familiar form—Ahyi's been through it all.

The girl with the chemical burns asked: What business contacts?

Don't be stupid, another girl said, already crying. She's talking about prostitution!

What an uncivilized word, Ahyi said. We much prefer to call our girls *imported goods*.

We could report you to the police, the girl with the chemical burns said. She was beginning to hyperventilate. You're illegal immigrants now, Ahyi said serenely as she held a plastic bag over the wheezing girl's nose and mouth. Breathe, she instructed. To the rest of them she said: I can assure you life with us will be more worthwhile than life in jail.

When the van came to a stop and the side door slid open, Bébé dove out of it, vaulting directly into the thickset arms of an older white man they would come to know only as the Corsican. He pulled Bébé toward him by her hair. Pity to scalp such a pretty face, Ahyi shrugged, but it's no problem to put a wig on you. As she stepped around to the back of the van, she pushed her quilted floral jacket back to reveal a holstered handgun. Please, Ahyi said, for your own sake, don't do something like that again. What do you take us for, amateurs?

THE CORSICAN-CHINESE Friendship & Trade Association was cordially established when Ahyi and the Corsican were wed almost a decade ago, having merged their hearts to consecrate their criminal potential. Ahyi's homespun syndicate ran a job agency in Shanghai that was a front for human trafficking, specializing in a Shanghai-Nairobi-Marseilles route and a Nanjing–Belize–Los Angeles route. The Corsican's crew ran a prostitution ring. Under the Corsican's aegis an assortment of third-world women—Bulgarian, Turkish, Russian, Chinese, Kazakh—catered to businessmen passing through Marseilles.

Mostly the clientele was French and Corsican, occasionally Spanish and Italian. Nationality regardless, they were curiously the self-same species of man: middling, middle-aged, and married, potbellied or pinched in polyester suits they filled out too much or too little. The transactional logistics took place in little motels around the edge of the city center furnished with fusty beds that felt used even when they were freshly made, to and from which the girls were heavily escorted. Ahyi, who spoke a fluent if sharply nasal French with a strong Nanjing twang that made it sound more Cantonese than French, gave all of them new names.

Fresh beginnings, Ahyi said.

Bébé found hers a letdown in this regard.

In French the vowels rose and in Mandarin they descended, but "Bébé" was to all intents and purposes a phonetic facsimile of "蓓蓓." For weeks she was repulsed that all things considered, there was room yet in her for so dainty a variety of disappointment. Even so, Ahyi hadn't explained to her that Bébé wasn't really a French girl's name the way Estelle or Margaux was. One hot day months and months later in Paris, when Bébé learned in the course of the volunteer-run beginner French lessons at the immigrant activity center that her name was the French equivalent of *baby*, as in *infant*, as in *a term of romantic endearment*, as in 宝贝, she put her hand up to go to the bathroom. How do we ask politely to use the bathroom, the teacher cooed, if you please? Bébé kept her eyes on the daisy charms of the teacher's spectacle chain as she recited, pronouncing the *puis-je* and the *de bain* too emphatically: May I please go to the bathroom?

In the bathroom Bébé thought she would throw up, but there was nothing inside. She ran the tap on high, washing her face with brisk, exaggerated motions. Smoothing back her damp hair in the mirror, she gargled her mouth.

Pas de baisers, Monsieur, j'ai dit pas de baisers!

4

A *kiss is still a kiss,* a man sang as he tickled piano keys on the TV screen in Marlene's darkened apartment. *A sigh is just a sigh.* It was late on a Saturday night, or early on a Sunday morning, and Marlene had fallen asleep watching *Casablanca* when the boy called for the first time last weekend. The rhythmic ringing rattled Marlene awake. By the glow of the TV, she located the telephone and before scrambling to pick it up thought: Someone must have died.

Miss Dietrich's residence, she said with an indeterminate accent to hide the tremble in her voice, who is calling? Over the line no greeting or name was offered. Instead a voice launched evenly into High German:

> All is so far gone and long passed over.
>> Even the star from which I receive such light
> has been dead for a million years.
>> I think I heard awful words exchanged
> on a boat that went by. On the hour, a clock strikes
>> —but in which house?

Excuse me, Marlene said, dazed. Is that not Rilke?
The voice on the other end of the line laughed: So—it's true.
What's true?
You are an actress who knows your Rilke.
I'm sorry?
The voice ignored her to continue:

> I should like to leave my heart behind
>> and step out under the vast sky.
> I should like to pray. And one out of all the stars
>> must surely still remain.
> I think, I know, which one it is—

In spite of herself Marlene interrupted the stranger, pulling her voice back to deliver the poem's end from memory:

—*At the end of her beam in the sky,*
   she alone stands like a white city.

A moment of silence followed, and she began to suspect that she was still asleep. This was a dream—not a bad one at that. A tad twee, but nonetheless something she could go along with.

She heard: Excellent, Marlene.

Where did you get this number?

You wouldn't believe me, even if I told you.

Who is this?

Only a German schoolboy in Paris who heard that Rilke was Marlene Dietrich's favorite poet and wanted to please her.

Write your own lines and get a life.

That's easy for you to say, Marlene. You were born in 1901. I was born seventy years after you. Now everything has already happened. No new art of adequate meaning can come from my industrialized soul.

Your industrialized soul?

So quoting Rilke is not overreaching or derivative. It merely acknowledges my own limitations in my given time and place.

What drivel, Marlene said. What are they teaching in the schools these days?

Drivel is quite right, the voice on the phone said. Schools are conformist instruments of the state. Books are the great equalizer, and I am merely a boy who reads.

Marlene snorted.

Do your industrialized soul a favor, she said. Don't call again.

She hung the phone up, her heart beating fast. Humphrey Bogart was smiling his invitingly weary smile at her from the TV, and it seemed as if he were the one Marlene had been speaking with. Ingrid Bergman looked up at Bogie: But what about us?

Bogie delivered his famous line with gentle panache: We'll always have Paris.

34   A M A N D A   L E E   K O E

Even though Marlene had slept through the movie, she found herself tearing up from muscle memory. She'd once cried at this precise
line when watching *Casablanca,* why not cry once more? She would
like—to step out of her heart and go walking beneath the enormous
sky. She would like—to pray. Now she was really crying. She had never
been able to shed a tear on command in a movie, and she was not a fan
of the Stanislavski method, but she saw now its merits. The physicality
of tearing up had led to the emotion, not the other way around. She
wiped her eyes on the back of her hand, and picked up the phone to see
if the stranger was still there.

He was not.

In which case, this was hardly a dream. Someone had called in
the middle of the night, and Marlene had answered the phone. Hi, she
whispered to the dial tone, I'm still here.

On the TV, Bogie lifted Bergman's chin so her eyes met his.

Marlene held on to the cord of the phone, beginning to feel indignant that ten years shy of being a hundred, this fist-sized piece of pulp
in her chest could still be conned into going faster by some schoolboy
pranking with a bauble of German poetry, and tear ducts fulsomely
activated just by watching Humphrey Bogart say his lines in a movie!
Standards around here had fallen to rock bottom. This beating heart
had been the dispassionate surveyor of the finest stock L.A./New York/
Berlin/Paris/Cannes had to offer. Hemingway had once written Marlene: What do you really want to do for a life's work? Break everyone's
heart for a dime? You could always break mine and I'll give you a nickel.

Clearing her nose on her nightdress, she picked up her binoculars
and focused on the TV. Marlene observed, in close-up, Bogie watching
Ingrid Bergman board a waiting plane, as she found herself thinking
that she would not mind if the boy called again. Who was he? And of
all things, for him to have picked Rilke's "Lament"! It was one of her old
favorites. How pleased she was with herself, too, that without hesitation she had dredged the poem up perfectly, not a word out of place.

The plane was taking off.

Bogie was walking into the fog, watching Ingrid Bergman fly away
from him, his gin joint, and Casablanca. If the boy was on the phone

now, she could tell him that should have been her, for Marlene had been eyeing the leading role of Ilsa Lund that spring of 1942. Just past forty at the time, Marlene was on the lookout for a prestige project. *Casablanca* was a Warner Bros. production and Marlene was signed to Universal then, but she'd arm-twisted her agent into a possible loan. Ronald Reagan was one of Warner Bros.'s top contenders to play Rick Blaine. As for Ilsa Lund, Ann Sheridan's and Hedy Lamarr's names had been mentioned, but Marlene was looking to mount a challenge. It was of vital importance for a film actress to demonstrate that her market value as a leading lady remained undiminished even though she was no longer in her twenties or thirties. Marlene found it outrageous that her male counterparts in their forties and fifties had no problems being cast as romantic leads, but already the scripts she was beginning to receive were markedly different from before.

For ten years she'd played, exclusively and to great effect, femmes fatales.

Marlene made these stock characters entirely her own not by vamping them up or showing more skin. Her genius, which ran contrary to intuition, was simple. Because she played them bored, her characters became complex. Love is a divertissement they have long since tired of. Having seen it all, her characters go through life unmoved, with twinkling-eyed fatalism, but they'll surprise the audience yet by dropping all worldly defenses for a moment of *amour fou:* after falling for the enemy and abetting his escape in *Dishonored,* X-27 declines a blindfold but reapplies her lipstick before turning to face down a firing squad.

That was one of her favorite roles.

Now she was being asked to play the older woman, the aging diva.

Was this the fate of every actress, or had her reputation tailed off ever since she and Josef von Sternberg broke up in 1935? It was still difficult for her to think about him. Jo was smart and generous, a true aesthete whose eccentricities made her laugh. What she liked best: behind the gristly veneer of his erudite skepticism, he had a soft-centered heart. But Jo was also jealous of everything, and she could not stomach the part of him that was convinced that he owned her because he'd spotted her in Berlin when she was a nobody and cast her in his movie.

The Blue Angel was a hit, it was true, and things moved quickly after that. Paramount wanted to bring Marlene over to Hollywood immediately to be their answer to MGM's Garbo. Receiving the offer, she had dithered before Jo came to Berlin to arrange everything for her.

I don't know anyone in Hollywood, she said.

You know me, he said. That's all you'll need.

Contracted to make six films for Paramount together, they were a golden couple. Hollywood ate that candy right out of their hands even if, or especially because, they cut an unlikely figure together—Marlene was tall and radiant, Jo short and strange. On the afternoon they agreed to end it, Jo was wearing sporty white flannel trousers. Marlene recalled this sartorial inconsistency with clarity, because just then she had been flirting around with Fred Perry, who'd brought the fashion for tennis whites off the courts and into her parlor. Jo had scoffed that the only sort of men who would wear white pants to lunch were those who were all brawn and no brains, but here he was standing up in white flannels to congratulate her on their breakup as "at last an adult decision," even advising her on which directors she should work with next. As he walked away, she saw that he was crying. Good luck, he said. They won't light you like I light you. Listen to yourself, she made herself say. He left with the door wide open, and it took her a long time to rise to shut it.

The next time she heard from Jo, he was in Yokohoma.

I'm never going to make another film, he wrote her. My end is here.

Jo, she wrote back. I promise you you're going to make more films. They just won't have me in them.

AFTER HER ROMANTIC and creative partnership with Jo ended, Marlene found that shopping for roles was more daunting than she'd expected. Jo was an auteur who had written all his films around her; without him she would have to go about it just like everyone else— a working actress vying for prewritten parts. She had high hopes for Ilsa Lund in *Casablanca,* and was deeply offended when Warner Bros. announced that Ingrid Bergman would star, alongside Humphrey Bogart.

Really? Marlene said to her agent. That Swedish goody-two-shoes who doesn't wear makeup?

Reading the script for *Casablanca*, Marlene had been shrewd enough to see from the outset that the movie would stand the test of time. What would remain was the love story. Not the anti-Nazi, anti-Vichy plot—it was, after all, a U.S. Department of War Films product. That would be forgotten in the blink of a future moviegoer's eye, registering merely as a period backdrop against which idealism could triumph glamorously over cynicism. Such themes were current and urgent in Hollywood now that America had caught up with the political climate since Pearl Harbor.

They had certainly taken their time with that.

Indeed, not so many summers ago, taking her routine summer vacation in Cannes, Marlene had been incensed by Joe Kennedy preaching the benefits of isolationism to a brunch table. It had been Marlene's summer of Joes. They were all staying at the same Riviera resort—Jo von Sternberg, Joe Kennedy, Joe Carstairs. Everyone was jealous of Joe Carstairs, whom Marlene called the Pirate for the salty tattoos on her toned forearms. The Pirate was a fine sailor and, as the heiress of Standard Oil, she often picked up everyone's bill. Many a morning Marlene would sail out to sea with the Pirate on her yacht. They would drop anchor in the middle of the Côte d'Azur and scissor in the sun. When they returned to the resort tanned and sated, the brunch table would be in full swing. On this particular muggy afternoon, Joe Kennedy pontificated freely: We must proceed with caution. It would be dangerous for America to fall afoul of a country like Germany, and a man on a meteoric rise.

A man on a meteoric rise, the Pirate said. Is that all you have to say about Adolf Hitler?

Joe Kennedy sputtered on about the prudence of an appeasement policy, and not being hasty—let's see what he does now that he is chancellor and president before we judge the man too soon—but he turned red in the face as Marlene chipped in: Isn't anyone going to do anything about him before it's too late, or do I have to finish him off with my altar of Venus?

The table roared with laughter.

The American ambassador was saved by the juvenile graces of his son, Jack, who had not yet turned twenty-one.

The boy held up his drink.

To Marlene, *Blonde Venus*!

Manfully the table echoed the toast. Listen, if you cannot prove your valor to a woman, you may still propose a toast to her. They clinked glasses and downed highballs in her name. With tact beyond his years, Jack excused himself to go to the pool. Marlene pulled her caftan around her as she announced that she, too, would like a dip. None of the men dared follow. The Pirate took out a pack of cards as she broke the silence: Poker, anyone?

MARLENE WATCHED THE boy stroke a graceful freestyle that sluiced through the water. As he approached the shallow end of the pool, Marlene dipped her legs in. Jack came up for air. She let the caftan slip from her shoulders, and he paddled poolside toward her, shading his eyes to meet her gaze.

You do beautiful laps, she said.

I'm on the Harvard swim team, he said, breathing hard. Catching his breath he added: Also I sail. Right away he blushed at the earnest addendum. She smiled as she gestured to the small of her back, above the dip of her swimsuit: Would you help me with my sunscreen, Jack? Her swimsuit was bespoke. She'd run into Pierre Balmain on this same stretch of beach last year. I can never get a proper tan with swimsuits cut the way they are, Marlene had complained to him, they leave such ugly tan lines. It wasn't as if she were a prude, she added, but she couldn't be expected to sunbathe in the nude, could she? Imagine the photographers, the papers! The next spring, she was couriered a backless swimsuit from Balmain, accompanied by a salutatory note signed "Pierre" by hand.

As Jack slathered sunscreen evenly onto her skin, she asked him about school, girls, the future. I don't quite know what I want to do yet, he said. Perhaps join the army, but my old man isn't so sure about that.

Marlene looked back at the brunch table.

All the Joes had been looking in their direction, but now they looked away together, like a cockamamy brood of country geese. She tucked her hair into a crepe swim cap as she indulged him: I'm sure you'll do great things one day, Jack. He grinned at her, lean muscles wet in the sun, as she glided into the pool. It had been a generic thing to say to a twenty-year-old boy. Who knew the kid would one day be the thirty-fifth president of the United States?

5

Was it a month or a year into her stay with the Corsican-Chinese Friendship & Trade Association that Bébé asked for a diary? She was given a half-used spiral notebook with blue lines. It had a laminated lenticular photograph of a sleeping tiger on its cover. Viewed askance, the tiger opened its eyes and jaws. The thin pages she filled with nothing but tally marks. For all the time that had gone by undocumented in Marseilles, Bébé rounded it up or down to a perfunctory fifty. Her fifty-first client, on a midsummer's afternoon, was Chinese. That was new. Other than that, he was reliably that median of man: middle-aged, potbellied, polyester-suited. He stepped into the room, kicked off his shoes, and declared in Northern-accented Mandarin: Best blow my load before shit hits the fan!

Won't you have a shower? Bébé said.

Chop-chop, the client said as he stepped out of his trousers. He removed everything but his beige socks, sour smelling in the windowless room, as he squatted on his haunches, fishing a cigarette out of a rumpled pack. He tried to light it, but his hands were shaking. Bébé took the lighter from him and curled her palm around the flame. Surprised by her gesture, he leaned in to catch the fire all the same. Upon finishing the cigarette, he grunted and went to take a quick shower.

When he came, he gave a long and strangled shout.

The octave of his cry made Bébé think he was in fact not Northern, but Fujianese. With great solemnity he told her that her 口交 technique was 顶尖. Completely against her will she burst out laughing. He lit another cigarette and offered her one. It was unusual for clients to remain in the room unless they wanted to try to go at it again, for which there were certainly additional charges. As a courtesy, Bébé informed him that her fee was tabulated by time, not activity.

That's fine, he said, waving a hand. Whereabouts on the old road are you from?

Shanghai, she said, although the answer should have been Taishan.

Ah, he said. A good city.

Yourself?

Fujian, he said. Quanzhou, to be precise.

Biting back a savage smile, Bébé accepted the cigarette. Before she lit up, she asked if it would be all right for her to put her clothes back on. Yes, he said defensively, of course. He remained unclothed as she dressed, but after a moment, saw fit to throw the scratchy blanket over his lower body. No offense, he shrugged, looking down at his loose paunch and the will-o'-the-wisps of salt-and-pepper engirding his nipples, as if noticing them for the first time.

Fully dressed, she turned and brought the cigarette to her lips.

With a steadier hand now he lit her up. He told her he was a small-press publisher and that he had just got off the last plane out of Beijing.

THE OTHER SMALL-PRESS publishers were small because they had specific aesthetic interests. They were too niche. That, or they were politically inclined, and needed to operate on the fly. He was small because he was essentially interested in publishing translations of European literature.

He was doing nicely enough.

The educated class was hungry for foreign culture after all those years of pastoral proselytism, he said. Let a hundred flowers kiss my ass! Things were stable. Deng Xiaoping is a clincher, my kind of man. An all-out capitalist, mark my words, you'll see, if he holds on to the hot seat China will be the most consumerist country in thirty, nah, twenty years. It was a good time for business. Place your bets. Balzac flew off the shelves. Not so much Chekhov or Tolstoy. Nobody bought Proust, ha-ha. Zola did pretty well, for some reason.

Some were reputable reprints of translations that had gone out of print. Others I hired the best translators I could. I paid them better than most. So I was breaking even, generally content, until last month, when some kid bought a copy of a translation of *Madame Bovary* I'd published. He was a handsome lad, a university senior. That all seems fairly innocent, am I right? How soon fortunes turn, you better believe it! This kid took *Madame Bovary* around to the villages, preaching it to peasant girls before proceeding to make love to them in the hay.

Why *Madame Bovary,* you might ask? Why not *Sentimental Education?*

In his fine hands he had turned *Madame Bovary* into a cautionary tale against the rural petite bourgeoisie. He whispered to them sweet nothings of their right to individual freedom. He sang to them ditties about anarcho-feminism and anti-statist Marxism.

As if they could tell an elbow from an arse!

But their hearts were kindled when with great restraint each time he stopped thrusting his hips against their flailing bodies during the climactic instant of copulation to demand: Do you want to go the way of Emma Bovary?

Only when they had formed the following sentence would he resume his pelvic locomotion: I do not want to go the way of Emma Bovary!

Kid was making a killing.

Having amassed some fifteen to twenty girls with my paperback edition, he brought them to Beijing. Now they were affiliated with the university's anarchist student group. In the day, his bevy of besotted rustics was coached in maxims of libertarian socialism. By night: rice wine orgies and folk punk sing-alongs. When the sit-in at Tiananmen Square began, they descended on the promenade with much ado. Even if you don't understand the principles, you can still chant democratic slogans, am I right?

Now that things have turned ugly, now that the Party has fired on student protestors in the streets, now that those still alive have been taken into interrogation—these peasant girls, when asked what they were doing there, what do you think their answer was?

Madame Bovary.

So the Party got ahold of a copy of the book and traced *Madame Bovary* to my publishing press. With some digging they find out that I helped produce Cui Jian's *Rock 'n' Roll on the New Long March* album, but hey, give me a break, this was *before* they'd banned the guy's music. How the hell should I have known that "Nothing to My Name" would catch on as the youth movement's anthem? I was pally with his Hungarian bassist, that's all. We were drinking buddies at foreign embassy parties.

That does it for them. I get called in for questioning.

When I see what they've written on my file—"The Sole Purveyor of *Madame Bovary* in Beijing"—I start to laugh. But I shut up real quick when I see their faces.

Heaven is blind. So is the Party. Don't quote me on that.

I wasn't protesting at the square or in the streets. Never even popped by out of curiosity. But what do they care? They tell me I'm in cahoots with what's transpired. They show me a copy of the book. And I realize that dog turd had photocopied my *Madame Bovary*—a terrible copy at that, pages misaligned—so I hadn't even earned the royalties off these dissident wannabes. Naturally, all these student activists are silk purses born after the famines, the purges, the sending-downs that we old-timers ploughed through like farm pigs just a generation ago.

In the blink of an eye trouble is nigh.

I'm blacklisted. I'm denounced, in turn, as a Western-loving impe-rialist, a revisionist, an *anarchist*, for translating, printing, and distribut-ing *Madame Bovary* in China!

EXCUSE ME, SIR, Bébé interrupted. What has happened at Tianan-men Square?

He gawped at her.

Are you living under a rock, baby sister? He was sweating from relating his travails with such force. Marseilles is far, but still. He wiped his forehead with the back of his hand. It's a bad time, he continued, a snake year. If you don't know anything, it's better this way. Informa-tion begets trouble. The long line of ash from his cigarette broke off, dusting the motel pillow. She relit the cigarette for him as she asked: Could you write it down for me?

Write what down?

The name of the author and the book you mentioned.

What do you want it for?

But Bébé did not want it for anything, so to that she had no answer.

She'd never before read a classical Chinese novel in full, much less a European novel in translation. He studied her face. She did not look away. Slinging his hairy behind over the bed, he bent to retrieve a pen from his jacket. His ass cleft was the color of unhulled bean sprouts. He turned back, depressing the end of the ballpoint pen against his chin.

福楼拜, he wrote on the back of the cigarette pack, 包法利夫人.

He tossed it to her. As he released the pen again on his chin with a satisfying click, he said: We even republished this edition of *Madame Bovary* with a note from the translator, to say that Flaubert is not a capitalist. Well, he is a rentier, but his sympathies lie with the people. But did they see my effort with that? Of course not. Listen to me, girl. People want to see only the worst in other people.

What will you do now? Bébé asked.

I've got old friends littered all over the place. I studied literature in Paris when I was your age. Such a beautiful place, you can't imagine! The old government paid for us to go. Of course now that's all gone out the window. Zhou Enlai was my senior in the exchange program. Paris, Berlin, Munich, Lyon, London. It was so hard to travel then. Impossible unless you were born into money or you were a stowaway. Chairman Mao applied for the same work-study program and was rejected. *I* made it to Paris and *he* didn't, ha! Where did that get the both of us?

He stopped to blow some air through his lips like a horse.

With a bit of grit and grease our kind can always start over. A noodle stand, or a hand laundry—stomachs are hungry and clothes will be dirty. A good coat can be made from gathering up enough poor scraps, yeah yeah. Something always comes up if you keep your eyes open. Hey, it's good to see a homeland chicken so far from the old road. Nothing like a Chinese woman's skin, you know?

6

Marlene and JFK had not kept in contact, so when she visited Washington on a day-trip in 1961 to receive an honorary peace prize, she was surprised to receive a call from his aide: Mr. President extends an invitation to the Oval Office for late-afternoon drinks.

She could not be certain what "drinks" meant in his book, but she was open to finding out, and just in case, she wore a nice pair of pink silk panties. Great minds think alike, she said, when two and a half drinks into their meeting he leaned in to kiss her.

He said: Huh?

Please don't mess my hair up, she said. I have a ceremony to attend later.

It was all over in a few minutes. He'd moistened her with a few sloppy licks before making his entrance, and she was just getting into the rhythm of things by the time he was done. Before he undressed her, he had told her that for security reasons the room was bugged. But not to worry, the aides could only *hear* them, not *see* them. Gallantly, she made sure to issue a few more husky sighs than the encounter warranted so as to protect his reputation. He cleaned up and turned to her, asking: Did you ever do it with him?

Marlene wasn't sure whom he was talking about. She asked: Him? He nodded. Incredulously she ventured a guess: Your daddy?

He nodded again.

Jack! she protested. I never did it with your daddy.

I knew the old devil was lying, he said, patting her rump twice. That's the only door I got in first.

Unsure if she should be amused or offended, Marlene excused herself to the bathroom. She had not made him wear a condom. Not because he was the president—it was an indiscriminate favor she extended to any man she bedded. They were always so grateful afterward. Vinegar douching was what she swore by, and she never went anywhere without said spermicide ever since stoically seducing her music teacher at boarding school. The vinegar method had been taught to her by the older girls. All you needed was apple cider vinegar diluted with water and a douchebag with a nozzle. On her way in to the Oval Office, Marlene had been frisked and patted down several times. Her handbag went through a scanning device. They picked out her vial of apple cider vinegar. My weight-loss potion, she said, and unscrewed it for them to sniff.

Mr. President was snoring when Marlene came out of the bathroom.

She tried to shake him awake, but he was heavy as lead. He smiled doggishly in his sleep, and she recognized the teenager by the pool in the sun.

It was a quarter to seven and Marlene had to be at the Institute of Peace on the hour. When she put her hand on the doorknob, the door opened from the outside. She almost fell through. Steadying her, the president's aide bowed deeply. Changing channels on his flesh-colored surveillance earpiece, he called for a chauffeur.

AT THE INSTITUTE OF PEACE a balding compere read out individual citations for the catalog of honorees, comprising in excess wizened white émigré men, dead and alive: Albert Einstein, Claude Lévi-Strauss, Raphael Lemkin, Joseph Brodsky, Thomas Mann, Béla Bartók.

Seated in the front row, waiting to receive her prize, Marlene almost dozed off herself. She leapt up from her seat when she heard her name.

Listening to Marlene Dietrich sing "Lili Marleen" on the black radio was as devastating as an air raid for German troop morale, the balding compere said as she took the stage. Hemingway said of her: Even if she had nothing left, she could break your heart with her voice. As early as 1933 she spoke out against the Nazi Party, and in 1939 rescinded her German passport to become a U.S. citizen, despite a personal invitation from Hitler to return to Germany under his direct patronage. During the war, she was a high-profile frontline entertainer for our boys, attaining the rank of captain for her tour of duty. Can I have a round of applause for Marlene Dietrich, who chose to throw her lot with us from the very beginning!

The 1961 U.S. Institute of Peace prize medallion was gold leaf, with a laurel of olive branches topping the institute's logo.

It was a bit much, but Marlene had put it in one of her boxes all the same. She hoarded jewelry, love memos on the backs of napkins, program sheets for premieres, magazines with her face on the cover. She had a special malachite box where she preserved intimate souvenirs: Joe DiMaggio's jockstrap. Frank Sinatra's guitar pick. A lone stocking unclipped from Edith Piaf's garter belt. The pink silk panties she'd worn for the president also resided there. She'd repurposed the peace-prize medallion as a paperweight in this cave in Paris. It held down the obituary notices of friends and acquaintances she cut out from the papers; of course she was keeping tabs. Top of the pile for now was Lucille Ball—ruptured aorta, ten days after open-heart surgery at Cedars-Sinai, and doctors had claimed the rupture had nothing directly to do with the surgery. Pshaw!

Everyone Marlene had known from before seemed to have died out by around 1980. There was no one left to admire or loathe or compete with. Not only had she outlived them all, she thought, she'd tried everything at least once, and she would like to do it all over again. A bell was ringing from far away, reeling Marlene back in.

It was the phone.

Marlene dipped her chin into the plush white collar about her neck, letting the feathers tickle. She stared at the telephone for three whole rings before picking up the receiver. Miss Dietrich's residence, she whispered, who is calling?

She heard:

> You wanted greater yet, but love
>   forces all of us down to the ground.
> Sorrow bends powerfully, but an arc never returns
>   to its starting point without a reason.

IT WAS HE in High German.

It had worked—she in her floaty chemise, her lipstick, her mascara, her swan coat, her diamond bracelet, all diamonds. She stifled the smile growing on her lips, putting on an airy tone to say: Let me guess, Schiller?

Close—but not quite.

Hölderlin?

Impressive, Marlene. Now would you like to hear the rest of the poem?

First you should tell me your name.

My youthful anonymity is my one good card. I should be a fool to give it up so soon.

I'm going to have to call you Bogie then.

Why him?

Casablanca was playing on the TV when you first called.

Ingrid Bergman is a bore compared with you.

How so?

Let's put it this way, the boy on the phone said. She's too real.

Marlene could no longer contain the smile on her lips.

I'm going to take that as a compliment, she said.

In which case, he said, you understand me perfectly.

BY THE TIME the maid returned with the Ladurée macarons, Marlene was in a buoyant mood. Bogie—he made her want to read Novalis again. When had she last made a new acquaintance; recited *Frühromantik* poetry? The maid was unboxing the macarons. Marlene picked one up and nibbled at it dreamily, saying to the maid: Isn't it nice to remember to feel special about yourself? The maid looked at her with uncertainty. You wouldn't understand, Marlene said, would you? She patted a corner of her bed and bade the maid sit. Here, have a macaron, she offered. Have you ever had a macaron?

The maid shook her head.

Try one!

The maid picked a rose-flavored macaron, pale pink. She bit into it, and Marlene watched her spread the ganache on her tongue.

Well?

The maid nodded. A blush was prickling her cheeks. The confectionery must have felt so delicate in her mouth. How amusing: her maid was having an aesthetic reaction to Ladurée! It must have been so easy for life to be interesting when you were exposed to so little.

On impulse Marlene slipped off her swansdown coat and held it out to the maid. For you, she said. The maid's eyes widened. Know what a swan is? Marlene flapped her arms, goose-honked. Those big white beautiful schleppers? They have the softest feathers. Put it on, I say.

The maid shook her head.

Now now, Marlene said, I insist! She pushed the silk lining over the maid's shoulders. Slowly, the maid slipped her arms into it. Stand back, Marlene said, and let's have a look. The luxurious coat was lovely on her slender frame. The maid did a spontaneous half twirl on the spot, as she brushed her cheek against the softness of the collar.

Then, remembering herself, she turned and smiled shyly at Marlene.

There, Marlene said triumphantly. This is just what I meant. Isn't it nice to remember to feel special about yourself?

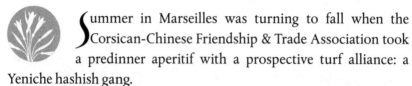 ummer in Marseilles was turning to fall when the Corsican-Chinese Friendship & Trade Association took a predinner aperitif with a prospective turf alliance: a Yeniche hashish gang.

The Corsican brought a multiracial selection of the bordello's best to trick out the entourage—a Russian; an Algerian; Bébé. The meeting took place at an air-conditioned Italian restaurant on neutral ground. Bébé was in the bathroom when the Corsican made an off-the-cuff remark that greatly offended the Yeniche. She was pulling up her stockings when the shooting began. She kicked off her heels and headed for the kitchen. A sous-chef and kitchen boy were squatting, hands over heads, under the stove top. She bolted through the service entrance.

Bébé did not know where she was running.

She did not stop until she hit a dirty canal. Her stockings were torn. She pulled them off and held on tight to the safety rails, trying to still the dry fire in her lungs. Throwing her balled-up stockings into the water, she startled a family of mallard ducks cruising in a V formation. She followed the ducks and the canal into town, sighted the main train station, and stole onto a train to Paris.

When she—Chinese, shoeless, in a skintight dress—got off at the Gare de Lyon, a patrolling officer asked to see her papers.

She shook her head. He clapped a hand on her shoulder.

Bébé began to cry. What she most wanted to tell the officer was that this was the first time she'd let herself cry in France, but she couldn't, and he wouldn't have understood anyway. *Non parler français,* she said. *Parler chinois.*

She was detained at a metropolitan police station.

The next morning, a police vehicle came for her. The rear windows were reinforced with wire mesh, and the height of the hard plastic seats had been specially designed such that detainees would have to cower to fit in the back.

Bébé was brought to a building with spotless floors and shown to a fluorescent-lit room. An immigrations officer, a pro bono human-rights lawyer, and a translator were waiting to take her statement. The lawyer shot up at once. She shook Bébé's hand, and the translator followed suit. Bébé was served an inert bun and a small paper cup of scalding-hot vending machine coffee. She took the food quickly, burning her tongue on the drink. The heat of the coffee spread through her as she closed her eyes, pressing her fingers against them, and opened them again.

I was involved in what happened at Tiananmen Square, Bébé said. I took the last ship out of Beijing. I am a village girl from Taishan. I did not know much. I do not know much. A young man came to my village with an overnight bag. He was very handsome. In his overnight bag was a translation of foreign literature. He stayed a fortnight. In the day he read us Flaubert. In the evening he sang us songs, lay with us in the fields as the sun went down.

When he left the village, we wanted to leave with him. He took us to Beijing. At his university, they told us about freedom. They brought us to the sit-in. We chanted slogans in the streets. When the soldiers opened fire, some of my new friends died. The rest of us were dispersed. Someone said we'd be blacklisted for life if we were caught by the wrong people. We should leave while we could. So I left on a boat. From the boat we got onto a ship. The ship sailed to Marseilles. But I wanted to come to Paris.

In other words, the lawyer said, you have come to Paris as a refugee?

Bébé was unfamiliar with the word. The translator explained, in brief, the term to her. Bébé did not dare answer. She was trying to look for cues in the body language of the lawyer, to see if yes or no was the appropriate response.

I did not think it was possible that they read Flaubert in China, the lawyer whispered, close to tears. Tell us, what of Flaubert did you read?

Madame Bovary, Bébé said.

And how do you find the novel?

Bébé hesitated, lowering her eyes. The lawyer leaned over the metal table to touch Bébé's hand encouragingly. She gave it a little squeeze.

I do not want to go the way of Emma Bovary, Bébé said.

Oh, the lawyer said, a tear falling down her cheek, bless!

Walter Benjamin
Is Recommended
an Overnight Motel
in Portbou

The glass of still water Anna May asked for never came, the tuxedo-swaddled men were disgruntled that she'd stopped dancing, and these two women were a piece of work. First the brunette who demanded a lowdown on Hollywood, then the winking blonde who spilled a drink on her. Though the dress was soaked through and it made no difference, the blonde was still dramatically stanching the champagne with her musky handkerchief.

The night was all balled up.

Anna May decided to be a good sport and laugh it off. The blonde began to laugh, too. Lapping up the kerfuffle, the photographer was still waiting. As they rearranged themselves, Anna May was amazed by the instantaneous effect of the camera pointed in their direction, effortlessly coaxing up bright smiles, like the three of them had known one another for years and were the firmest of friends. Thanking them, the photographer was about to move on when the blonde asked what magazine the picture might appear in.

I freelance for *Life*, the photographer said.

Life magazine! the blonde exclaimed.

Anna May saw the brunette blink superciliously at the baldness of the blonde's excitement. The blonde went right on flirting with the photographer in German, saying something to him while pointing at her legs, and shortly after was called away by an acquaintance passing them by who had rhinestones pasted in a line from cleavage to collarbone, at which the blonde immediately wolf-whistled. The Bergfilm brunette was quick to pull Anna May aside to explain to her in an apologetic undertone that the blonde was "only a chorus girl in a cabaret, not a serious actress, always cracking dirty jokes and dancing barefoot with the transvestites. You mustn't think it's typical!"

The brunette was presumptuous, and that put her off.

Don't worry about it, Anna May said, I never think anything is typical. But the brunette had already turned to a man who must have been very wealthy, by the looks of his large diamond cufflinks. Smiling up at the man and grasping him by the elbow, the brunette slipped Anna May a calling card and signaled to her that they would catch up another time.

ANNA MAY HAD not known anyone at the Berlin Press Ball.

Briefed that it was a highlight of the city's social calendar, she was on the guest list courtesy of the director she was working with for her first international feature, a German-British-French co-production. Instructing her to stay put and promising to introduce her around the room, he pottered off to procure some canapés and had not returned. No matter; the women were garrulous (Do Chinese women really wash their face in rice water? Is Charlie Chaplin a card-carrying Communist? What slimming cure would you recommend to achieve your flapper figure?); the men wanted to dance. An orderly queue had formed, and it reminded her of the time her father took her to the world expo in L.A. as a child. You can learn a lot at exhibitions, he said. She'd been excited to go because it meant everyone else would be left at home.

Reaching the front of a long queue marked "Congolese Mature Female," Anna May was given the opportunity to shake the hand of a reclining nude—dark skin oiled to a shine, eyes drugged down to half mast, breasts small with nipples as long as rubber bands—but instead she burst into tears. The tremulous reason she provided her father later: Because they took away her clothes.

No, her father explained, she never had clothes to begin with. It is natural to her, where she is from. In that case, Anna May said, anyone who wants to shake her hand must first remove *their* clothes. Liu Tsong, her father laughed, you have your ideas, but they don't make any sense.

They make sense to me, she answered.

But, my girl, he said gently enough, you are not the world.

·   ·   ·

FOR THIS DEBUTANTE sojourn out of America, her first trip to Europe in the spring of 1928, Anna May packed fourteen alligator-skin valises. What to bring or what not to bring to Berlin, London, Paris, these frolicsome metropoles where surely everything could be had?

Only the common, who have nothing of worth to bring with them, travel great distances with a single bundle tied to the end of a bamboo stick. Worse yet, merely the clothes on their backs. That is how your grandfather left Taishan, her father reminded her whenever he could, with nothing but his shirt and trousers, less than a dollar in his pocket, when he planted his two feet down on American soil.

Packing for the trip, Anna May loaded up those suitcases for the ghost of her grandfather, too. Heaven has eyes. Let him see her now, twenty-three-year-old rising starlet as portended by film magazines on both sides of the Atlantic, crossing an ocean in a first-class cabin with fourteen valises bursting with the finest garments! Seasick on the voyage, she slept it off. She was accompanied by her older sister, who was availing herself of Anna May's success to explore Europe's capital cities. Her entire family would have tagged along if they could—Anna May had to explain that this was a work trip, not a holiday. It would hardly do to have the whole Wong clan on her heels as she ran a busy schedule, and besides, it would cost plenty to book extra rooms or cabins wherever she went. Her mother clucked her tongue. No one's asking for an extra room, she said to Anna May in Cantonese, we can all sleep in one place. Your father and I will take the floor, she added, and you children can have the bed—just the usual!

Her father had been more reasonable.

Liu Tsong is traveling for work, he said. We'll get in her way.

Her mother soldiered on about the opportunity to travel on the dime of Paramount Pictures, and God only knows what those white devils might do to their beloved daughter were she unaccompanied in a faraway land. Even though her father did not approve of Anna May being an actress, he'd given her a little nod, as if to say: Let me handle your mother, and for that she was grateful. Before she left, he pressed into her hands a safety amulet and a travel-sized Bible. The amulet was requested from a Taoist spirit medium, and the Bible had been borrowed off the pastor. Their household practiced ancestral worship, but they also went to the Chinese Baptist church on Sundays. Growing up this way, Anna May had accepted the harmony of believing in both until she was old enough to notice, one day, at random, how incompatible they were. Her mother's unimpeachable logic shushed her up: The more spirits the merrier. Double blessings! Anna May took along both amulet and Bible to keep her parents happy, but what she really wanted on the luxury liner out to sea was a map of the world, and someone to tell her where they were. Drink of the water and think of the well, her father had drummed into her over the years. Though our bodies sleep in California, our hearts dream in Taishan. But I've never been to Taishan, she said, confused. Doesn't matter, he assured her. Anna May wobbled when the ship berthed in Hamburg, after which there was yet a train to catch to Berlin. A white-gloved chauffeur with a sign met them at the Hauptbahnhof. When her sister reached over to open the passenger door herself, she was admonished by the chauffeur, who doubled over quickly and primly to seat both ladies.

IT TOOK NO time at all for Anna May to decide she liked Europe more than America: much nicer to be apple-buttered here than to be bullied back home. For the longest time she'd wanted to be just like everyone else, but now she was beginning to see just what she might be able to do with not being the same. Was this a new game in which she'd gained an unexpected advantage, or the same old one trussed up in a different suit? Walking through back alleys in downtown L.A., it was common sport for white joes to set their dogs on Chinese passersby, so much so that when a pit bull was unleashed on Anna May one afternoon, she was instantly relieved that she would no longer have to worry about when it would happen. Her father scooped her up though she was already twelve and no longer a small child, turned to the dog's owner, and recited a limerick she failed to understand. It ended this way, in a silly singsong tone: Two wrongs don't make a right / Like two Wongs don't make a white!

The white man chortled, calling his dog to heel.

Nice, he said. Haven't heard that one before.

Putting her back down on her feet, her father bowed, and they were allowed to pass unscathed. Anna May could parse the telling of the joke in their moment of danger, but she found that she was unable to accept that scraping bow, after the pit bull had been called back.

Why did you bow? she asked her father, trying to keep the scorn from her voice.

Do you want to have rabies? he said.

I'd rather be bitten by a mad dog, she thought, than to see you bow to that man. But her father was glowering at her, and she did not dare say it aloud. That night, when her mother came to tuck her in, her mother said: Do you know how much your father loves you? Anna May turned away. I don't want to know, she breathed into her pillow. She held close to her heart the proud belief that she, unlike her father, would never have bowed down—a high horse she was unseated from at fourteen, when told to "scream like a Chinese" in her first appearance, as an extra, in a Hollywood movie.

It was a silent film. The producers wanted ambience.

She stepped aside as they set up the scene.

I don't know how to speak Chinese, she said to the line producer.

Doesn't matter, the line producer said, just make it up. Make it up? Anna May asked. Take this one out, she heard someone say to the casting manager over her head. Sub in another.

Wait, she said, I can do it.

What she ended up screaming was a nonsensical patois of kitchen Cantonese and playground Spanish, which she'd picked up from shooting marbles with the Hispanic boys just outside of her neighborhood. The film was Alla Nazimova's *The Red Lantern*. Nazimova played both lead roles, half sisters, in Boxer Rebellion Beijing: the half-Chinese Mahlee and the full-white Blanche. Anna May was one of five hundred Chinese extras culled from Chinatown. She was on a delivery errand when a street-casting assistant had approached her. The release form she took home required her parents' signature. She was careful to practice her forgery before setting ink down to paper.

Her role, uncredited: *Chinese lantern bearer.*

Before reporting to Paramount that morning, Anna May fished around her mother's dresser drawer for her cake of white rice powder.

After rubbing it all over her face, she feared it was too pale. Unable to find the rouge paper, she tore a corner of a red packet she'd received lucky money in for the new year, smearing its chalky red pigment onto her cheeks in circular motions. Before she slipped out of the house, she noticed that the powder had obscured one of her eyebrows. With a black crayon from her school satchel, she drew a straight line where her brow was. Arriving at the gates of the hallowed studio, Anna May was more nervous about being caught by her parents than she was about reporting to Paramount for the first time. There was a sign for the *Red Lantern* extras to proceed to hair and makeup. Her walk was brisk and her stride wide, but as she reached the trailer, she slowed it down to tiny graceful steps lest anyone mark her down for rushing around. A woman with a clipboard saw her face and started laughing.

Look at this chinky tomato come to try out for the circus!

Her face was swabbed left to right with cold cream on a towelette. Although Anna May was indignant about having her handiwork ruined, having all these grown-ups fussing over her made her feel important, and she sat up straighter as her hair was pulled back into two tight braids. Then she was given a torn cotton smock with Chinese buttons to change into. When the costume designer wanted to add more dirt to the smock, Anna May tried to shrink away from the spray nozzle. Movies should make you more than you were, not less, and she did not want to look like a beggar. Anna May would have asked for her costume to be swapped, but all the other extras were in similar dress, and already they were being briefed. When you move across the street and hit this mark on cue, a tall man was saying loudly, you should not look like you are reaching a destination, and whatever you do, do not look into the camera.

After a few takes, the position of the camera would be changed, and they would have to do it again. Waiting and repeating, Anna May observed that all the movies she'd ever watched were no more than an hour long. Already they had been scuttling around for more than that. How many hours of footage made one movie?

She did not leave when the extras were dismissed.

Sitting very quietly on the edge of the set, she got to see Alla Nazimova rehearsing. Dressed like a goddess, she was the only person in her scene. How long did Miss Nazimova have to wait to be taken for a real actress, and when had she known?

SINCE AGE TEN Anna May had been practicing every day. The duration of her exercises depended on how long she could use unnoticed the one large mirror in their shared bedroom. Escaping from helping out in the laundry by invoking homework, she made up scenes in her head while lying on the bed. When she could hold it in no longer, she turned to the mirror, looked into her own eyes, and began.

Pursuant to her understanding, in crucial moments handsome men at least six feet tall walked into rooms with throwaway panache, fired pearl-handled pistols without missing their mark, cocked their heads as they saved the day, and kissed the girl. Looking into the mirror, Anna May urged them not to leave her behind with a well-turned-out shoulder, chemise slipping right off, close to fainting in their rugged arms, inhaling the note of aniseed in their pomade as she moved toward a declaration that would make them stay. I need this wild life, Anna May burst out once, hands draped around an imaginary neck, I need you! It was a line she'd memorized off an intertitle card in a movie. Opening her eyes she saw her father's reflection in the mirror. How long her father had been watching, she did not know. She dropped the posture right away, faltering for something to say, but her father had already walked back out without saying a word.

The following Saturday Anna May was taken to the spirit medium in Chinatown, who gave her a paste of ash water to drink from. On Sunday to the reverend in the Chinese Baptist church, who preached in both Taishanese and English. Out! Out of this flower maiden, this tender child, they chanted respectively. Hungry ghost, craven Satan, out I say! When her father asked the reverend when the spirit possession would end, Anna May threw up her hands.

I am not possessed, Father, she said, addressing the reverend as she stared unblinkingly at her father looking on aghast at his lippy daughter, I'm an actress.

.   .   .

NOW THAT SHE was, in fact, an actress, it was undoubtedly glamorous to be attending an endless swathe of high-society parties, to be requested as a front-row presence at seasonal launches in designer ateliers, but Anna May found it strange that all these things were expected of her when none of them was in any way relevant or essential to acting itself. She supposed she could have said no to such invitations, but turning down these frivolous benefits was harder than she'd expected. She found this aspect of her character disappointing, though she reasoned that it was less a blanket greed than an anxiety over squandering away what had been hard earned. Having grown up so modestly, perhaps this was understandable. It was something to work on. She hoped in future to be a person who could say no without apology, and without regret. Was it not permissible to show up on set for work, but other than that, to have a perfectly ordinary private life?

You'll grow into it, her agent said, this is part of your job.

He was arranging her publicity schedule in Europe—social events, photo shoots, interviews, meetings. Without the right image, he counseled, work ethic and natural talent come close to nothing. What's the right image for me, Anna May wanted to know but did not dare ask her agent. There was no other actress who looked like her in Hollywood. Perhaps she could model herself after Dolores del Río, the Mexican crossover beauty, but even Dolores had tried to pass for white in L.A. At casting calls, Anna May had grown used to being the only Asian in the room, trying out for side characters, but surely there would come a point when she would get to audition for leading roles, too? Having not found that answer in Hollywood, Anna May was here to see if Europe would give her more latitude, but she felt overwhelmed in this bright ballroom in Berlin.

Now she was simply trying to make her way to the powder room, but someone had stepped up to her and was inquiring enthusiastically after "the Chinese way of life." No reason to explain she knew more about Christopher Columbus than Confucius, not when it was so easy to enchant these people with a few choice nouns: *dragon; kumquats; silkworm; chopsticks!* This pantomime was disorienting for Anna May only because she'd striven so hard to rid herself of any trace of it back in L.A. The expensive face powder that was too light for her skin tone, the hot irons to curl her dead-straight black hair, studying glamour shots of Mary Pickford to paint on cherry lips, trying to contour in the impression, at a glance, of double lids with eye-shadow palettes.

Anna May hurried on but was waylaid again.

Excuse me, an elderly woman in a heavily embroidered shawl exclaimed. You look just like one of those porcelain figurines in the shop window at KaDeWe.

Thank you, Anna May said.

Also, the stranger went on beaming, you speak such good English!

Part of Anna May wanted the elderly woman to know English was the only language she spoke well. Killing off her half-past-six Cantonese had been fuss-free, it faded on its own accord as soon as she moved out of her family home; as for Mandarin, she'd only ever been able to count from one to ten and pronounce her own name. Another part of her did not see what the point of telling this lady would be. After all, it was clear she hadn't meant any of the things she was saying in a bad way. Thank you very much, Anna May said to the elderly woman and bowed out of her way. People were slick, she stank of champagne. Strangers were tripping over themselves to accost her not because she was attractive, no: she was impossible to miss because she was different. The dress stuck uncomfortably to her skin. She'd almost reached the powder room when someone touched her shoulder.

To Anna May's surprise, it was the blonde who'd spilled the drink on her. Almost lost you there, the woman said with a smile.

What is it? Anna May said, more brusquely than she'd intended.

The blonde was holding up a glass of water. Here, she said, thrusting it toward Anna May, I heard you calling after the waiter earlier. He never got back to you, did he? Fancy being at a party where there's enough cuvée to fill a spa town, the blonde went on, but not a drop of still water to be had. Anna May drained the glass in two mouthfuls. Then she did not know what to do with the empty receptacle.

The blonde took it from her hand.

Come now, she said to Anna May, are you quite all right?

三

The powder room was very fine: marble sinks, polished fixtures.

So, the blonde said jauntily, it's your first time in town? Let me take you out. I've got a fantastic clothier. Affordable, too. We'll make you a new dress—my way of apologizing. Anna May told her that wasn't necessary, she just wanted to get rid of the champagne smell for now.

What smell? the blonde asked, genuinely curious. She sniffed at Anna May. The other women in the bathroom stared at the blonde. Anna May tried to ignore their gaze as she thought about how to describe the scent of champagne exposed to air. Like wet limestone, she said. For some reason the blonde found this funny and started to laugh. Her laugh sounded like a goose honk, and she did nothing to suppress it into something more seemly. Now she was leaning closer to Anna May and taking a big whiff. I must be a plebeian, the blonde finally declared, smells like freshly baked bread to me. Anyway, she suggested, if you remove your dress, I can help you wash and dry it off. Anna May passed her dress to the blonde as she stood half naked in the cubicle, feeling like a fool in nothing but her long string of pearls and an underskirt slip. Soon she heard the floor pedal and the hand dryer, then the knock on the door. Opening the door a slice, the woman slid into the cubicle like a cat. Toasty, she said, holding the dress up to her cheek.

She presented the dress, clean and warm.

Thank you, Anna May said. As she breathed, the long string of pearls rose and fell ever so slightly against her skin. The blonde reached out and touched her necklace.

Saltwater pearls?

In fact they were freshwater, but she found herself wanting to please the woman.

Yes, she said, South Sea.

The blonde was touching the necklace without touching Anna May's skin, instead allowing each bead she had fingered and warmed to fall back onto her body.

South of what?

WHEN THE BLONDE put a hand under her slip, Anna May stiffened, but she did not ask her to stop. Firstly because she was rude and attractive, a combination Anna May disliked in men but had yet to come across in a woman; secondly, it was clear that the woman had done this before; and finally, far from home for the first time, it struck Anna May that the last thing she wanted was to come across as conventional. Let no one think that all Chinese were wet socks from the boondocks on her account. She was a city girl, and faster than most. Besides, it was safe: there was no chance of running into this woman once she got back. Berlin was Berlin. L.A. was L.A.

The woman was smiling.

She must have discovered that Anna May was not wearing drawers or panties. Anna May wanted to explain that she was not a minx who went to parties naked down there; she'd been worried that underwear would show beneath her dress, but the slip had already been unloosed. It fell, soft and useless, around her ankles, and now the woman was a halo of blond on knees, bringing a warm tongue and cold fingers to her in considered succession, as women entered and exited the powder room outside, carefully gathering up silk and taffeta and velvet skirts in their hands as they lowered themselves over toilets, minding their multifarious rings and bracelets as they soaped and washed their hands, arranging their hair in the mirror as they exchanged notes on so-and-so's dress pattern, a clear copy of the latest display in Paul Poiret's atelier, and did you see that low décolletage on Jeanne? How repellent it looks on her with breasts so proud! The blonde had hardened her tongue, egging Anna May on till she broke to exclaim an amorphous semivowel much too loud for a public bathroom.

She caught herself immediately, afraid.

The blonde wiped her mouth on the back of her hand, and the back of her hand on Anna May's slip. Don't you worry, pet, she said, as she took out her rouge case for a two-stroke touchup, smacking her mouth to spread the color, Berlin is a noisy city.

THE BLONDE LIVED in a modest but charming apartment.

Fully cut books and half-smoked cigarettes with lipsticked ends littered a large table and several shelves. The woman had touched each part of her more boldly than a man would, but without pugnacity. Or perhaps the woman was utterly pugnacious, but the softness of her eyes and cheeks and arms was enough to beguile another woman into mistaking her pugnacity for something gentler. The champagne-stained dress was limp over the back of a chair, and everything smelled of tuberoses. Dashed to the ground early on by one of their wrists from the bedside table, a broken vase pooled petals on the floor.

You're a fast learner. The blonde laughed. Can you stay the night?

Anna May's bangs were damp as she pressed her forehead against the blonde's shoulder. Every other part of you is soft, the blonde said, but your hands are rough. Why is that? Laundry hands, Anna May said, as she ran her chapped palm up and down the blonde's bare leg. Keep going, the blonde said with a shiver, I like your laundry hands.

ANNA MAY'S LAUNDRY hands had been many years in the making, roughened from scrubbing on washboards. Not allowed out to play till she had finished up the daily load of tablecloths, uniforms, and bed linen, she still had her fun wending through drying sheets in the luke-warm comfort of lye and soap. Hide-and-seek with her sister could last for hours. There were so many choice spots for hiding. She'd once fallen asleep under an ironing mangle. Aerating the sad iron with a bellows to crease that neat line down the front of customers' trousers, she'd learned to be careful of hot coal chips. She knew how to press her own cotton tunics flawlessly, to make them look more expensive than they really were.

There was a living space above the laundry, with one bed. Although her mother was the one who insisted the children must have the bed and would not allow them—especially her *baobei erzi*, her youngest son—on the floor under any circumstances, that did not stop her from being full of complaints. The wind in her achy bones came from the cold hard floor, she moaned, but that was necessary, absolutely. Parents have to eat bitterness so their children can taste a sweet future. You'll understand this when you're a mother, she said to Anna May. What Anna May wanted to know was: What's so great about being a mother? Silly girl, her mother said. It's not about greatness. It's the natural way of things. They had one rickety table, two chairs, and a few stools. This was where they ate, and also where they did their homework. To store their belongings, each member of the family had a wooden crate, gathered by her father behind a fruit grocer's.

Anna May thought everyone else lived the same way, till the day she was invited to a classmate's birthday party. It was the only party she'd ever received an invitation to, and she put on her Sunday best. At the entrance to her friend's house there was no counter—only a fence, a lawn, a front door. Inside, it was not humid. The air was cool, and there were no hanging clothes, no exposed lightbulbs. There was a leather sofa set in a well-lit living room, which led to a dining room and a patio. There was an upright piano, a black nanny, and a fluffy-haired dog. Anna May thought that the living room was where they all slept, but later she saw that there were individual bedrooms for every member of the family. Each room had its own door, bed, dresser, and wardrobe. When the nanny noticed her admiring a sterling silver hand mirror in her friend's bedroom, she told Anna May that she might please return to the parlor. After that party, Anna May couldn't look at her own home the same way again. Each time she walked past the hand-painted sign for WONG SAM SING'S CHINESE HAND LAUNDRY, horizontally in English and vertically in Chinese characters, it did not fail to embarrass her, even if she was alone on the street.

Because she had not told anyone in class how her father earned his keep, Anna May had assumed that no one knew he was a laundryman. By the time she found out everyone knew, courtesy of the craniometrist's son, the class had already constructed a jingle: All you have to do is shake her sandpaper hand / To know her father is a laundryman.

While making her delivery rounds after school one afternoon, she received a few coins from a nice white lady who sent them her bedsheets. She smelled of hot scones and answered the door in a frilled apron. Anna May hid the money in her shoe, under the insole. She was walking home by a roundabout route, prolonging her enjoyment of the uncomfortable sensation of coins under her heel, testing out how it would look and feel to walk with a limping gait, when she saw an advertisement in the front of a shop for Thomas Edison's "Chinese Laundry." *Magic for a nickel,* it promised, *they move like rubber!*

Anna May did not know who Thomas Edison was, or why there was a sign for a Chinese laundry here, and besides, this did not look like a laundry at all. It did not have steamy windows, or the overhanging maze of damp clothes visible behind the counter of Wong Sam Sing's Chinese Hand Laundry. She stepped in and found the space dimly lit, with two rows of machines flanking the walls. A man collected a nickel and told her to step up. She needed a stool to be level with the machine. When she put her eyes to the sights, there was a tiny black-and-white Chinese laundry shop just a few feet from her face. Two men were in a thrilling chase. How could they be moving in there? She'd seen photographs and was fairly certain that the uncanny lookalikes had remained completely still. Her father had taken her to open-air Taishanese opera shows in Chinatown some Sundays, but it was clear that the men in costume were standing before them. This was a machine, the men were tiny, and they repeated their actions as long as you continued watching. In class the next day, she boasted to her classmates of what she had seen. Magic for a nickel, she repeated the tagline, trying to make the words sound like they were her own. Everyone knows about the nickelodeon, the craniometrist's son said. Guess you haven't been to the theater down North Main.

What's there? she said.

The real deal, he told her.

After recess, the students were told to return home, there was a smallpox epidemic. Anna May went on foot to North Main. The theater was manned by a Mexican man in a cowboy hat who kept a toothpick between his teeth. In as adult a manner as possible she asked for a ticket to the next show. Chaplin, he said, smiling at her, but she did not know what he was talking about.

It was a matinee, very empty.

The hall smelled of wet carpet and caramel corn. She made her way to the front of the dark theater and sat in the first row, counting the number of seats on each side so she could sit exactly in the middle. Her eyes went googly when the picture started because it was too close, but she did not move. The title card flashed before her:

THE TRAMP

She was *here*, but she was also *there*, and so was the Tramp. His face was sad, but how he made her laugh, and what a gent he was! Why wouldn't the Lady tell her father she wanted to be with the Tramp? How could the Lady have had another lad all along? It took everything Anna May had to keep from shouting her recommendations out loud to the Tramp on the screen. The movie ended with the Tramp skipping and swinging his cane, back on the road where he belonged, the same way it had begun. Nobody understood him, and he was alone—she wanted to go on the road with him and be his gamine.

She began saving up her lunch money.

Skipping meals gave her bouts of bad gastric pain. That was easy to bear, as long as she thought of the cramps as a secret baptism that made her worthier than the other girls and boys in class who yawned and pulled on their hands, waiting for the school bell to ring. Once it rang, they shoved books and pencils into waxed-cotton satchels and raced out of the classroom, but where to and what for?

She bided her time, working hard in the laundry, helping out around the house. When she'd saved up enough lunch money, she asked her father for permission to visit her classmate's house on Sunday afternoons. To learn to play the piano, she said. After all, she added with hitherto unversed cunning, we do not have one at home.

In this way, she snuck off to the movies for a few hours every week, seeing everything from *A Message from Mars* to *Dr. Jekyll and Mr. Hyde*, though Chaplin remained her favorite. What adventures the men had.

How fine the women looked as they walked down a street, turned a doorknob, looked angry, became happy again. The clothes they wore, the places they went, the feelings they had. Everything was bigger and brighter than it should have been. More than anything else, Anna May wanted to be there, too.

You're cut like a filly, the woman observed as they dressed.

Waking past noon, the woman raked the tips of her fingernails up and down Anna May's back, and this time they were both content to take turns rubbing up lazily against the other, till mellow friction crested over into agreeable heat. Discovering simultaneously that they were ravenous when they were done dallying, they began attending to their toilette. When they stood naked shoulder to shoulder looking in the full-length mirror, Anna May was a trifle taller than the woman. What are you, the woman said to their reflection in the mirror, five feet six and a half?

Five feet seven, Anna May said.

The woman fiddled around in her closet and had Anna May try on a dress with a V-shaped neckline, then a belted tweed skirt suit, which seemed to please her. She held Anna May close by the lapels. She did not want Anna May in heels. Don't you want us to be just the same height? she teased, passing her a finely made pair of oxford flats. They made up their faces, jostling each other for more mirror, preening as they curled their lashes and accentuated their cheekbones.

THE BLONDE TOOK Anna May to an old dance hall restaurant with dark wood paneling and a large mirrored ball. The tables were lit with candlesticks. There was a bar at the end, and a polished dance floor in the middle. This is where I learned to dance, the blonde said, I used to come here all the time with my mother. We'd share a beer and jive for hours. It was after the war and packed to the ears. They knew just what to cash in on—marathon waltz parties for widows. Those lonesome biddies could really dance. My god, they'd had so little action for such a long time, it all came out on the dance floor, you know? Anna May shook her head as she laughed. The blonde did not talk like anyone else

she knew, and she certainly could not imagine going drinking or dancing with her own mother.

What? the blonde wanted to know, giving her a heavy-lidded stare.

I'm trying to see you as a girl, Anna May said, here with those
women.

I was a fat kid, the blonde informed her. Too many cream puffs. Her
eyes were solemn, but her smile was wicked. Anna May wanted to run
her fingers over that clever mouth. I loved dessert, the blonde went on
fervently, still do. When I was sent away to boarding school and sweet
treats were forbidden, I hid pastries up in my bodice so I could smuggle
them into bed. Cream Tits! That was my code name in the dorm room.
Everyone wanted a piece of me.

This woman could really make her laugh.

It was very late in the afternoon, and the only other patrons were
a man with a sketchbook in a corner, and a husband and wife pair
with their young daughter in tow. The girl would not stop staring at
Anna May and the blonde, not even when chastised by her mother. The
blonde had perched her derby walking cane over the edge of the table.
Every time she laughed it clattered to the floor. The maître d' frowned,
but the fresh-faced waiter would rush over to pick it up. Whenever
he returned her cane, the blonde covered his hand with hers briefly,
ruddying the tips of his ears and the sparse configuration of pimples
across his forehead a hapless red.

After their mains, Anna May ordered a cappuccino, but the blonde
leaned over and asked the waiter to send over her usual instead.

Two demitasses of espresso were served up, with a tiny bottle of
grappa on the side.

Take your coffee, the blonde said, but leave just a few drops, at the
bottom of the cup. She demonstrated all of this for Anna May. Swirl
in the grappa, then drink it down in one sip. When she threw back her
head, her curls shook. There, she said, smacking her lips, can you feel
that little ball of fire going down your throat? When it reaches your
belly, you'll be ready for anything. Roguishly she toed Anna May's
ankle under the table. Afraid someone would notice, Anna May moved
her foot away as she downed her cup, and they tussled to pay the bill.

Exiting the restaurant, they passed the table with the family, and the blonde stopped to chuck the young girl under the chin. The girl blinked. Promptly she began to wail. *Entschuldigung*, the blonde said, tipping her hat to the parents, as the bedazzled waiter bowed them out of the establishment.

NIGHT HAD FALLEN, and the fashionable women-only club on Bülowstraße was superintended by a sensuously curvy bouncer in a Grecian toga who kissed the blonde full on the mouth in greeting. Onstage, a broad-shouldered singer with cropped hair was dressed smartly in an Eton-boy suit. As Anna May passed the stage with the blonde, the singer catcalled.

Mar-lay-nah!

A thin woman with an aquiline nose in a draped dress took the blonde by the waist and spoke to her in a rapid rush of Berlin dialect. She appeared to have no breasts, an effect that set off her attire beautifully. She threw a pointed, quizzical look at Anna May. The blonde pinched her friend on the forearm and introduced them.

Anna—you'll never forget our Ingeborg, she's an ambulance driver.

Gamesomely batting the blonde with her fan, Ingeborg brought them to join her table. To a velvet boothful of half-silhouetted women near the front of the stage, the blonde introduced Anna May in a hushed tone as a Hollywood actress.

A number of the women had some English, which they trotted out in generic greetings as they announced themselves: Eva, Liesel, Cornelia, Lotte, Klara, Sonja. A dark-nippled waitress in nothing but a harness brought over two glasses filled with a jade-green liquid, topped by slotted spoons and sugar cubes. Have you never had absinthe! Ingeborg said as she poured Anna May a drink, melting giggle water over the sugar cube, clear jade green dissolving into milky opalescence. The absinthe left a hint of fennel on the back of her tongue. After the singer in the Eton-boy suit was done with her set, she joined their table. Inching out Ingeborg, the singer sat next to the blonde. Unbuttoning the top button of her cheviot jacket and loosening her ascot, the singer set down a proprietary palm on the small of the blonde's back.

Crestfallen, Ingeborg turned to Anna May.

Fair warning, Ingeborg said. She does that.

Who does what? Anna May asked.

Ingeborg shook her head and poured herself more absinthe.

So, Ingeborg said, how's Hollywood treating you?

We're skating around plenty, Anna May said, but I'm keeping my options open.

And where are you from?

Los Angeles, Anna May said.

Before that?

Anna May shook her head, repeated herself: Los Angeles.

But where were you born?

Los Angeles, she said.

All the skirts were night owls who knew just how to flush up a dance floor. When Anna May said she had to be going, she had a social appointment the next morning, the blonde said she would leave with her. Ingeborg did not look happy about this, nor did the other women at the table. Standing outside the club, a newsboy came hustling up with the morning papers. The blonde bought one, then she smiled at Anna May as she bought another.

Two of the same morning paper? Anna May said.

In case you decide to come home with me, the blonde said, we can each have a paper of our own to read in the morning. I am, at heart, she added, a gentleman. She whistled for a cab in a louche way, and as soon as it pulled up they jumped in together. Back in the woman's apartment, when they were fully undressed and the woman was openly admiring her body, Anna May said: I can't make this a habit.

Come here, filly, the woman said.

Her body went.

The woman laughed and licked her own finger.

ANNA MAY WOKE only because a man pushed open the bedroom door and poked his head around. She thought he was a thief or a rapist, but then he said in a familiar way: Mutti? The blonde hardly stirred as Anna May pulled the sheets up to cover her bare shoulders. When the man saw that there was another person in bed, and that it was a woman, he smiled, giving her a curt nod, which she did not return. The blonde opened an eye.

Papi? I have company.

I can see that.

So come back later; go to Tami's, or the corner café.

The man left the room, taking care to close the door behind him. When Anna May heard the heavier front door close, she turned to the blonde, who had hung her wrist comfortably over the dip between Anna May's waist and hips.

Who was that?

Mm?

The intruder—you know him?

Know him? The blonde laughed, her eyes flying open. Sweetheart, that's my husband, Rudi. Anna May's lips turned quite dry, but the blonde had already shut her eyes. I'll introduce you next time, she mumbled drowsily. How long are you in town for again? Catching sight of the time displayed by the walnut clock on the bedside table, Anna May started. I have to go, she said, standing up, I have a meeting to see to.

Sounds dull, the blonde said. Must you really?

I'm already late, Anna May said, and it's an interview.

Oh, the blonde said, sitting up now, looking impressed. With whom?

Die Literarische Welt.

Die Literarische Welt? The blonde sounded amused. That's a literary magazine, she said, and now Anna May could not be sure if the woman was just being playful, or if there was a disparaging edge to her tone as she asked: What would they want with an actress?

Anna May moved through the delicate motions of putting one's clothes back on, article by article, in the appropriate order, under an unfamiliar eye. The blonde had lit a cigarette, as if to better enjoy the show. Look, she said to Anna May in a tender way, you have a run in your stocking. Balancing her cigarette precariously across the edge of an unwashed coffee cup, she got up and walked across the room naked, putting one hand on her derriere as she browsed her wardrobe with the other. Here, she held out a navy pantsuit of worsted wool, the leg tailored straight and sharp, paired with a light-blue blouson. Then she dived back into the wardrobe and fished out a gold cravat. They'll look delicious on you. Anna May hesitated. Are you or aren't you a Hollywood actress? the blonde said. You shouldn't be seen in the same outfit twice in a row. Anna May began putting the blonde's clothes on. And tonight, the blonde said, tapping ash on her floor. Shall I see you again?

As she tucked the blouse in, Anna May managed to say: I didn't know you were married.

Anna, the blonde said her name with a hard *A*, two hard *A*'s, her goose-honk laugh throaty and profuse, her eyes cold with delight. *I* didn't know *you* were so bourgeois!

五

The Chinese American actress was more than an hour late to their scheduled interview. As she entered the konditorei in a fluster, Walter was surprised that she was dressed in a navy pantsuit, paired assuredly with a gold cravat. His impatience subsided as he admired how even from a distance, she could suggest so immediately and implicitly two aspects of herself. The one that was superficial, and the one that was secret. What she did in being he could do only in thought, in writing; how the life of the mind fell short the moment you placed it next to life itself.

Mr. Benjamin?

She approached his table uncertainly, having run her eyes over the crowded back room of the bakery, guessing perhaps by his spectacles, the way the table was set. He found her effusive enunciation of the *j* in his last name as a palatal consonant, in addition to the title *Mr.*, earnest and touching.

Miss Wong, he returned.

She took a seat and apologized. She'd made a wrong turn, she explained, finding herself lost on her way here. Berlin was for Walter so neat and self-satisfied a prison—at least within his upper-crust circles—that he was envious, for a moment, that a Chinese American woman could, of course, well lose her way here. Someone like him had first to travel at least as far as Naples to experience properly that delightful sensation of being dispersed, porous, commingled. He wanted to tell her that he would have liked to see Berlin through her eyes, but fearing that this implied undue intimacy, asked instead that generic question: if she was finding his city to her liking. I don't know, she said with a fidgety smile. How should I put it? Your city has made me surprise myself. Her Californian cadence was so strong he had to strain to catch the flattened vowels.

She was slipping her hands out of her gloves.

He marveled at her wrists. They were thinner and finer than he'd seen on any European woman, her fingers longer and paler. The flesh under her unpainted nails was pink. As to her skin, it was not yellow. She was fair almost to the point of translucence, and he could sight the veins snaking under her skin. He was curious, too, about the epicanthal fold of her eyelids that was always exaggerated in artists' impressions and popular depictions, but he tried to refrain from looking at them, focusing instead on her eyes. How evenly black her pupils were! There was no part of her for him to land on that was neutral, and he found it amusing that he was being thrown off by a woman's appearance. But it was not just any exterior, he countered, it was her very essence. He wanted to see her as just another woman, but how should he go about this when she was unlike anyone else he'd encountered?

Walter was no provincial turtle gone to ground in his shell.

He had the wherewithal to be well traveled in the questing tradition of the Enlightenment, enriching his spirit by surveying far-off places and acquiring new experiences. He'd shared a propeller-powered sleigh with melon-breasted babushkas in Moscow who had a basket under one arm and a child under the other, and smoked hashish in Marseilles while bowing at wispy *dames de la nuit* in pink shifts, but most people he came into contact with were one thing or the other. This woman before him was both. As she pinned a loose strand of long black hair back into her low chignon he could not help but let his imagination bolt backward, reading in the precise elegance of her fingers the entire arc of her race right back to the imperial courts of bygone dynasties in ancient China, where courtesans had to be skillful with their fingers on bamboo flutes, but in the next moment he was jarred out of his delicious flight of fancy as those selfsame fingers clicked one against the other to snap an idling waitress to attention as the cosmopolitan before him ordered an espresso. Make it a double, she intoned. He blinked. And why, Mr. Benjamin, she asked, turning to him, would a literary magazine be interested in interviewing an actress?

Was she being self-deprecating, or was she fishing for a compliment?

Walter could hardly say it was because he was quite fond of actresses, and he found himself unwilling to verbalize to her how the extemporaneous interpolation of various spheres of her being—

actress, Chinese, American, flapper who had Europe wrapped around her little finger—was nothing short of scrumptious for someone like him, as if he were afraid to jinx it for her: that once he said the words she would no longer be authentic in her unwitting (or so he presumed) embodiment of the simultaneity of those signs.

Eichberg, he said, clearing his throat. We review Eichberg's films at *Die Literarische Welt*.

Yes, she said, of course. He could see her shifting gears as she prepared to talk up the new Eichberg Anglo-German coproduction she was in town for. Its English title was *Wasted Love*, she said, whereas its German title was *Dirty Money*. From the way she told this anecdote, he could tell she'd reused it any number of times. Her character's name was Song, she said. She was an urchin who got by catching lobsters on the beach, spotted by a knife thrower who incorporates her into part of his routine. It was her first lead role in a movie, she said, and also the first time she played a heroine—she saves the male lead's life, twice. When *Wasted Love* wrapped, she would move on to London to shoot *Piccadilly*, where she would again be one of the top-billed performers in a movie. This had never happened for her in Hollywood before, she said, and it was no longer possible now, in fact, for they had just introduced the Motion Picture Production Code stating expressly that depictions or suggestions of racial miscegenation were forbidden onscreen.

I had to look up *miscegenation* in the dictionary, the Chinese actress said. And I laughed, then I cried, because, let us be honest, every story is a love story. If it is illegal for me to kiss a white actor, where does that leave me? What that really means is that my character will always be a side character, Mr. Benjamin. In America my character dies in nine and a half out of ten films because a white male lead has to end up with a white female lead.

As she told him about her childhood, growing up poor in a hand laundry, he caught himself thinking how exciting and textured that all sounded. His own childhood had been pampered but colorless. On his travels through cities now he found himself turning in to the grimiest of back alleys, riding the most cramped of street trams, to steep in the mess that had been disallowed him. In Naples he'd found wonder in the fact that children were up at all hours, barefooted, and wrote in a travel column for a German newspaper: "Poverty has brought about a stretching of frontiers that mirrors the most radiant freedom of thought." The moment he saw it in print, Walter wished it could have been expunged from every circulated sheet. Only the most privileged of men could have written such a giddy, obtuse sentence. This, he thought, was in general the bone he picked with the academy, and the reason for his reluctance to fall in with the doctrine of theory. He still had a long way to go before he found a satisfactory means of expressing his ideas, but he was determined to make it his own.

A pastry flake had hitched itself onto the rounded edge of the Chinese actress's lower lip, and he was distracted by it. Walter wanted dearly to brush the crumb away. Not to touch her, but because that cherry-red mouth should remain pristine. When he queried her on modes of accessing interiority in her performance, she suggested girlishly: Might writing not be acting, on the page?

For him writing was more like blocking, when the director arranges the movements of his actors in relation to how he wants to move the camera within the space in the scene, but perhaps that was a matter of the distance of the approach, and he would doubtless be a far more reserved performer than she. Before he could offer any reply aloud, she retracted her opinion. You will forgive me, Mr. Benjamin, she said. Sometimes I think I feel everything but I know nothing.

But don't you see, he said, his eyes on the spot where the crumb had rested on her lip, though it was no longer there. You are an actress, so knowing is the same as feeling.

She smiled.

The effect her smile had was to make it seem as if her body were inclining toward him, rendering everyone else in the café absent, when in fact she had not moved, sitting perfectly still as she said: Thank you, Mr. Benjamin.

AT THE END of the interview, Walter paid for their pastries and coffee and they waited some time for change to be returned. He asked if she might be considering a move to Europe. Opportunities here seemed better for someone like her, the Chinese actress said, but L.A.

was still home, and she would prefer to remain there. His change still had not arrived, so Walter called over the manager, who said he would be happy to check with the waitress on duty.

Circling back to their table shortly after, the manager explained in polite German that the waitress was sure she'd already returned the change. Perhaps there has been an inadvertent mistake, Walter said in equally formal tones, my apologies in advance for discommoding you, but might you be able to check again? He'd put down a fifty-reichsmark banknote, and the bill had come up to only a little over six reichsmarks.

The manager excused himself.

Is everything all right? the Chinese actress asked. She must have been trying to follow the proceedings, and Walter was growing very embarrassed. Not to worry, he said to her with a nod, there is no problem. When the manager came to them again, his parlance was decidedly more direct than before. Sir, he said. My staff is certain there is no mistake. Walter did not want to make a scene in the crowded café, and already a few customers were beginning to turn their way. In that case, Walter said, standing up, we shall be taking our leave. The Chinese actress remained seated. Wait a minute, she protested in English to the manager, I was here all the while, and I saw with my own eyes that no change was returned. Instead of replying directly to her, the manager exchanged a look with Walter, as if to say: Take your woman in hand.

Come, Walter said, Miss Wong.

This is outrageous, the Chinese actress exclaimed indignantly. This is daylight robbery!

I am afraid, ma'am, the manager said in English, that you are disturbing the atmosphere of our coffeehouse, as a consequence of which I will have to ask your good self and your patron to leave our premises.

Outside, Walter flushed scarlet as he stumbled into an apology.

I cannot begin to express my copious regrets—

Don't be sorry, she averred, we should go to the police!

He shook his head.

Mr. Benjamin, she said, I am thoroughly prepared to be your eyewitness.

Thank you, he said, but I have no wish for you to undertake an abortive endeavor. He explained that there had been an incident reported recently in the papers where a Jewish guest's purse had gone missing from his escritoire during a hotel stay. When he went to the police, they contended that many Jews were inventing such stories so as to claim insurance money. Incensed, the man lodged an official complaint with the judicial authorities, which first ruled that he should pay the hotel damages for defamation, then threw his subsequent appeal out for "contempt of court," with legal fees for all parties to be borne by the plaintiff.

Therefore, Walter concluded, I submit that it would not do to waste Miss Wong's valuable time on a fool's errand while she should be enjoying her time in Berlin.

So you're Jewish, the Chinese actress said. I'm stupid about such things, you white people all look the same to me. Taken aback, Walter wanted to say that he wasn't white, and nominative declarations of categorical polemics were fraught with peril, but he was afraid to come across as chastising a Chinese woman, and he was dazzled, moreover, by the candor of her statement. He braced for a disparaging remark to follow, but she was smiling as she went on to relate, in a fond tone, an anecdote about a birthday party for a Jewish classmate in elementary school. I was the only one who turned up to her party, she was saying. After she dried her tears it was still just the two of us, so we gorged ourselves on the spread. I had a grand time. When I got home and told my parents all that had happened, she added, my mother expressed her approval. "A natural friendship," she called it, and I asked her what was natural about it. Do you know what my mother said, Mr. Benjamin?

He waited for her to go on, and she did so with a wry sort of relish he had not expected: What she said was, "After all, we Chinese are the Jews of the East!"

She began to laugh, a subtle, silver-toned sound, and Walter could not help but join in with his gravelly smoker's chuckle, even though it felt peculiar and inapposite to find any of this humorous. That girl had the prettiest hand mirror, the Chinese actress recalled with a sigh, backed in sterling silver. I'd wished for my own portable looking glass, too, so I could practice my acting wherever I went. Walter watched as she stopped to skip stones into the river. She was good at it. He wanted to share something with her, too, but he did not know what to say, and he would have picked up a pebble had his stone-skipping skills been any less dismal. They stood in silence for some time, then began walking toward the tramcar. She was due at a house party in Charlottenburg, she said, where she would be performing a Chinese tea ceremony for some artists, writers, and impresarios. Her sister, who had accompanied her on the trip, would also be meeting her there. He offered to escort her to the house party, in case she lost her way again.

It's true, she said, isn't it? I am prone to going around in circles.

He blushed, explaining he had not intended to imply her ineptitude with directions.

Mr. Benjamin, she said slowly, do you ever get the feeling that where life really happens is off the tracks?

I believe I do, he said. If he'd known her any better, and this was not their very first meeting, he would have replied: All the time. Now her professional demeanor was returning to the fore—it was so kind of him to chaperone her on her way, she said, and he would be welcome to join them as her guest. Walter was not one for parties, but the journalist in him knew it was bound to yield gainful material for his article. He accepted her invitation, and she admitted to being nervous about the tea ceremony she'd acquiesced to. May I confess, she said, that I don't know anything about tea? I'm more a soda-fountain type, but I couldn't tell them that, could I?

Couldn't you? he prodded, then snuck a sidelong glance at her willowy, pantsuited frame. She shrugged as she said with a smile: Who wants to see a Chinese girl drink Coca-Cola?

When Anna May received a copy of *Die Literarische Welt* a few months later back in Los Angeles, the bespectacled journalist had included an English translation of the article he'd written up on her so she could read it.

Everything that had happened in Berlin seemed so far away now.

The movie she'd shot in Europe had been edited and scored, but it was not yet out in America. Occasionally, when she saw a dark blonde with a soft perm on the streets or in a store, she might think of that woman she'd spent the night with. It was good that she was on a different continent—and married. There were no bothersome consequences to deal with when there was an ocean between them.

Anna May was beginning to think that married people started up affairs with her precisely because they could see the end in sight. The only serious relationship she'd had was a few years ago, with the director Tod Browning. She was only nineteen then, and he'd been married, too. Looking back, she did not know what she had been thinking. She'd not even decided if she really did fancy the man—he had a long, misshapen face, his front teeth were false, and he smelled of hard liquor at any given time of the day—or if it was just his movies she was drawn to, but quickly her parents were talking about disowning her, and the press had a field day flaming her every which way.

Shaken by all this opposition, she began to see that her only way out was to act like she knew exactly what she had been getting herself into, or no one would take her seriously henceforth. Everyone thought it was wrong, but for sham reasons. Not because she was underage and he in his forties, nor because she was single and he was married, but because she was Asian and he was white. It had taken a good half a year for the press to cool off, during which time reporters hounded not only Anna May but her family: What do you think of your daughter's interracial contamination? Her mother had come crying to her, begging her to end it so the family would no longer have to shoulder her disgrace. Haven't we brought you up well, Liu Tsong?

Compared with the drippy sensationalism Anna May was used to, Walter's article was hardly like a piece of journalism at all, and more like a mannered fairy tale. Walter certainly had a way with words, and although these words had been employed to flatter her, she noticed that he'd printed her name as May Wong rather than Anna May Wong, and the only reason she could think of for this was because the former sounded more Chinese. Also, he had gone heavy on the Oriental metaphors. On first read, she enjoyed them, they were so lyrical. Then when she looked at the article again she began to find it a touch ludicrous. As to what she had been wearing, he'd written—"one would like to know a Chinese poem for it." What would that have to do with a voguish pantsuit? She couldn't imagine anything less appropriate. She wrote back to thank him, though she did offer the comment: Does my name really remind you of "tiny chopsticks that unfurl into moon-filled scentless blossoms in a cup of tea," Mr. Benjamin? How so?

Walter's response came by express mail.

Ignorance is a dishonorable bulwark, the letter began, and a man could do better than to hide behind it, but might it count toward a mitigating circumstance that you are, indeed, the first Chinese woman I have met? He had not realized it beforehand, he wrote, but this must have exerted an influence on how he thought he had to write about her—namely as ethnography, or dream. Rereading the piece, it unsettled him to admit that it seemed more enamored of the poetic potential of presenting her as a Chinese woman than it was invested in decoding her intricate entanglements as more than that: an American; an actress. He had been ill equipped, in a social and thereby ultimately semantic sense, to transcribe their encounter in plain words. Why are we able only to aestheticize or abhor difference? Metaphors are a poor proxy, he wrote in closing. You will forgive me. There must be a better way ahead.

IN THE FOLLOWING years they kept in touch with the occasional letter. They went, gradually, from "Dear Mr. Benjamin" and "Dear Miss

Wong" to "Dear Walter" and "Dear Anna May." Walter enjoyed maintaining correspondence with a Chinese actress, and Anna May took pleasure in exchanging letters with a German critic.

She wrote him that she was slated to appear in *Daughter of the Dragon,* as an aristocrat who discovers the villainous Fu Manchu is her father. Fu Manchu would be played by Warner Oland, whose career was skyrocketing on yellowface roles. His popularity in both America and China had soared with the Charlie Chan franchise, wherein he played a globe-trotting Chinese detective incapable of speaking idiomatic English.

In China they hate me, Anna May wrote, but then, why do they love Mr. Oland? Each time she appeared in a movie, she told him, China printed in their papers: ANNA MAY WONG LOSES FACE AGAIN FOR CHINA! Whereas, to her stupefaction, the Chinese media sang Oland's praises. His portrayal of Charlie Chan was intelligent, genteel, capable, upstanding! There were even two Charlie Chan spinoff productions, one in Hong Kong, the other in Shanghai. Chinese actors tried to mime Warner Oland's mannerisms and gestures as meticulously as they could, Chinamen in a bid to outdo one another in emulating a Swede's caricature of a Chinaman.

Encouraged by Walter, Anna May took to the act of writing, too.

Sometimes she sent him drafts of essays she was hoping to get published in the papers, mostly Californian papers or women's magazines or entertainment weeklies, asking if he had time to look them over, though, she wrote, my words are surely so trivial next to yours.

He wrote her: You have no reason to self-efface to the extent that you do.

Alas, Mr. Benjamin, she replied, self-effacement is part of my rich matrilineal heritage. That is to say, as a Chinese girl, I was brought up phenomenally well.

In truth he *did* think her trivial, but all the more noble because of her triviality. She wrote impassioned little tracts on race and identity and stardom with popular titles, published on slow news days in second-rate papers. If collected in a dossier and read through one after the other, some proved flagrantly contradictory—"Beyond Racial Representation," she sent him, and shortly after, "Chinese Ways of Expressing Love"—but when read separately, they were diverting enough.

Her thought was neither sharp nor perspicuous enough to be original or savvy, but he read her—as she would be read nonetheless by strangers thumb and nose in newspapers—because she was a beautiful actress, and reading what a beautiful actress had written was a way of being with her.

She pandered in her writing, and so it disappointed.

But as an actress she had already abstracted and performed everything she could hope to assay in the curl of her wrist, the arch of her back, in a Chinese brocade costume or a slouchy flapper skirt. He read in her acting complicity and resistance at the same time, each enhancing the other. He read in her writing only one at a time, both cheapening themselves in turn.

He did not know at what level to address her drafts, and most often sent back niceties and piddling copyedits. Occasionally, he wrote her about how their new right-wing chancellor was cause for concern, but no one was doing anything about it, because what was there to be done, when he had come to power by democratic vote? The people had spoken. Even though the mixed spa Walter frequented in Wannsee had put up a sign to say they were "co-religionist," he no longer felt comfortable there—someone had daubed a swastika, in red lipstick no less, on the bath towel he'd left on a deck chair while he was soaking in the water. In other cheerless news, Heidelberg had rejected his dissertation on the origins of tragic German drama for being too frothy, and his father, a prominent banker, had curtailed his allowance significantly, disappointed that after enjoying an advantaged upbringing and unbounded financial support, not only had his son failed to make significant headway in his academic career and cultural portfolio, he was veering toward dialectical materialism: Already we are Jewish, must you also be Marxist?

He was trying to survive on freelance work, even as a radio scriptwriter, if she could imagine that, but with the newest Law for the Restoration of the Professional Civil Service, no one would hire him. His preferred Teutonic pseudonyms—Herr K. W. Stampflinger and Herr

Detlef Holz—had run their due course, and he could not even legally own a typewriter in Berlin. Still, he wanted to finish up his translation of Proust's *À la recherche du temps perdu,* but it never seemed to end. That would appear to mirror his on-again, off-again affair with a Latvian Bolshevik woman. For now it was on again, and as usual he was of two minds about it. Like you, he wrote, she, too, is an actress. But an agit-prop theater actress, who believes that children's theater could be used as a cornerstone for the education of the underprivileged offspring of the poor proletariat who otherwise have no opportunities for peda-gogical enrichment and social advancement. He would have wooed her with zeal, he wrote, but she was already married. She is a woman of ideas, he wrote fondly, that is to say, an ideal woman for me.

ALTHOUGH THEIR EPISTOLARY friendship was firmly platonic, Anna May felt a small pinch reading this letter. Not because she was jeal-ous that Walter admired this woman, but because the woman, "also an actress," sounded so much more sophisticated than she. Compared with this woman, she felt crude and unlettered, but was it really neces-sary to marry one's politics with one's art, and wouldn't it be for very wrong reasons if at the end of the day what Anna May wanted was not to change the world, but to garner for herself some measure of savoir faire?

She wrote Walter that she, too, seemed to fall for individuals who were already married, and that in her personal experience, none of those affairs had ended well, but then again, it could be because she was an Asian American woman and none of her white partners had taken her seriously. As a German Jewish cultural theorist wooing a Latvian Bolshevik theater actress, he would have more of a chance than she, she sincerely thought, and this might sound witless and ditzy, but she did truly believe that in life we all deserve to be happy and must muster up some measure of fool's courage to pursue that end, even in less than ideal circumstances.

Their correspondence tailed off after several years, when some of Anna May's letters to Walter were returned unopened. He must have moved to a different lodging, forgetting to update her with his new address. Often he wrote her from disparate locales—Ibiza, Svendborg, Nice, Paris—and she envied his mobility. As a freelance writer, he must have been able to work from anywhere he pleased, did not have to be tied down to an industry and a place, the way she was with Hollywood and L.A. It was too bad to lose touch. There had been something liberating about having no friends in common, no social pressure to meet in the flesh. She'd enjoyed their exchanges. Perhaps it was easier for them both to speak quite freely because they were each remote enough from the other in so many ways.

All her letters to him she had signed in this manner, arch and unvarying:

Orientally yours

七

DIE LITERARISCHE WELT

6 July 1928

Conversation with Anna May Wong

A CHINOISERIE FROM THE OLD WEST
Walter Benjamin

May Wong—the name sounds vibrantly edged, robust and light like tiny chopsticks that unfurl into moon-filled scentless blossoms in a cup of tea. My questions were the tepid bath into which the destinies it encloses are supposed to surrender a little of themselves.

In this hospitable Berlin house, we formed a small community that had gathered around the low table to follow the proceedings. But as it is said in the *Ju-Kia-Li:* "Pointless chatter about people's affairs frustrates important conversation."

At first nothing came of it for a long while and we had time to create an image of each other: the influential and worldly inhabitant of this room, who wished to offer us the final hours before her departure ("You encounter a person, he asks you for a favour; if he is pleased with you, then you become his friend"), the novelist, who later asks May Wong whether she rehearsed her roles before a mirror; the artist whom May Wong indicated on the left, the American journalist whom she indicated on the right, and Anna's sister who was accompanying her in Europe. The two of them came here from America all by themselves, and when they stood at the Hamburg train station, there was nothing left for them to do but to listen attentively and follow the group where they heard the word *Berlin* fall.

May Wong, as we know, is in the middle of the big film now being made under the direction of Eichberg. Of course, we learn very little about this film. "But the role is perfect," she said, "it belongs to me as no role before." Vollmoeller had written it just for her. And for this reason, there is sure to be much suffering and misfortune, for she loves tragic scenes. Her weeping is famous among her peers.

A full countenance like the spring breeze,
Plump and mild tempered

as it said in the fifth chapter of the *Dschung-Kuei*. That is why she loves to play her sad scenes in mature, weighty roles. "I don't like to always play flapper girls. I like mothers, most of all. I played a mother once, at the age of fifteen. Why not? There are so many young mothers."

She will, I told myself, come to speak about what we wish to know of her, of her own accord and for that reason all the more precious, the more skillfully I know how to distract her. "Do many aristocratic Germans"—as they say so beautifully in "Götz," when they want to make conversation—"now study in Bologna?" Or "Do the Chinese love film? Are there Chinese directors? Do they make movies in China?" Certainly they make movies. Of course they love it. Are there any people on earth who can escape film, either in love or fear?

Only, they began too late in China, at least if one trusts the impression of what was recently screened in Paris as "the first Chinese film." "The Rose of Pushui" is a work in which the most unscrupulous American method of direction underplays the infinitely subtle material, which the Mongoloid facial expressions portray for the film. Only a dilettante could dare to encapsulate in a few catchphrases the distinctiveness of these facial expressions and this approach to film acting. After all—be it due to the reticence, the speed, the quickness to smile, the abrupt shift into horror—in Europe, the emergence of the Japanese actor Sessue Hayakawa has not been forgotten to this day, even after ten years. His acting created a school. All the more strange how long it took in America for Chinese to be allowed or appointed to act in movies.

May Wong cannot imagine her existence without movies, and when I asked: "What medium would you reach for, if film was not at your disposal?" her sole response was "touch wood," and the entire group playfully hammered on our small table. May Wong makes a swing out of questions and answers: she leans back, reappears, sinks away, emerges again, and I feel as though I am giving her a little push from time to time. She laughs, that is all.

Her dress would not at all be inappropriate for such a garden game: a dark blue lady's suit, light blue blouse, embellished by a gold cravat—one would like to know a Chinese poem for it. She has always worn such clothing, for she was not born in China but in the Chinatown of Los Angeles. When her roles call for it, however, she dons the old costumes with pleasure. Her imagination works more freely when she wears them. Her favorite dress, which she wears at home from time to time, was tailored out of her father's wedding coat. With that we were back from "Bologna" and in Hollywood once more.

When it was first suggested to her to be filmed she found it strange, she wouldn't believe it. Of course, what fell to her was just a minor role. But we imagined the feverish excitement with which she sought her first appearance on the silver screen, and her boundless disappointment that it came to nothing. She had put such effort into it. For she had been interested in films from early on. She still remembers today the first time she stepped into a cinema. School was out that day due to some epidemic. With her pocket money she bought a ticket. As soon as she got home, she reenacted before a mirror all that she had seen. For, as it is said in the story of two cousins, in the chapter about the departure of the crane and the return of the swallow: "One's career in life is a matter to which one must turn one's thoughts early on."

She has long since had no use for mirrors—neither a glass mirror nor a distorting paper mirror that replies to her as public opinion.

Friendly and hostile criticism matter little to her. "Because," this Chinese saying comes from her directly, "one hears the bitter truth only from enemies. I want to hear the bitter truth also from friends." "Do you have role models? Teachers?" "No. There are actresses whom I admire, but the only time I picked up another's gesture, it was from—according to the general conviction of Hollywood—the most stupid, most untalented actress around."

We had already wandered into another room. May Wong quickly found her reclining position again. She seemed to feel comfortable here, letting loose her long hair, arranging it to resemble "a dragon frolicking in water," stroking it at her brow. Right in the middle, it cuts in at a deeper angle, creating the most heart-shaped of all faces.

Everything that is heart seems to be reflected in her eyes.

I know I shall see her again, in a film that may be similar to the fabric of our dialogue, of which I say, along with the author of the *Ju-Kia-Li:*

The fabric was divinely worn,
  But the face was finer still.

八

The morning he finally decided to leave Marseilles, Walter took his time finishing up the last of the ersatz coffee, roasted from acorns. The nutty taste he'd found nauseating in the beginning had grown on him. He studied his emergency U.S. entry visa as he waited for the water to heat up. Even the umlaut in his full name was accurately reflected: Walter Bendix Schönflies Benjamin.

The kettle whistled a gentle boil.

Staidly he observed that he was far less anxious when there had been no visa. With no practicable way out then, he was quite free to go about his daily business. Now, alas, he was faced with a dancing bear's obligation to perform the grandiose escape he'd been putting off for years. When the visa first reached him in Paris months ago, painstakingly procured and securely forwarded to him by Adorno and Horkheimer in L.A., Walter had chucked the whole envelope casually on a pile of old newsprint in a corner of his rented pension. Such travel documents were in very short supply. Most countries had officially closed their borders off to German Jewish refugees; no one wanted a mass influx of someone else's problem on their hands. War had been declared, and Walter was an enemy alien in Paris, but he'd wanted to start on a new book—about Baudelaire. Instead of ratifying the visa at a consulate and making his way to America as soon as possible, Walter went to the Bibliothèque Nationale to renew his library membership card, so he could carry out his research uninterrupted. It was only when word came that the Wehrmacht was pushing into Paris that Walter entrusted his *Arcades Project* manuscript to Bataille, returned all the Baudelaire books to the library, and fled, first to Lourdes, then Marseilles.

The kettle was screaming now, but Walter's inertia had expatiated beyond the room. If he did not have the energy to turn it off and make his morning coffee, how would he be able to climb a mountain and cross a sea? It had been impertinent and irresponsible to set larger wheels in motion when he had no real certainty as to whether he could bring himself to follow an arc till its end. By the time Walter got to Marseilles, it was no longer so easy to set sail from this busy port with its indelicate miasma of oil, urine, printer's ink. Article XIX of the Franco-German armistice had been signed, requiring the French government to surrender on demand anyone the NSDAP wanted extradited to Germany.

Walter was most certainly on that list.

The Gestapo had put in a repatriation order with the German Embassy in Paris fairly early on after getting wind of the "Paris Letter," in which Walter had written unequivocally: "culture under the swastika is nothing but the playground of unqualified minds" and "fascist art is one of propaganda." He did not have a death wish, but surely, in writing, one strives to tell the truth as clearly as one can, or why write at all? Paris had not spat him back out to Berlin then, but circumstances were different now. Vichy France was already borrowing from the populist nationalism of Germany's swastika. Leery of that scuzzy mix they now termed the Anti-France—namely Protestants, Jews, Freemasons, foreigners, Communists, homosexuals, and Romani—they were setting up their own special commissions to take care of these aforementioned public enemies. Together with the left-wing government that had been in power, these rotted apples must surely be responsible for their country's effete standing. Once they were rid of these undesirable persons, they could make France *magnifique* again. Better to have a strong authoritarian government that cared for and cultivated its real sons than a namby-pamby republic: high-minded promises for rootless cosmopolitans full of hot air.

Without washing out yesterday's dregs, Walter prepared his coffee.

Waiting for it to brew, he ran a free hand along the spines of the last few books he carried with him, enjoying the amicable sound this made. What he missed most in exile was his personal library, and the beloved rare books he'd saved up for on errant paychecks. Walter had accumulated twenty-eight changes of address in assorted cities for seven years prior, parting with more and more of his collection with each move. Also, he'd lost touch with most friends and acquaintances:

it was no longer safe for him to give out his address, even under a false name. Between looking over his shoulder and settling down in yet another makeshift place, Walter fleshed out concurrent manuscripts. When there was no more paper, he resorted to using both sides of the page, a breach in etiquette he found distasteful, and when even that had been exhausted, he wrote his notes between the lines of his own handwriting. Given that he was always on the run, with fresh paper in short supply, he realized that the precariousness of his daily life was forcing him to think and write, more and more, in elliptical paragraphs. It was all he could manage of late, in flight. If any of these provisional drafts were ever published, what a lark it would be if readers considered their fragmented form a pure element of style.

Nursing his acorn coffee, he watched a black ant cross the threshold of the rickety table, sizable morsel hoisted over its exoskeleton. How he admired the ability of the common ant to bear loads hundreds of times in excess of its own body weight! He flicked it off the table. Then he tried to look for it on the floor, but it was nowhere to be found. Later in the day, after trimming his moustache very short and patting on cedarwood aftershave in the spots he'd knicked, Walter packed a black leather suitcase crammed full of his papers, one change of undergarments, and the visa. There was no space for his books, and so he left them behind.

FROM MARSEILLES, WALTER caught a train to Port-Vendres, meeting up with a socialist-democrat photographer and her son who were hoping to make the same passage. Like Walter, the two possessed an entry visa into America, but not the relevant exit visa out of Vichy France. For this reason, they had all been counseled that the best way to attempt their exit would be to cross overland from Port-Vendres, the southernmost tip of Vichy France, where it met the northern cusp of its neutral Spanish neighbor, Portbou, between mountain and sea. After entering Portbou, they would head on to Lisbon and sail for America. Fresh lace doilies brightened the worn headrests in the communal train carriage. The photographer had a small stash of bogus food stamps, with which she'd obtained some bread and tomatoes. She shared them with Walter on the commute. Upon reaching Port-Vendres, the trio made a discreet survey of the track they would take, cutting across a stretch of the Pyrenees mountains on foot to reach Portbou.

Circumspection and his infirm heart led Walter to propose his spending the night up on the mountain after the recon so he would not have to exert himself on the same route the very next day, when they embarked on the track proper.

They tried to dissuade him, but he was firm.

You must understand, he said, I do not wish to retrace a single step.

And so Walter spent the night alone with his suitcase in a small stand of parasol pines, the scent of fermenting grapes reaching him on the nighttime wind. Regrouping the next morning, they were ready to walk from one topography of fascism into another—it had been nary a year since the Spanish democrats fell to Franco's nationalists in the Guerra Civil—one that, for now, better suited their logistical predicament.

They tried to make themselves look inconspicuous among the vine workers, but with his spectacles and the black leather briefcase, Walter was sure they stood out. He wanted the photographer and her son to go ahead of him, but they said it was better to walk together. Calmly, he explained his reason. They would have none of it. Also, he confessed, he feared his stamina was giving out. It had been several hours of hiking upward, fording unpaved dirt roads, climbing over limestone boulders that littered overgrown slopes. They were not family, he counseled, and had only just made the other's acquaintance by pure chance, so there was please no need to feel constrained.

Still they refused to leave him on his own.

Every ten minutes, Walter stopped to rest for one minute, and they waited with him. Silently grateful for their comradeship and wary of slowing them down, he counted every second on his wristwatch, forcing himself up at forty-five or thirty. When Walter well and truly could walk no farther, the photographer relieved him of his hand luggage, and her son propped him up to cross the last, steep vineyard. Seeing the middle-aged woman struggle with his heavy briefcase when she herself was traveling without trappings, Walter was beset by guilt, but still he could not bring himself to discard his life's work. Ma'am, he said. You should not be bearing my burden. I can only hope you will believe me when I say that these contents are more important to me than my life itself.

I believe you, she said simply, without irony.

Topping the ridge, they sighted the stark cerulean repose of the Mediterranean Sea below them. The sea was so blue it took Walter's breath away. It was a beautiful late-September morning. He'd written Adorno and Horkheimer drolly that even if a fossil piece like him survived the arduous journey with his diseased heart and sooty lungs, personally, he did not see the draw of being wheeled around and exhibited as "the last European" in America. Los Angeles is not America, Adorno had written back, it is Weimar under palm trees. Here the climate is wonderful, and you will do your best work.

Walter had to concede—perhaps he had been wrong to dismiss wholesale the idea of a new life—he was looking forward to seeing his friends again. Coughing, he allowed himself to entertain the thought: If I reach Los Angeles in one piece, I'll owe it to myself to quit smoking. A lone gull flew by, wingspan prodigious, and Walter felt his syncopated heart soar with it.

AT THE FRENCH-SPANISH overland border, Walter, the photographer, and her son presented themselves to the authorities of Portbou. They were informed on the spot that without the relevant exit visa out of Vichy France, they were being denied entry into Francoist Spain, which had recently canceled all transit visas for German Jewish refugees. The provincial Spanish border police at Portbou had been briefed to expel any such persons as soon as reasonably possible back to Vichy French authorities, who would in turn rotate them on to their Nazi higher-ups.

Don't look at me that way, ma'am.

We are just following protocol, and you do not possess the required paperwork. We reserve the right to refuse entry. It is regrettable, but consider it from our point of view. Surely it will be a problem for us if our country runs amok with Protestants, Jews, Freemasons, foreigners, Communists, homosexuals, and Romani.

We apologize for any inconvenience caused.

We will arrange a train carriage for your deportation in the morning. For an overnight stay, we recommend the Hostal França.

THEY PAID UP front for their rooms.

The Portbou police posted a sentry outside the motel.

The photographer and her son shared a twin room. Walter asked for a single. The courteous Spanish *abuela* who kept the establishment spick-and-span showed him to room number 3. There was absolutely nothing to do. Walter deeply regretted not packing a book to read. Glancing at the heft of his unfinished manuscript in the suitcase, he thought it was unforgivably egotistical to have lugged these papers along. They should be burned at once. In any case, when was the last time he'd derived the scholarly satisfaction of a thesis smoothed over? He never had that luxury on the run. It was hard for him to believe that things had come to this, when he was just a man who liked to write and read. Each time he put on his round, thick spectacles and peered at the worn-out, rabbity reflection in the mirror, it made him want to laugh. This was the face of a man who was being hunted down by the secret police?

He unpacked and repacked his suitcase, and started to shave.

On the little vanity he arranged his shaving kit and the fifteen tablets of morphine he'd carried around with him ever since Hitler had been sworn in as chancellor, hidden not without ignoble mirth between his change of underwear. The tablets were eight years old, and he could only hope they had not lost their potency. Walter had asked the apothecary all those years ago: You are most certain this amount will suffice? If it came to it, he added, it would be best to err on the side of caution in this sort of matter, you understand. Sir, the apothecary assured him, it would do well enough to finish off a prizefighting bull.

After shaving, Walter made sure his teeth and fingernails were clean.

Before administering the lethal dose, he smashed his watch, so it would not distract its owner in his last hour with its faithful ticking.

Crunching down on the watch face under his boot momentarily took the edge off everything. It gave Walter a good thrill, in equal parts sacrilegious and satisfying. As a small child, Walter recalled coming up to just the pendulum bob of an enormous Winterhalder & Hofmeier grandfather clock in the corner of his family's antique shop. In order to better mask their wealth, his father had taken to saying he was only an antiques dealer, not a banker. The standing clock had a moon dial, and peering at the weights and cable pulleys visible through the beveled glass panels, Walter had had a magnificent view of the anagogic workings of time. Having now destroyed his timepiece, he could not be sure how much time had passed, but sometime later, recumbent on neat bed linen with the drug dribbling through his bloodstream, completely alone in a small town whose randomness bothered him more than its desolation, moving a shoulder and hearing the old creak of a loose spring in the mattress, Walter began to regret what he had done, but of course it was too late.

He twitched.

He was curious to know if the twitch was his own doing, or an effect of the morphine. It was hard to say. He reminded himself that at the bottom of it all, things were only mannequins. Everything was simply a matter of sooner or later, and at least this way, he would go by his own hand. If there was only a way to know how close he was to the end, he would have felt better. A blackish anxiety of losing control over his final thoughts was starting to slip over everything, and his breath began to shorten up into shallow, gasping intervals.

It took Walter every last shred of his will to calm himself down, and re-create with exquisite precision the scent of his library. It smelled of pinecones and cinders, and called to mind two of his favorite things: coffee and rain. Looking through the book crates that had just arrived, Walter was surprised to see that his collection had been delivered in its entirety. All of them were in one place again. He'd forgotten he owned this volume. What to place next to that?

I am unpacking my library, he thought. Yes, I am. The books are not yet on the shelves, not yet touched by the mild boredom of order. I cannot march up and down their ranks to pass them in review before a friendly audience. You need not fear any of that. Instead, I ask you to join me in the disorder of crates that have been wrenched open, the air saturated with the dust of wood, the floor covered with torn paper, to join me among piles of volumes that are seeing daylight again after years of darkness, so that you may be ready to share with me a bit of the mood—it is certainly not an elegiac mood, but, rather, one of anticipation—

The Malayan Orangutan
Has the Key
to the Basement
of the Leipzig Zoo

II

Life is short but art is long. Leni chanted her scales outside a trailer high up in the Bavarian Alps. *Ars longa,* she articulated at different pitches, slightly out of breath, *vita brevis.* One more set of calisthenics to go—she was warming up her voice and body at the same time.

Life is short but art is long, she panted, *ars longa, vita brevis!*

Upon nailing her last jumping jack she bent over to touch her toes, taking a quiet moment for herself before the rush of the workday began. A director was the eye of the storm, a general who commandeered by example. Leni adhered to the same morning routine on shoot so she could ground herself for the unpredictable challenges ahead. Making a movie is just like being at war, she often told her crew. Another favorite proclamation of hers: How splendid this mountain air is! Such statements might have sounded glib, but they were intended, in good part, as reminders to her crew of how lucky they were to be working on her movie. *Tiefland* was about a young gypsy dancer torn between an innocent shepherd and a greedy marquis, a mountain movie that had nothing to do with reality. Down below, across Europe, it was all hair and teeth and eyes. The minimum conscription age was inching lower by the day, the maximum higher.

If her crew didn't pull their weight, she might have to let the incompetent ones go.

Leni knew everyone in the safety net of her employ was trying to remain in her good graces for that reason, and she had to take their compliments with a pinch of salt, but even then, when they'd praised her performance in unison the day before, she was so pleased she didn't need to pop a nighttime muscle relaxant to help her fall asleep.

Tiefland is going to be gold, her assistant said. Martha is such a sympathetic character, and dare I say, Miss Riefenstahl, you've given her so much soul, she dances right off the screen!

Blood still pumping from her exercise, Leni felt refreshed and ready this morning. She brushed her hair back and put on her trusty camel overcoat. Double-breasted and slimming when belted, it photographed wonderfully for production stills and never appeared to get dirty. Whenever she thrust it off, the assistant, who trailed behind Leni with a clipboard, a tumbler of water, and a jar of smelling salts, was expected to catch the coat before it touched the ground. Her bladder colic was better today, too. Though it was still thick and foul smelling, there was hardly any blood in her urine as she squatted in the outhouse they'd constructed at the back of their encampment. The pain, while troublesome, was manageable—she'd just received a fresh batch of methadone painkillers direct from the good people at IG Farben. Quality stuff, synthesized specially for field surgery on injured soldiers, it was not sold on the market. Morphine had been effective, but it made her drowsy. She could not afford to look woozy, not when she was both lead actress and director.

In the large-scale documentaries she'd shot for the Party, there were as many as a few hundred men under Leni's thumb, running around doing whatever she told them to. Line producers, cinematographers, unit managers, film loaders, assistant directors, sound grips, location scouts, script supervisors, lighting technicians, boom operators, crowd controllers. Everyone was waiting for Miss Riefenstahl to call action, say cut. She expected complete allegiance to her vision, and there were those who found her directing style too controlling.

An older male cinematographer once walked off Leni's set.

In the middle of a take, she'd given him an exasperated look and gestured with a flurry of her hands that he was not moving fast enough to cover the action. Speed up, she mouthed. He turned to her, halting the production. With all due respect, Miss Riefenstahl, he said. If you have determined all my start and end points, as well as every last angle and the speed of the coverage, without including me in the discussion, overriding all my opinions, what room do I have to breathe?

I don't need you to breathe, she told him, I just need you to move the camera!

Looking at his face she was afraid he was going to hit her, but with a quick glance around she felt confident he would not dare to do so in front of everyone, and went on unruffled: Look, if you listen to all I say, you know there is a good chance you will win a prize next year.

I'd ride you below the crupper, bitch, the cinematographer said, only you're too high-strung for anyone to have a good time.

Men would mouth off without thinking twice about who they were crossing. Never having to fight for anything made them complacent and impulsive. She wanted to scream: You're fired! But she bit this back just in time. No matter how firmly she'd planted her feet, any day she could have the carpet yanked out from under her—best to retain a sense of scale when your opponent was losing his—and now she sensed the crew's sympathies tilting toward her. Why lose their favor just to have the last word? She dug her heels in. A vulnerable silence would serve her better. True enough, they came up to her after he left, asking if she was all right, offering her a hot drink. She shook her head and smiled bravely. Let's go on with the scene, she said. When the crew relayed that story down the grapevine, there was, more or less, only one way it could end now: Miss Riefenstahl was a true professional.

WHEN SHE RECEIVED the phone call from the Reich Ministry of Public Enlightenment and Propaganda to inform her that *Tiefland* was green-lit, mute tears of relief slid down Leni's cheeks, though over the line she preserved perfectly the clipped tone of official bureaucratese. Financing was in place and they were good to go once she submitted her crew list, and the Ministry had verified that everyone was in good blood standing. They would set up a date so she could sign the paperwork for the Doctor.

Thank you, she said, I can't wait to begin.

Clicking the phone back onto the receiver, she did a victory jig around the table alone in her kitchen in Berlin—she intended to spend as long as she could on this movie, up in the mountains, far away from what was going on in the cities. As soon as she started sketching out ideas for *Tiefland*'s production design, the migraine that had been bothering her for months lifted. Everyone knew H favored her from the beginning, but what no one knew was how it had been growing much trickier to do what she wanted without putting the Party off. If she wanted the NSDAP to continue funding and prioritizing her projects, she had to remain relevant to them while making her own art.

The best way to make use of someone is to make them think they are making use of you. H had a soft spot for her, and they could easily spark each other into a creative tizzy when speaking of an upcoming collaboration in abstract terms, thus clearing a wide berth for her: Of course she wanted to make *Tiefland* because the mountains were so resplendent, they reminded her of the Volk! A gift to the people, a return to the mystical, a tribute to the land. Yes, it looked like she might have to play Martha, the lead character, herself, since she'd once been a classical dancer—it would seem there was no Party-approved actress more suitable for the challenges of the role. How fantastic that her personal desires dovetailed with the Party's vision for a new order. My aesthetic aspiration, your political intent. In different tongues we speak the same language, moving toward an unshakable purity for the future.

As usual, the one with doubts was the Doctor.

Yet another mountain movie? He steepled his fingers contemplatively. I do wonder—at this point, what would we do with one of those? You know we admire your movies, but we can only fund something that makes sense for us. I'm certain you understand?

The Doctor saw right through her. She hated him for it.

In another universe, she once entertained the disgusting thought for a second, they could have been good together: an ambitious duo who understood each other perfectly. Under current conditions, he was an obstacle poised to inconvenience her at every turn. Yet the Doctor could not stop her, as long as H was there to back her up. This was the sorest of points for the Doctor. In the beginning Leni had childishly flaunted it, but as soon as she saw that the Doctor's resentment of her special closeness to H went beyond the professional, she knew better than to continue provoking him.

As the Minister of Propaganda, not only did the Doctor control the purse strings for the arts and the budget of your production, he decided whether you and your work were German or un-German. Rub the Doctor the wrong way, and with one piece of paper and a rubber stamp, he could ensure with immediate effect that you would never work in this country again. He was the one who led the book burnings and the fire oaths: No to decadence and moral corruption! Yes to decency and morality in family and state! I consign to the flames the writings of the Weimar revisionist Thomas Mann, the milksop traitor Erich Maria Remarque, and the debauched foreigner Ernest Hemingway. Burn them all!

EVERY NIGHT LENI prayed Germany would win the war.

She prayed hard, not because she was a patriot, not because she was loyal to the Party, not because H could do no wrong, but because, honest-to-goodness, she did not want to go down with any of them. If they won, she might come up tops again. Was it really so wrong to want the best for yourself? She'd put all her eggs in one basket. Everything seemed so promising in their early years together—the economy had stabilized, the NSDAP was revered, her films were celebrated. Things were different now. These days, Leni never undressed fully before bed. It was safer to go to sleep with your clothes on. If something happened you could throw on a coat, lace up your boots, and run. Often in her dreams she was sprinting dry-mouthed with no end in sight, but when she turned around there was no one behind her.

Most mornings Leni woke frightened, but she could not show that troubled face to the crew, not when *Tiefland* felt like a plentiful commune protected by a spell: if one person broke down to ask why they were making an alpine movie about a shepherd and a dancer when the world around them had gone mad, everything would turn to dust— they would all be back in the city, queueing for rations and cowering in bunkers. That must not happen.

She would be the magic pillar everyone leaned on.

Swallowing the pills and supplements she needed to get through the day—light barbiturates for the anxiety, methadone for the bladder colic, St. John's wort for everything else—Leni grabbed some breakfast from the cook's tent and headed to the editing cabin. Reviewing the rushes that had been printed and prepared for her on the projector in the editing cabin this morning, she was not too pleased with what she saw. You can't trust anyone's eye other than your own—Leni thought her face looked stiff. There was not enough light on her as she entered, and more fog was required so that when the mountains (moments ago so artfully obscured) were revealed, the viewer could be lifted into their grandeur. Thankfully, all of this was remediable. They would reshoot the scene today—as many takes as were needed to achieve what she wanted.

As long as they were here, hard at work on *Tiefland*, everything could seem all right.

This was their world, not the one down below. Each morning Leni buzzed her scales, feeling the ticklish susurrations of her own voice and lips in her ears, on her cheeks. Life is short, she droned, art is long. Till the scales and words were just air vibrating through larynx, and there was no more doubt left, only the one clear objective: *Ars longa*— she was not responsible for anything else, other than making the best film she could—*vita brevis*.

III

Morning light is cooler and softer, Hans Haas could hear Schmitz say if he closed his eyes while on dawn patrol around the mountain valley. The sun shines in from the horizon, not the way it beats down at midday. Its angle is sharper. Use a blue low light, close to the rear. Overexpose ever so slightly, but check if the director finds it acceptable. We have to be very precise with the lights, so the director can be free.

Amid this idyllic set in the mountains, Hans Haas felt calm. If Schmitz could have been here, too, everything would have been perfect. In the daytime, there were quiet moments for Hans Haas to look out and observe the quality of the light, the way it filtered through the mist. Sometimes he still woke in the middle of the night expecting to rub fine sand from his face, with the impulse to grab his rifle, but he had only to open his eyes and breathe in the mountain air to assure himself that he was not back in the heat of the North African desert, he was on a clean straw pallet in the Bavarian Alps. He was not being jostled this way and that by a leathery-skinned platoon leader in dusty fatigues, he was being instructed by a sharp-looking woman in a sleek camel overcoat. He was not on the losing end of the Afrika Korps campaign in Sirte, he was on the set of a state-sanctioned Bergfilm with a generous budget. There was clean water: not only to drink, but to bathe in. Three hot crew meals were served daily. Yesterday Miss Riefenstahl had even passed around the toffee candy she normally reserved for the child extras. The warmth of buttermilk fat melting on his tongue left an unexpectedly sour aftertaste.

Hans Haas had been on set for only a week or two, and like everyone else here, he hoped to remain as long as the war went on. They were safe here. He oversaw the security of the animals and the extras, assisted Miss Riefenstahl's gaffer with the lights. Handling bounce boards and gobo stands he was in his element again, no more Astras and Karabiners. There was something about gunmetal that made his hands go cold when reloading the magazine, even if it was just practice.

Having taken part in two Wehrmacht campaigns on the North African front, Hans Haas was being rotated back to Berlin for his rest when Riefenstahl Film GmbH, upon receiving a new batch of extras for its production, had wanted to borrow a few Afrika Korps servicemen on furlough to beef up security. Candidates with technical experience in the movie industry were preferred so they could help out on set at the same time. Passing through Tyrol on the way home, the commander had asked if any one of them had experience with film production. Hans Haas had been one of the few selected and dispatched since he'd worked as a best boy at UFA, known to be the premium motion-picture production company in Berlin.

PASSING THE HAIR and makeup trailer, Hans Haas overheard Miss Riefenstahl telling the makeup artist to lay on the foundation thickly. He felt a little sorry that no one dared to tell her that that only made her look older. This would have been less of a problem if she had not hand-picked such a young lad to play the male lead: Franz boasted to anyone who would listen that Miss Riefenstahl had plucked him right off a ski slope in St. Anton, for "being her type." It was fine that he'd never acted, what was important to her was that he had the exact right look to play her love interest. Be that as it may, he was an atrocious performer, and they made for an awkward onscreen couple: Franz was not yet twenty, and Miss Riefenstahl must have been over forty.

Hans Haas watched them rehearse the scene where shepherd Pedro and dancer Martha meet in the meadow. Gaze at me with desire, Miss Riefenstahl commanded. Franz tried to make his eyes soulful and stirring, widening and narrowing them repeatedly, as he breathed audibly and stamped his foot like a donkey.

Everyone else was in silent stitches.

Miss Riefenstahl called for restraint. Hans Haas could see that she was trying to pretend she had not noticed that everyone was having a laugh at her expense in order to remain in character, but it all flew over Franz's broad shoulders, till finally she called out in exasperation: Gaze

at me with desire, but like a virgin! Hans Haas sneezed. Miss Riefenstahl snapped out of character. Is something the matter? she demanded
in the general direction of the crew. I hire you to play to my strengths,
not to jeer when we are experiencing technical difficulties.

If Schmitz were here, Hans Haas was certain they would have
locked eyes and burst out laughing. Then he would have been in
trouble, but Schmitz had a knack for getting him out of things. Hans
Haas had been Schmitz's apprentice. Everyone in the industry knew
Schmitz was one of the best gaffers in Berlin, and Schmitz had taught
him everything he knew.

THE FIRST TIME he met Schmitz on a UFA production lot in Berlin,
the set was lit brightly. People were moving around like wind-up toys
finding their positions.

Sunrise slants, a voice called out. Lower all key lights on set!

The lights were lowered. The man calling out instructions was
thickset, his russet hair somehow clashing with his large frame. When
the line producer introduced Hans Haas to him, he scowled and said
as if Hans Haas were not present: Long arms, yes, but like matchsticks!

Later, when Hans Haas burned his fingers on a red light, Schmitz
said to his subordinate, addressing him in the third person: Of course
young Haas already shows how fit he is. What's your eelskin stuffed
with, pudding? Schmitz flicked him a damp towel as he moved the
red light on his own. Welcome to the world of light and shadow, Hasi.
Hans Haas watched the lead actress step on set in a forest-green coat
as Schmitz suffused the interior set—an entire boulevard, replete with
streetlamps—with a fresh, early-morning glow.

Though light was integral to films, gaffers came and went completely unrecognized and uncelebrated. That did not stop Hans Haas
from looking up to Schmitz as an artist. When he told this to Schmitz,
he received a smack on the head. Who wants to be an artist, Schmitz
said, they're bootless faggots! Call me what I am—a craftsman.

Hans Haas admired that his mentor was practical, but imaginative.

He could create a naturalistic, late-afternoon light on an enclosed
set with just a single source of hard light, rigged to a studio beam, dif-

fused with muslin, and distributed with the clever use of mirrors. He was quick to think up eccentric but effective solutions. Hans Haas had watched him put on a double layer of gloves before lifting a portable light source, swinging it evenly from left to right to mimic the passing movement of cars, take after take, with unwavering precision. When the director wanted a certain effect from the light and the cinematographer had not achieved it precisely, Schmitz knew immediately what to tweak. He would call for a different lens to be added to the light to narrow it down or spread it out. His hands, always gloved on set, were nevertheless scarred heavily with burn marks. He spoke firmly to Hans Haas, giving him clear instructions on setups, but in between takes he discoursed with more sensitivity than Hans Haas would have expected. Light should tell a story without calling attention to itself, Schmitz would say. Diffusion softens imperfections. By pulling light farther away from the object it hits, you create harder shadows. That's all the rage in Hollywood now, but everyone here knows we did it first in *The Cabinet of Dr. Caligari!*

Schmitz gave Hans Haas credit when it was due, while shouldering Hans Haas's mistakes as his own. On one production, Hans Haas was rigging up a Hal 500 when a malfunctioning screen door dropped right beside the ankle of the Czech-sourced actress Lida Baarova. She burst into loud tears. The producer wanted Hans Haas dismissed, not just from the set, but from UFA altogether. Schmitz stepped in.

It didn't even touch her!

Look, the producer said. Do you know who she is?

Hans Haas nodded.

I can't be sure, Schmitz said sarcastically. She is—Lida Baarova?

My friend, the producer said. You know just what I mean.

Hans Haas nodded again.

They had all seen the Minister of Propaganda visit the set, where he was shown to a special seat behind the director. Herr Doktor Goebbels had even been heard boasting that Miss Baarova possessed the most adorable belly button in all of Germany. They'd all seen Miss Baarova leave in the Doctor's chauffeured ride after they wrapped for the day, not even waiting for the car to pull out of UFA before she melted into his arms in the backseat.

So, Schmitz said. Are we NSDAP doormats now? I don't see why I should be, when I'm not a Party member. Neither are you, nor is baby-cheeks Haas here. How is it anyone's business some Reichstag rat-face is messing with a Czech muffin? Let's have some principles. If you want to fire Haas, you'll have to fire me, too!

The producer eyed Hans Haas. Don't get too big for your breeches just because you've got yourself a crusader, he said before going on his way. Schmitz patted the producer on the back and stepped to the side for a smoke. Hans Haas followed behind as he watched Schmitz roll his tobacco. Thank you, he said. Schmitz shook his head and exhaled as he offered up a drag. Although Hans Haas did not smoke, he took it, trying for casual as he inhaled. You got it all wrong, kid, Schmitz was saying. Doing the right thing is nothing personal, see?

Hans Haas returned Schmitz his cigarette.

Schmitz stuck it back in the corner of his mouth. He frowned.

Haas, my man, Schmitz said. It is very bad etiquette to take a puff of someone's cig and return it wet! I can never understand this; it's outside your mouth, not in it. You'd better figure this out right away, or I'll fire you myself, you hear?

IV

Before retreating to the mountains for her shoot, Leni had to meet with the Doctor to get his signature for the paperwork in regards to the funding for *Tiefland*. For the meeting, she dressed as modestly as possible: stiff fabric, dark colors, thick stockings, covered shoes, unwaved hair, minimal makeup.

Following the state's incorporation of the once-private UFA film studio as part of the Ministry of Propaganda, Leni's eponymous production company, Riefenstahl Film GmbH, was one of only three production companies permitted to operate autonomously of the Reich.

The funds for *Tiefland* had been authorized from H to her, but that was not to say that it had come easy: after the Doctor's lukewarm response to her proposal for *Tiefland*, she'd gone out on a limb, writing to H and explaining her concept to him, without sending the Doctor a carbon copy of their correspondence, as she knew he much preferred her to do. She was touched—what with everything else on his plate—that H wrote back in no time at all to say that she should go ahead, he would support her with whatever budget she found appropriate. Forgive the Doctor for being practical, he wrote. He has the Party's best interests. I do, too, but just as importantly, I have so much faith in you. I can only hope I won't let you down, she ended her response to him.

His reply was brief: You can't let me down. It is not possible.

Oh, she felt herself turn pink, it was better than love! H and she did not see each other much—even when they met, it was rare for them to divulge any respective personal details, as if the sanctity and solidity of their friendship must be protected at all costs from the germs of the banal and the maudlin, and they were allowed to speak only of visions and ideals—but she knew they shared an elemental bond: how they craved for the world to be brighter, the stage larger. Trumpets in her head and flowers in her chest when she read H's letter, but she would have to downplay her victory when she went in to see the Doctor. Each time she bypassed the Doctor to go directly to H, she knew she would have to be prepared to pay for it in some way, at some point. He had his mealy-mouthed, double-edged ways of getting back at her.

THE DOCTOR WAS said to have a proclivity for actresses, and Leni had fully intended to use this to her advantage, but there was something in him that was closed to her, that caused him to keep her at arm's length.

Leni did not understand this until she decided to befriend the Doctor's wife. Magda was a Party secretary, and another woman who enjoyed H's special confidence. It seemed to Leni that all of H's confidantes were female. He did not have any friends who were men, just as everyone she personally relied on was male. A small price to pay for large achievements. Men were intimidated by H, she thought, just as women must be resentful of her. In any case, male or female, keep your enemies close, and their spouses closer. Bring them expensive cream biscuits when their other halves are out of town, and you might learn something new.

Sure enough, midway through the one-on-one afternoon chat, Magda dropped the decorous niceties, and after checking that the children were absorbed in a spelling game with the nanny, looked at Leni quite hungrily, cantilevering her bosom over the tea tray to say: Tell me, please. What is it like to know him as an artist?

Leni was dismayed.

Dunderheaded Magda must be experiencing marital woes—she was worried that Leni was having an affair with the Doctor. From the outside, they must appear to work so closely together. Leni could only hope it was not a widespread sentiment! Before she could say anything, Magda had gone on: Have you ever thought about how lucky you are? The only reason why I married Joseph was so I could be closer to *him*. Oh, don't look so shocked, Leni, it's an open secret in the Party, not a confession from me to you; I wouldn't burden you that way. As you know, our leader has to remain unmarried, it is important for his image. But between us I will say this: it is not the same. *It is not the same!* He will never look at me the way he looks at you. Even with Joseph, he looks at Joseph like the good stage manager he is, but we've seen him look at you, Leni. He looks at me like—like a woman—but he looks at you like you are a great artist!

Magda did not think she was having an affair with the Doctor. It was H she hankered after. Leni was appalled by the directness of this woman's wild-eyed proclamations, but a part of her wanted to crow with pride: If you want him to look at you that way, why don't you go ahead and see if you can be a film director instead of a desk secretary, and oh-so-run-of-the-mill!

Then it struck her—why the Doctor threw his tempers—he, too, was jealous.

Tea was cleared, and Magda suggested a little tour of their home. Leni went along with it. In their study, Leni found out that the Doctor had a PhD in Romantic literature from Heidelberg and had tried for many years to become a published author. None of his plays had been staged nor his poetry printed, Magda told her, but one work of fiction had appeared in book form. A coming-of-age novella called *Michael*, it was inspired by Dostoyevsky. Leni was not much of a reader, but thumbing through the Goebbelses' personal copy in their library, even she could sneer at the Doctor's shallow juvenilia. Don't tell Joseph I showed it to you, Magda said. He's sensitive about it, but the way I see it, a book is a book, isn't it, Leni?

Of course, Leni agreed, writing is a most worthwhile endeavor.

I knew a creative woman like you would understand. Magda smiled at her as she replaced the browning paperback in the bottom drawer. I'm so glad you stayed for tea, Leni. I hardly get to have a real conversation with anyone these days. You'll come again, won't you?

AT THE APPOINTED time Leni showed up at the Doctor's office in the Ministry of Propaganda to get her money. She knocked on the door and was told to enter, but he appeared to be dictating a note to his secretary as he viewed a projection. Each time she saw the Doctor, he was more tanned than the last, even in winter. Picturing him flipping around naked on a sunbed like a pancake made her queasy. He held up a hand, but it was not to say hello. Rather, it was a signal that she should not interrupt him. She stood awkwardly until the Doctor motioned for her to have a seat as he wrapped up. Leni positioned herself adjacent to him on the two-piece sofa.

On the screen before them was a Hollywood movie.

Every age that has historical status is governed by aristocracies, the Doctor was saying to his secretary, weighing the words slowly on his tongue, eyes on the screen. Aristocracy with the meaning the best are ruling, he continued, without looking at Leni. Peoples never do govern themselves. That idea—no, better—that *lunacy* was concocted by liberalism.

He paused to rub his temples.

His speeches were cotton candy, Leni thought. When the style melted away nothing was left at their center. H spoke like a mystic, but with purpose. It made you want to pull yourself up by the bootstraps, not float away on a breeze. As the Doctor droned on, Leni saw to her surprise Marlene Dietrich cross the screen. Marlene's fair hair was in tight ringlets. She was wearing a frilled corset with dark lace insets and a hat trimmed with a trail of fluttering marabou feathers, as she sauntered into an American West–styled saloon. How could she be dressed in such an outlandish outfit and not look foolishly out of place? It was a natural-born talent Leni knew she lacked. Her own clothes were sensible, expensive, and well made, but she could never have pulled off whatever Marlene was wearing, not even in a movie. Leni had walked into the meeting prepared to be in control, but seeing Marlene's assured likeness in the same room, radiating outward from a Hollywood movie, threw her off immediately.

For the role, Marlene had a prominent beauty mark kissing the tip of her cheekbone. Perfect, Leni thought bitterly, she should wear it all the time, it suited her so consummately, making visible her vulgarity! Marlene was crass shimmying around with her beauty mark and skimpy outfits in this Western; she was crass as a bit-part player in Berlin who overplucked her brows and painted her lips whore red; she must have been born crass, and she'd done so little to deserve her success. It was some ten years past now, but Leni could easily recall her heart sinking that afternoon in 1929 when the phone call came from Josef von Sternberg's assistant, informing her she had not been selected for the part of Lola Lola in *The Blue Angel*. She liked Jo, admired his movies, and was hoping to manufacture an opportunity for them to work together. It was bound to be a fast track into Hollywood, which she had been trying to break into with no success.

Leni bit her lip and asked: May I know who got it?

When she heard "Marlene Dietrich," her throat constricted as she pronounced into the phone: How wonderful, please send my regards! Slamming the receiver down, she dashed a half-empty teacup onto the floor, and then the saucer, too. Cleaning up her mess later she'd cut her foot on a shard of broken porcelain. Even now, when Leni caught sight of that faint scar, she felt a pinch. How had that boorish nobody ousted her good self, an actress on the rise with a respectable catalog of movie credits to show for? Marlene must have been willing to fall into bed with Jo right away. Best regards to the two cheaters. They were both married—not to each other—and they were eloping to America to make movies together! But no matter, Leni thought sagely then, a fat cow like Marlene with a suburban barmaid's sensibility would never go far in Hollywood. That sophisticated scene was sure to wait it out for someone like Leni. She hated how wrong she had been about this. Every time she saw Marlene in a new Hollywood movie, or even heard her name, it left Leni cold and rattled.

How well the Doctor knew her, to have arranged this welcoming touch. Now he was dismissing his secretary. Let's stop there, he said. We'll continue after my meeting with Miss Riefenstahl. It would be impolite to keep our golden girl waiting. Before Leni could collect herself and ignore the life-sized projection of her archenemy batting false lashes, the Doctor played his hand. Leni, he said, turning to her solicitously. Where did you come from?

He poured them each a drink from a decanter.

Nowhere, she said, determined to remain calm. Home, if you will.

Ah, he said. That wasn't apparent to me. Your dressing—I was concerned, I thought—Dear me, has she just come from a funeral? Leni did not respond. Happy to hear that isn't the case, of course, the Doctor said, passing her the drink. Cheers?

No thank you, she said.

No?

I don't drink, she said truthfully. Alcohol makes me tired and dizzy.

That explains everything, the Doctor said as he took a sniff of the drink he'd poured her. If you don't ever get off, it's no small wonder how high-strung you are! He clinked glasses with himself and drained them one after the other. When he was done, he smacked his lips and nodded toward the screen. Our very own Marlene's latest romp, he said. *Destry Rides Again.* Taking L.A. by storm, isn't she? Here we are in the middle of a war, and this is what she sees fit to play in: a Hollywood cowboy movie. The Doctor leaned forward. And what do you suppose her character is called in the film?

Leni shook her head.

Frenchy, the Doctor pursed his lips, she is called Frenchy. Of course she knows how hurtful this is to us, when we are at war with those frogs. He slid a finger over the rim of his empty glass, producing an awful squeak. Leni, he continued, we are so lucky to have you. You are the only one of the stars to understand us. Zarah Leander and Marika Rökk are lookers, but they are imports. Mercenary women. Lida was Czech but—personally speaking—I'm able to report she's certified German at heart. She turned down Hollywood offers to be with us, it's too bad we had to send her away. But you, Leni. You're the paragon of a good German woman, aren't you?

Leni sat tight on the sofa, wishing she'd accepted the drink just so she would have had something to hold in her hands. She gave an indefinite nod, as the Doctor went on: Marlene sent back her passport. We have a bounty on her person now. Just a little lower than Einstein's. They should be taken alive of course, so we can use them. He chuckled—a wet and clammy sound. She did not know if his bounty list was a metaphor. Remind me again, he added. Did you see Marlene when you were in America?

No, she said warily. I did not meet with Marlene.

Pity.

We never got along.

No?

Well, I should think that Marlene has always seen me as competition.

Oh I see, he said, appearing to think it over. Why would she? Anyway, he went on smoothly like he hadn't just insulted her, what about Clark Gable?

What about him?

Didn't you ever get to meet Clark Gable in Hollywood?

Leni did not know why the Doctor was playing these games with her, asking questions he knew the answers to. It was not the right time, she said. I should hardly have to remind you why.

The Doctor smiled, reclining into the couch.

But surely you are not challenging the Party's judgment? That would not be right, and our leader would be so surprised to hear that. We ask. He gives brilliant replies. I love him. No question. We have a vested interest in your success, of course. Your international approbation has an effect on our nation's standing. But we need scalable returns. There are any number of artists and writers my Ministry has dropped like hot potatoes. Have you heard about Max Ehrlich?

No, she said evenly, I have not.

Put it this way, the Doctor said, you won't be hearing from him anymore.

A strained silence passed between them. The Doctor put his hand on her knee. His fingers were cold and limp. Somehow, it was obvious to Leni in the quality of his touch that he had placed his hand there to frighten, not to make a move. A horrid consolation: Hurrah, this man is not in fact harassing me physically, he is only trying to intimidate me psychologically. Breaking it down this way, it was easier to react practically, and not emotionally. She made like she was scratching an itch behind her calf so as to move her knee from his hand. It worked. Where were we? The Doctor removed his hand and tapped his temple. Ah, yes. Clark Gable. What I meant to tell you earlier was that he is on our bounty list, too.

What does Clark Gable have to do with anything?

Hasn't our leader told you before? Clark Gable is his favorite actor.

But Clark Gable is American.

He hasn't told you, then, the Doctor said, excited. He told me Clark Gable looks like a real man. And I agree. Don't you? The man has an unassailable feeling about him. If we ever get a hold of Clark Gable, we'll send him to you.

Whatever for?

Have you seen *Gone with the Wind?*

This surely was a trick question. Leni was relieved she had spotted the snare. Of course not, she said. Where would I go to see it if the Ministry has banned it?

Leni, Leni, the Doctor patted her knee, at the exact same spot he had touched her before. You would come to the Ministry to see it, of course. He smiled at her. On the screen, Frenchy was dancing on the bartop, gun in her holster. We consider *Gone with the Wind* superb, the Doctor went on. Something rousing to keep the people's imaginations occupied, so they don't get swept away by every street-corner rumor. He thinks Gable would be wonderful in a Volkisch-style *Gone with the Wind*. You could direct it, after you are done with this mountain movie of yours. Admittedly, we are all waiting for you to make another *Triumph of the Will*, but that isn't what you want, is it? You want to try something new! Our agents in America say Frank Capra has been commissioned to attempt a rebuttal to your masterpiece, and it might please you to know what he said: "Riefenstahl's prowess—it's intimidating." God only knows why you want to waste your talent on Bergfilms. What is it with you and mountains, anyway, my girl?

He moved to the desk to retrieve some papers.

A contract for seven million reichsmarks, awaiting her signature on the dotted line. Even on the higher end, he harped on as she initialed the bottom of every page, a feature film in Berlin costs half a million reichsmarks at most, but as he understood it, she had been given special permission. With a budget like that, who can we expect to be starring in it? Was she going to bring in a marquee name from abroad like Clara Bow or Garbo, or could she be lining her own pockets with all that gold? He would be taking a personal interest in those expense sheets, keep them neat! Given that her budget was fourteen times the cost of an average movie, they had correspondingly high expectations of *Tiefland*. In wartime a movie can be only one of two things: a call to arms, or a bedtime story. Was hers going to be a snooze? The sooner she finished it the better. When the war was over and they were victorious, she would surely be asked to film the victory parade, with an even more enormous budget! Could she sink all the state coffers with just one movie? Then everyone could eat cake, and she would be free to play with all the big-ticket toys she liked: cranes, tracks, miniatures, the newest range of Arriflex precision lenses!

Wouldn't that be something to look forward to, Missy Director?

The Doctor's voice had grown higher and higher, thinner and thinner, as he mocked her. Not wanting him to know how much he got to her, she managed to keep her face calm, though her breathing had quickened and she felt her chest heave. The Doctor had noticed, too. He let his eyes wander over her before fixing his gaze on her breasts moving up and down. He did not take his eyes off her chest until she opened her mouth to speak. Yes, Leni said, forcing a smile even as she felt her lip quiver, I look forward to all of that. Splendid, the Doctor said, returning her smile with an equally cold one. I would expect nothing less of you.

Leni stood to leave. The Doctor bowed.

It was wonderful of you to stop by, he said, but will you let my secretary back in on your way out? We have got to get on with real work. You'll drop me a line any time you need anything, won't you?

From the screen, Frenchy blew a kiss to a man with a pint of beer.

SEVEN MILLION REICHSMARKS sounded colossal, but money disappeared so quickly on set. When Leni emerged from her trailer to inform the crew that they would be reshooting yesterday's scene, the assistant director said in front of everyone: We're all ready for the scene with the wolf right now, Miss Riefenstahl. Resetting will cut us back at least an hour and cloud cover is forecasted later this afternoon. Are you sure you don't want to start with the wolf scene?

I'm sure, Leni said gently but firmly, and I want us to all be on the same page. Let's get Martha's scene right first. It won't do to get ahead of ourselves, what do you think?

We'll focus on Martha then, the assistant director said to her deferentially, I'll get them to put the wolf back in the pen. We'll be reshooting "Martha Enters the Village," he called out to the crew. Reset, reset! Prep the extras! Put the wolf back in the pen and warm him down!

After everyone had dispersed, the production manager circled back to her.

Miss Riefenstahl, he said. I shouldn't like to be the one to say this, but the budget isn't holding up so well. It's the constant reshoots and the sick days. This was just what Leni did not want to hear right now. Was he a fool? If they finished shooting the movie, everyone would have to go back down the mountains. Or was he trying to hint to her that for the shoot to go on, she would soon have to reach out a hand for more money? The unsavory prospect of cabling the Doctor and risking a visit from him was substantial incentive to be more prudent, but for now she would chance that. Turning to him with a weak smile, Leni rounded her shoulders as she said in a small voice: Klaus, are you really going to berate me about my bladder colic?

He was flustered.

Miss Riefenstahl, that was not what I meant.

I try so hard, Klaus, she said. You know the day before, when I'd strapped the hot water bottle to my abdomen, I wanted to go on, but it was so painful—

Certainly, you must get your rest, he said. I'll make sure everyone is ready and I'll manage the budget. It'll work out. Thank you, Klaus, she said. I couldn't do it without you. Ah, don't say that, Miss Riefenstahl, the production manager said. We're all here to support your vision. It might be my vision, Leni said with as much warmth as she could muster at short notice, but this is *our* movie. I don't want any of you to forget that for a second.

Making her way to the lighting crew, Leni located the gaffer.

He was rigging a setup with the new best boy they'd borrowed from the Afrika Korps. The best boy was young. His face and arms were very tanned, but he had an unnerved look about him. She wondered if he knew firsthand that the victory promised them was falling out of reach. But continuing with this line of thinking was sure to trigger a panic attack. This was war, she told herself, and things could change with one brilliant pincer attack. Leave that to H, focus on what is at hand.

Listen, she said to the gaffer and the best boy. For a filmmaker like me, lights convey just as much as performers in a scene. The lighting did not emote enough in yesterday's scenes—it was only arbitrary. Is there something you can do about that?

As we are shooting outdoors, Miss Riefenstahl, the gaffer said, there's not so much control, but I'll try to think of something.

I'm sure you will, Leni said. She turned to the new best boy and stuck out a hand. He looked surprised to be addressed directly, as he gave his name: Hans Haas at your service. There were already four or five other Hanses on set. She barely registered his name, but it was good to make everyone feel valued, even if only for a minute.

I hear you were at UFA, she said. That's quite impressive.

I have a long way to go, he said, and I appreciate this learning opportunity on Miss Riefenstahl's set.

Good, she said distractedly, as she spotted her co-actor in the distance, stretching the trunk of his body. He'd rolled up his sleeves, probably to show off his muscles. This was not a beauty pageant; she would have to go over and put him in his place. Very good, she finished up here, I'll expect you to assist Dieter as best you can. Let's give this our best shot. Remember, I am not going for Wandervogel naturalism. More mythical, less naturalistic. Together we must strive for an elevation of the senses!

V

A tough lady to please, the cinematographer said to the gaffer and Hans Haas grudgingly after Miss Riefenstahl was out of earshot, but you have to give it to her, she really knows what she's talking about. Sure that's how she got to where she is, the gaffer said. Knowing her stuff. Can't hurt to know your stuff, the cinematographer agreed, on top of spreading those legs wide as a tripod stand.

Have you *seen* her legs, though?

Muscly as hell. Big calves, you can't miss them.

I like them frail; she's too sporty.

Do you reckon it's true the Doctor has only one testicle, same snag as Napoleon?

Come on, Dieter, we've been through this before, she can't be hopping from the wolf's lair to the rat's nest, you don't think that would be a problem?

And what did I say the last time, Jorg? Obviously they're in it together, holy trinity. Hitler on her front porch, Goebbels through the back door.

Well, we'd best get going before she comes over to show us one or two of the things she knows.

I have no problems with that, Jorg, why do you think I keep a light on in my cabin at night? For the moths?

Hans Haas knew how the tech crew liked to get jazzy with off-color lingo, ad-libbed on macho set after macho set in Berlin, but Miss Riefenstahl had been so nice, he was surprised they talked like that behind her back. Lead actresses got it all the time. There was so much waiting around on a big set, and dead time needed to be filled. Yet as far as Hans Haas knew, there had never been a lead actress who was also commanding the tech crew as a director, like Miss Riefenstahl. One moment she was having her makeup touched up, and the next moment she was briefing the cinematographer on the blocking. A woman did some things differently, it was true. She'd taken the time to ask for his name and shake his hand. None of the male directors he'd worked with ever did anything like that. Often, for crew in junior positions, no one noticed you or asked your name unless you made a mistake and they were about to give you a dressing down, dock your pay, or fire you.

The cinematographer was commandeering him around as they set up for the scene: Miss Riefenstahl would be riding in on horseback. She wanted more light on her than they had arranged yesterday. They agreed on heavy-duty fog from the smoke machine, which would allow the light to catch onto its particles for a dewy quality. What would Schmitz have done? Light to the story the director wants to tell, Schmitz liked to say. Don't tell the cinematographer, Hasi, but shots do not compose a frame. Lights do.

Hans Haas proposed a setup Schmitz had taught him: a carbon arc spotlight that would follow Miss Riefenstahl, setting up many layers of diffusion between her and the source. On camera it would look like she was glowing. They tested it out, and even the cinematographer agreed it looked better than before. I was trained by the best, Hans Haas would have said, but he did not want to step on the toes of the gaffer.

Contingent on Miss Riefenstahl's bladder colic, they might or might not be shooting one more scene after lunch. If her colic flared up, they would be done for the day. He would dismantle the lights when they cooled, transport them back down the mountain, do a head count of the extras, and secure their dormitory. Then there were the animals to feed: oats for the dappled-gray horse, scraps for the wolf. After that, he would enjoy a hot meal himself, and then hope for a deep and dreamless sleep. In Sirte, even when there had been proper food and they were not eating rations under tarp, no matter how many miles they had marched or how tired he was, Hans Haas could not sleep through more than three quarters of an hour.

Best Boy, Schmitz would turn to him and say, sure you don't want to share the Pervitin?

Rumor that Hans Haas was strung up on amphetamines caught on. Before the first campaign, his tentmates requested a share of his stash. Uppers were a boon. Soldiers who could get their hands on some popped them before battle so they could stay alert and fight harder for their lives. I don't have any, he told them, as Schmitz mouthed to them: Best Boy doesn't want to share! Hans Haas's eyes rolled back in their sockets from fatigue, but his eyelids jumped open at the slightest noise, even the soft-pedal hum of his own thoughts. Why were they crawling about in the desert, risking their lives for the words of men who sat in overstuffed armchairs in the chancellery back in Berlin? But he did not dare to ask Schmitz any of this, so he watched Schmitz's sleeping face till he dozed off, too.

AFTER THE UFA production studio fell under the auspices of the new Ministry of Propaganda, the Doctor had made a speech at the Tobis Film Palace. This was a war they had to fight in many theaters, including that of culture, Herr Doktor Minister Goebbels intoned. The continued service of creative professionals in the motion picture industry to produce Ministry-approved German films was as indispensable as that of soldiers going into battle. Some of the crew found it absurd that films now had to be approved and censored by a governmental body before they were green-lit for production or distributed for public consumption, but what was there to do besides making a couple of quibbles and going on with your work, if you wanted to keep your job in this unstable economy?

Senior crew who had worked for more than ten years in the industry could apply with an upcoming project, signed by a director, to be exempt from conscription. Most of the other crew stayed on gladly, scrambling, simpering to get the remaining state-sanctioned directors in Berlin to sign them on to their projects, but Schmitz was one of the few with other ideas.

One weekend they were having a drink at their usual tavern when a dispute began to escalate. Hans Haas was not sure he followed.

There were so many parties, fronts, coalitions, and putsches it was hard to keep track of them all, the SPD, the KPD, the NSDAP, the DNVP. The production coordinator was trying to drown everyone out in a loud voice about "us workers against the goddamn old boys' club." The film loader, the most educated of them, talked about job creation through rearmament and living space going hand in hand with "breaking the chains of shame of Versailles and putting an end to the system that abandoned us to slavery." The boom operator, barely audible, suggested "the necessity of compromise." Democracy is for the weak, the production coordinator said to shut the boom operator up, and the film loader agreed, it had to be all or nothing. Someone made a joke about how the only thing that brought the left and the right together was when they united to bash the middle, hö-hö. War is war, and schnapps is schnapps!

Hans Haas was a little tipsy. Though he was not really grasping their boozed-out arguments, he was still enjoying their rowdy camaraderie, when all of a sudden Schmitz banged his fist on the table.

Friends, he said. Talk is cheap.

Schmitz took a piece of paper out of his pocket and passed it around. It was an enlistment slip with his name on it. The boom operator was very drunk as he held the paper up to the light.

Who're you fighting for, Schmitz?

Everyone knew that Schmitz was not active with any of the parties, left, right, or center.

Parties change hands, Schmitz said, country is forever.

The boom operator laughed and lunged for Schmitz's crotch.

His pecker is too big for his underpants! Schmitz is himself the man!

Runts, Schmitz said. Piss off or shut up.

The night ended in typical fashion: lindy hop; broken glass; a trouncing. They were all kicked out of the bar when the production coordinator crowed like a rooster, Egyptian-walked all the way to a chubby waitress, reached out, and started to massage her sizable breasts in his hands as he called out: Hello, breakfast! He received from the feisty girl a kick in the nuts, and the well-lubricated group disbanded outside the bar, knocking heads and shaking hands, as Hans Haas walked with Schmitz until the junction of Alexanderplatz.

I'll follow you, Hans Haas said as they parted.

I'm going home, Haas.

I mean—I'll join up, too.

Get stuffed, Haas.

I'll go where you go.

What's it to you?

I'm your apprentice.

You're a pain in the ass!

HANS HAAS TENDERED his resignation alongside Schmitz.

Kid, Schmitz had said to him any number of times. It's war, not an adventure.

But it was simpler than that for Hans Haas, who never had someone to look up to. His father was a ne'er-do-well who went out to play skat and came home just to slap his mother around. The one time Hans Haas tried to put his body between them, he was punched up so badly he'd lost most of his milk teeth ahead of their time. He never tried it again. The day he left home, he'd asked his mother tremulously: You'll be fine, won't you? Yes, she said, I will be. Her voice was so firm he could almost look past her wet eyes. Apprenticing with Schmitz, Hans Haas found someone to learn from, and believe in. Though he looked imposing, Schmitz would have been the last person to throw his weight around. He could have had his assistants move all the equipment on set for him, but he would chip in and they would do it together. Out loud he might make a joke or two about you, but in a pinch he would stick his neck out for you, no questions asked. That was why Hans Haas wanted to go wherever he went, but of course he said nothing of this sort to Schmitz. Schmitz hated sentimental nonsense and would cross his eyes at him when they were lighting a schmaltzy scene for a production. Everything good he knew about life had come from Schmitz, and under his charge he'd built up a quiet confidence. There was a long way more to go before Hans Haas could be as good a gaffer, but that could wait.

Before they received their marching orders and after they collected their prorated paychecks, Schmitz took Hans Haas to the brothel he frequented on Ku'damm. Look, Hasi, Schmitz said. The longer you put it off, the harder it'll be to live down when you're older—You'll thank me when you've got yourself a wife, she won't think you're a nancy— besides, what if you died a virgin on duty? Not going to have that pinned on me!

Schmitz offered up his go-to girl to Hans Haas.

It's your first time, Schmitz said. Say hi to Gunda for me.

Gunda was much older. Hans Haas swallowed nervously as he entered the room. She had thin lips, and bewitching stretch marks on her belly and under her thighs that he wanted to touch but did not dare to, as she moved expertly to lick the shaft of his penis. She laughed when he tried to hide his erection from her. Didn't Schmitz tell you I don't bite, she said, or your money back? She wore her hair piled in a precarious chignon, and Hans Haas put a hand on her head, not to push her, but to see if the chignon would unravel. The moment her hair came free to frame her face was lovelier than the moment he tried to push himself clumsily into her. For the love of Thor, she said, it's not like a spear you throw into the dark. She guided him with her hand. Hallo, he said to Schmitz in his head. So this is where you go to when you're lonely? When it was over and Gunda put her hair back up, Hans Haas was amazed that it was just the same disheveled chignon as before. He tried to pay her. She waved him off, informing him that Schmitz had already prepaid in kind: silk stockings, hashish, chocolate liqueurs.

The man looks like a mountain bear, Gunda said, but I grant you, he's got taste. First time he's brought someone here, she added. Who're you anyway, his kid cousin? Hans Haas told her they worked together at UFA. Schmitz is the best gaffer in Berlin, Hans Haas said proudly, and I assist him. Gaffer, Gunda said, so that's what he is. The burns on his hands!

Hans Haas tried to tip her, but Gunda told him she didn't accept cash. She'd not used paper money ever since the death of her sister— Edda had jumped into the Spree because a loan of four hundred marks she took out in 1921 had turned into forty-five trillion marks in 1923. A fish stinks from the head, but they were rid of the Kaiser and his cronies now. Things were looking up, the NSDAP was doing an admirable job of stabilizing the economy, all in good time, but it was best to live hand to mouth. What did *freigeist* riffraff like her need paper money for anyway? To stoke the fire?

VI

Leni's collarbones shone. The hair and makeup unit was working their magic. She brushed loose bronzing powder off her blouse with the back of her hand, moving her neck and shoulders to see how best to position them when she mounted and dismounted the horse in her scene. Perhaps there was too much around her décolletage, but she was pleased with the result in the mirror.

Leni watched as the extras stood in line.

The makeup artist shaded their faces with dark eye shadow and blush so they would look ruddy and dirty, darker complexioned: the extras were playing Moorish peasants. Other directors or actors might prefer to hide away in their own trailer till everything had been set up, but she liked nothing more than making her rounds and looking out for details, however tiny, that she could improve by pointing them out. Everything was of consequence on camera.

At the front of the line was a little girl.

More kohl around the corners of her eyes, Leni said. The girl fidgeted as the makeup artist worked. Unable to hold her eyes open to accommodate the movements of the pencil around their edges, the girl started to cry. There, there, Leni turned to the girl, have a toffee! She clicked her fingers at the assistant, who produced a paper bag of sweets from her waist pouch. Made from real butter and caramel, these sweets were hard to come by, even on the black market. From the look on the girl's face, it must have been some time since she last had a treat. She'd stopped crying. Leni sat the girl on her knee, stroking her hair. The girl sucked on the toffee with loud, smacking sounds. Madam Riefenstahl, the girl said, unsticking her teeth and looking up hopefully at Leni, may I please have another? Leni patted the girl's soft head. Of course you may, she said, pressing a big piece into her hand. And please, call me Tante Leni.

Tante Leni, the girl said solemnly, when I grow up, I want to be an actress, just like you.

What is your name, my dear?

Zazilia, the girl said, but you can call me Zee.

How adorable children were! Someday, Leni thought, she was bound to make a fantastic mother. She was impatient with everyone else, but with children she could be endlessly accommodating. That would show her own mother, who'd commented that Leni would be best off not procreating, she was so self-centered she would not even be able to keep a houseplant alive for more than a month. *Schau*, Mama! She stroked the girl's soft, tangly hair and told the hair stylist to comb through the curls till they shone. Leni shared her mirror with the girl: Aren't you pretty? The girl smiled up at her. When she was ready, she made a fist around the extra toffee and ran off to the holding area, where an older woman was watching with a worried look on her face. Leni gave a little nod in their direction to show that it was all very well, but just then she noticed one teenaged extra with a striking face.

Leni pictured her in a scene.

The extras had to blend into the background so that the leads could pop in the foreground. Give that girl there a scarf to wear, she told her assistant. Her face is too strong. It was done right away. Leni watched as the girl tucked her hair into it. Pretty faces had a head start, and Leni was a practical woman. She had a clear-eyed view of where she stood in every department. Her own face was not the one that would be noticed in a crowd, but from very early on she had understood her audience to be men, and learned to spin a portable world around her that they would look in on and fail to understand. As creatures of ego they saw in their failure to understand only the allure of a woman. And that point of indistinction was where she cut it on the bias, took them by the hand, and hinted that she needed them. In planting her need she seeded their want, in such a way that it would seem to them innate by the time that want surfaced. As far back as she could remember, it had always worked for her this way. There was first a Chilean expatriate who bought her a tennis racket. Leni did not know how to play tennis, but why should that stop her from showing up on the courts of the see-and-be-seen Berlin tennis and ice-skating club in white socks, folded down twice to expose her ankles?

Let me teach you, the Chilean said when he saw her.

I was hoping you might say that, she said.

One summer a Romanian Jewish producer with an aristocratic underbite chatted her up on a beach, where she was improvising dance in a monokini, throwing jetés inspired by the lusty tide, reaching upward toward the sky as she turned her face exultantly to the wind. He was enamored enough to wave away her amateurism as avant-gardism, to rent out entire concert halls to showcase her "free association" dances. When she broke her knee, she wept and asked him inconsolably: Tell me, wasn't I Germany's answer to Anna Pavlova? He kissed her shins. I will pay for the best physician in Berlin, he said. You must dance again.

Waiting to board a train to consult with an esteemed physician on the subway platform at Nollendorfplatz, Leni saw a movie poster: *MOUNTAIN OF DESTINY*. On it was a silhouetted man climbing a magnificent mountain, arm and leg lifted midstride as if in a choreographed dance sequence. Her train arrived. She let it pass. In a trance she hobbled to Mozart Hall, a few blocks down, where the poster indicated the movie was showing: snow, pathos, beauty! When the film ended, she knew with clarity what her new destiny was. She could no longer be a dancer? She was going to be a world-famous actress. The stage would forget you. A film reel could not.

IT TOOK LENI some time, but eventually she buttered up the right socialite from the tennis club's circle and secured a meeting with the director Arnold Fanck at the Rumpelmayer pastry shop on Kurfürstendamm. How old are you, he asked. Twenty-three, she said. And have you played in bit parts? No, she said. She was saving herself up for a leading role. Ah, he said. She asked if he shot his movies on location, they were so stunning. He said yes, and mentioned that because of the extreme weather conditions, his actors rarely did their own stunts. They all had body doubles, professional mountaineers. If you cast me, she said, I would be very happy to do my own stunts. Surprised, he said he had not known she was familiar with mountaineering. How many expeditions had she made, and where to?

None yet, she said. But I know I can do it if I make my mind up to.

At the end of their chat, he said he would consider her for his next movie, but he did not have a new script yet. He was experiencing some writer's block, he admitted. Trust me, she said, inspiration will flow if it's meant to be. After he left, Leni went from the café directly to the nearest hospital, with neither appointment nor overnight bag, and coaxed an orthopedic surgeon into operating on her in the morning. Knee surgery was not the sort of thing anyone did on a whim, and Fanck had promised her nothing, but if things went as Leni hoped they would, she had to be one step ahead. Her knee had healed superficially, but it would not withstand the pressures of mountain climbing.

Your case isn't an emergency, the surgeon said.

It's more urgent than that, she said, I am about to be in a movie.

As she went under the ether at dawn, she saw clouds, precipices, mountains. When she woke at dusk, she had the invoice sent directly to her Romanian Jewish admirer, and she cabled the director-geologist to let him know what she'd done. Fanck arrived in her ward the next morning, and it was even better than what she'd imagined: from under his coat he handed her a bundle of paper wrapped in newspaper. I have to admit, he said, I was going to ignore your cable. But then, I couldn't stop thinking of you—a young woman who asks you out for coffee, and twenty-four hours later, she's gone for knee surgery so that, *in case* you are to cast her, she is ready to do her own stunts in your next Berg-film. She smiled at him, licking unrouged lips. Since you kept me up all night, he said, I wrote you this.

She unwrapped the newspaper to find a manuscript entitled:

THE HOLY MOUNTAIN

It would be the first of numerous collaborations between them.

True to her word, Leni successfully performed all of her own stunts, getting better at it with every new movie they made. *S.O.S. Iceberg*, slated for a fall release in 1933, would take them to the Arctic, and she'd even choreographed the action sequences. Leni was looking forward to the adventure and took it upon herself to train up strength and stamina for the role. Every alternate weekday she brought weighted shin guards to the Sportpalast and ran at least four times around the track. This particular afternoon, entering the arena, she was annoyed to see that it was entirely filled and she would not be able to use the facility. It appeared to be a rally for the upcoming federal elections. She had never been to one and was surprised they were so well attended. Since she was already here, she strapped on her weights all the same and did knee bends as she listened to a man with a small moustache and side-parted hair who spoke into a bullhorn: Whenever I stand up for the German peasant, it is for the sake of the Volk. The podium was far away but he had a clear, spirited voice that pricked Leni's ears to attention. I have neither ancestral estate nor manor, he went on. My interests are yours. I believe I would be the only statesman in the world who does not have a bank account. I hold no stock, I have no shares in any companies. I do not draw any dividends. We are not fighting Jewish or Christian capitalism, we are fighting every capitalism: if you allow me, *I would like to make you completely free.*

Leni's calves began to tremble in their weighted shin guards.

She could not see his face in detail from the back of the stadium, but his last words had curved round the arena to touch the tips of her bare shoulders. She had to squat briefly to regain her balance. When she stood up, the crowd erupted into a penultimate wave of Heils that carried her forward. Who is he, she asked the stranger next to her in the midst of the rabble. The one who will finally show the world what we are made of, the stranger said as he raised his hands.

IT WASN'T HARD to find out more about the man with the moustache.

His anti-big-business, anti-bourgeois, and anti-capitalist speeches were growing very popular with frustrated workers struggling to earn their keep and afford basic necessities. Everyone agreed he was a brilliant speaker, even his opponents. He had been to prison for attempting a putsch and was now the leader of the Nationalsozialistische Deutsche Arbeiterpartei, the far-right NSDAP. This man was on the rise, Leni mused. It would be great to get to know him personally, and surely there was no harm in reaching out for a chat. The worst that could happen was not hearing back. The elections were a mess and things could swing any which way, but you never knew, and if he *did* get to the top, it would be too late by then. Now was a good time to put in that bid, even if she wasn't sure yet how they might work together. No loss for her if the NSDAP fared badly at the polls: there were always other men for an ambitious woman to telegram about a cup of coffee.

Time was a little tight. She was scheduled to travel to Greenland in a week for *S.O.S. Iceberg,* but all the better, she would work that into her letter: It is very silly of me to send you this letter, especially as we are about to go shoot our newest Bergfilm in the Arctic, with forty tents, two tons of equipment, and polar bears borrowed from the Hamburg zoo. See if that wouldn't intrigue him—soon she would be many miles away, making art in an inhospitable place.

A day before her trip to Greenland, a phone call: Would Miss Riefenstahl be able to come to Wilhelmshaven for an afternoon tomorrow? The leader of the NSDAP would like to meet with her. If she left Berlin early, she could arrive by four in the afternoon. The Party would reimburse her fare. They would pick her up at the train station and drive her to Horumersiel, where he was at the present moment. Would you promise me, Leni said breathlessly, that this is not a joke?

That morning the perennial problem that so ails nouveau-bourgeois women: the wardrobe, the bureau so full of clothing, but what to wear? Her life, she thought, with a meticulously measured dash of exaggeration, depended on it. She chose a white rayon-crepe afternoon dress and bobbed her hair.

At four she was on the platform at Wilhelmshaven.

A tall man in plain clothes escorted her into a red Mercedes. The conspicuous brand and color took Leni by surprise. In the car she tried to keep up conversation. Why had she been honored with so swift a response? She had not even expected her letter to be read. No, really!

We were walking along the beach before a rally, the adjutant said, talking about films. Our leader has begun to think of whom he would like to work with for media coverage of the Party's image. I suggested a few names, but he did not seem impressed. He looked out at the water and asked me if I had seen the lead actress's dance on the sea in *The*

Holy Mountain. He said that the lead actress was also beginning to direct some very fine movies of her own. Leni Riefenstahl. You should take a look at her work, he told me, we might use her. A woman? I asked—you will excuse me, I hadn't known there were women directors. And he said: Why not? When I got back to the hotel later, your note arrived, forwarded alongside mail collected from the Brown House. I told him, You mentioned Leni Riefenstahl at teatime.

He said: Yes?

She has written you.

He took the note from me.

Everything happens for a reason, he said to me as he read your note. Try to reach her.

The Mercedes slowed to a stop, and the door was held open for her. Leni stepped out and there he stood, against the sea. He was wearing a dark-blue suit with a white shirt and a plain navy necktie. He did not wear a hat. His shoes were polished, and he had a pair of binoculars around his neck. They exchanged formal greetings, and he asked if she might accompany him for a stroll along the shore. The air, he said, was unseasonably warm. She wanted to say something that would impress him; she felt as if she did not know how to conduct herself around him.

She repeated brightly: Unseasonably!

Looking out through his binoculars, he began telling her about all the different types of boats at sea. That's a large cutter, he explained, the one with the sails of different sizes. This, an open gaffer. Here's a skiff. And that big one there? Probably a herring drifter. He switched conversational topics seemingly at random: one moment it was Wagner (I *love* Wagner! she managed to squeeze in), then King Ludwig of Bavaria. Finally he came to the motion picture. When they had exhausted broad remarks, he cleared his throat and saw fit to say, almost shyly: I have seen all your movies. Once we come to power, he added, I hope you will make all our Party films. Right then Leni realized she had the upper hand: he was the one who wanted something from her. She knew to prolong the chase. Oh, she said, I know *nothing* about politics!

All the better, he answered right away. What I want is an artistic document of our times.

He was most taken by *The Blue Light,* he said. Need he mention how much of an impression it made on him that she, whom he had thought of as the actress—the star—was also its writer, editor, and director?

Leni did not want him to think she was an overcontrolling person who would be difficult to collaborate with, and so tried to deflect this by explaining that the only reason why she would cast and direct herself was because budgets were tight and she was trying to save money by keeping the production small. In truth she despised acting for an inferior director or directing an inferior actress and was certain she would be able to do a better job both ways if left to her own devices, but surely to admit this mode of operation made her sound monomaniacal.

He frowned.

I'm surprised to hear that, he said. Perhaps I am mistaken?

I'm sorry? she said, frazzled.

Her conception of Junta was pure, he pronounced. He'd assumed that that purity was manifestly apparent because she had knowingly taken control of every element of her movie to ensure it would not be contaminated in any way. It was precisely what he sought for Germany, too. It is easy to find followers, he added. It is not so easy to find contemporaries.

Yes, she changed tacks at once, you are right. But I am just starting to strike out on my own, and I am a woman. It would not do for me to speak so boldly, not when Fanck and Pabst and Lang—

He held his hand up.

Do not compare yourself with others, he said. His voice was taking on the edge it had in the stadium. You insult yourself, he went on, and you insult me: I am familiar with their work. But I have asked expressly to meet with you because I saw in *The Blue Light* that you know what it is to burn.

To burn?

If you want to shine like the sun, he said, first you have to burn like it.

She could barely breathe.

If she started off with bread-and-butter work for the Party, she thought, and he liked what he saw, he might even go on to finance her fiction films one day. Fanck had been supportive, but they'd drifted apart ever since Leni struck out on her own. Her solo efforts were receiving considerable attention, and some people had mistakenly assumed that Fanck had directed them. That irked her, and she wanted to distance herself from him. Far better to rely on an entity, a Party with whom you could have a professional relationship, than to bank on the goodwill of an aging mentor, the whims of one well-to-do scion, the commercial prospects of a production house's box-office receipts. And there was something special about H. True, he was far more shy in person than Leni had expected, he was not much of a looker (for starters, she thought he would look better without that moustache), and she had imagined him to be taller, but the longer you spent in his presence, the less you wanted to leave. Was it the quiet confidence? The NSDAP had not even won their seats yet, and here he was talking about what sorts of films he wanted to commission after the elections. Or maybe it was the poetic seriousness with which he spoke? In her films, he was saying, she sought a unity and stability lacking in their current environs. A mythic vision from the past, about the future. He shared the very same. They had to find the language for that.

Behind him a blood-orange sunset slipped off the horizon.

Stay for dinner, he said.

She should like nothing better than that, she said, but alas she had to catch the first train back, in order to board the Arctic-bound crew ship from Hamburg the next day.

Stay the night, he said, and we will arrange a private plane for you in the morning.

A private plane? she said. You must be pulling my leg?

I tend to follow through on what I say, he said. You will join us?

AT DINNER, LENI noticed immediately, even before she was seated, that she was the only woman at the table. She sat poised in her chair, back straight, letting the shape of her breasts show against the white rayon, forearms touching the edge of the table as lightly as possible. Before the entrée, he told the assembly that they were blessed to be dining with her: Miss Riefenstahl is about to shoot a new movie. She smiled as modestly as she could and told the table it was her pleasure to be here with them. They wanted to know what the movie was about. I play a female pilot searching for her missing husband, she said. He's a scientist lost on the ice. We set off for the Arctic tomorrow.

Everyone was suitably impressed, and in the moment Leni could not help but feel like a gracious wife helping to enliven a dull dinner party, as she took it upon herself to keep the conversation flowing. She made amiable eye contact with all the men present, but her eyes kept returning to H. He nodded and smiled at her from across the dinner table. She observed that he ate only the vegetable side dishes, skipping the main ones, and drank only mineral water, not even apple juice or a digestif. After the meal, he did not take coffee but tea, and Leni counted the seven teaspoons he heaped from the sugar bowl into his teacup.

We should have Miss Riefenstahl over for dinner all the time, one of his associates said.

Yes, H said, as she met his eye. She will soon be making our films.

Leni wanted to say that she had not yet agreed, but it would have been rude to contradict him in front of his associates. They were drinking now, to a momentous election and a marvelous collaboration!

Lying in bed in a large guest room, covers pulled up to her nose, it took Leni a long time to fall asleep that night as she replayed the day's events, H's voice in her ear: *A herring drifter*—Had she played it too innocent? What did he like?—*a skiff*.

She was excited to see him again the next morning, but at breakfast he did not meet Leni's eye or make conversation with anyone else at the table. Everyone followed his cue, eating quickly and quietly. The mood was completely different from the night before. Even though this made her jumpy, she found it striking that he had such a pervasive effect on those around him. As she was leaving, Leni was disappointed that he had not come to say good-bye. Just before she stepped into the red Mercedes that would take her to the plane he'd chartered for her to Hamburg, he appeared.

Wordlessly he took her hand and led her into the car.

Enjoy Greenland, he said with a tiny twinkle in his eye. Be careful of the polar bears.

Leni wished she had keener wits, for she knew even as she re-

sponded that it spoiled the wonderful lightness of his remark: Be careful of assassination attempts.

His face darkened, but he laughed as he saw her off. What a strange
woman you are, he said. You are prone to saying the wrong thing, but
at the right time, and that is refreshing. I have no doubt we shall be seeing each other again.

VII

The day's reshoot went well enough, other than that Miss Riefenstahl asked for an eye light when she was riding into the village. The gaffer went to prepare it. Hans Haas assisted him, though it made no sense for Miss Riefenstahl to have an eye light, not when the sun was behind her, and the shot was so wide.

They were given the rest of the day off as the cinematographer shot some cutaways, since the extras were back in costume and the sun was still out. Hans Haas watered the dappled gray, then led it back to the makeshift stables for a brush down. Franz, still kitted out in his breeches, wearing foundation and blush, was telling him that the horse had belonged to Queen Wilhelmina of Holland. When we took the Netherlands, Franz explained, the horse fell into the custody of the NSDAP, so it was loaned out to the production. Hans Haas was studying Franz's face. Are you wearing blush? Hans Haas asked as the dappled gray twitched under the dandy brush. Franz put a hand to his cheek as he asked: Is it really so obvious?

Bursting into the makeshift stable with the animal handler, the line producer said: Sort this out.

Is something wrong? Franz asked.

One of you had better find it, the line producer said. I am not going to lose my job because of some low-level dimwits!

Have you told her? the animal handler asked tearfully.

Of course I did, the line producer said, I can't keep something like that from her!

Haas, the animal handler said unsteadily, you brought the wolf back to his cage this morning, didn't you?

Yes, Hans Haas said, I did.

And later, the animal handler said, Did you forget to lock up?

The wolf is gone, the line producer said. When Riefenstahl heard, she had to be sedated.

Sedated? Hans Haas said.

We had to carry her back to her cabin, the line producer said.

Didn't you go to warm the wolf down after I locked him up? Hans Haas said to the animal handler. I met you on your way up.

I was supposed to, yes, the animal handler said, but at the last moment I went to the field instead to set up the sheep—

I don't give a hoot whose fault it is, the line producer said. Yours or yours, it's the same difference. Find the wolf, or I can't guarantee you'll be allowed to remain on set.

THE MIST WAS low and thick as it snaked through the lowlands of the valley. Hans Haas turned east, the animal trainer west. They had not discussed just how they would apprehend the wolf if they encountered it, but each man brought with him some items from the shed: guns, rope, sturdy nets. The film crew had depleted the tranquilizer gun when shooting the first wolf scene. New darts had not yet arrived. Good luck, Hans Haas wanted to say as they parted, but the animal handler had already left. If they were fired, they would be reconscripted as able-bodied men and sent to one of the fronts.

After a few hours, Hans Haas could not be sure if he was coming around the ravine a second time. He began whistling in time with his step. When he realized it was jazz, he stopped himself. He backtracked and went down the stony path that led toward the cliff face. The drop of the cliff was sudden. Looking out at the landscape, he was surprised to see the wolf at a distance. It lay in the shade of an acacia tree on a lower point of the knoll. Hans Haas got off the path of the cliff face, net in one hand, gun in the other, treading lightly, careful not to step on even a dry leaf. When he was about fifty yards apace, the wolf woke. It looked directly at Hans Haas. He lifted his gun. Looking through the sights, he saw that the wolf had yellow irises.

The wolf looked at Hans Haas in a neutral way for a long time.

Neither of them moved. Then the wolf turned away, yawning with a shake of its head. It stretched its hind legs fully, first the left, then the right, finishing up with an involuntary tremble before it moved away. Lowering his gun, Hans Haas watched as the wolf trotted away at a comfortable pace without looking back.

By the time Hans Haas got back to camp, the crew was finishing up their dinner, and he saw that Miss Riefenstahl stopped eating at once. She came over to him: Well?

Hans Haas shook his head.

The animal trainer, who had returned earlier, empty-handed, offered to resume the search at first light, but Miss Riefenstahl said that wouldn't be necessary, she'd rented a hunting dog from one of the Italian farmers in the Sarntal Valley. The farmer thought the dog might be able to track the wolf if it sniffed out the wolf's pen. If there were no results—

Miss Riefenstahl, the animal trainer said, standing up. I believe I would be more useful to you here. My expertise is more specific compared with the Afrika Korps boy, I am trained to wrangle animals, and there are many in your script. Hans Haas saw the dirty look Miss Riefenstahl gave the animal trainer as she walked away from the food tent. The rest of the crew resumed their dinner.

I'm sorry, the animal trainer said to Hans Haas, I didn't mean—

Of course you did, Franz cut in, as he offered Hans Haas the dinner plate he'd saved up with his portion of food. We all heard you loud and clear.

THE SMELL OF hot, freshly ground coffee the next morning made Hans Haas feel lucky to be alive. He downed it and filled a second mug. Who knew how much longer he had up here? He was surprised that he did not regret letting the wolf go. If he was going to be sent back to the front, so be it. For now there were still duties to be performed and the tiniest of pleasures to be taken. On set, the mountain water the coffee was brewed in was crystal clear, and he could taste the roast of the bean. In Sirte, they had overestimated their water requirement, and so were oversupplied at the start. The hapless Italians had not provided them with any useful ground information. With allies like these, Schmitz liked to say, who needs enemies? They faced a water shortage in the later part of their campaign, but in the beginning, with the surplus, they had a platoon commander who ordered coffee brewed at almost every layoff, even short halts. By the time it got around to the privates, it was little more than sandy dregs, but they made what they could of it with tinned milk and sugar. Hans Haas handed the mug back to the cook's daughter and went down to the valley, where he would match the equipment to the cinematographer's shot list.

Hans Haas was sorting out cables when he heard the dogs. They barked with authority as they reached the camp. Behind the dogs were two Italian farmers, one of them pulling a donkey cart, the other limping. Strapped to the cart was the wolf, tongue out of its jaw. Miss Riefenstahl ran from where she was rehearsing in the meadow with Franz.

It tried to bite me, the first farmer said. So I aimed for its leg, but—

Half of the wolf's face had been shot off.

Hans Haas heard Miss Riefenstahl scream.

She squatted down, placing her head between her knees, and her hands on top of her head. Her assistant ran to her with smelling salts, but Miss Riefenstahl dashed them away. Her shoulders were heaving as she shouted: Give me space to think! One farmer called out brazenly over the top of her head: I hope we will still be paid? At this Miss Riefenstahl clambered to her feet and turned to face the farmers. Paid? she spat. If you know what's best for you, don't let me see your dirty face around here again.

Late in the night, when everyone was asleep, Hans Haas got out of bed. He put his boots on, took up his rifle, and made a show of patrolling the grounds. When he was sure that no one was watching, he went to the pen where the wolf was chained.

The wolf was still alive.

It was lying on its side, its breathing labored. When it heard Hans Haas's approach, it opened its eyes. It must have been in too much pain to growl or even bare its teeth, for it simply shut its eyes again. Hans Haas could see part of its skull where the bullet had torn through, a patchwork of white bone and skeiny ligaments.

He pointed his rifle at the wolf, hands shaking as he aimed.

He would most certainly be sent back to the front if he shot the wolf dead. Miss Riefenstahl might still keep him around to assist the gaffer if he kept his head low, with any luck. He stood there aiming the sights at the wolf's head for a long time, but he did not release the safety catch. I'm sorry, Hans Haas said. The wolf pinched its eyes open at the sound of his voice. Hans Haas watched the wolf's flank heaving unevenly a minute longer. Its breathing was growing more ragged. He put down his gun and left.

THE WOLF DIED before the sun came up the next day.

In the morning, Hans Haas saw Miss Riefenstahl and the art team standing in the wolf's pen. If we skin it, someone said, could we drape the fur over a dog? Am I surrounded by idiots, Miss Riefenstahl said with a hand to her temple, *or am I surrounded by idiots!* She prodded the wolf's dead body with a stick. Move this away, she said, I'll think of something. She turned to the line producer. Push back the scenes with the wolf, she said, let's go on with the other scenes we have for today. Everything else went uneventfully, and after dinner, as Hans Haas passed the dump where food scraps were discarded, he saw the wolf's body in a corner, beside some carrot peelings and chicken bones.

Hans Haas lay wide awake again that night.

When all was quiet, he dressed and went to the dump. The wolf's body was still there. Flies had begun to settle. He chased them away and dug a hole with his bare hands. It was not as deep or wide as he would have liked for it to be. When he was done burying the wolf, he plucked a wishbone from a chicken carcass to mark its grave. He stood up and shook the dirt off his palms. Turning around he heard a rustle. It was just the cook's daughter. He put a finger to his lips. She nodded and gave him water to wash his hands with. Hans Haas cleaned his hands, walked back to his pallet, and closed his eyes. But sleep would not come, so he picked at the dirt under his nails till dawn broke.

VIII

The wolf had been born in a forest in Czechoslovakia at the foot of the Ore mountains. When it was fully grown, it forded the mountain pass and crossed over into Leipzig.

It had been hunting a hare when it was itself pursued and tranquilized at the craggy foothills of the Rhine mountains. A black bear specialist from the Leipzig Zoo, collecting ursine stool samples farther afield, had sighted it.

The last wild German wolf was thought to have been shot in the 1880s.

There were hopes for wolves to return to the land, what with the Animal Protection Charter the NSDAP had initiated and signed into law. Conservationists at the zoo were delighted with the new antivivisection and antihunting laws, and bemused by the meticulous extent to which the fine print conveyed the particularities of their leader's sensitive nature. The final item in the second section of the Charter read: "It is forbidden to tear out or separate the thighs of living frogs," and the papers had reported that a restaurateur in Munich had been fined for boiling a lobster alive.

THE LEIPZIG ZOO inducted the new wolf into their grounds with much fanfare. In a man-made enclosure, it joined a pack of gray wolves, gifted by the Americans as a diplomatic gesture years ago. Given its relatively timid nature, the new wolf was bullied by the pack. As a lower-ranking male, it did not mate with the alpha female, but it seemed to have found some luck with one of the young beta females and was just beginning to display courtship behavior when Leni approached the chairman of the Leipzig Zoo. Hoping to dissuade her, the chairman mentioned to Leni the limitations on animal use for entertainment, as meted out by law in the Animal Protection Charter. She would need a trained wolf, domesticated from youth. Perhaps they could donate a pup to her if the alpha female birthed a pack in good time.

You will excuse me for being straightforward, dear sir, Leni said to him, but perhaps you have misunderstood my standing with our leader. My film is a direct commission. The wolf is an animal that is close to his heart. Did you know that "Adolf" is old German for the Nordic *athalwolf*? He shall be so disappointed to know the Leipzig Zoo was uncooperative. No pressure, of course. I'll leave you to consider my request. The very next morning, Leni was pleased to receive an official letter of release. All the best with your movie, an enclosed postscript read, and we wish you every success.

TOWARD THE END of the war, American freedom bombs fell on the Leipzig Zoo.

The bull elephant from the Kingdom of Siam died immediately, his stomach blasted through. His mate and their baby would not leave his body. The sole Somalian hippopotamus drowned, pinned by debris to the bottom of the outdoor pool. A troop of twenty Pakistani rhesus monkeys escaped together, screaming and swinging from tree to tree. One by one, they all died within the hour, having drunk water contaminated by incendiary chemicals. Before he was evacuated with his wife and children, the chairman of the Leipzig Zoo ran into the ape house. His favorite Javanese white gibbon reached out to him, bloody stumps in place of graceful limbs. The white gibbon had lost so much blood and was in such a severe state of shock the chairman could hardly find a vein for the injection. After it stopped breathing, its kinked tail twitched once. The chairman ferried those he could to safety, carrying armful after armful of baboons and golden tamarind monkeys to a disused basement, locking them away from enemy fire—but who to feed them, and how would they leave if need be?

The chairman left the key to the basement under a gaily painted fruit bowl with scalloped edges trimmed in gold gilt. Taking her hairy palm in his and walking her over, he pointed out the key's location to the oldest orangutan matriarch from Malaya.

Do you understand me, Dewi? he whispered. Blink if you do.

She stared back at him with her wise round eyes.

The next morning, a U.S. fighter craft flew in low, firing at any-thing that moved. Its first hit was the Leipzig Zoo's last giraffe. There had been three, all female, two reticulated and Ethiopian. The last one standing was a new acquisition from the Nuba Mountains in Sudan that the zoo had been particularly proud of for her striking markings and her height. Tall as she was, it seemed to take her a long time to hit the cratered ground.

Josef von Sternberg
Pays a Visit to a
Zen Buddhist Mental Asylum
in Kyoto

九

In these madcap years people have yet to understand that the motion picture is the only medium of consequence for our sycophantic times. What photography did for painting, the film is doing for the novel: freeing it from the drudgery of realistic description.

I had wanted dearly to be a writer before I was bewitched by the bold vicissitudes promised by the movie camera's radical juvenescence and formal despotism. The experience of a reader is one of collaborative consent toward the perceived intent of the author. The experience of the moviegoer is sentient surrender to the multisensorial will of the filmmaker. The filmmaker's pen might not yet be amply flexible, but this is part of the thrill of the early chase: Where are we now in 1932 but thirty years into the early cradle of motion picture history?

In the sleepy fishing village—you can be sure they call it the world republic—of belle-lettres they hark back most oft to Cervantes circa 1605, but let me put my boot down to declare *Don Quixote* a laggard to the quarry. A Heian court woman, Murasaki Shikibu, wrote the epic *Tale of the Genji* in 1021! Nine hundred and ten years later, now that writers are at last in the quandary of the modern, they are reaching beyond their cuffs to combat form with form, to slay the slain. But alas the hour is late for the writer. There is too much to unlearn. The reactionary shackles of their chosen medium's advanced age ossifies the moving parts of their vague exertions toward the avant-garde.

Vague—by virtue of fraternization with the reader.

To truly be visionary, my dear ladies: there is no social contract between the audience and yourself. Their patience for an emergent narrative wears thin? Likewise my expectations on their nascent intelligence! Why should *I* have to imagine an audience, why shouldn't the audience imagine *me*?

. . .

EVEN THE DIRECTOR'S brows were moving at the same highfalu-
tin tempo as his speech, so there remained the possibility that what
Anna May had heard before—namely that Mr. Josef von Sternberg had
appended the *von* to his *Sternberg* not as a means of ingratiating oneself
with the blue-blooded, but as a dig at the philistine German obsession
with titles—was true.

She was so tired of hearing men go off on hyperextended flights of
fancy as if they owned the world and you were only a clockwork toy in
this regard, having to sit, listen, and nod at all the right times because
they were paying for dinner, they pumped the most sugar into the production, they had cast you in their movie.

But where was I, Miss Wong?

The director mused as he sprawled in the wicker chair. They were
taking tea in the Polo Lounge's arbor. He pushed his jacket sleeves back.
The jacket was expensive light wool, cut two or even three sizes too big
for his frame, paired with tan jodhpurs and black rhinestone cufflinks.
He had a droopy moustache, "Oriental-style," that is, shaped thin to a
fault in the fashion of a man not hirsute enough to grow a full beard,
and a mahogany cane, even though he walked perfectly well.

Ah, yes, he caught up to himself, here I am.

In fact Anna May was not listening.

She had leaned back into her chair and was watching, as discreetly
as she could, every single movement of the hand belonging to the director's companion, as it slipped a fresh cigarette from case to mouth. I'm
not about to audition you, the director continued in a more reasonable
tone as he nodded at Anna May, so please feel at ease. You know from
Paramount the role's already yours, you're our Hui Fei, but I wanted to
meet you beforehand, and of course I wanted you to meet Marlene, our
Shanghai Lily.

Anna May did not know if she was grateful, disappointed, or
surprised—from the way Marlene leaned over and gave her hand,
it was likely that she had not told von Sternberg they were previ-
ously acquainted. She'd avoided looking directly at Marlene while he
pontificated.

Miss Wong, Marlene said, as their eyes met now. A pleasure.

She glanced away briefly to keep her cool as she returned: Likewise, Miss Dietrich.

She did not know if it was her imagination, or if Marlene had allowed her hand to idle in hers a few beats longer than was necessary. Marlene's hand was soft in her palm, nails unpainted but topped with a clear varnish. Anna May's hand trembled, she hoped imperceptibly. Three years could scarcely be a precise and meaningful measure of time, not when this Marlene before her looked much younger and much older at once. Was it the hair, set back from her face in finger waves and bleached platinum? That week in Berlin, it was a comely if homely shade of dirty dark blond. Her brows were bleached to match—and where else? The brand-new image had been presented in the studio's publicity shots, but in person Anna May saw that Marlene must have been ten pounds thinner, maybe fifteen. Who had told her to lose all that weight? She'd been lovely as she was. She was wearing a simple and sporty jersey dress, which casually showed off the lines of her trim body. There was no trace of the merry mishmash of colors and textures the woman she'd met back then had favored.

A waiter came to take their order.

Jo—Marlene called him that; Anna May took her lead—ordered a coffee, and Marlene said she would have the same. Anna May ordered malt whiskey. As the waiter took her order she saw Marlene give a wily smile. Anna May verged on changing to coffee, not wanting to appear to have ordered a malt whiskey in the afternoon just for effect, but Marlene had spoken: Now Miss Wong has put me in quite the mood for Scotch! Perhaps it would not be too extravagant, the waiter offered, for Miss Dietrich to enjoy both coffee and whiskey? Marlene looked to their director, guiding Anna May's eye toward him. Together, the two women observed that Jo looked prepared to find anything Marlene did unreservedly enchanting. A splendid idea, Marlene said to the waiter.

The whiskey arrived before the coffee.

Remarkably, Jo had not talked stopping. His two actresses had barely said a word. Marlene raised her glass. The clink redounded lightly in Anna May's fingers as Jo shifted in his seat, checking her profile. Asians are slighter of build. He patted Marlene's knee absently as he addressed Anna May. Our Marlene here had to lose almost twenty pounds of blubber, can you imagine? Jo, Marlene said. Will you quit embarrassing me in front of a beautiful woman I've just met! She swatted Jo's hand off her knee. He replaced it around her shoulder, looking into her eyes, and Anna May excused herself to the bathroom.

She was powdering her nose when Marlene entered.

Immediately she snapped her compact shut. Then she wished she had not done that—she opened the compact again. She was glad that there was another person in the space, a frowsy bathroom attendant in the corner arranging hand towels in a pyramid, or she would not have known how to carry herself. When Marlene walked up toward her, she was afraid that one of them would be tempted to mention something from the past now that they were almost alone, so it was a relief when Marlene said: Isn't Jo quite the handful?

A woman in a cocktail dress walked into the bathroom.

As the woman recognized Marlene, Anna May watched her swallow her double-take as she washed her hands in proximity to the hotshot actress who'd come out of nowhere and taken L.A. by storm. Every local paper and magazine in the last couple of years had done a Marlene Dietrich feature or three. I am looking forward to working with you, Anna May said politely to Marlene's reflection. You will excuse me if I return to the table first.

BACK IN THE arbor the waiter held Anna May's chair out, and Jo continued even before she was reseated. Your characters, he said, indicating Marlene's empty chair, are opposite but the same. Yin and yang—am I saying it right? Women who live by their wits, high-class courtesans, blood sisters. You ply the Chinese coast together on the *Shanghai Express*. Anna May drank her whiskey as Jo went on. Shanghai is a true city, Jo said, the way a man might say a woman is a real woman, whatever that is ever meant to mean. Have you been there?

No, Anna May said, but I would love to visit.

This she always said about China—it seemed the right thing for a Chinese person to say—but she was not so sure about it. Everything

she knew about China, for the most part, came from her father's secondhand folktales and Pearl S. Buck novels. Women had bound feet
and married early. Men pulled rickshaws and took on concubines.
There was not enough rice to eat, but everyone was addicted to opium.
Where is the farthest you've traveled? Jo was asking. The farthest our
Marlene has ever traveled is Cannes. She tells me she has no practical
need for anything farther afield when each summer the beau monde
kisses her hands in the South of France. What do you make of that?

I make that Miss Dietrich's career is going very well, Anna May
said as Marlene returned to the table, and that I would do well to visit
Cannes this summer.

When last we were in Cannes, Jo said, we met the Pasha of Marrakech. He asked why we had not called upon him when we were in his
country. Why, I said, I have never been to your country, to which the
Pasha said, but I have seen that movie of yours, *Morocco*! So I had to tell
the good Pasha that this was my fault, a shortcoming of my production, to have been unable to avoid such similarity, alas. We were shooting right here in L.A., Jo explained to Anna May, avoiding telephone
wires and street signs in our shots, sweating our skins off: this looks
nothing like Morocco. We worried about becoming a cheap laughing-
stock, not even stylized enough to say it was our faux take on faithful
reality. How does L.A. pass for Marrakech, the Mojave for the Sahara?
But then the Pasha of Marrakech wants to know why you did not call
when you were in his domain!

Be very careful of this man, Marlene leaned over to say to Anna
May. He will let you walk out barefoot into the desert at 120 degrees,
after which he will not inform you that you've completed your scene—
because he has just enough sunlight to shoot the next scene, in which
you are not needed, so you keep walking. Fainting in the heat, you are
brought back to the tent, and when you wake at his feet, asking out
loud in a fever dream: Do you need another close-up, what does he do?
He corrects the pronunciation of your English!

Marlene turned to Jo, her hand stroking his: Is that not right, Jo-Jo?

But Jo was still on the tail end of his own commentary. They were
speaking over each other, and only Anna May was listening. Style never

asks, Jo said, style never apologizes. The coffee arrived, and the waiter set down a cup for each of them. Style never hesitates, Jo gesticulated. Style necessitates. He knocked over the sugar bowl but went right on: One day I meet a Russian at a screening of *The Last Command,* and I ask the Russian whether Russians behave as they do in my film. No, the Russian answers me, they do not, but they *should*!

Jo *loved* Asia. This proclamation was perhaps not half as facile as it might appear to be. He was proud that he'd put his body through some motions firsthand, having bathed in the Ganges River within sight of burning corpses in Varanasi, tipped a Burmese temple's rosewood alms collection box in U.S. dollars after he touched the androgynous toes of the biggest Buddha statue and a fair bit of his or her limestone toenail chipped off, clapped his hands in a twelve-stoned Shinto garden in Kyoto that had been landscaped with the eye in mind such that at any one point you could only ever see eleven stones no matter your vantage point, had an indestructible hexagonal lump of his earwax extracted with a flaming candle and moxa needles as he prostrated himself on a bamboo mattress in Shanghai.

On all his journeys farther east, Jo would track down the equivalent of theater or live performance in that part of the world. In this way he had been privy to kuda lumping in Jakarta, where men in sarongs danced with rattan horses and chewed grass in a trance, or jo-ha-kyu five-act plays in Nagoya, a concept of modulation and movement applied to composition and pacing, translating imperfectly into *beginning-break-rapid*.

He had every admiration for what he termed the Oriental aesthetic, where craft was taken no less seriously but art had no qualms about commingling with life. Transcendence was muddied, not pristine. Jo learned this in a packed wooden playhouse in Manchuria as humid as a sauna, observing gender-indeterminate performers with painted faces and voluminous sleeves singing onstage in castrati voices, as the audience shouted for tea refills and threw pumpkin seeds over their shoulders. No one minded that the viewers were as loud as the performers themselves, and little Chinese children had clambered over his thighs and calves to make their way onto the stage, where they danced or laughed, mimicking the actors or chirruping among themselves.

When they got bored, they slid back down his lap to their parents.

The performers were completely indifferent to the children rolling at their feet, sidestepping or crawling over them as necessary. Toward the back of the small stage, there was a single hooded figure, all in black. The figure had his arms raised, though he did not move. His face was obscured, pure shadow. Jo thought he must have been a personification of death. Fascinating to include a literal figure of darkness static onstage without lines, but surely he would intervene in the action at some point?

After half an hour Jo was given to understand that the hooded man was a tea server.

From time to time, the performers would break character as they pleased, turning their backs to the audience, reaching for a small tray hidden behind the sleeves of the hooded man, to sip lukewarm tea from tiny porcelain cups. The tea server's black garb indicated that he was meant to be invisible to the audience. After the performers returned the cup to the tray, they readjusted their beards or lily sleeves or headgear, carrying on right where they left off in their twangy falsettos. Enamored of the deliberate histrionics and natural restraint, Jo did not think the poker-faced Chinaman emoted less. He thought their emotions were more fluid, but that they did not simply allow their feelings to seep into and out of every pore without due consideration.

Anna May was the first Asian American performer he had worked with, and from everything he had seen her in, she was a natural. From *Across to Singapore* to *Flame of Love,* he found her to be an underutilized actress of the highest order. After a bout of acrobatic lovemaking, when Marlene had demanded to know whom else—other than herself—he thought to be a fine performer, he'd tried to sidestep the ambush by naming men (Emil Jannings, Charles Laughton, and you can't deny that Bela Lugosi is deliberate but effective), but she forced it out of him all the same. All right, he conceded, all right. Hedy Lamarr, Anna May Wong—

Anna May Wong?

It's too bad the studios are sticks in the mud about color, he said. Wouldn't it be bold to see Anna May Wong play Catherine the Great?

I would like to play Catherine the Great, Marlene said coldly.

You already are Catherine the Great, Jo said, where would the fun in that be?

In any case, Marlene said, the studios would never sign off on a movie like that. A Chinese lead wouldn't be able to make them any money.

To hell with the studios and money, Jo said, I am concerned with *cinema*!

AMERICAN CRITICS FOUND him so new and yet so old. The Europeans were intrigued but confused: Is he one of us, or one of them? Jo knew he was able to give off this old-newness and us-themness because Jonas Stern was born by the Danube in Vienna, Austria; Jo Sternberg had grown up in and dropped out of Jamaica High School in Queens, New York; and Josef von Sternberg was now making movies with one leg in Babelsberg, Berlin, and the other in Hollywood, L.A. For him, "us" and "them," "here" and "there," "new" and "old" were neither "either" nor "or." He was able to accessorize himself convincingly with all of these contradictions at once, further augmented by and realized in his choice of self-presentation: the artful dandy lost in time. The equestrian jodhpurs and ill-fitting jackets, his thinned-out moustache and imperial affectation had all been carefully selected and puckishly performed.

If you do not entertain yourself now, who will when?

And so with gusto and glee Jo exploited different aspects of himself, improvised in loving accordance with his environs. In Berlin he thought like a New Yorker, talked like a New Yorker, moved like a New Yorker. In L.A. he thought like a German Jew, talked like a German Jew, moved like a German Jew. Was it pompous and pretentious to say he was as influenced by Japanese kabuki as he was by German expressionism as he was by Hollywood Prohibition gangster flicks? He was pompous and pretentious, then. Would Western critics see the kabuki in the Viennese-German-Jewish-American? Not in a hundred years. Would his contemporaries, in the complacency of their unseeing insularity, deride the curiosity of his cosmopolitan cupidity? In a heartbeat. Perhaps this, too, was what he liked best about Marlene: her lust for bothness. The German press gave Marlene a hard time for becoming American without realizing, Jo thought, that as with everything else she did in her life, she played it both ways: she looked as good in a skirt as she did in trousers, she was married but she philandered without concealment or deception, she was not a simple opportunist in her career but she was game to try everything once. By their very nature decisions tended toward narrowing life's possibilities, but Marlene had a knack for making decisions that opened rather than closed, shrugging labels off like they were fleas.

On his part Jo never resisted any label.

He had foresight enough to see that the more labels were attached to him in theory, the more leeway he had in practice. But he supposed that was easy for someone like him to say about himself. He could collect labels freely and flick them away as easily as the ends of cigarillos when he was done using them, but on someone like Anna May, labels once availed of could not be so simply obliterated.

Even so, he thought that with the rise of talkies, what would have placed a limitation on the roles Anna May could play was her voice. And frankly it had nothing to do with being Chinese, but everything to do with being Californian. Her voice was alto, colored with a regal sadness, but the diction was quite flat. You did not notice it much when she was a side character with a throwaway line or two, but it would have been noticeable had she needed to carry an entire film. Jo had preempted the sound problem for Marlene, who had a thick Berlinische tongue that wrapped itself helplessly around English. The moment she docked in New York he'd gifted her a bottle-green Rolls-Royce and hired for her the following personnel at significant personal expense: an accent coach, a dietician, a personal trainer, a hairdresser. Marlene accepted them all, no questions asked, other than the personal trainer: I'd rather starve than exercise. Powered by Prussian willpower she shaved off the pounds in no time. Her dark roots never showed under their bottle-blonde cover, and her mid-Atlantic accent—littered with a few last German idiosyncrasies he scolded her aloud for, but in secret found utterly endearing—was soon crisp.

.   .   .

WHEN MARLENE MADE her first public appearances in New York and then L.A., glowing on Jo's arm and a full head taller than him in her heels, he said to entertainment reporters: I am Marlene—Marlene is me.

Editorial responses ranged from the unimaginatively obsequious ("premium artistic collaboration of our here and now, this Trilby and Svengali") to the concerned ("smitten as he seems, one senses a latent, insalubrious misogyny on the part of this director"), but there was one reporter who had picked up on the Flaubertian aspect of his comment ("it was almost a hundred years ago when Gustave Flaubert was asked how it was that he could write from a woman's innermost self so spellbindingly without the experience of being a woman, and the author had answered: I am Madame Bovary—Madame Bovary is me. When Mr. von Sternberg effected the same response at the Astor Place hotel yesterday evening following the arrival of his muse to New York City, before they move on to Hollywood and go straight into production, for Paramount has hastened to sign the starlet even before the ship sailed, we see that he is even more of a master illusionist than we know him to be: where does the foppish gent end in Marlene Dietrich, and the astute seductress begin in Mr. von Sternberg?").

The only regret he had in regard to his wife (that this was his only regret either spoke poorly of his character, or showed he had never loved the woman) was that she had left him thinking he and Marlene were a half-baked cliché: ingenue meets director, ingenue sleeps with director. Humor me, Jo, close this loop with me, will you? His wife drew a circle in the air between them with her finger, where it lingered. Director makes ingenue a star, ingenue leaves director.

It's not what you think, he said hotly. You wouldn't understand.

I wouldn't understand, she said in a defeated way, quiet tears wetting her cheeks, and then she screamed so loudly and angrily he jumped: I wouldn't understand? Rubbing his temples vigorously, he wished she could settle down and shush, her crying was giving him a grand headache. Marlene could be dramatic and unreasonable, but she was never one for tears. He liked that about her. He put his hands up, gesticulating for language. Marlene and I, he began. Marlene and I, we are: a glove puppet tattooed onto the back of a hand; a recursive matryoshka nesting doll set that never ends; a trompe l'oeil twice reversed in a magic mirror; a hermaphrodite sea star cartwheeling across the ocean floor—

He thought his wife had broken down into ever more hysterical sobbing, but then he saw that he was much mistaken: she was laughing. Her hoarse contempt shocked him into silence. He did not dare go on. *A hermaphrodite sea star,* Jo? she whispered when she caught her breath. I'll sign the papers.

He hoped his ex would read the Flaubertian editorial (he was of poor character *and* he had never loved the woman). How lucky he was to have found Marlene. It had come so close to not happening, too. He had considered many other German actresses for the role of Lola Lola in *The Blue Angel*—Trude Hesterberg, Lucie Mannheim, Leni Riefenstahl, Käthe Haack—when a friend took him and his producer to see a comic play in a cheap theater to round off their evening with something lowbrow.

Marlene was in the play.

She was awful, an amateur. Her acting was sheer melodrama, but nobody could look away from her. The ass is not bad, someone said, but doesn't she need a face, too? Another warned: Be on your guard, she is one of those new-age ambisexuals. The next day, unbeknownst to his friends, Jo sent Marlene a memo to come audition. Promptly she came, but not the way the other hopefuls arrived, looking as if they would fizz out if you spoke one word with them. Jo spotted Marlene in the waiting room, reading a book. When he passed by her, he said: What are you reading, poetry? Close enough, she said with a shrug, barely looking up. He squinted to scrutinize the spine. It was Schopenhauer. He blushed and said he would see her later. For the audition and screen test, they wanted her to sing the same song in German and English, "You're the Cream in My Coffee." She said in a bored tone: Can't I just smoke a cigarette?

Later he saw just how clever and funny she was.

There is nothing a director finds less interesting than an actress who is dying to be cast in his film, and there is nothing more intriguing for a man who needs to be in control than the self-possessed comportment of a woman who has casual sex with both men and women by

night after closing a rowdy cabaret act as the last girl in a chorus line—
and her nose in a book by day. Under his baton, which she yielded to
like a clever marionette, she was the brightest star on both sides of the
Atlantic, courted and coveted by scions and studios, but she had not
forgotten who had turned her into one. Wrapping up a Paramount
press conference announcing *Shanghai Express,* the minder selected a
reporter to pose his final queries. Mr. von Sternberg, is Miss Dietrich
the most talented actress you have ever met?

But you must be sorely mistaken, Jo said. Talent is far from the
most essential quality in an actress.

What is the essential quality, Mr. von Sternberg?

Radiance, he said.

Without looking at her, he could feel Marlene smile next to him.

Last question—to Miss Dietrich—is Mr. von Sternberg really as
sadistic as they say?

Jo watched his leading lady uncross her legs and lean forward, as
she raised one rakish eyebrow: Ought a sculptor be labeled a sadist for
chipping his stone or pounding his clay?

At the penultimate wardrobe fitting for *Shanghai Express*, Anna May observed that some of her dresses were more embellished. Compared with Shanghai Lily's fur and feathers, Hui Fei's wardrobe had been quite dull and modest. Now the fabrics were richer, the cuts sharper. Nice work, she told the costumer as a stray sequin was stitched into place.

Miss Dietrich said you were to be allowed more glamour, the costumer said.

Anna May was surprised that she had it in her to feel offended by this, but she slipped on the upgraded brocade robe anyway and proceeded to set. Was this, indeed, what Shanghai looked like? Though largely constructed from papier-mâché, it was made by production designers to be bustling and attractive, with so much street life even Anna May forgot she was on a production back lot. There was a train and a quarter mile of functional track borrowed from the Santa Fe Railway. A cow and her calf were lowing by the side. They were to feature prominently in a scene where the *Shanghai Express* chugged by, only to be stopped short by an animal suckling her young on the tracks. Anna May heard that Jo had arranged for the cow to birth and nurse her calf right next to the station at La Grande, so that mother and child would be undisturbed by the cacophony and thoroughly prepared for their cameo. A rooster crossed her path, wattles quivering as it edged forward. A Chinese child extra was chasing it, but when he saw Anna May, he stopped short and hid behind one of the pillars, the better to gawk at her. Don't lean on it, a production manager hollered after the boy, it's plaster of paris!

Anna May saw Jo perched on a ladder propped against the train.

An assistant with a dark-gray paintbrush moved in accordance with what Jo pointed to. But, Mr. von Sternberg, someone said, the train is black. Of course it is, Jo replied calmly. I am painting the shadows of clouds on the back of the locomotive, can't you see?

He was called away toward an effluvium of blond at the other end of the studio, where they were moving key lights around Marlene. As per Jo's direction, the cinematographer and gaffer had set up a screen and lighting test. Marlene's cheekbones were resplendent. She wore a dress that began at the neck in a swirl of dark feathers and ended in black Chantilly lace at her feet. Marlene and Jo had spent an entire day going through thousands of feathers to find the perfect iridescence that would show on black-and-white film, finally going with the black-green tail feathers of Mexican fighting cocks. Anyone with eyes could see that everything on set was arranged to flatter Marlene: lighting, blocking, costume textures, production backdrops. It had been exactly ten years since Anna May had first scored a credited role in a Hollywood movie, 1922's *Toll of the Sea*, and a decade later, she had yet to enjoy such privileges, secured by studio stars and auteur muses. Everyone consistently praised Anna May's performances, and at twenty-seven now she considered herself to be in her prime, but she was still waiting for Hollywood to cast her in a lead role.

I'm telling you this sooner so you won't regret later, her father said early on, you know you can't be doing this all your life. At first she thought he meant it rhetorically, but he went on to ask: Liu Tsong, have you ever seen a Hollywood movie where the lead character is Chinese, and played by a Chinese?

She was shocked that her father, whom she considered outmoded, slow-witted in the measures of the world, was the one who clued her in to this. White men could play all the yellow emperors and brown sheikhs in the world, but she would never play a European countess, or even an American housewife! How had it honestly not occurred to her that a good number of roles automatically excluded her? She'd thought she was doing well enough. Before even turning twenty, she was booked for role after role in Hollywood—a Spanish honky-tonk girl in *Thundering Dawn*, a Mongol slave in *The Thief of Bagdad*, an Inuit in *The Alaskan*, and the Native American princess Tiger Lily in *Peter Pan*. It was true none of them were lead roles, but she'd assumed she'd not been invited to try out for those because she wasn't yet ready, not because she was Chinese.

Even if this profession wasn't so indecent, her father said, you'd have nowhere to climb. I'll find my own way, she said to him, refusing to show she was shaken. How will you survive? he asked. You are completely out of touch with reality.

ONE AFTERNOON HER father had held up a newspaper to her face. Sit, he said. You think I'm blind?

A photograph of her in a brassiere and Douglas Fairbanks Jr. in a turban had been making its rounds, not only in local papers, but even those in China. That's a publicity picture for our new movie, Anna May explained, it's nothing personal. Her father said: Who is going to want used goods, Liu Tsong?

He showed her the Cantonese clipping: ANNA MAY WONG STRIPS FOR WHITE MAN.

She wanted to know: What does what I wear or whom I see have to do with China?

Her father did not answer that.

All artists are perverts, he said. You might not see it now, but I can't condone such behavior in my household any longer. I have arranged for you an amicable solution, he added, passing her an envelope. When she opened it and saw several photographs of respectable Chinese men, she threw the whole matchmaking packet to the ground like it had burned her hands and started to scream as loudly as she could.

Liu Tsong, her father exhorted, be civil!

You be civil, she cried, backing away from him, working herself into such a fit she had to be taken to the hospital. From the hospital she checked herself into a hotel. It was safer there. Her whole life still lay ahead of her, if she was willing to protect it from the people who claimed to know her best. Other than that she had been born their daughter, what did they see in her?

Her mother pleaded with her to come home.

Someone's wings have hardened, her father mocked, referring to her in the third person even though she was in the same room. I'm telling you, she thinks she's too good for us now.

Shortly after, Anna May signed the lease to an apartment.

Moving out had been well within her means for a few years now; her paycheck was paltry compared with that of the other stars, but it was still more than the hand laundry earned in a month. Living at home was an embarrassment that cut both ways now that her fans had begun to show up at Wong Sam Sing's Chinese Hand Laundry. She was embarrassed to be seen in the laundry; her father was embarrassed that she had fans. She'd not dared to move out sooner because of what had been said when she brought up the matter. Only loose women live on their own, her father said, outside of marriage and family. At home we do everything for you, her mother added. Where else will you get that?

Living alone was a revelation Anna May reveled in wholly.

Her apartment she decorated not just to her tastes, but to how she imagined the apartment of an actress ought to be. With care she considered the tone and shape of each thing she put around herself. The apartment had to be modern, individualistic, contrarian. Far Eastern garnishes littered her household with careless precision, to be read by the right people ironically and by the wrong people literally. Bold abstract artwork on the walls, bonsai in porcelain troughs, traditional calligraphy scrolls whose words she could not fathom. Home was a blank slate she could fill in with how she wanted herself to be. The last thing she wanted was to look down on her family as she learned to like herself, but was there any other way out of that odd-angled corner she'd backed into? The setup was painful in its clarity: either she disappointed them, or she disappointed herself.

In her new bedroom Anna May had a handsome vanity table of rosewood.

It had a large triple-paneled mirror with beveled glass edges and a matching rosewood stool. She sat here after watching the roles first-billed actresses got to play, as she thought about how she would have interpreted them, had only she been allowed to audition.

Repeating these leading-lady lines, she never needed to drop articles, vowels, and adverbs the way they liked to make her do when she was performing as a Chinese side character.

Me likey chop su-ey, you no likey?

She might not have been able to change the lines, but she never played it dumb, servile, or cloying, when it would have been so easy to indulge that which the studios wanted. She played it sharp. The lonely whetstone she threw her edge against: Chaplin.

Unbeknownst to him, or anyone, for that matter, he was her sparring partner in becoming a better performer. Practice might not make perfect, but you were bound to improve if you worked at it. She bought her own projector and all his reels, took notes on his keen timing and wry performance. Abjection could be comic, but she recognized in his irony a certain decency she wanted for herself: the world is not as you want it to be, but it is still the one you wake up to and conduct yourself through with dignity.

Was this as Chaplin intended, or was she reading him too reactively?

Actors seemed to have more room for characterization in their roles than actresses. Anna May never wanted to be a prop, playing for chic, but no one seemed to care about the difference between a good actress and a bad one, as long as the actress looked good on camera.

What she loved about acting was not the attention. Had it been up to her, she would not have gone to any of the parties or posed for any of those pictures, but she had been told they were necessary in order to maintain a certain image. If that was not looked after, it could hurt her bookings. What Anna May loved about acting was the craft. Even after all these years, to have a fresh script in hand and a new character's skin to get under gave her a thrill, no matter how few lines she had or how disproportionate her salary was compared with everyone else's on the credit roll. The process of living truthfully under imaginary circumstances was what she was addicted to. Could a bad actress suffer as much as a good one?

nna May flinched as she heard Jo shout, "Cut!"
You're faking it, he added, you're a bore! One take
ago it was: Get back into it and let me love you, and before
that, simply: What is wrong with you, Miss Wong?

The scene was a simple one.

Mrs. Haggerty entered the train cabin Hui Fei and Shanghai Lily
were in, where they lounged in capricious postures, trading senten-
tious remarks. But next to Marlene's languid Shanghai Lily, Anna May
was limpid and unfocused, and she had been flubbing her lines.

In all her years of acting, Anna May had never before been chastised by a director. She watched nervously as Jo relit his pipe.

Turn your shoulders away from me and straighten out, he said to
her, and if for some reason you can't stand to look at Marlene, then
just count to six and gaze at that lamp as if you could no longer live
without it!

Marlene was already back in position.

Before they went for the new take, when everyone was busy with a
speck of dust to be cleaned off the camera lens, and a touchup for Mrs.
Haggerty's streaky foundation, Anna May turned to Marlene, breaking
character to ask: What did you tell Jo?

I told him nothing, Marlene said.

Don't you understand, Anna May said. I can't afford to have your
reputation.

Marlene leaned so close to her ear Anna May could feel her breathing. Anna, she whispered, what *is* my reputation? Surreptitiously she
kissed her earlobe as she asked: Why haven't you learned to live a little?
At first, all Anna May could think of was whether anyone had seen
what Marlene did, but then she saw that no one was watching. Everyone was busy, and she began to relax. She looked Marlene straight in
the eye, and Marlene stared back at her. Very slowly Marlene started

smiling, and Anna May deliberately mirrored the movement of her scene partner's mouth, as they held an even gaze like a straight line penciled out between them.

Now they were ready to begin.

ON "ACTION," MRS. Haggerty slides open the train cabin's doors.

Shanghai Lily checks her appearance in the mirror while Hui Fei plays solitaire. They turn to regard each other coolly as the dowdy Mrs. Haggerty introduces herself, yammering on about her dog and the boardinghouse she owns in Shanghai, which houses only "respectable people." Shanghai Lily asks if Mrs. Haggerty doesn't perhaps find respectable people terribly dull.

Rattled, Mrs. Haggerty turns to Hui Fei for moral support.

I must confess, Hui Fei says with delectable disdain as she smokes and reads the calling card Mrs. Haggerty has passed to her. I don't quite know the standard of respectability that you demand in your boardinghouse, Mrs. Haggerty. Hui Fei returns the calling card to the scandalized woman, insouciant and unhurried.

Cut, Jo said crisply, that was perfect, Miss Wong. I don't know what you were waiting for before this, perhaps you thrill to performing under pressure?

FOR A WHOLE week Anna May glowed.

Relaxed and light-headed, she could feel that she was opening up not only her own performance, but also Marlene's. What's more, there was nothing to it. She just had to look at Marlene and remember to breathe. Every scene between them was dispensed with ease in two or at most three takes, and the whole crew was abuzz with talk of their chemistry. Jo was not one to condescend to praise, but it was plain to see he was pleased with his two actresses. He'd turned a harsh eye on Clive Brook, who was playing Captain Doc Harvey, Shanghai Lily's love interest, after coming off back-to-back box-office successes as Sherlock Holmes. Look at the women, next to them you're a cement mixer! Do you want me to slap you, so you can at least have an expression on your face?

Between takes Anna May retired to Marlene's dressing room, much larger and more luxurious than her own, listening to records with the door left open, not rehearsing their scenes, just talking and touching in the manner of new acquaintances, formal, demurring, solicitous, avid, as a runner brought them iced coffee with striped straws, in each hand a cigarette they forgot to smoke. When Anna May was not in a scene, she stood behind Jo, where a spare stool would be brought to her. She'd noticed that Marlene had her own lawn chair with her name embroidered in cursive across the back, and thought of paying for one out of her own pocket on the side, but did any of these status tokens really matter, when she could not help but look on and smile as she heard Marlene's bossy voice ring out: Thin those false lashes down by half, I do not want to look like Garbo!

The crew adored Marlene, and Anna May saw why: Which other diva, upon hearing a crew member sneeze or sniffle, would task herself to locate the person with the flu, and no matter who it was, third dolly grip or props builder's assistant, present to them the next day a container of Dietrich's home-brewed chicken soup?

Anna May even made her own modest contributions to Marlene's publicity machine.

They were watching Jo's gaffer adjust his signature butterfly lighting, arranged so that it almost formed a glowing nimbus around her forehead, cheekbones, and hair, when Anna May commented that Marlene was lit so beautifully she looked like she'd been dusted in gold foil. Overhearing this remark, Marlene's manager exclaimed it would be tip-top fodder for the rumor mill, and spun it like so, as printed in the papers: "Every morning before going on set, the actress Marlene Dietrich has a $50 nub of solid gold ground into dust, and sprinkled on her hair."

It was the prettiest lie. Marlene loved it.

So did Anna May, who would have been more than happy to spend her unoccupied moments thinking up gold-tinted press gossip for her costar. She wasn't the only one. Returning from lunch once, the

Shanghai Express cast passed the adjacent lot where another Paramount production was shooting with Tallulah Bankhead. Tallulah spread her legs. She'd painted the insides of her thighs gold and was calling out saucily: Guess who I had for lunch today?

Come on, Marlene retorted. You wish!

IN THE SCENE Anna May likes best in *Shanghai Express,* Shanghai Lily wears a coat with a silver fox collar. When Shanghai Lily looks at Hui Fei in the corridor, her chin tucks sumptuously into its fullness.

Hui Fei's hair is loose. From nowhere she unsheathes a knife.

It is small, but very sharp.

Seeing Hui Fei draw the knife, Shanghai Lily strides through the cabin and holds her companion in an embrace from behind. Shanghai Lily does not know that the Communist warlord Chang (played to the hilt by Hollywood's favorite Chinaman, Warner Oland) has just raped Hui Fei, and Hui Fei says nothing to her either. There are no tears in her eyes. Her mouth is set in a very thin line. Shanghai Lily takes Hui Fei's wrists in her hands. Hui Fei turns to her slightly. The blade of the knife glints. Shanghai Lily's eyes beseech as she rests her chin on Hui Fei's shoulder and says softly: Don't do anything foolish. Shrugging Shanghai Lily off, Hui Fei considers the point of the blade. Her nipples are visible under her cheongsam, tight silk catching the light, she's not wearing a bra. Without a word she moves down the corridor, leaving Shanghai Lily trembling alone in her furs, as the train rumbles on.

With just the knife, Hui Fei takes on Chang and murders him by her own hand. Then she goes up to Captain Doc Harvey.

You better get her out of there, Hui Fei says, I just killed Chang.

Have you got a gun? Doc mutters, but Hui Fei has already walked away.

THEY WERE REVIEWING the rushes for this scene when Jo remarked: Forget Doc, now it seems as if Shanghai Lily and Hui Fei are lovers!

Anna May started to flush a deep red as she tried to push the color away from her neck, her cheeks, but everyone else was laughing.

Marlene caught her eye.

Very nice, Jo went on, and nothing overt about it either, we won't have to worry about the censor's scissors. Those self-ordained Hays Code despots are too stupid for anything that isn't cussing and fornicating right before their eyes.

In public there was the expediency that it was all part of the irresistible shuck and jive of being two beautiful women in a room together in front of other people, but when their costumes were hung up onto racks, Anna May felt herself recede, wishing they could still be filming. Could Marlene really want nothing from her in real life? Yes, there was Jo, and there was the husband, but might there not be something she could give Marlene, that she alone was good for? It made her feel sick to think this way whenever Marlene was near, and she began to make up excuses to be alone. Her lines remained perfect and her performance impeccable, but she no longer visited Marlene in her dressing room or hung behind to watch her do a take, chatting with the crew. It would be best to finish the movie and forget about Marlene. See her every now and then on someone else's arm at a Paramount party and exchange a few pleasantries, that was how it would be. Soon Anna May took to leaving Paramount right after her last scene of the day, before they'd even cleaned off her makeup, hiding out in the hotel. In the bath on the night before the last shoot day, the concierge buzzed Anna May for a flower delivery. A vase of lilies was sent up. The accompanying card, unsigned, read: Call me. Five minutes later, another call from the concierge. More lilies, the same note. For the rest of the hour this repeated itself. First it was charming, then outrageous—who sends over a roomful of the sender's favorite flower, rather than the recipient's?

There was no more tabletop space.

She looked around at all the lilies.

What Anna May liked about Marlene, right from the start, was that she seemed to be that rare woman who truly did not care what anyone else thought. People would talk? Let them sing and shout! Before she met Marlene, Anna May never imagined a woman could have such a life. Marlene's sense of self never flickered—playing bit parts back then; having made the big time now—she remained the same person. She knew who she was, and reveled in that knowledge, and so

appeared effortlessly *Marlene* at all times. Now half of Hollywood had
the hots for her, but Anna May thought, with some measure of pride,
that in fact they did not know what it was they liked about her. They
only wanted to be part of the glamour the studios had built up around
her image, but they did not know that behind the shiny publicity was a
real woman you could fall for.

If Marlene wanted her, too, why should she be so afraid of what
others would think?

Anna May was so tired of living a lie for everyone else's benefit.
As early on as she could remember, the most important lesson she'd
taught herself was to keep anything she wanted a secret. Too many
times, she'd found out the hard way that what she wanted was wrong.
Now she was older and knew better, but it was too late. How she saw
herself, first and foremost, had been set in stone by others: she was an
indecent person who was bound to give her family a bad name. She
knew this was neither fair nor true, but what you knew was more often
than not separate from what you felt. Already her parents had wanted
to disown her for being an actress; what would happen if she went
with Marlene on top of that, too? They would have died of shame if it
became public knowledge, and the Chinese press would certainly be
tripping over themselves to ensure the scoop was spread far and wide.
They'd called her a degenerate for acting with a white man; they would
have run out of names for her if they found out about this.

She picked up the phone.

Before she could close herself up again, she dialed Marlene's number. If she did not get to see Marlene tonight, part of her would go
quiet. That silence might be permanent and tremendous. Inside of it,
she would never be able to unlearn anything. When the phone was
answered, Anna May closed her eyes as she said: Do you want to come
over?

Yes, Marlene said, I would like that very much.

REMOVING HER STOCKINGS drying on the radiator Anna May
knocked down a vase of lilies. She drew the curtains open, then shut
them again. A warm flurry settled between her chest and stomach, and

though she was nervous, she was very glad that she'd called. She made the bed, tipping the pillows and her pulse points with a few drops of her favorite Penhaligon's. It was the closest scent she'd found, over the years, to that of Marlene's handkerchief when first they met. She had only a popular jazz piano record, so she put that on. She stepped back to survey the room. Worrying everything would come off too studied, she hastened to disarray a cushion and the coverlet as the doorbell rang, jangling several times in quick succession. Just a sec, Anna May called out. She wished she'd given herself something to drink before answering the door. When she opened it, Marlene was leaning her head against the doorframe. Hi, Marlene said casually. She was wearing a bouclé jacket and her face was flushed. Anna May watched as Marlene tottered over to the armchair by the window and took out a cigarette. You don't mind if I smoke, she mumbled after lighting it, or perhaps you do? Before Anna May said anything, Marlene snuffed out the cigarette on the cuff of her jacket, burning a hole through the curled yarn.

It's only the latest Chanel, she giggled.

She was obviously drunk.

Are you okay? Anna May said.

I'm selfish, Marlene said solemnly, reaching over to take Anna May's hand, pressing it fast to her forehead like she was miming a fever. I love providing, but only because it binds others to me. I'm never interested in playing a character, she went on as she brought Anna May's fingers to her lips and bit on one of them lightly, I'm merely interested in a character being me.

With her other hand, Anna May swept Marlene's curls back from her moist forehead.

That's what he said, Marlene said, sitting up straighter.

Anna May did not follow.

Jo is a big fan of your naturalism, Marlene said, more loudly now. He says you are a generous performer, so you must be a generous person. It follows. You let other people play off you, whereas I only ever play off myself. He told me to learn one or two things from you, can you imagine?

Her fingers, still interlaced with Marlene's, went cold.

That's why you sent me lilies? Anna May said.

She wanted to remove her hand, but Marlene was gripping too tightly.

The lilies, Marlene exclaimed, yes, of course! Let me tell you about the lilies. She looked around to acknowledge the flowers. Jo-Jo sent them to me, Marlene slurred. So predictable—men—am I right? He's said his piece and wants me to call so we can patch things up now. What does he think I am, a pushover? So I helped him forward on *all* the lilies to you, since he admires you so much. Let's see, she nodded curtly at the vases like she was counting out the important people she recognized at a premiere, that's a lot. How do you like them? Must have cost him a pretty penny.

A jaunty Gershwin hit went on playing in the background. More than anything, Anna May wanted to turn the music off. How could she have thought that Marlene was playing for keeps? She should never have called. Silence was remote, but at least it was safe. There was nothing to take back outside of it. She wanted to be alone. I think you should go, Anna May managed to say. With a lot of control, her voice came out just right, neither too loud nor too soft. She did not want to see Marlene now, and in fact she did not want to see her again, but the woman had curled up in the armchair and closed her eyes.

Why are you still here? Anna May said. We have a long day tomorrow.

Marlene ignored her, but her left hand kept time with the music against the side of the armchair. Anna May walked over to the player on the table and took its arm off the record. Right away, Marlene's eyes flicked open, affronted, as if this were her room and Anna May had just walked in and silenced her music. Well then, Anna, Marlene said, sitting up, should we practice our scene, and you can show me how to do my lines? If you keep up the good work, Jo might even cast you as Catherine the Great. He doesn't care that it'll bomb the box office, isn't he a real artist? Suddenly, before Anna May could say anything, Marlene began to sob. I'm a horrible person, Marlene said, pulling Anna May toward her, I know I am. She burrowed her face into Anna May's caftan. Jo said if it weren't for him, I would never have made it in Berlin, much less America. She wrapped her arms around Anna May's midriff and looked up at her hopefully. Don't make me go, Marlene said, please

Anna, I'm sorry. Tears were still running down her face. She tugged on Anna May to make her sit on the couch beside her.

Anna May sat.

Thank you, Marlene said. Thank you, she whispered again, as she took Anna May's hand, brushing it across her own forearm, back and forth. Laundry hands, Marlene said. Remember? She smiled weakly at Anna May. Anna May felt herself soften as she continued the movement on her own accord, running her palm over Marlene's smooth skin to comfort her. They were quiet and close this way till Marlene closed her fingers around Anna May's wrist. Your pearls, Marlene murmured, when first we met. They were freshwater, weren't they, filly?

十三

hanghai Express was America's highest-grossing movie in 1932. Paramount Pictures was justifiably elated— they'd trounced archrival MGM's all-star *Grand Hotel* at the box office. Dietrich/von Sternberg had prevailed over Garbo. *Vanity Fair* reviewed the sensational smasher as follows:

> Floridly vulgar, Mr. von Sternberg trades his open style for fancy play, chiefly upon the legs in silk, and buttocks in lace, of Marlene Dietrich, of whom he has made, once again, a veritable slut. The Sternberg problem is not one of ability, but taste. His umbilical perseverance is fixed on the navel of Venus, as meanwhile the inimitable Anna May Wong outclasses Dietrich, Brook and Oland in every scene she appears.

Jo, who read reviews for laughs, was used to the capricious pronouncements of the press. One moment it was "a brilliant impresario ahead of his time," the next it was "Who taught him drama? Hitler?" Not so Marlene. An argument ensued about who was doing whom in, who would be nothing without whom, who was leaving whom right this instant. Every time they fought personally, which regrettably was often enough, one of them would threaten to leave Paramount professionally, though they both knew they were hog-tied together by a watertight six-picture contract.

Shanghai Express was the midline. Three down, three to go.

If they brawled in the middle of a shoot, Jo would ready himself to receive the studio bigwigs who would hightail over to his place uninvited, one of whom even went right down on bended knee, begging him to make up with Marlene ("Anything it takes, my man. Bill us the flowers, the champers, knock yourself out") and not get the company in serious trouble by turning their prize horse into a hayburner.

When in a fit of anger Jo said to Marlene that she wasn't that great an actress, just an oversized personality on legs, she swore she would never speak with him again.

In fact I didn't mean it in a bad way, he tried as she walked out the door. Surface is the only thing that's real to me, he called out after her sincerely; what's more, I know all your faults and love them like they're my own! She was too busy revving up the bottle-green Rolls-Royce to listen, so he tried: Who bought you the fast car? At that she looked him in the eye. But only to shut down the engine, throw the keys into the bushes, and stalk off the property in stilettos.

Woman, he screeched at the gate, I'll give you three hours to come back to me, or you can pack your bags and get out of my house!

As always, when she returned, barefoot and blistered, he washed between her toes and kissed them.

A COMMON CUSTOM in Hollywood then was for the director to applaud after a scene, in particular if it was difficult. Oftentimes "difficult" merely meant "emotional," and was played big to compensate. Some directors even clapped after every scene. Jo found this idiotic; it would be like applauding himself. He believed that whatever performers appeared to have done onscreen was possible only because of the psychophysiological state the director had coerced, lulled, or tricked them into. The higher up you went in the movies, unlike theater, there was rarely a good or bad actor at the bottom of it, only a good or bad director. Jo had seen many a fine acting talent squandered by a director with no vision, and on the other hand, there was, every so often, the ordinary man or woman transformed by the way a director presented him or her in a film.

Circumnavigating the same old social circles through later years, it was not uncommon for individuals from Marlene's bevy of ex-lovers to come up to Jo and rue the disservice he'd done them by endowing her with traits not her own on the screen. I did not give to her anything she did not already have, he would defend Marlene by saying each time, I only dramatized them. You saw what you wanted to see, don't let's be bitter.

Still, there would be a shred of solidarity between Jo and such men, having been through all of that: It was good while it lasted. Did she make you believe? Because she was a narcissist and so was he, it could have been love, just as likely as it could have been vanity. As long as they trusted each other, any distinction between those two emotional states carried no practical significance.

For a substantial period Marlene had refused to be loaned out to and used by any Hollywood director other than Jo, and he was touched by her loyalty. After they'd broken up irrefutably, when he was ready to subject himself to the pleasure and torture of watching the woman he'd talent-spotted, trained up, brought over, and shared a bed with in someone else's movie, he saw that in standing by him she might simply have had her own best interests at heart. Next to his talent for making her beautiful, he might have been completely incidental.

He missed her face.

He'd written entire scenes, designed whole sequences just to watch her light up a cigarette, put on a hat. Pity the contractual agreement was complete; they could no longer use it to extort from one another as they pleased. Were seven opulent films worth a lifetime's heartache? The line he wrote with his own hand and coached Marlene to deliver in their last movie together: If you really loved me, you'd have killed yourself. All the reviewers had latched onto the observation that both male protagonists in *The Devil Is a Woman* physically resembled Jo so closely. He couldn't have cared less.

BEFORE GOING OFF on a long voyage to Japan to purge himself of Marlene and wean her off him, Jo told her in good faith that her next best chance was with Rouben Mamoulian or Ernst Lubitsch. Already he sensed that she was the one who would be remembered, and he dismissed in time as a diminutive oddball in ill-fitted suits who was lucky enough to have had a big bite of a beautiful woman once. Almost turning back at the harbor, he forced himself to board the ship. With Marlene everything was bright, but there was no future.

On the ship he exaggerated for himself a bachelor's debauchery, subsisting on oysters and liqueurs that he regurgitated to starboard in tears. Arriving in Tokyo he whored himself silly before hauling himself onto a Kyoto-bound train to seek out a nameless kabuki actress he'd been hoping to meet. She was the descendant of a Meiji-era courtier, and had achieved a hallowed reputation as a performer of great versatility, although she had never been allowed to perform professionally.

Kabuki was an old boys' club. Her troupe upheld the *onnagata* tradition of male actors trained specifically and stringently for female roles. The Noh stage was highly symbolic, so there was absolutely no need for a woman to play a female role. That would only lead to a backsliding in tradition. Further, her nature as a woman was too soft. She would not be able to produce the differentiation between gentle movements and the forceful actions that were essential to the shape and dynamism of Noh. She was allowed, however, to join in the troupe's training as a fashionable hobby, an accomplished amusement, but only because of her father's reputation in Noh circles. Learning from distinguished *onnagata* she might even improve on her feminine character along the way!

After decades of cultivating her craft on the sidelines, just two or three more gifted than her, a handful her equal, and the vast majority mediocre, the woman was committed to a Zen Buddhist asylum when she lost her mind at a *shūmei* naming ceremony, where year after year she had gone unhonored as the men around her were promoted, their names and designations recorded for posterity in the troupe's annals.

It took Jo a week to get to the Zen Buddhist asylum.

Far out in greater Kansai prefecture, it was a gated compound with a rock garden and a slim moat. When Jo inquired as to the architecture of the asylum, what he understood from the monk was that the moat (finger tracing oval perimeter) was to keep the external pandemonium (flurry of hands, circling wide) of the world at bay (hands making a barrier) so it couldn't disturb the personal entropy (whizzing of finger to the temple) of the patients' rich (fists clutched to chest, blooming outward) interior lives.

For a comparatively sane person encountering its thoughtful architecture, the Japanese asylum was quaint and restful. Some years later, when commissioning Richard Neutra to erect a mansion in San Fernando, Jo asked for just the one bedroom, high windows retrofitted for privacy ("You are a modernist in exile, you will find an aesthetic yet practical solution"), ample space for entertaining but no locks on any bathrooms ("On the few occasions I am in the mood for guests I do not want lachrymose thespians slitting their wrists in my sinks"), and a sinuous moat all around the mansion ("to keep the generic madness of the world from infecting the particularities of my personal idiosyncrasies").

When Jo reached her garret, the kabuki actress was in a frenzy of performance. One moment her wrists were listless, the next her fingers could have strangled a cow. Although her hands were empty by her sides, her eyes gave the impression of looking out from behind a paper fan. The safety bars across the window striated her face in discontinuous shadow. In great agitation she cut a *mie* pose, holding on for three beats and crossing her eyes before letting her body fall back into a drunkard's leaden swagger. But she was only falsifying her weakness, and floated straight back up right away, with a clear and light countenance to show the hidden aspect of her character.

Jo had only heard of *haragei*.

In *haragei*, the same actor takes on different characters on the Noh stage without changing costumes or speaking styles. The change had to be indicated to the audience from within. "Belly acting" was technically demanding. It could take more than ten years for a novice to learn, and twenty more for a virtuoso to master, but once he was adept, the triumphant pride of devouring the tidal energy of the audience recognizing and riding on the actor's emotion was unsurpassable.

The kabuki actress came up right to him.

A nose away from Jo, her eyes locked onto him without seeing.

Jo wept noiselessly into his elbow.

He did not know what she was performing, but he could feel the internal landscapes of her characters burning. She was on fire, beyond the ambit of a prop, the feudal prejudices of the troupe, the highest honor of having an audience member call out your stage name, followed by your father's stage name, when you had accomplished an inspired *mie*. Despite being barred from performance, for years she had trained relentlessly for the dream of hearing their patronymic heralded. Now, disintegrating in solitary confinement behind bars, she had forgotten everything there was to regret: her lines, her sex, her name.

Nothing separated her from her craft now.

The Collection Camp
for Nonsedentary Persons
of Roma and Sinti Descent
in Bucolic Salzburg

IX

Cut, cut, cut! Leni said, putting a hand to her temple to steady herself, I told you this would never work. A German shepherd will not look like a wolf, just as the transvestites on Bülowstraße do not look like women! Return this dog to wherever you got it from. If there's turpentine to spare, remove the gray paint we daubed over its fur. Now if you cannot locate for me a tame wolf, I told you, I will find one by myself, but do not try to convince me otherwise with knockoffs! I must cut close to the bone. I require authenticity. And how about the eighty sheep for Pedro's flock? Have we secured them? I want Merino sheep. Not the ones with horns, and not the ones with black faces. *Merino.*

Even Leni could not recall the original deadline for *Tiefland*. She'd bulldozed past it again and again, and kept everyone on full payroll as the project dragged on. It was the fair thing to do, and as much as possible, she liked to think of herself as a fair person. She respected the crew's time and commitment. Since reports had to be sent to the Doctor and the Ministry of Propaganda for every extension, it was getting harder and harder to justify each time. In that respect, her bladder colic was a blessing in disguise. Anyone who could chastise a sick woman about adhering more efficiently to the planned schedule was surely going to look bad.

As for logistical complications, she let them play out in full. That often took good time.

Leni had written the film to be set in the fictional town of Roccabruna. She had envisioned shooting in the Catalan lowlands. Location-wise, the Doctor advised that Spain was dicey, but Italy was a safe bet. They were on good terms with the Duce. After scouting, she settled on Krün, a village wedged in a mountain plateau on the Bavarian side of the Alps for the primary shoot, and the Italian Dolomites for some establishing shots.

She oversaw elaborate architectural designs for Moorish arches and wrought-iron filigree that would match her vision for the set. She okayed the design on paper, but after the sets had been constructed and brought to the mountains, she complained that they weren't rustic enough. She wanted everything rebuilt from scratch. It was done. Much better, she said of the new ones, though they were hardly distinguishable from the old.

Then there had been the problem of the extras.

As much as possible, Leni never liked to stint on her environments. The real thing was always best. This certainly applied to extras and animals. That was why she had taken so much trouble with the wolf. Surrounding yourself with the right objects and textures amounted to a rich patina on the screen. *Tiefland* opened with Martha—herself as a Moorish beggar dancer, full of far-flung color, exotic mystery, spirited flamboyance—riding a horse into town, gazed upon admiringly by the street urchins of Roccabruna, and she wanted those extras to have the right look. Production assistants suggested recruiting the children of mountain farmers from the nearby Sarntal Valley to play the street urchins. She took some test pictures of them. The children of the mountain farmers were corn-fed, blond, and blue-eyed.

It will show on the screen, she said.

We're shooting a black-and-white, Miss Riefenstahl, a production assistant said. Would the difference be noticeable?

If we were back in Berlin, Leni said, you would be fired.

LENI WROTE THE Doctor, asking if it would be possible to travel to Andalusia to recruit some dark-haired extras. She would need adults, too, as villagers in later scenes. He wrote back that it was not merely too expensive, but also dangerous, given the combat situation.

Leni turned back dispiritedly to the pictures of the Sarntal Valley inhabitants. The makeup artist suggested dyeing their hair and rubbing soot on their faces. After one potato schnapps too many, the line producer joked: It was too bad they couldn't use some Jewish extras. They could well pass as Moorish. And casting would be so convenient, too; they need only visit one of the Party's collection camps! Leni disregarded his prattle, but the next morning she went up to him and squeezed his arm. You've given me the perfect idea, she said. Of course we can't use Jews, but who else is there? *Gypsies!*

With alacrity and exuberance she wrote the Doctor.

He was not opposed to the idea, agreeing that, for her intents and purposes, gypsies were an ideal stand-in for Moors. She was hereby authorized to visit one of the Party's holding camps for nonsedentary persons of Roma and Sinti descent, and to pick as many extras as she needed. If she was still in Krün, the camp nearest to her was Maxglan. Arrangements were made for her to be received by camp officials. She should send the Doctor a name list of those she found suitable. He would get someone to file official paperwork to facilitate the procurement.

Camp Maxglan had been only a short drive away.

There were two hundred and seventy Roma and Sinti inmates being held there. Presented in neat rows in a cramped courtyard, they wore threadbare clothing and had dirty faces. I can't take these people like this, Leni said when she arrived. Can they reclothe themselves and come back out again? There was an odd silence before the camp commander cleared his throat and told her this was as good as it got.

Fine, Leni said, trying to regain her composure. I'll take it from here. Marching up and down the lines and peering at their faces, Leni held up her index fingers and thumbs against each other to simulate the aspect ratio of her Arriflex. It was distracting to have to look at them as a bedraggled flock of humans, and that smell! Isolating them face by face, body by body, as rectilinear objects to be placed in focus, Leni sifted out forty to have a second look at. There were a few who were too thin, so she whittled it down to thirty. From there she picked twenty-three. An NSDAP official was on hand to take down her selection. The oldest was a seventy-five-year-old widower, and the youngest was three months old, born at the camp. As she left the dismal place, Leni noticed that it was surrounded by barbed wire. She shrugged to herself. Times were so volatile now, they were safer in there.

Information was sent to headquarters to be processed and cleared. I hope you will be able to expedite this matter, she cabled the Doctor. *Tiefland* is waiting for me.

Back at headquarters, the twenty-three handpicked Roma and

Sinti extras were certified by the NSDAP to be, the administrative notation read, NOT FROM JEWISH TRIBES. A contract was drawn up to stipulate terms clearly. There was to be strict isolation of the extras from all other personnel. The set was to follow the same regulations as did the camp. This included latrine use and ration portions. Security measures were not to be overridden for artistic matters. Armed guards borrowed from the Wehrmacht would be sent to accompany the loan. Should the need arise, they were not to be obstructed in performing their duties. Leni Riefenstahl GmbH would arrange for and bear the costs of housing, feeding, and transporting the extras. Extras were to be recompensed for their labor at a wage of seven reichsmarks per day for adults. Three children were to be counted as one adult. Further, the contract stated, in italics, these wages were not to be paid to the Roma and Sinti inmates directly. They should be made out to the Salzburg branch of the NSDAP's Gypsy General Fund, to defray the overhead of running camps like Maxglan.

Leni received two copies of the contract in Krün.

She browsed through them quickly, signed the papers, and couriered them back posthaste, impatient to begin.

THE GYPSIES WERE natural performers and provided the homespun verisimilitude Leni wanted for the villagers of Roccabruna. When the scene had to be reset, they resumed their original positions quickly and quietly, as if they had already been trained to gather and disperse. Leni was glad that she had held out for this dark-eyed Roma and Sinti bunch—they were so well behaved, the Wehrmacht Afrika Korps guards were hardly necessary.

Sometimes Leni would join the hair and makeup supervisor on continuity checks, trimming fringes and beards and hair lengths so they would look the same as they had across the long shoot. One evening, the line producer came to ask her if the gypsies were allowed to sing before their bedtime.

Of course, Leni said. Why would we forbid that?

It was not permitted them in Camp Maxglan, the line producer said. If we want to follow protocol, we probably shouldn't—

This is my set, Leni said. I permit them to sing here.

Leni was friendly with the extras, but she found them to be nervous around her. Only little Zazilia greeted her every time she saw her, hoping for more toffee. Everyone else was careful to give her a wide berth whenever she passed. Fame has that kind of effect, Leni guessed. Even if you didn't parade it around, people noticed. You could only try to reassure them that you were just like them, too.

One of Leni's scenes as Martha had her galloping in on the dappled gray at high speed, and it was quite dangerous. To be safe, she picked out five female extras who could be passed off as her from the back or at a distance. None of them had equestrian experience, so Leni simply picked the one who resembled her the most. The girl had dark hair and must have been in her twenties. She was almost the exact same height as Leni, though a good deal thinner. To beef her up, they gave her a few more clothing layers to wear underneath. Her hair was trimmed and curled to match Leni's, and she got to wear Martha's dancer costume. The body double was frightened before they started shooting. Leni offered to share her antianxiety barbiturate with her. The girl shook her head. *Gott im Himmel*, these people were so antsy about modern medicine!

It'll all go well, Leni cajoled. What's more, you'll be paid more as a body double than an extra.

Our wages, her body double said hesitantly, they go—to the camp.

Look now, Leni said, trying not to lose her patience. I didn't dictate the terms of your work here, but I'll owe you a favor, how about that? Take this pill like I said—you'll feel much better. With a most mistrustful look on her face, the girl took the pill from Leni. My dear, Leni said, I'm not having one myself only because I already did so at breakfast. What do you think it is, poison?

X

Hans Haas kept his voice gentle when he corralled the Roma and Sinti extras together in the mornings. He felt bad that they would stop talking whenever any of the film crew was within earshot, even though no one on set understood Romani. The extras could speak German fluently, too, but they did not use it among themselves, and in general they did not speak with the guards or crew unless necessary.

Most of them tried to avoid eye contact with Hans Haas, but the girl who'd played Miss Riefenstahl's body double had grown bolder than the rest after being singled out for that scene. Hans Haas had been the one leading the dappled gray back to its mark as they went for multiple takes. Waiting beyond the frame, she'd asked him quite casually in German: And if the horse throws me? Not knowing how else to answer, he reassured her: I'm sure you'll be fine. She gave him a haughty smirk that made her look very pretty, especially in Miss Riefenstahl's gypsy costume, as she mounted the horse and looked straight ahead, waiting for their cue. The horse reared in one of the takes, but the girl kept her wits about her and they managed to continue shooting the scene at various speeds, till Miss Riefenstahl was satisfied. Wonderful job, Hans Haas heard her say to the body double, you're such a natural!

In the mornings, when Hans Haas came for roll call and to take them to the holding pen for breakfast, she held his gaze steadily, nodding at him as he passed them by.

She was the one who'd asked the line producer if they might be allowed to sing.

When permission came back in the positive, Hans Haas supplied them a little handbell he'd found in the supply shed, which made them so happy. The body double thanked Hans Haas, and he saw her eyes soften for a moment. That's no problem at all, he said, staying a while to listen. Without instruments, the extras layered their chesty vocals one over the other. Hans Haas could feel their song in his gut, although he did not understand the words.

Another time, the body double asked Hans Haas: How long more will the shoot last for?

I'm not sure, Hans Haas said, I am on a temporary contract myself.

Could you ask someone who might know? the body double said. Hans Haas agreed to help find out. Without saying it is I who wishes to know, she added. Once the words left her lips she looked like she regretted them, as if she had disclosed a weakness best kept private. Hans Haas did not see what she was worried about and tried to reassure her, but she shook her head. At lunch the next day he asked the line producer. The line producer did not answer, but he held up crossed fingers. No one can be sure, Hans Haas reported to the body double, but it is hoped that the shoot will go on till the war ends. So that everybody can remain here.

The body double nodded, thinking it over.

Then she looked at him and said: Who is "everybody"?

Hans Haas was taken aback.

She lowered her voice to say: We've done no wrong, sir.

He was silent.

She tried: You're a good man. He was getting uncomfortable now. She looked at him even more closely. You're not like the others, she said. Have you lost someone?

Miss, I will have to ask you to go back into the pen, he said. As you know, it is against the rules for us to be communicating at length. I could get into trouble. She looked at him. We could both get into trouble, he added. Still she would not stop staring, so he prodded her lightly with the butt of his rifle to face away from him and turn around. He ushered her back in, locked the gate, and was careful to avoid her after that.

THE LIBYAN SAND had been as fine as talcum powder, and it got into everything: their eyes, their ears, their boots, their underpants, their food, their truck engines. In the mornings, it leaned toward dun, and in the evenings, ash, but at noon, when the sun scorched its limestone base, it blazed white. Neckerchiefs had been in vogue among the 15th Panzer and 5th Light divisions of the Afrika Korps ever since their high commander, sporting one in striking turquoise, officiated a parade. This page had purportedly been taken out of the French cavalry's book. It was spiffy, it absorbed one's perspiration, it protected the back of the neck from sunburn.

Much to Hans Haas's amusement, even Schmitz had taken to wearing a colorful neckerchief he tied like a cravat. Not everyone in Sirte had the good fortune of being availed of a piece of fabric that suited the requirements of the look, but in a pinch a triangular segment cut from an undershirt would do the trick. Schmitz's improvised cravat, in a pleasant shade of violet with a hand-rolled white border, had been Gunda's fichu. She'd handed it to him as a keepsake and talisman, accompanied by that singular exhortation issued from the lips of any number of women—mothers, wives, sisters, whores alike—in different tongues, across continents: Come back in one piece!

HANS HAAS AND Schmitz were caught in a sandstorm crossing the two hundred meters from their dugout to the mess tent for one midday meal. They heard the wind even before they saw the lightning or felt the sand. Schmitz tossed his neckerchief to Hans Haas.

Hold it over your nose and mouth, Best Boy.

And you?

Schmitz yanked his field cap over his nose and mouth and pulled Hans Haas down with him as the wave of sand sliced through. Hans Haas breathed the sweet-sour odor of Schmitz's sweat through the fichu. When the storm passed, Schmitz laughed at Hans Haas hopping on one leg to knock sand out of his ears, teasing him for looking like a sawdust doll. They had not brought out a map or a sun compass, since the distance they were covering was so short, but they were adrift for nearly two hours. By the time they got to the mess tent food service was over, and they were late to report for afternoon terrain training. There were limited blanks to be fired for target practice, but even when there were no field exercises, they were told to get a feel of the desert.

When the time comes, the commander said, you don't want unfamiliarity to hamper survival.

The desert heat, the sand, and the ever-changing direction of the desiccating winds all made for maximum discomfort. Hans Haas could not stop scratching his skin. Quit it, Schmitz said gruffly each time, and Hans Haas would stop, but soon after without noticing he would start over. Schmitz cuffed him. What are you, Schmitz said, a mongrel with fleas? Hans Haas saw that he'd scratched through the skin on the side of his elbow. Schmitz leaned over to disperse the sandflies that were beginning to alight on the raw flesh beneath.

At night in their desert tents, they listened to the radio, played poker on hand-drawn cards, shared pictures they'd brought of wives, girlfriends, movie actresses. One of the other two corporals masturbated unfailingly to a picture of his wife. When he came, he made it a point to whisper: Ger-da.

What a devoted little rooster, Schmitz would say, but the corporal did not mind.

Most of the pocket actress picture cards Schmitz tossed off to were autographed, and their tentmates often borrowed them for this reason—those lily hands, they've touched these very corners! Schmitz stowed his collection in the flap of his satchel, and anyone was welcome to share. When Hans Haas was looking through them, he found a passport-sized photograph of Schmitz. As far as Hans Haas had seen, men regarded the camera sternly for their portrait, but Schmitz had turned up his collar and was giving an open-mouthed smile, like he'd been caught by surprise. Hoping Schmitz wouldn't notice, Hans Haas slipped that passport-sized photograph into his own satchel. One evening as they were returning to the tent, Schmitz asked Hans Haas: Are you a believer, Haas?

Hans Haas shook his head.

Why not, Schmitz said, it is easy to believe.

I am not a believer, Hans Haas said, slowly, because I would like to believe that we get to decide.

They both grew silent, then Schmitz asked: Haven't you at least been baptized, as a child?

Hans Haas shook his head again.

So if one of us died, Schmitz said, it is unlikely we would ever meet again.

Hans Haas nodded.

In that case, Schmitz said, how about staying alive?

Hans Haas did not want this conversation to end, and so repeated idiotically: How about it?

I swear you annoy the hell out of me, Schmitz said as he reached over and caught Hans Haas's neck in his elbow, squeezing it so tight he gasped out loud. What would I do without a dunce like you to look out for, eh Hasi?

LYING IN THEIR four-men tent, Hans Haas and Schmitz were listening to a Reichstag cover of Cole Porter's "You're the Top." Ordinary jazz was forbidden to Germans as degenerate for its free-flowing improvisatory nature, but Herr Doktor Minister had assembled a private live band in a state-of-the-art studio in the Ministry of Propaganda, from which the only licensed jazz channel on the Rome-Berlin-Tokyo Axis radio operated, where German riffs on American café standards were broadcast as far as South America:

> You're the Top
> You're a German flyer
> You're the Top
> You're machine gun fire

The two other corporals they shared the tent with were out on sentry duty. When the song ended, Schmitz began to fiddle with the radio. The signals sputtered, and then a song came on. As the signal grew clearer, Hans Haas realized it was an American jazz song, a real one. Listening to enemy shortwave—not even dispatches, just music— could have you tried for treason, the penalty for that being summary execution. Hans Haas was nervous.

Schmitz patted him on the shoulder.

We're at war, Best Boy, he drawled. Let's take our chances.

They were lying on their stomachs over their sleeping bags, the radio between them, volume dialed low. And that, boys, was Bing Crosby's "Rolleo Rolling Along," a fresh schoolgirlish voice said in an American accent, so you'd best be rolleo rolling along this afternoon.

What a doll, Schmitz said. Can't you hear it, just from her voice?

He flipped onto his side and undid his fly.

Up next, boys, Dinah Washington. This is GI Jane on GI Jive.

There was a split second between Schmitz undoing his fly and Schmitz touching himself. Hans Haas spat on his palm and reached over. If Schmitz was surprised, he did not let it show on his face. There was nothing unnatural about camaraderie between comrades as long as it did not become a peacetime preference, when there was a steady supply of women to be had. It was hygienic to release pressure, nerves. What happens in the desert stays in the desert—and surely they could not be the only ones. Schmitz closed his eyes, but Hans Haas kept his open as he moved his hand faster, Schmitz tilting slightly to give him more room as he struggled to undo his own pants.

When Schmitz opened his eyes, Hans Haas turned over.

He felt Schmitz's warm body cover his. Without first moistening himself, Schmitz forced himself into Hans Haas. It was so painful he tensed up, wanting to cry out, but he was afraid that would make Schmitz stop. Hans Haas could feel the ample fold of Schmitz's beer belly over his backbone, and his hands on either side of his hips. He braced his body to support Schmitz's weight better. Over the pain was a sensation that fanned from the end of his tailbone into the rest of his body. They were no longer in Sirte. He sighed just before Schmitz came. The liquid was warm and he clenched his muscles to hold it in. Schmitz pulled out swiftly. When Hans Haas turned around, he saw that blood and a bit of excrement had smeared Schmitz. He wanted to apologize, make a joke, help clean, but Schmitz had turned away from him and was wiping himself on a rag. Schmitz tossed the rag aside and secured his pants.

The radio was still on, low.

Fight hard, boys, we are right behind you!

· · ·

EVERYTHING WAS THE same but of course it was different, and Hans Haas kept the sensation of Schmitz inside of him like a prayer. Whenever invoked, he could make his body respond with a keen shudder as he went through the motions of target practice or terrain training, on a march or over a meal. Each time, he held his breath until the shudder passed, willing it to last longer.

In the beginning he had been afraid that Schmitz would avoid him.

The morning after, he was relieved that Schmitz treated him just as before, horsing around at his expense as they marched and ate and bivouacked together. But soon he worried that things were normal because Schmitz did not think anything of what had happened between them. When the water supply went short, they were allowed only upright showers from water packets. Hans Haas had to tiptoe to hold the pack over Schmitz's head, controlling the flow of water as Schmitz shut his eyes and scrubbed himself under the arms, behind the ears. When all this is over, Schmitz said, know what I'm really looking forward to, Best Boy?

Gunda?

Schmitz rapped the top of his head. Hasi, he said, you have got to get your priorities straight. A bath, Best Boy. A real bath back home. The tech crew had a favorite bathhouse they went to for scrub downs and steam saunas at the end of a long shoot. Hans Haas realized he'd already forgotten about the place. He asked Schmitz: Do you think we'll crew on another movie together?

Of course we will, Schmitz said. Under the right circumstances.

What are the right circumstances?

But Schmitz could not answer that.

Some nights Hans Haas went hungry, skipping supper so his ass would be clean and empty, just in case. He tried to make excuses to be alone with Schmitz, waiting for Schmitz to approach him, but night after night Schmitz did no such thing. Yet as long as they were in a group, Schmitz had not stopped touching himself in front of Hans Haas. With the radio tuned to the German jazz channel, the four Afrika Korps men beat themselves off wildly in the middle of the desert. Intermittently Hans Haas would look over at Schmitz, but he'd avert his eyes before long, afraid their tentmates would notice. One night, when he could bear it no longer, Hans Haas kept his eyes on Schmitz the whole time and tried to match his rhythm. When Schmitz saw what Hans Haas was doing, he stopped short.

Early discharge, Schmitz?

Shut up and get back to your Gerda, I need to take a piss is all.

Schmitz left the tent. Hans Haas followed.

As soon as they were out of earshot Schmitz turned around.

What are you playing at, Best Boy?

Hans Haas dropped to his knees, trying to undo Schmitz's pants. Schmitz kicked him away. He got back up and lunged for Schmitz's leg. Schmitz fell and they struggled in the sand. Schmitz pinned Hans Haas down easily. Quit it, Haas! He would not. He tried to reach for Schmitz's crotch. Schmitz punched him in the face and stood up. Hans Haas lay in the sand, holding his face in his hands. Schmitz pulled his woolens down and pissed right next to Hans Haas's face. It was a cloudless moonless night, and the air was so dry it hurt to breathe.

If it weren't for you, Hans Haas said, I would be safe at home now.

Schmitz said nothing, but the steady stream of piss stopped for a second. Then it resumed, taking an arc before it hit the sand.

What do you think I came here for, Hans Haas said, the war?

Still Schmitz said nothing. Hans Haas could have screamed. Watching the steam from the heat of Schmitz's piss evaporate into the cool night air, he turned his cheek and stuck his tongue out toward it. Schmitz stopped pissing at once and kicked him in the ribs.

God damn it, Haas, Schmitz said. What do you want from me?

Hans Haas opened his mouth: I—

But he did not know what he would have said either, for Schmitz kicked him again. Now it was so painful he could hardly bear to exhale, and Schmitz was walking away, breeze smoothing over his footprints as he left them in the sand. Hans Haas wanted to cough up blood into the earth, let it pool into quicksand so he could sink through the desert, cross a subterranean tunnel, and renounce comrade, platoon, army, country. His only plan in life had been to go where this one man went. He'd followed him into the heat of the desert, but either it was too much or it wasn't enough. Now the mirage was over. Why not swim across the sea toward Athens or Naples, scupper his body to the bottom of the ocean floor with the heaviest weight locked to his chest. Something poked him in the side. He opened his eyes.

Schmitz was prodding him with the toe of his boot.

Get up, runt, Schmitz said.

He could have been a Viking giant or a Norse god, what with the sky and stars behind his strong shoulders, and the messy red hair sticking out from every direction behind his ears. You look like a king, Hans Haas wanted to tell Schmitz, with no intention other than stating what he saw, but he did not want to scare Schmitz off, not when he had come back. What are you waiting for with that birdy look on your face, Schmitz said, a family of scorpions to come bite your pecker off?

Schmitz reached out a hand.

Taking it to haul himself into a sitting position, Hans Haas winced from the pain in his ribs. He saw that Schmitz noticed, so to hide it he lied and pointed up ahead: Look, a shooting star. Schmitz turned to look at the sky, where nothing moved. He turned back.

It's passed, Hans Haas said, you just missed it.

What do I care? Schmitz said as he boosted Hans Haas onto his feet. Please don't tell me you made a wish. Hans Haas could only laugh, the vibrations of his laughter needling the ache in his ribs, glob of pain thrumming so close to his heart it was hard to say which was which, as together they walked back to the tent and fell asleep, side by side.

IT IS AN early-morning melee.

On paper it is a thing of beauty, designed by one side to surprise the other before dawn in the desert. Let the historians or the generals declaim from the cozy repose of their armchairs the tactical genius of a combined arms maneuver for on the ground, in blood-hazed sweat and scorched metal, there is no time for glory when there is barely time to breathe. Machine fragments and human parts dot the sandscape.

Hans Haas is trying to flank Schmitz as they go forward. His ears will not stop ringing. When Schmitz turns around to check if he is still following, he wants to tell Schmitz, Don't look back, I'm right here, but there is no time to speak. A wrap party in the beer garden, the first time he got sloshed, Schmitz holding his head up as he retched himself dry. Keeping still for a take, watching the damp red hair uncurl on the back of Schmitz's neck. He can almost see it now at the base of the helmet before him. How he knew what light or filter or stand Schmitz wanted from just a look, a movement of the hands. Caught in that sandstorm, bodies hugging close together. They are charging ahead when from the corner of his eye Hans Haas sees a gun aimed at Schmitz from some twenty feet away. Instead of covering Schmitz, Hans Haas ducks instinctively to protect himself, curling low to the ground as his skin ripples from the shockwave of gunfire. Less than a second later, Schmitz is down in the sand. His body is in one piece but there is too much blood. Hans Haas scrambles toward Schmitz. None of this should have happened—if he could do it again right away, he would be prepared to act differently this time. Schmitz is struggling for breath as he reaches out his hand. Hans Haas grabs it, looking around for someplace safe they can hide. He shuts his eyes, but when he opens them it's still the same. He begins to panic. He pisses his pants as he cries out for help. No one hears him. Somewhere behind them, a grenade goes off. The ground heaves, his teeth are chattering, everything is louder than he is. Then he feels Schmitz squeezing his hand, calm and firm. That familiar grip brings Hans Haas back and he remembers to breathe. The ground has stopped moving, too. Schmitz is trying to say something. Hans Haas leans close. Cool dry lips part against his cheek, but the words never make it. As the strength in Schmitz's fingers slackens, Hans Haas bends over to hold as much of him as he can.

AT NOON THE sky is clear blue.

One side is victorious, the other is not: the way it has always been. A kettle of vultures surveys its luncheon, circling on high. It is the official cease-fire, called for both sides to recover their dead and wounded. The silence is stark but comradely. Both sides must work fast. Behind the right-minded aim of laying each fallen soldier to rest individually is the inevitable utility of an en masse burial. The heat of the desert accelerates decomposition, and the stench will be unbearable if the bodies are not buried by tomorrow.

One side finds one of their own, alive, on top of one of their own, dead. Both bodies have their eyes open. One of them can't be much older than twenty. The other must be nearing forty. The younger man blinks, the older man stares straight ahead. They must have lain this way, cheek to cheek, without moving for some time: a thin layer of shifted sand covers them both, undulating patterns on their uniforms. The younger man refuses to budge. They check him for injuries, but when they try to pull him up, he digs his nails into his comrade's shoulders. They do not have time for this. Together they pry him off the dead body.

Let me stay, the younger man says. I want to stay right here.

Clearly, he is in shock. His lips are parched, but he appears unharmed. They sit him down and offer him some water. He does not drink. Someone is bending over to help close the older man's eyes. Don't, the younger man says. They go on with what they are doing. I said, Don't touch him! The younger man is lunging for them, upsetting the precious canteen of drinking water. Someone has to hold him down. It is not so easy to shut the eyes now that the body has been dead for some time. Please, the younger man begs as they restrain him. A more experienced combatant reaches over to massage the tissue around the eye sockets, still supple, to release those muscles caught in motion. Now the lids of the older man are slid down smoothly. They let go of the younger man. He turns away from the older man's face. Behind the now-closed lids are eyes he won't be seeing again.

The body is carted away, to join the others laid out in the sand.

From afar it is quite hard to tell all the bodies apart, but when the younger man turns back to look, there is no mistaking him for anyone else: red hair, broad shoulders. A big gust of wind blows. He worries that grains of sand will enter his friend's ears.

Behind the lines, each side begins to dig a shallow mass grave.

XI

The new wolf was obtained personally by Leni, after substantial flattery and bribery, from a Spanish baron and collaborator who had a penchant for wild animals that festooned the menagerie on the rolling grounds of his estate. This wolf had its canines and claws removed as a pup, was trained to beg for scraps at the table, and even to offer up its paw. Her producer was deeply relieved that this was much safer for everyone, but Leni was unhappy that the wolf was eager to please, with no savage streak. After play-fighting with Pedro, it padded up to her for a treat.

There were not so many scenes left, and she was running out of money.

The *Tiefland* shoot would have to come to an end soon. Leni did not want to go back down, where everything had grown so very confusing. Teething problems, she told herself. Things had to get worse before they could get better. But how bad is worse? She could admit to no one that she was afraid. Others who had voiced doubts had fallen firmly out of favor with the Party. A few had even been tried for sedition against the state. Sometimes, when it all got too much and she was worrying herself sick about what to do next once they wrapped this production, Leni would catch herself thinking yet again: If only that dratted Josef von Sternberg had chosen me for *The Blue Angel*. Then I wouldn't be in this mess. I would be living it up in Hollywood, where people would be waiting to kiss my hands. But if it weren't for this country and this time, she countered uncertainly, would you have made such beautiful movies? Of course I would have, she retorted just to end this sour thought on a high note, I can make magic wherever I go, it lives in me. Where and what are secondary. Who and how are key.

Watching Marlene's star rise steadily in America then, with Jo penning role after role for that woman, less movies with a plot than chamber pieces to show off his muse, Leni told herself that Marlene may have made it, but it was all Jo's doing. Well, there was no honor in that.

Leni had promised herself that when *she* moved to Hollywood, it would be different.

She'd tried to make plans to visit with a project as early as she could, but full Party approval came only in the fall of 1938, by which time Marlene had had an eight-year head start. The Ministry of Propaganda brokered Leni's maiden visit to America: *Olympia* was doing well on the international festival circuit; they wanted to capitalize on that momentum to sell American rights to distributors. Leni's personal ambitions coincided with the Party's interests in building up an international profile for Germany, and her junket was fully underwritten by public funds. New York had been a most delightful start. On deck, Leni was busy admiring how the parting fog made Manhattan's silhouette even more imposing, when her chaperone tried to redirect her attention. What is it? she asked shortly, jolted out of the mental note she was making on how this natural effect could be re-created artificially in a movie. People who couldn't understand an artist's need for space would interrupt you about any dumb thing, it was ridiculous! What did she care that a swarm of small boats had sailed up to meet the ship's entry into port? The people in them were flailing their arms for attention. They had notepads in hand. When she listened closely, she realized they were calling out the same name.

Over here, Miss Riefenstahl!

They were American reporters, and they were here for her. Leni noticed that some were cradling doves. What's with the birds, she asked her chaperone. Passenger pigeons, he explained, if you give a scoop, they're sent back to the printing press to beat the other papers.

When a woman had substance, she did not need to ride on the coattails of an older male director who would open doors hitherto closed to her. A woman of substance did not even need to pay minders to arrange a press conference in the ritziest hotel in a foreign city she was visiting for the first time. The press would row out to meet her with their fastest pigeons. Cap that, Marlene!

Miss Riefenstahl, are you Hitler's girlfriend?

Leni turned in that direction.

No, she called out, but then she couldn't resist peppering her denial with a touch of coquetry. You mustn't believe everything you hear!

BREAKFASTING AT THE Pierre the next day after a restful slumber, Leni brought all the newspapers she could gather to her table, eager to see what they had to say about her, which picture they had printed.

Pretty as a swastika, one paper wrote.

Her favorite picture was the one in which she'd posed like the Statue of Liberty.

Leni sailed down Fifth Avenue, pulling down her sunglasses expectantly, hallo America! When she intimated to the Ziegfeld girls at City Hall that she, too, was a dancer, they all wanted her autograph. The manager at City Hall, the biggest theater in America, was keen on buying screening rights for *Olympia*. They would meet up in Hollywood with his lawyer to sign the contract. Leni was thrilled by the scale and speed at which things happened here. Someone took her entourage to a black revue, and she commented gaily that the rhythm was fantastic but it was all jungle ability! Everyone in her company laughed. At MoMA, viewing new work from French postimpressionists ahead of their special screening of *Triumph of the Will* as part of the museum's art film program, she was asked her opinion of Cézanne. The imprecision of form in his new body of work bothered Leni, the waffly clouds and the cobblestones lifting off of themselves, but she knew the high regard in which Cézanne was held in these circles and so made a generic statement of approval.

At the least she did think he was a more acceptable painter than his German contemporaries. She saw in the work of Kirchner, Grosz, the whole faction that tried to dignify themselves with an innocuous name like "New Objectivity" something altogether unsanitary. That evening after her MoMA visit, before the news broke, a confidential memo came to her from a New York–based Gestapo agent: Miss Riefenstahl, you are advised not to speak on the incident, and to return to Berlin immediately.

What incident?

Soon you will hear.

When the news poured in, what she read was shocking, but Leni did not elect to return to Berlin. Right away, she invited journalists to speak with her in her suite at The Pierre. The editorials in American papers covering "The Night of Broken Glass," stating that hundreds of Jews had been murdered and thousands arrested in a single evening, describing the destruction of two hundred and sixty seven synagogues, property damage amounting to hundreds of millions of reichsmarks, the community fine of one billion reichsmarks to be collected by compulsory confiscation of 20 percent of the property of every German Jew, she dismissed in one impassioned word: Slander! She might not be the most savvy about the ins and outs of bilateral relations, but everyone knew that things were tense between Germany and America. False nonsense was printed in the papers all the time, with both sides trying to make the other look bad, but surely this was taking it too far.

What can you say about Hitler, Miss Riefenstahl?

What can I say? Leni said. Radiance streams from him.

ARRIVING IN L.A., Leni was disappointed that it was so much uglier than she pictured it to be. What a bleak, sprawling, lifeless place! This was where the movies were made? She cheered up once they checked in to their accommodation, a large bungalow at the Beverly Hills Hotel. Now the town was beginning to live up to her expectations: flowering bird-of-paradise, orange and grapefruit trees, multiple swimming pools. L.A. had such a carefree mood, she wanted to feel like part of it. She repaired to the luxurious bathroom to shave her legs, so she could remove her stockings and paddle bare-legged by the pool. On her way back out she was met by an L.A.–based Gestapo agent. Excuse me! She exclaimed indignantly, gathering her bathrobe protectively about her décolletage.

Miss Riefenstahl, he said, you must stop speaking to the papers.

I am trying to make things better, she said.

They are only getting worse, he said.

How could that be, she said, unless the reports are true?

It's complicated, he said, but for you, it is straightforward. Keep your opinions on the pogrom and the Party to yourself. Sell your movie before it is too late, and head home.

That very afternoon she was startled to see on a full page in the papers:

THERE IS NO PLACE FOR HITLER'S FILMMAKER IN HOLLYWOOD.
GO HOME LENI RIEFENSTAHL!

What a shocker, especially when it had all been so lovely in New York! The notice was signed by the Anti-Nazi League in America. She called for an assistant to cable them immediately: I am not a member of the NSDAP. Politics do not interest me. Art does.

It was too late. Meeting after meeting that had been lined up for her in advance was canceled. Distributors, production houses, directors, and actors who had been eager to meet with her just a few days ago wanted nothing to do with her now. Disconcerted, she dashed out a list of acquaintances with connections in town, whom she could call on within the realm of reason. She wrote Jo, with little hope she knew—even Babelsberg Studios back in Berlin had been buzzing about him and Marlene. Sternberg's poor wife had filed for divorce, and even attempted to sue Marlene for being "a love pirate." Leni tried to contrive a meeting with Charlie Chaplin, who had been in attendance at the MoMA screening of *Triumph of the Will* in New York. He'd looked surprisingly dapper as himself and not the Tramp, but had disturbed the mesmerized audience by emitting a throaty guffaw every now and then. His laughter had Leni befuddled. Was he being rude, or paying a compliment? Did a comic have no meter for aesthetics? Still she hoped to speak with him, but he'd left swiftly after with a bunch of French filmmakers who had awestruck expressions on their faces. She penned Chaplin a note, but before posting it found out he was one of the most prominent members of the Anti-Nazi League.

No one wrote back to Leni.

Only Walt Disney kept the appointment he'd made prior to her visit. She went on a tour of his animation studio, trying to look enthusiastic as he showed her sketches and layouts. Would you like to look through the multiplane camera? Leni observed a contrite Mickey chase a huffy Minnie across a busy street. There she was, at long last, in L.A.—talking to a man about a cartoon mouse!

In other words, she'd blown it with Hollywood. When she got back to Berlin, she cried for days, sickened to learn that how the world outside saw her was completely at odds with how she was used to seeing herself back home. The world was unfair, full of falsifications. Her truth was much simpler: she'd befriended a man who admired her work, he gave her some money to make movies. What he did beyond that had nothing to do with her. It was hitting below the belt to lump them all together, Leni and the NSDAP, her movies and their actions, when she was not even a Party member, just an ordinary citizen. True, upon sighting a yellow-and-black armband pinned to a coat, she might cross a sidewalk earlier than she had to, so their paths remained separate. Noticing a Star of David painted on a shop window, she might avoid patronizing the place henceforth, not because she particularly supported the "Don't buy from Jews, support German businesses" campaign, but just so she wouldn't get into any trouble. That was all—and everyone she knew did the same thing, too. Now they were saying it was true that glass had been broken and people had died. No doubt that was terrible, but what did that have to do with her art and her person?

XII

Some of the Roma and Sinti extras cried when it was time for them to go. Leni took it upon herself to shush them. The whole crew would be leaving the Dolomites soon enough. Most would return to Berlin. She'd managed to secure for herself a ski cottage high up in Kitzbühel where she would begin editing *Tiefland*. Before they parted, they posed for a photograph together against an unspoiled view of the Sarntal Valley. Zazilia sat on her knee.

Tante Leni, she said hopefully, do you have any more toffee?

I'm afraid not, Zee, Leni told her.

Leni nestled herself in the middle of the front row, adjusted her dirndl, and smiled. Her assistant counted to three. After the photograph was made, the twenty-three Roma and Sinti extras were loaded up onto the truck, one by one. Leni stood there with her crew to see them off. Last to board was the girl who'd played her body double. Before she got on, she said formally: Miss Riefenstahl, we would like to thank you. You have been so nice.

It was wonderful having all of you, too, Leni said, turning to nod to everyone in the back of the truck. The body double approached Leni, but was prevented from coming too close by the Afrika Korps best boy.

Do you remember, the body double said quietly, you said you owed me a favor?

The truck's engine was idling.

When Leni did not respond, the woman went on: For being your body double on the back of the horse, because it was too dangerous for you, you could have been injured? Or have you forgotten?

Sure I remember, Leni said, trying to sound offhand. What might I help you with?

Can you do something for us, the body double said, about the camp? We don't know where we will be taken after that, and we have heard stories—

Rumors would be rumors. You could not fix everything for everyone, much less a gypsy. They should not have been allowed to sing. Give them a concession out of the goodness of your own heart and all of a sudden they expect you to bend backward and cartwheel for them like you owe them a living—

Like I said, Leni said, it was wonderful having you on set, but I'm afraid the contract is up. I can show you a copy, if you want, she added. I can't do anything about it, even if I would like to.

We hear that you know people, the body double said, no longer in a quiet voice. Perhaps you could put in a word for us, change their minds—

It's quite clear you've never dealt with bureaucracy—

Please, Miss Riefenstahl!

The body double's voice broke into a cracked wail as she bowed her head, hair just like Leni's own falling over her face. Leni felt a wave of nausea. The familiar pangs of bladder colic began to radiate from hip to groin. The body double was on her knees now. Before the Afrika Korps best boy could stop her, she'd touched Leni's shoe. Leni moved her foot away quickly. How embarrassing this was becoming, and in front of her whole crew, too. Never trust an itinerant to have enough dignity to engage in a civil conversation without resorting to something tricksy and dramatic. I need the bathroom, Leni said to the Afrika Korps best boy. Clean her knees, get her back on her feet, and load her up.

When the Afrika Korps best boy stepped forward to handle the body double, she shrugged herself free from his grasp.

Don't you dare touch me, she said to him, I will go on my own.

The body double heaved herself onto the back of the waiting truck. She said something to her people in Romani. Some who were crying stopped crying, and some who were not crying started. Only the children seemed to still be in their own world, looking back out at the set with no emotion. The Afrika Korps best boy jumped into the truck with them—he was to oversee their safe return to Camp Maxglan. The body double turned to Leni's crew. Her fingers, gripping the edge of the truck, were white. Tell her, she said. Tell her our blood is on her hands, and she will never make another movie as long as she lives.

The truck had already begun to pull away when Leni reemerged from the bathroom. It looked like her crew had done well to handle the sticky situation efficiently for her; the extras were all in the back of the truck with the Afrika Korps best boy guarding them, ready to set off. Sometimes it was easier when those of lesser power dealt with those with no power—the latter would not make ridiculous demands of the former as they would with someone in charge.

Her assistant rushed forward with the contract, her painkillers, and a canteen of water. Thank you, she said, tucking the contract under her armpit for good measure. If the body double wanted to challenge her again, she would show her the clause as printed. She washed the methadone down with a cool gulp of water. The truck began to move off. From the back, a small hand began to wave. Squinting, Leni saw that it was Zazilia. A few other children copied the girl and began to wave, too. Leni found herself wiping away a tear. Oh, Leni said, I didn't have time to say a proper good-bye, she was my favorite. Beside her, the line producer raised his walkie-talkie. He could radio the truck driver back. Leni shook her head. Let them be on their way, she said, they shouldn't be late.

The truck trundled forward.

Bye-bye, Tante Leni, the girl shouted. I'll never forget you!

Good-bye, Zee, Leni hollered to the little girl, funneling her palms around her mouth so her voice could carry. I shan't forget you, too!

She dabbed her eyes as an upsurge of colic pain dug into her side.

I think I'll just go right ahead and pop one more methadone, she said to her assistant. The pill was given to her. She was sweating as she swallowed it. Leni waved and waved, stopping only when she could no longer see the little girl's hand swinging from side to side.

XIII

The drive to Camp Maxglan was less than two hours long. It was a quiet afternoon. The path was steep, and the truck was moving at a very slow speed. In the rear, where he was keeping an eye on the extras, Hans Haas did not dare to make eye contact with any of them as he held on to his rifle.

The extras did not talk, but midway through the trip, a middle-aged woman with deep-set eyes started clapping out a rhythm with her hands. She began to sing, alone. Then Miss Riefenstahl's body double harmonized with her. A few others joined in. When the song ended, the body double stood up slowly. She kept her gaze level with Hans Haas's as she backed away from him. In a few steady steps, she was at the edge of the back of the truck. She turned, pushed past the tarp, and jumped off. Through the gap in the tarp Hans Haas saw the body double rolling into the brush as she broke her fall and raised herself up.

The middle-aged woman who had started singing the song stood up with a child in her arms. Hans Haas clenched his rifle. The woman crouched down, turning immediately to shield the child with her body. But when nothing happened and she saw that his hands were shaking, she went low on her knees and slid toward the back of the truck.

Hans Haas did not move.

If he fired now, the ringing would be so sudden and bright his eardrums might shatter. How disgusting to be unable to distance himself from this body. Was it really his? A body was a liability. He could not be responsible for how it needed to be fed and watered, night and day. He could not be responsible for how it wanted what it wanted, how there was nothing better than that pressing sensation in his tailbone, no, that had nothing to do with him. He could not be responsible for how he was up and about in the Dolomites while Schmitz was now rotting a few feet deep in North Africa. His wish on the desert star that never fell: that they could go home together.

Where it had mattered, his body had chosen itself, but now that he was here, after all, without Schmitz, he could not say any of this was worth it. If he had nothing left to lose now, why was he still afraid? He was passive and tractable even as a schoolboy, always the one turning the rope, never the one jumping, but he had been sure that at the base of it all, he was a decent person. Naturally, most people must think that of themselves, and how many of them were just as wrong, when push came to shove? Here was a chance to rewrite his story, even if no one would tell it. All he had to do in the back of this truck was what he did best: nothing. His heart pounded so loudly in his chest he was sure everyone could hear it. Hans Haas did not know what the extras were running away from, but it had to be something frightful, if they thought that jumping off a truck in the middle of the mountains with no supplies was better than being brought back to the camp.

He'd put his gun down.

The middle-aged woman clambered off the back of the truck with the child. Everyone rushed to the back. A bent old man was helping a girl into a woman's outstretched arms. If they all got away on his watch—Hans Haas's eardrums rang. It was only then he realized he'd lifted his rifle again and pulled the trigger.

XIV

No one needs to hear about this, Leni said to the truck driver and the Afrika Korps best boy when they returned. The Doctor is just waiting for me to make one misstep so he can pounce on the production. Do I make myself clear?

The extras had tried to jump off the back of the moving truck, but the Afrika Korps best boy fired a warning shot and they'd stopped and given chase. After expending a few more bullets, one of which hit an old man in the leg, they managed to get everything under control. The twenty-three extras were then tied down to one another with rope, and they were delivered back to Camp Maxglan without further incident. We should have chained them up from the start, the producer said. Can you imagine how much trouble we would be in if any of them got away?

Early the next morning, when Leni saw Franz running toward them screaming, she thought he was practicing the scene in which he discovers that Martha the gypsy dancer has been married off to the evil marquis of Roccabruno.

I can't take this anymore, she said to him, this is not the opera.

Hans Haas, Franz said, Hans Haas—

Who?

The Afrika Korps best boy—

What about him?

The tree, Franz gagged.

AFTER THE BEST boy's body was retrieved by the gaffer and the cinematographer and placed out of sight under a sheet, they all sat shaken around a fire, drinking hot cocoa to assuage their nerves, everyone slowly converging on the unspoken agreement that it was definitely a puzzle: nothing out of sorts had happened, and while the best boy had been quiet, he had never seemed unstable. Why had he taken his own life out of the blue, when they had it so good here?

Imagine, Leni's assistant said, he could have turned his gun on us!

That's enough now, Leni said sharply.

She was determined to do right by the poor boy, to send his body back to his loved ones in Germany with a personal letter of appreciation. The army personnel who came to collect his body said they were unable to contact his next of kin, listed as a certain Schmitz.

It was too bad then, she would give him a proper burial here.

She tipped her assistant to handle the matter.

Leni's assistant hired a Catholic priest from the village for a quiet ceremony. The best boy was buried in the valley at sunrise, alongside the scant personal items they found in his satchel: a woman's purple fichu and one passport-sized photograph of a jowly man with an upturned collar and a jaunty smile. Only Franz and the cook's daughter were in attendance. The rest of the crew was busy preparing for the day's first scene. Franz had carved up a small remembrance into a stone to mark the best boy's resting place up here in the mountains. All it said was "H." The cook's daughter brought with her a chicken wishbone, which she broke over the body. As the sun rose in the valley, misty peach over clear blue, the Catholic priest administered the Twenty-third Psalm in peasant Italian, and they all bowed their heads as they intoned together: Amen.

The Failed
Socio-Situationist Sculptor
in Düsseldorf

8

Before the hot plate, Marlene prepared her meals by balancing an aluminum tray over her beaded bedside lamp. Heating up a tin of baked beans took up to an hour, and even then the canned mush remained tepid. Once Marlene made her mind up about anything, she was prepared to be prodigiously resourceful, and had survived ably without leaving the apartment by activating her fan base.

Don't send love, she wrote them. Send me something I can eat.

So the French sent pastries, the Germans liverwurst, the Swedish pickled herring, and on one occasion, from Japan by air, the sweetest vacuum-sealed cod roe, all to 12 avenue Montaigne. Marlene developed a taste for eating old-fashioned sausages straight out of the packet. Sauerkraut was a good one, too. It never went bad, could be left out a whole fortnight uncovered on a Tiffany dessert plate. Tiffany's was the dullest jewelry shop in the world, but their bone china? Lovely. Of course, there were offers from wealthy, worried fans who wanted to cater her three gourmet meals daily, but Marlene had turned them down. This worn-out body was the last thing left under her control, and plying it with processed food made her feel sharp. Convinced that all these years of living badly might one day come in handy if she needed to guilt anyone into anything, Marlene was of two minds when the Chinese maid purchased the hot plate, with money saved from all the times she had been told to keep the change. Marlene could hardly believe how daft the maid was. You have to look out for yourself before you look out for others, she scolded, or do you really want to be a servant for the rest of your life? But the maid was already unearthing some groceries she'd bought to test out the new contraption.

They started small.

No-frills foodstuffs and properly heated canned food, but as Marlene recovered her taste for a good, hot meal, the maid began to pick out fresh produce each week. Asparagus, potatoes, beets, eggs, pumpkin, collards, whitefish, chicken breasts. Marlene's mouth watered, but she was too proud for eagerness, and so made sure to go through the motions of misgiving. Soon enough, she saw that there was little need for pretenses with the maid. This struck Marlene as a great novelty, and by degrees, she began to drop the poses, big and small, that she was so used to defaulting to. All her life there had been the pressure of not being Marlene enough, but she marveled one day, as it came to her, abrupt and belated: Choupette, you have no idea who I am, do you?

The maid looked up from her cleaning with serious eyes. Madame?

Marlene cackled with delight.

TODAY MARLENE HAD sent the maid out with a long list of ingredients made out in a spidery hand: beef shanks, marrow bone, onions, carrots, celery, rutabaga—she was sure she had forgotten one or two things, but she would never get started if she was counting on herself to remember everything first.

She wanted to make pot-au-feu for Bogie.

Her pot-au-feu had once been as legendary as her legs, and through the years, Marlene knew full well she'd begun to play the love fool whenever she caught herself reeling off the ingredients in her head, floating down the well-lit aisles of gourmet supermarkets in a printed scarf and dark glasses, haggling at the butchery, as a matter of principle, over the price per pound of beef shank and bone marrow.

In retrospective appraisal, she divided her affairs not by gender or duration, but those for whom she'd cooked pot-au-feu and those she had not. The last beau to receive the special stew treatment was probably Yul Brynner. Although she was almost twenty years his senior— and had been much annoyed when the press termed their romance "not autumn-spring but winter-autumn"—he, like all her other sweets, went to the ground before her: lung cancer, four years ago. Now the coldest season had come to pass—Marlene would not have guessed that she had one more pot-au-feu left in her, and for an anonymous caller no less.

It had been only a month, and already she could not imagine her days without Bogie's weekly intervention, every Sunday around noon.

Marlene had no idea what the voice over the phone looked like, but for once, that suited her better. Her life, once overpopulated with options, no longer offered opportunities for the exercise of her discretion, and it was her turn now to be the floozy at the whim and fancy of another. But even that had not led her to mistaking Bogie's phone calls, and her indulgence thereof, for what might be called love: it had always been clear to Marlene that what was more pleasurable than being in love, was acting like it.

The summer Marlene was sixteen she understood this for the first time. The one she acted for was a countess, a friend of her mother's, wedded to a humorless aristocrat four inches shorter than she, who wore two-toned wingtips with three-inch heels. The countess had agreed to take her to see *Tannhäuser,* which was being performed up in Weimar. For a fortnight beforehand our intoxicated mädchen halved her meal portions, sending herself to bed with no dessert, so as to fit into a velvet dress so tight it pinched her sides. In the train cabin, the countess kept her gloves on but removed her court shoes, sliding on pink slippers finished with ostrich puffs along the toe line. How tiny her dear feet were! Whenever she moved them the feather puffs shivered. On her hands, the fine sable gloves were so snug they looked wet across her knuckles. Every time they went into a tunnel, Marlene bent to kiss her hand in the dark. The older woman chided her each time they approached another underground passage: Marlenchen, are you really going to kiss that dirty glove?

The next summer, Countess Gerdorf came to visit again, and Marlene was cut down to size by her own contempt for the same woman, a year on. Was this really the one whose used-up silken cigarette tips she'd hoarded on the sly? The one to whom she'd written: Don't you know, if you were not married to the Count and I were not under age, I would do anything to get you?

That was when she knew that it was the act she courted, hardly the person, and that for her there was no contrition or contradiction in this. To be able to wear feelings lightly while experiencing them deeply was a rare sort of freedom. As for possible harm caused to others— there must be something in it for them, too, if they did not stay away. When she came of age, she added domesticity to her repertoire and savored, for a limited run, the role of virtuous hausfrau to the hilt. She liked people who liked to eat. Men who did not have an appetite were seldom good in bed, and one of the purest delights in life, when living with a woman, was finding her sitting loose-haired in your kitchen in the middle of the night, mopping up leftover stew with a huge hunk of bread. Whenever Marlene began cooking, the domestic treatment hoodwinked many an innocent paramour into thinking it was going to last a while now, just as Erich Maria Remarque had when his tears fell into her pot-au-feu on a balmy evening around 1940. All sorts of things were happening in Berlin, Remarque said, and he was soaking up the sun in L.A., developing an idea for a new novel. This was life?

How thin he had grown in loosey-goosey California!

Although the gauntness lent his face an attractive, ascetic touch, Marlene took it upon herself to fatten Remarque up immediately. He was one of those Germans who could not or would not forget for a moment that he was *here* and not *there*, in circumstances such as these. Early on in 1933, Goebbels had banned and burned Remarque's books, and in 1938, the NSDAP had revoked his German citizenship. His youngest sister would soon be tried in the Volksgerichtshof, and found guilty of "undermining morale," just for having been heard stating that she considered the war lost. Your brother is, unfortunately, beyond our reach, the court judgment would say. You, however, will not escape us. The invoice for 495.80 reichsmarks, billed to Remarque, for his sister's prosecution, imprisonment, and execution by beheading would not reach him until the war had ended.

In the safe harbor of L.A., Marlene talked the Paramount boys into hiring Remarque for a script, something to take his mind off things. *All Quiet on the Western Front* had been a hit—Remarque was in a far better position to negotiate his transatlantic crossover than the other German literati beginning to pile up in L.A. like so much flotsam that summer. She knew that Adorno, having settled in the Pacific Palisades, was trying to arrange for the safe passage of friends like Hannah Arendt and Walter Benjamin back in Europe.

Some made it over. Others did not.

Marlene donated a quarter of her pay to the European Film Fund, set up by her agent, Paul Kohner, who managed everyone from Greta

Garbo to Maurice Chevalier—almost all of whom tithed 10 percent of their weekly salary. Tirelessly Kohner made out daily affidavits and fake work permits for performers, writers, and artists trying to leave Germany. For those who reached L.A., hotel bungalows on long-term leases to Paramount and MGM that had been used for executive meetings and scriptwriting pow-wows were fast being converted into half-way houses for those with papers stamped ENEMY ALIEN in America.

IT HAD TAKEN Marlene some time to get that far with Remarque, and even to urge him over to America. The first she saw of him, his monocle was glinting across the ballroom of the Hôtel des Bains in Venice, in 1939. They danced together that night but retired to their own rooms, a blemish on her personal record.

Marlene woke the next morning ready to set things straight.

She made up her face very lightly and put on a pair of lounge pajamas. She rolled the sleeves up, then down, then up again. Unable to decide, she walked out into the parlor with one sleeve up and the other down. Up or down? she asked her husband, Rudi, and his mistress, Tamara, with whom she often traveled: three interconnecting rooms, two bathrooms. Marlene gave Rudi as long a leash as he gave her. They had no quarrel, and were happy together. Rudi and Tamara, used to her extracurricular activities, voted for Marlene to wear her sleeves down. She unrolled her sleeves. As she was leaving the room, she noticed her dog-eared copy of Rilke's *Complete Poems,* a gift from Aunt Jolie, just like the diamond-paste bracelet. The book had been Marlene's travel companion since she was eighteen, and she knew most of the poems from memory. Where the pages had come loose, she had stitched them back together by hand. With this prop under her arm, she sauntered out of the hotel in sandals. Crossing the boardwalk she saw Remarque sitting in a spot of sun, gazing out at the choppy Adriatic Sea. She passed before him, making sure the worn spine bearing Rilke's name was visible.

Of course, Remarque said shortly, without greeting her. All movie stars read poetry.

Marlene smiled, pressing the volume into his hands.

Choose a poem, she said. Tell me only the title. He condescended to browse and asked for "The Panther." Marlene declaimed the first two stanzas. He removed his sunglasses, the better to look her in the eye, as she recited the last stanza:

> Only at times the curtain of the pupils
>   lifts without a sound—Then enters an image
> through the gliding stillness of arrested muscles
>   straight to the heart where it ceases to be.

Remarque flipped the pages again and stopped at random. "Leda," he said, and she recited it by heart to perfection. "The Gazelle," he said, and she gave it back, too. Did you memorize all that Rilke just to impress me? he said, amused. Surely a movie actress has better use for her time? I like your novels, she said, but you shouldn't overstate your case. After midmorning sex in his room, they slipped into mono-grammed hotel bathrobes, and she threw open the balcony windows.

Her Rilke lay quite forgotten on the deck chair.

There was hardly a boat out at sea, and as they looked out Marlene told Remarque to move to L.A. before it was too late. She would help him out if he needed anything there. She told him that Rudolf Hess had been to New York to see her over Christmas in 1936, and had extended a personal invitation back to Berlin, direct from Hitler and Goebbels. I can assure you, Hess had said, that you will be moving around in the highest circles. What Marlene said to him: Merry Christmas, I am late for a party. Please don't come again.

Remarque said: You could have been killed. Marlene said yes, she knew. Hess had publicly commented that anyone who could change his last name from the German spelling Remark to the French spelling could not possibly be a real man, Remarque told Marlene. Hess was also the one who took down Hitler's dictation of *Mein Kampf* on toilet paper in prison, after the failed Beer Hall Putsch.

Can you imagine, he said, all of that, on toilet paper?

Absolutely, Marlene said, I'd clean my ass on it.

· · ·

WHEN MARLENE TOLD Bogie over the phone that she had herself wooed Remarque with Rilke's verses all those years ago, Bogie wanted to know what happened later. He plumped up, Marlene said, and I got bored. He dedicated one of his books to me, before shacking up with Paulette Goddard.

Lucky for me, Bogie said. You can't get bored of what you don't know.

Bogie had a voice and manner out of his age and time. Crisp and pristine, it was a voice made to read women classics and hold court in High German. He had none of the Berlin drawl she herself slid into. His syntax was formal, his accent refined. This decorum engendered a sense of courtship. They partook in classics that circumambulated cultural time, that would not age the way mortals did, that made her clean forget she was ninety and he eighteen. It could just as well have been the other way around.

She asked him the same thing each week he called, before they said their good-byes.

Bogie, are you sure you won't tell me your name?

Milady, he teased. Why ruin a good thing with empty convention?

That's hardly fair, she said, given that you know mine.

Come on, Marlene, he said, laughing, as he slowly rolled her name off his lips, let's be above board here. Your name has not belonged to you for years. Everyone can put your face to it, without knowing anything about you—it's nothing but a symbol!

9

When he first refused to tell her his name, Marlene dropped her voice to whisper: Is there a *von* in it? At this he had to laugh. He did not know anyone in his life who could be classed as of noble birth, not by a long shot. Ah, she said conspiratorially, I knew you were titled, you are so well spoken. I shan't ask more now. Surely she could not be serious, she was just an actress through and through, game for any bait that came along.

Born in North Rhine-Westphalia in a welfare ward, he did not cry as a baby, even after he was spanked a second time. Other than his silence, he was healthy in all regards, and the doctor proffered generic congratulations to his parents, who were peering at their rumpled miracle: It's a boy!

He looks white, his mother was thinking, but did not say.

He looks brown, his father was thinking, but did not say.

They named him Ibrahim Max Müller.

His father, an avid football fan, considered this joining of two national sporting heroes—Max Morlock and Gerd Müller—a stroke of genius on his part. Didn't it have a nice ring to it! Ibrahim was his mother's addendum, against what his father considered better judgment: Don't you want our child to have a future? Even if he's fair enough to pass, the name will be a burden.

HIS MOTHER WAS a Turkish Kurdish guest worker from Urfa. His father had cuckolded her Turkish husband. They worked at an open-field lignite mine. The Turks were miners. The German was a line supervisor. When the Turkish husband was rotated temporarily to a neighboring mine, the German supervisor took his chances. To his surprise, the Turkish woman did not resist. Her body was as lovely as he'd guessed, under the rough-hewn, navy-blue work suit rendering all workers lumpen. When her husband returned to the mine, the woman told him the line supervisor had seen her hair and body. The Turkish man head-butted the German line supervisor. His work permit was canceled, and he was sent back where he came from. The Turkish woman and the German line supervisor were not formally married. Divorce would have been impossible from a sharia court. Simply, she was far enough away from Ankara and Urfa to ignore the letters from both sides of the family—those from hers more virulent than her deported husband's. One of her uncles wrote: If I lay my eyes on you, I'll kill you and castrate the foreign scumbag who brought a whore like you astray.

Ibrahim grew up speaking German to his father and Turkish to his mother. Although his mother could speak some German, she spoke to Ibrahim exclusively in Turkish. His father knew no Turkish whatsoever, and sometimes his mother would tell Ibrahim things in Turkish she did not want his father to hear.

Max, his father would ask, what is your mother saying?

His mother called him Ibrahim and his father called him Max. Even before he could understand it was happening, he grew tired of being tugged to and fro between them. It ended when he was about eight and his father told him to tell his mother that he had fallen in love with a Swedish woman. Ibrahim told his mother: Papa has fallen in love with a dog. His mother reached out to hug him close to her, but he did not let her. His father stopped coming home, but he continued to send them money all the way from Travemünde, where he had moved in with the Swedish woman, who ran an economical chalet on a nudist beach.

Look, his mother said to Ibrahim. Your father still loves us.

They sent him letters, his mother writing in the Turkish alphabet.

Papa can't read them, Ibrahim said.

No, his mother said. He will feel them.

A FEW WEEKENDS after his father left them, his mother packed some sandwiches and they boarded the train to Travemünde. It was Ibrahim's first time at the beach. He ran right up to the tide as it pulled away, jumping back as it rushed in. They walked past a stretch of holiday homes and chalets.

When will we see Papa? he asked.

Soon, his mother said. Didn't I promise to let you build sand castles first?

They packed wet sand with their hands.

Ibrahim's sand castle had turrets and a moat that could be filled with seawater. The sea breeze was strong. When it blew his mother's headscarf off, he thought she would be angry, but she merely swept her hair with the backs of her sandy hands and laughed. I'll go get Papa, she said, kissing the top of his head as she stood up. Wait here.

His mother was away for a long time.

The back of his neck began to hurt from sunburn. Growing tired of refilling the moat, Ibrahim began to worry that his parents must have gone off without him. He did not dare move, for fear of their returning and not finding him there. It started to get cold when the sun went down. A kind elderly couple, cocooned individually in stripey beach towels, stopped to ask where his parents were. They found the address of the chalet in the backpack the mother had left with him.

THE RECEPTIONIST AT the chalet was blond, with very large breasts. She was filing her nails when Ibrahim came in with the couple. She was not wearing a bra. The elderly man tried to keep his eyes from slipping below her chin to her chest as he asked for the boss.

That would be me, the blonde said, putting the nail file down, crossing her arms under her chest. The elderly man looked at a loss. He cleared his throat, turning to his wife. Well, it's like this, she kept saying at the beginning of every sentence, I'm not sure what the situation is, and I don't want to judge. At the end she managed to round it off quite respectably with: We are just trying to help the boy.

When Ibrahim's father appeared, he went down on a knee, as if expecting Ibrahim to race into his arms. Ibrahim shuffled over, pulling on his lower lip with his fingers. Why didn't you write or ring in advance? his father said, ruffling his hair. Do you want something to eat, Max? Ibrahim was ushered into the bosom of the blond receptionist, who, postembrace, bent down and introduced herself as "a very good friend of your father." Her cleavage was deep, decorated with a few wrinkles. In a child-sized bathrobe that was too short for him, and adult-sized bathroom slippers too large, Ibrahim ate baked beans and sausages and potatoes in the motel's office as the adults had some sort of a discussion outside.

When his father came back in, he said: You'll sleep here tonight.

Where's Mama? Ibrahim asked.

She'll be here for you tomorrow, his father said.

The large-breasted blonde opened up a small cot for him in the manager's quarters that night, a large room located at the back of the property. When she leaned over to put on the bedclothes, Ibrahim saw the pinkish-brown spread of her big nipples. She kissed him good-night, leaving the smell of sun and sunscreen on his cheek. He tried to turn to catch the smell, but he couldn't, it drifted in and out from under his nose only when he wasn't trying to smell it.

The next morning, they breakfasted together.

Ibrahim had muesli with milk as the blonde and his father took their coffee.

Could I please have some coffee, too?

He's so sweet, the blonde said, letting him drink from her cup. Her lipstick mark was on the rim, and he put his mouth over the mark to match it, hoping for sun and sunscreen, but it came up crayons. Two policemen came to the resort and were shown to the office. His father sat with them in a corner, where they consulted in hushed tones. The blonde tried to interest Ibrahim in a crossword puzzle, but it was too difficult for him. A seven-letter word, the opposite of homesickness. She crushed him close to her. Carefully he leaned a shoulder into her breasts, which were practically sitting on the table, as he filled out the puzzle. He did not know the answer, but she told it to him, letter by letter: F-E-R-N-W-E-H.

Before he could finish filling out the tiny boxes on the paper, his father came back to the table. Max, his father said, they found your mother's body in the sea.

LATE THAT NIGHT, Ibrahim lay very still in the cot with his eyes closed, barely breathing.

He could hear the blonde crying softly.

I don't want that woman buried in Travemünde, she said. I don't want her here.

I don't want that either, his father said, but you saw how much it cost to freight the body back to Westphalia.

Can't you just cremate it?

How bad d'you want me to look? I told you, she's Muslim. They don't do cremation.

Oh, it isn't *your* problem! You weren't even married to her! Why is this happening to us? The blonde blew her nose. And the kid? she whispered. You're not planning to let him stay, are you?

The following morning, the boy's mother's body was buried in a corner of the local Travemünde cemetery. A few days later, Ibrahim's father took the train back to Siegen with him to arrange matters. Ibrahim was to remain in school there, "where all your friends are." Money would be sent to a guardian every month. A week later, when the paperwork was settled, his father boarded the train back to Travemünde. Chin up, m'boy, he said, as he left Ibrahim with a big bag of Haribo gummy bears. "To everyone's surprise" (so began the letter from the social worker to his father; another year: "Against all odds"), Ibrahim did well in school and proceeded to gymnasium. He did well in gymnasium and passed the Abitur at seventeen. The social worker encouraged him to enroll in civil engineering for higher education. Lots of openings in that sector for the foreseeable future, takes a long time to build a carpet-bombed country back up.

No, he smiled. I would like to be some sort of an artist.

Art doesn't quite pay, he was informed.

Why should it pay, Ibrahim thought, when it might be a reason to live?

10

The rust smell of beef broth hung heavy in the still air of Marlene's apartment. Waiting for the stew to be done and expecting Bogie to call, her eyes were on whatever was playing on the TV, but the scent of the meat had reminded Marlene of how pot-au-feu had been taught her by her mother.

There was no meat in their pot whatsoever, only root vegetables, which they were thankful for, in the midst of that first world war. Marlene was to treat the rutabaga and potatoes like beef shank, the occasional carrot like bone marrow. Her mother would rap her smartly across the knuckles if she did not chop and prepare each cut of "meat" as if it was real sinew and gristle. Sitting down to sample their vegetarian pot-au-feu, Marlene competed with her mother to make the most platitudinous remarks, as they spooned tasteless broth into their mouths. How the meat slid off the bone and melted in your mouth!

In those years, Marlene invented with her mother all sorts of humdrum private games that made no sense outside of their household. Recalling all this, she was surprised that she now considered these some of her happiest days.

Her favorite was the Peter game.

For Marlene, the best part of the Peter game was that she alone controlled its duration. As long as she wore her father's watch on her wrist, her mother had to call her Peter. Which one of them had originally devised the game neither of them could later recall, but it had been within the week the watch was presented to them in a velveteen-lined box, along with the certificate to confirm that the head of their household had died a hero's death, while on reconnaissance patrol.

However many times she turned it over in her head and in whichever direction, Marlene could not see how it was heroic for a man, much less the one who had brought her up so sternly, to have died not in battle but on patrol. When her mother found that offending line of the certificate besmirched by charcoal in a childish hand, she slapped Marlene so hard her ears buzzed, after which, bent over a kitchen chair, she was whipped over the backs of her legs with a birch switch. As Marlene undressed and drew her bathwater that evening, the afternoon's upset all forgotten, her mother saw the crisscrossing welts the switch had raised on those pretty calves and hastened to hide her tears. The morning after the beating and bath, Marlene found her father's old watch under her pillow, and soon after, the Peter game was invented. When Marlene was Peter, her mother, who affected a stoic parenting style, spoke to her in a softer and higher voice, touching her more often. The Peter game ended when her mother remarried. Suspecting the game's untimely demise, Marlene had secretly worn her father's watch under the lacy cuff of her itchy dress on the day of the wedding, and flashed it at her mother right after the ceremony, during the guest reception.

Not today, her mother said.

Not today *who?* Marlene said.

Not today, Marlene, her mother said, as young Peter burst into tears.

> But paradise is locked and bolted
>   and the cherub is behind us.
>   We must make a journey around the world
>   to see if a back door has perhaps been left open.

It was Kleist Bogie served up today. Marlene recognized it instantly.

What a treat, she said, I love Kleist. His short stories were always reprinted in the evening papers in Berlin. I had a favorite one about a man who meets an old friend in a park, and they begin to talk about dancing bears and marionette theaters.

Can you imagine, Marlene, Bogie said. Kleist was in your evening papers. Have you seen what passes for writing in a paper these days?

Young people today were fanciful for nothing, Marlene thought abruptly, with no emotion. They wasted their imagination on any silly thing they laid their hands on. There's nothing to imagine, she said to Bogie irritably. That's just how it was. Then, regretting her tone and afraid it would turn him off her, she went on quickly with what she'd planned. Bogie, she softened her voice, which arrondissement are you in? If it isn't too preposterous, would you like to come down to avenue Montaigne for my homemade pot-au-feu? My mother's recipe. You're not allowed upstairs, of course, but if you are agreeable, I will send my maid down with a bowl in an hour and a half. She is a Chinese girl in a pink uniform, there is no way you will miss her.

AN HOUR ON, the shanks had turned out dry and chewy. As none of Marlene's windows could be opened, it was going to take some time for the smell of overcooked beef to dissipate. The stew was too thick and salty. When Marlene added half a glass of water, the consistency was irreparably weakened. She could not possibly send the maid down with a bowlful of this, and she was too proud to have her help wait empty-handed to inform Bogie that the dish had not been fit for his consumption. He would have to be stood up.

Take this away from me, Marlene said to the maid, pushing the bowl away. Get rid of it.

The maid stayed put, spooning up a mouthful of the stew.

She was saying something in her thick Chinese accent, blowing on a spoonful of stew and bringing it in Marlene's direction. Marlene flipped the spoon away from her. The stew hit the side of the maid's cheek before it slopped down her shoulder.

Are you an imbecile?

The maid looked at her.

I said, are you *dumb*?

The maid's face fell. She cleaned her cheek on her sleeve and took everything away to the kitchen. Marlene channel-surfed to calm herself down, stabbing at the remote control every few seconds, not long enough for anything to settle.

Speed is how the cheetah survives as a predator that can't defend itself in a fight—

You're pretty good at giving orders, metal-mouth—now let's see how good you are at taking 'em. Move away from my friends!—

Ruptured tank sends eleven million gallons of crude oil into the Alaskan—

Marlene muted the TV.

Straining her ears, she tried to listen out for the sound of crockery and running water in the kitchen. She heard nothing. The maid must have left the apartment without saying good-bye, and she was sitting alone in the dark again. Panicking, Marlene wanted to call out to the maid, but she could not remember her name. Had she never known it before?

Choupette, Marlene shouted, help!

The maid came running in, hands in sudsy kitchen gloves.

Madame?

So the maid was still here, as she well should be, and there was nothing to worry about. It's all right now, Marlene said sharply. Carry on! The maid stood in the doorway as Marlene pushed the volume of the TV back up: In Honolulu, an ailing Ferdinand Marcos has offered to give back 90 percent of his holdings to the Filipino people in exchange for being buried next to his mother—

All right, Madame?

Go away, Marlene said. Don't you know when to go away?

The maid left, holding up her gloves so as not to drip dishwater on the carpet. Watching the maid walk away from her, Marlene began to cry. She could not say why. The maid was unperturbed when she looked over her shoulder. She returned to the bed, removed her rubber gloves, and touched Marlene's shoulder. When Marlene did not stop crying, the maid squeezed past the tables, took her shoes off, and lay next to her. She put one arm around Marlene and began to rock her gently. Marlene felt the warmth of her body. She was sobbing now. The maid began to sing in Chinese. God knows what she was singing, but listening to her nasal voice calmed Marlene down. The maid smelled so clean. She smelled of washing detergent. When the maid finished singing, she let go of Marlene, climbed off the bed, put on her shoes, and looked embarrassed. Marlene herself had not felt embarrassed in a long time, but the maid was making her feel self-conscious now. Not knowing what to do to make everything less uncomfortable, she fished out a twenty-franc note from under her sheepskin and passed it to the maid.

The maid shook her head.

Take it, Marlene snapped.

No, Madame, the maid insisted.

Marlene brandished the note as far as she could. The maid stepped back, where Marlene could not reach her from the bed. She put her hands behind her and shook her head again. Ugh, Marlene said as she stretched over the bed. The maid burst into a bright peal of laughter. It was the first time Marlene had heard her laugh. She began laughing, too. The maid perked up and asked: Want to try to walk, Madame? The maid came over, supporting Marlene's weight by slipping her shoulder under her arm and holding up her torso. One by one she slid Marlene's legs to touch the floor as she heaved her up into a standing position.

Left, right, left, right, Madame. See?

Very slowly they bisected the room, from the bed to the TV.

When the bad bones began to hurt, Marlene felt her body tense up. Noticing this, the maid supported Marlene's weight more fully, hefting her into a half piggyback. Marlene tightened her arms around the maid. Is okay, Madame? Marlene nodded, digging her chin into the maid's shoulder. They reached the bed, and the maid bent her knees for Marlene to roll over. What would happen if she didn't let go? The maid's body was so warm. Madame? The maid was still in a crouch, waiting for Marlene to settle herself. Trying to kill me, are you? Marlene complained aloud as she shrugged herself off. I could have had a heart attack!

Without a word the maid left the room.

Marlene sat very still as she waited to see what would happen next. If the maid did not return, she dared herself, I'll never move again. No, she added on with a dash of bravado, if she doesn't return, I'll set the room on fire. Anxiously she regarded the doorway. A short while later, that now-familiar silhouette reappeared, carrying two steaming bowls of reheated stew.

About time, Marlene said primly, I'm starving.

With relish they shared the overdone pot-au-feu.

11

At the end of Ibrahim's freshman year in Berlin, a pig's head was hung on the door of his dorm room with the words GOATFUCKERS GO HOME TO ANATOLIA scrawled in black marker across the snout. The school administration expressed its concern and apologies for "a tasteless prank," but declined to reveal the identity of the perpetrators.

As long as the perpetrators were unnamed, Ibrahim refused to allow the pig's head to be taken down.

He skipped classes to guard the festering pig's head, but still the culprits went unpunished. Finally a fleet-footed janitor was sent to remove the offending article in the middle of the night. After this, Ibrahim was known around campus as Pighead, and no one would go near him. In his second year, in addition to dabbling in photography (in the style of Daidō Moriyama, whose photo books he had first chanced upon in the Orientalisch section of the library, rather than the Fotografie section; he took it upon himself to rectify this, to the puzzlement of the librarian, a nice lady who paired her bifocals with pastel florals), classical German and French literature (with a focus on Sturm und Drang Romanticism), and a bit of philosophy (German idealism, and in particular Schleiermacher), Ibrahim proposed as his final-year project an attempt to remove the ARBEIT MACHT FREI sign above the old Sachsenhausen concentration camp on the outskirts of the city, alongside a paper on lexical semantics. What could WORK SETS FREE mean in a time of genocidal totalitarianism then, and a split capitalism-communism Cold War dichotomy now?

If I had only half your ambition, his advising professor quipped, thinking it was an elaborate joke. I look forward to the paper.

MIDWAY THROUGH THE semester, Ibrahim went alone, armed with a diamond-blade reciprocating saw, a monkey wrench, an extendable two-step ladder, a portable trolley with cable wire ties, some rope, and a big sheet of canvas, all stuffed into a large backpacker knapsack, to Sachsenhausen. He'd dressed in a special outfit he'd assembled from several visits to thrift shops: an American football jersey (Minnesota Vikings #7), cargo pants that ended midshin, Velcro-strapped sandals, and a baseball cap. He laughed out loud when he saw his reflection.

On the way, he listened to *Rank* on his Walkman, the Smiths' latest. The Smiths was Ibrahim's favorite band.

Johnny Marr played a clever guitar, but Morrissey wrote lyrics that could stand up and walk off the page unassisted by a melody, emotional and cynical in equal parts. When Ibrahim grew up, he wanted to be his own Morrissey. Too literate to be concerned with modernity, he would locate for himself just the same autodidactic noblesse in rebellion. Morrissey had been born into a working-class Irish Catholic immigrant brood and was bullied for all of those things in Manchester, where he'd grown up in social housing with a poster of James Dean on his bedroom wall and all the Oscar Wilde books he could borrow from the public library. If Morrissey had made it through, Ibrahim thought maybe he could, too. Ibrahim had read in a fanzine that when Morrissey was eighteen, even as an unpopular loner with no friends who was flunking his way out of school, he'd written in his diary:

I want to be famous NOW
NOT when I'm dead

A fair number of visitors were milling around the Sachsenhausen concentration camp memorial when Ibrahim reached the premises in his American disguise. There was a visor-clad Japanese tour group, whose guide held up a little white flag with a red circle in the middle of it. There were skull-capped Jews. There were actual Americans in Bermuda shorts and waist pouches. Some had their cameras out, pointing them at their companions, who put on pensive expressions against the backdrop; others had their hands clasped before or behind them in studied repose.

At half an hour before closing time, Ibrahim slipped under one of the replicas of the slatted bunk beds that prisoners slept on, five to a bed. When the ushers closed up, he tucked his legs in and held his breath, but they didn't even walk his way. He waited several hours more, napping intermittently, before he wiggled out quietly.

With no one around, and the lights turned off, the camp felt more real to him. It was no longer a photo opportunity or a simulacrum of calamity. There was an austere coolness to the compound. The ARBEIT MACHT FREI sign was not as highly mounted on the gate as it had seemed, and Ibrahim could reach it without much difficulty. He set up his stepladder and held the diamond-blade reciprocating saw to the sign at a forty-five-degree angle. The noise from the saw meeting the iron was stark and angry, amplified in the dead of the night in pastoral Oranienburg. One corner gave. Ibrahim held on carefully as he started working on a second corner. When he saw bright headlights approaching, he jumped off the stepladder, as two officers got out of the car and gave chase. In detention at the police station in Oranienburg, Ibrahim was asked: Who paid you to do this? What would you have done with the ARBEIT MACHT FREI sign if you had removed it? Are you working with other accomplices or organized networks? Do you have neo-Nazi or white power affiliations with any individual or organization in Germany or Europe?

Because he was of mixed descent, the accusations of *neo-Nazi* were not as strident as they would otherwise have been, but those of *poor migrant integration* were surfaced. As he was not yet eighteen, he was tried in juvenile court back in Berlin.

Reporters visited his university.

Everyone was quick to claim a degree of familiarity with Ibrahim: Pighead reads Saussure, digs the Smiths! No one could trace a clean motive for his action, though one reporter went so far as to dig up and quote from a term essay Ibrahim had turned in, which ended with the words "history is not a teleology."

The reporters' questions after the trial Ibrahim ignored or answered this way: If I said my gesture was formal and not moral, would you believe me? Or would it be easier if I told you I was bored? Yes?

A pretty journalist shoved a mic under Ibrahim's nose as he left the courthouse. Ibrahim, you say your gesture is formal. Can you tell us something about your ideas on form?

Her heels clacked as she ran after him.

Before he was made to duck into the police car he managed to say: Form follows fascism. Ibrahim smiled at her as the police shut the door. She caught her breath and waved good-bye. What a pretentious prick, one of the other reporters, a fat man in sports shoes, said.

The pretty journalist glared at him.

FORM FOLLOWS FASCISM became a headline that week.

It was too epigrammatic for editors to resist, even though no one could say for sure what it meant. Working backward from each media outlet's wildly differing interpretation of Ibrahim—Neo-Nazi acolyte; teenaged Kurdish delinquent; historical revisionist; anarchist proto-artist; attention-seeking youth—one could guess at their subjective disposition, which said more about them than about him. A right-wing paper expounded on the dangers of racial mixing and called for moni-tored repatriation of foreign workers and tightened border control. A centrist op-ed with a fancy prose style even made a big show, awk-wardly finagled, of quoting Adorno's "To write poetry after Auschwitz is barbaric." The pretty journalist infused her article with heartfelt staccato exclamations:

> Ibrahim Max Müller is not a neo-Nazi, nor is he a violent migrant. He is an aesthete! This is not a criminal gesture, it is an artistic one! The new gallery is not the white cube. It is history, it is bureaucracy, it is public memory! With one gesture, Ibrahim Max Müller has exposed our privileged hypocrisy.

For attempted grand larceny of the ARBEIT MACHT FREI sign in Sachsenhausen, Ibrahim Max Müller was sentenced to paying repair costs, and three months in detention at the JVA. Because he could not pay, his sentence was extended, in lieu of payment, from three months to six. He was also expelled from his university. At the JVA youth deten-tion center in Berlin, Ibrahim received a considerable number of offers of boy-on-boy hand jobs and even blow jobs, which, he soon discov-ered, seldom if at all carried with them an emotional implication, and that he accepted in any case without encumbrance. For a short spell he received a spate of fan mail, opened up by wardens before being passed on to him. Most of it was from young women who sounded like carbon copies of the pretty journalist. He'd known that type on campus. Girls who wore colorful knitted tank tops and pinned Antifa badges to their hemp shoulder bags but were snooty whenever he tried to start an actual conversation.

There was one long letter from a man who introduced himself in sprawling cursive as "a failed contemporary artist who, alas, was compelled by principle to cease my socio-Situationist sculpture after participating in just one operation, an offshoot of the 'Demonstration for Capitalist Realism' action in the Berges furniture store in Düsseldorf several years before you were born. Ever since I have been every day reshaping the boundaries of my practice in my mind and through the daily tribulations of my lived experience, without so much as touching a lump of clay or a scrappy piece of aluminum wire for the last twenty-six years, to little avail. But hearing of your trial and your actions I was able to read them, very clearly, as a call to arms and a Ready-Made Social Sculpture."

The failed artist expounded on his opinion that Ibrahim was "nothing less than an incipient visionary." He should not be unduly anxious about his incarceration. In retrospect, it would serve only to exemplify how his gestures could not be read in the time he was producing those gestures. Germany's publics were not yet ready to reckon with him—"and that is only to say, my boy, that so many of us remain contemptibly unwilling to stand up to the refraction of our very own souls and mirrored selves at an oblique angle"—but the passage of time would vindicate him, showing Ibrahim "not merely to be a blazing frontrunner in the new plastic arts, but one who, despite tenderness of age, and recent trends in our wider cultural sphere toward the sterile veneer of bourgeois abstraction, is willing and able to engage, exultantly, within yet beyond our pockmarked history, with serious philosophical questions of humanity and art-making." He ended the letter quoting Joseph Beuys in full lines, floridly scribbled, his handwriting growing larger and loopier as it reached the end: "Only on condition of a radical widening of definitions will it be possible for art and activities related to art to provide evidence that art is now the only evolutionary-revolutionary power. Only art is capable of dismantling the repressive effects of a senile social system that continues to totter along the death-line: to dismantle in order to build 'a Social Organism as a Work of Art.'"

IBRAHIM FOUND THE letter pitiful—this man had not failed at art, he had failed to live—and posted no response. The days were monotonous, yet time passed sooner than he'd expected, and when Ibrahim got out of JVA, he took a transit train to Hamburg and hopped on a ferry to Manchester. In the club district he crashed his way through gigs, and at Hacienda midway through a New Order set, he found out from a Mancunian raver with a buzz cut that the Smiths had split up. More than a year ago, mate, the raver shouted over the ending of "Thieves Like Us." Where were you, hey, out in the woods?

Someone surfed past his head, white rubber toe of a dirty Converse sneaker splitting his lip as the irresistible electronic opening pulse of "Bizarre Love Triangle" dropped hard and fast. The whole floor went up in screams. His lip was throbbing. Without swallowing he tasted the blood. Watching magnetized bodies flail helplessly together to the beat—livid wrists and limp fingers detaching themselves from shoulders in the air, eyelids sewn shut to faces but still jumping, treacly hair slicked to backs of necks—he saw that he was the only one who was not moving. He was alone, and he had been alone for a long time.

In the middle of the bursting club he began to sob.

To hide the crying he tried to dance, pressing his body onto the girl in front of him. When she turned around, he managed to latch his mouth onto hers without even seeing her face. She froze, then struggled, and when he would not let her go, melted into him, before they were parted by the moving crowd. Very soon, the music became sharper and tighter, the band had moved on to the dark foliage of "Truth" with its polyphonic labyrinth of delayed amps and layered synths. Strobes began to flash, and they would not stop. Their pattern was senseless. Needing something to hold on to, Ibrahim reached out in front of him again. A fist went into his ribs, a Cockney accent practiced itself over and over on "Suck off, faggot, suck off," and when he tried to stand up, the last thing he saw was combat boots and flannel pelting down before he was dragged out.

For the next three days he thought: Ibrahim's up and gone.

He did not move, he was not hungry, and he could not be sure if he was asleep or awake. It was a pity that he was left with Max Müller. He was not sure what any of this meant, but for the first time in a long time he let himself miss his mother, without reservation. Each time he thought of her, he had been afraid to use up what he could scarcely remember. He was certain that every sight, sound, and smell had a limited, little life. Now he wanted to spend it all and be done. On the fourth day, he woke in the cardboard collection area behind a grocery store. He could stand, and walk in a straight line. He had not been stabbed or mugged. In a public bathroom he drank for five minutes straight from the faucet, checked out the purple-yellow bruises on his torso, washed himself up as best he could, and caught a ferry to Paris.

The lights were brighter than they were in Berlin, and though it was prettier, Ibrahim found Paris slow and proud. He was walking behind a doddery white gent when the man tripped, and Ibrahim lunged to support him, clutching his elbow. The old man steadied himself, turned around, and tapped Ibrahim smartly with his cane. Don't think I don't know what you're up to! He patted the shape of his wallet in his breast pocket. It's because of you lot that I keep it here.

Ibrahim pulled the cane from the old man, leaving him sprawled on the pavement.

He hung around music venues in the 6th arrondissement, trying for a job at the Ritz and La Cigale, but they were too chi-chi. Once a shopgirl gave him a pat of butter for a bag of rolls he'd begged off a bakery at closing time, and he felt a disproportionate gratefulness. When a cross-dressing manager at La Java in the 10th arrondissement said yes, he could do with extra help, Ibrahim kissed his hands.

Call me Le Tigre, the manager said.

La Java was tucked in the back of a very old shopping arcade, below the curve of an art deco curved iron staircase in the basement. Le Tigre allowed Ibrahim to sleep in the liquor storeroom, told him to double up as the day watchman. With two duvets and a sheet of cardboard, Ibrahim bedded down on a tessellation of beer crates, listening to the Smiths. Because Morrissey delivered the lyrics slightly off the beat, his songs always sounded new to Ibrahim's ears. Peeling themselves away from chord structures in 4/4 time, his words were never quite in the place anyone expected them to be, and they kept the squeak and scratch of mice in the walls at bay as Ibrahim fell asleep:

I'd like to drop my trousers to the world
I am a man of means (of slender means)

I COULD BE wrong, Le Tigre whispered to Ibrahim on a quiet week-day night behind the counter, shifting his eyes to indicate a tall thin man with a bouffant hairstyle, but isn't that David Bowie?

A group of eccentrically dressed men sat on poufs around a low table, ordering round after round of dry martinis. I mean it would have been okay if Fassbinder had directed *Just a Gigolo,* the bouffant-haired man was saying to the group in English, but with Hemmings, it became a joke. Promise me you won't see it, it's my thirty-two Elvis movies rolled into one.

What's he saying, Le Tigre, who didn't know any English, whispered to Ibrahim.

That he was in a very bad movie, Ibrahim whispered back.

It was horrible, the bouffant-haired man went on. There was a scene where Commies and Nazis fought over my body. The only reason why I said yes to the movie is because they dangled Marlene Dietrich before me. I never got to meet her, in the end. She wouldn't return to Germany. She shot everything on a soundstage here in Paris, designed to look like our set in Berlin. An editor stitched it together—

When I was still with the recording studio, a man with bushy cat-erpillar eyebrows interrupted, they had this fabulous idea of getting Dietrich to read translated German classics out loud, beginning with Rilke. Twenty thousand dollars a session. They give me her phone number. I call. Miss Dietrich's residence, the person who answers the phone says. I can't place the accent. Somewhere between Catalan and German. I explain my business and she says, Please hold. Then Marlene Dietrich comes on. Hello, she says, and I realize at once that *she* was the same person who'd answered the phone! Marlene Dietrich was pretending to be the maid so you wouldn't think she was all alone!

The whole table cracked up. A finger was lifted for more martinis.

Le Tigre prepared a round, and Ibrahim served them up as the man with the caterpillar eyebrows went on reenacting his conversation: Miss Dietrich, I say. We hear your favorite writer is Rilke.

Yes, she says. That is so.

I reexplain my business and she asks, What of Rilke will you have me read? We had yet to decide, and of course the old broad is fudging, I'll bet she's never really read Rilke. I mention the only thing of his I recall. Perhaps, I say, *Letters of a Young Poet*? She starts to cough. A real, hacking fit. I'm on the line thinking, Jesus, should I call an ambulance? She is trying to spit something out between coughs. It's *Letters to a Young Poet*, she croaks finally, not *Letters of a Young Poet*! Shame on you, she screeches like a schoolmarm, and slams down the phone. The table howled with laughter. Clearly the man with the caterpillar eyebrows was enjoying the attention. Having been sidelined, the bouffant-haired man remained silent.

Could you do that maid accent again, someone said, that was gold!

I might do better, the man with caterpillar eyebrows said. He clicked his fingers at Ibrahim. Is there a phone in this bar? Ibrahim brought them around the counter of the bar top. Le Tigre raised an eyebrow. The man took out a black notebook from his coat pocket and put the phone on speaker mode. He nudged the bouffant-haired man: I'll dial, and you'll sing her a song. The bouffant-haired man said he wasn't up to it. The man with the caterpillar brows took out twenty francs from his wallet and eyed Ibrahim. How about you, lad? he said. Every minute you keep her on the phone, you get a bonus ten francs.

He tapped Ibrahim on the chest with the crisp twenty-franc note.

Deal, Ibrahim said, watching closely as the man with the bushy eyebrows began to dial the number on speakerphone. No one knew if the number was real, but in a moment it began to ring. What could he possibly have to say to Marlene Dietrich, one of the men joked. "They stiffed on my tip today?"

Hey, the man with the bouffant hairstyle said, don't be rude now.

The prank call went on for far longer than anyone expected. Ibrahim had managed to stretch it out to a full ten minutes. They'd all held their breaths when they heard Marlene Dietrich answer the phone, but the zinger was when Ibrahim broke into Rilke. By the time Marlene Dietrich got to "Do your industrialized soul a favor, don't call again," they were transfixed, and when the phone clicked, the room was silent for a good five seconds before the man in the bouffant hairstyle started to clap. Kid, the man with bushy eyebrows said, who are you?

Like I said to her, Ibrahim said. Just a boy who reads. Now can I have my money?

The man with the bushy eyebrows counted out seventy on the table. The man with the bouffant hairstyle topped it up to a hundred, pressing the additional thirty into Ibrahim's hand directly, saying: You've got potential.

Sorry to ask, Ibrahim said, but are you really David Bowie?

The man with the bouffant hairstyle smiled.

At the end of the night, someone threw up over his own moccasins. After Le Tigre left him to close up, Ibrahim cleaned the floor up with some paper napkins doused in dishwashing liquid and a moldy mop.

ALL WEEK, IBRAHIM thought about what Bowie had said to him. He had the potential—but what did he have the potential for? It seemed clear that if his estranged father or deceased mother could start over, they would not have chosen to have him again. The one thing he was sure of being was the worst mistake of two people's lives. He should never really have been here. Scoring a perfect grade-point average got him a pig's head on the door. Breaking an old man's fall he was taken for a pickpocket. Reciting Rilke by heart—he was still a clown. As long as they saw his face, he was always going to be the wrong person, in the wrong place, at the wrong time. His hand was trembling as he dialed the number he'd memorized off the man with the bushy eyebrows that night. He did not wait for a hello as he recited:

You wanted greater yet, but love
  forces all of us down to the ground.
Sorrow bends powerfully, but an arc never returns
  to its starting point without a reason.

She *was* good. She guessed Schiller. It was Hölderlin.

Listening more closely this time, Ibrahim heard her voice quiver. She was trying to hold it in, but it made her excitement only more pronounced. Although she was somebody and he was nobody, it was his game to play once he realized, however improbably, that she was just as lonely as he was. An old woman could want nothing more than to be treated the way he would treat her: like a teenage girl. She was Marlene Dietrich and, just like him, she had no one. He wanted to impress her each time, but sometimes her needs were much less fussy than he could have anticipated. Once she asked him to describe what he saw out of his window. Ibrahim did not have a window, but he closed his eyes for her, and described all that he saw in his head. The pavement was still damp for there had been an early-morning shower, he told Marlene. There was a neat mound of fallen leaves collated invisibly by road sweepers. A woman in a mackintosh was crossing the street, although the pedestrian sign had yet to come on.

I can see it, Bogie, she said. He heard her voice catch. I can see it all.

ON THE THIRD Sunday, she told him he was the only person she'd talked to in a long time who treated her like she was a real person. He wanted to laugh, to tell her that was his whole life. That can hardly be helped, he said instead. Who wants to talk to you like a real person when you've become a sordid figment of the cultural imagination? That's what a goddess is in our century, Marlene. A face that can circulate outside of time.

She was quiet. Poof, he said, and she laughed.

He could make her laugh, he thought. He could.

· · ·

ON THE FOURTH Sunday, Marlene said she wanted him to try her cooking. This caught Ibrahim dreadfully off guard. He had never expected or experienced this: a woman who wanted to cook for him. To his shame, tears came to his eyes. He dashed them off the back of his hand. He would leave her to rot. Let a famous hag find herself a new plaything. It was pathetic—how she was desperate enough to listen to him. He'd told no one, not even Le Tigre, about the phone calls. He'd wanted it to be something he could have for himself, but he felt certain now that no one would believe him if he told them anyway.

I hope you like meat, he heard her say.

He took a deep breath. I love meat, he said.

She gave him the address of her building, 12 avenue Montaigne. He was not allowed to see her, of course; she had not entertained a single visitor in years and she could not make an exception for him, he must understand. I understand fully, he said. There is only one image of you for me. This seemed to please her, and she told him to wait across the street till he saw a Chinese maid in a pink uniform come outside of the building with a bowl of pot-au-feu, in about an hour. He waited for three hours on avenue Montaigne, first across the street, along the odd-numbered side, and then when he was chased off by a doorman, on her even-numbered side, till he was chased off by another doorman, too.

Hiding in a phone booth down the street, he kept an eye out on the building till finally he saw a petite Asian girl come through the revolving door. She was in a pastel-pink uniform, just as Marlene had said, but she was not holding a bowl of stew. Slung over her shoulder was an expensive-looking coat, which appeared to be made from white fur. He could not tell if her face ought to be considered beautiful or ugly. Her single-lidded eyes made her look melancholic, or was it her thin but precise lips? He followed her at a distance as she walked down the street in white canvas shoes with a brisk stride. Was she unique, or was it just her juxtaposition against this environment?

Turning on the corner, she walked into a consignment store.

The Chinese girl went straight to the counter. Ibrahim stood behind a hat stand, twirling it slowly, looking at her through fedoras and boaters. She placed the coat carefully on the counter. The owner of the consignment store raised an eyebrow when she saw the designer label. She looked at the Chinese girl and shook her head.

Take this away, the shop owner said. The nerve!

The Chinese girl looked puzzled.

Whose coat did you slip off a rack when no one was looking?

No, the Chinese girl protested, a gift!

Thief, the woman said, get out of my shop before I call the police.

Ibrahim stepped out from behind the hat stand.

You have no right to talk to her like that, he said.

The shop owner looked stunned for a moment. Then she regained her composure and said: I knew it was bad news when you walked in one after the other, you're in this together! What do you want? What do you want? I don't keep big bills here!

Ibrahim swept the coat off the counter and put his arm around the girl's shoulder, hightailing her toward the door. Come on, he said. When the shop owner saw that he was not armed, she turned to her telephone. I'd like to report a scam, she said. Two foreigners.

Ibrahim knocked over the hat stand. The shop owner screamed.

He took his time to pick up a trilby with a kingfisher-blue feather that had fallen to his feet, setting it on his head and turning to look at the Chinese girl full in the face. What had he thought he would find on her—surprise, fascination? She stared at him, blank and appraising, with no expression. The shop owner was giving the police her address.

Ibrahim bent to pick up a cream wool beret.

He arranged the beret on the Chinese girl's head, as if to outflank her aloofness with comic timing. She did not stop him. Ibrahim opened the door for her with a flourish. She stepped through it, graceless but nimble, just as he would have liked her to. The shop owner slammed the phone down, charging out of her shop, and they began at the same time to run. He kept one hand on the trilby on his head and tried to take her hand with the other, but she shook him off. Afraid she could not keep up with his pace, he slowed down, but she sped up.

Running down the main thoroughfare, he spotted a movie house. Here, Ibrahim said. They'll never think to look for us in here.

She followed him into the same compartment of the revolving door. What do you think you are doing, she turned to him in soft, dis-

dainful French, out of breath. When he did not answer, she said: You
are maker of problems.

He said: But what would life be without problems?

She stopped pushing through the revolving door to glare at him,
making a scoffing sound at the back of her throat. The door stopped
turning. Someone entered the partition behind, and they were conducted through the carousel, into the mirrored lobby. They caught
sight of their reflection. Both of them still had their hats on. Hers was
askew. Very casually, she regarded herself in the mirror. Then she
reached out, solemn and unsmiling, to rearrange the cream beret on
her head as if it were completely natural that she should do so. She did
not look at him. Ibrahim could not stop watching her. The coat was
still over his arm. He held it out for her, and without hesitation she slid
into it, one arm and then the other. The beret went perfectly.

The ticket lobby was quite empty.

Ibrahim went up to the box office to ask if there was a picture playing. A matinee had started fifteen minutes ago. Ibrahim paid for two
tickets. She watched him with grim suspicion.

Popcorn? he asked.

What is popcorn? she said.

He should have liked to kiss the back of her hand.

Anna Karina has nothing on you, he said.

She said: Who is Anna Karina?

12

On weekdays, Bébé was a clockwork spring wound just tightly enough for the day, nothing more nothing less.

Waking at five thirty cut it fine. The walk to the station was twenty minutes, and the commute from her dormitory to the Ministry just under two hours.

She reached the Ministry at eight.

Aside from the forty-five-minute lunch break, she worked steadily on her feet, scrubbing out toilet bowls, mopping floors, emptying bins, polishing mirrors, refilling liquid soap, hand towels, and toilet paper. Bébé was careful to ensure the floor was clean but never wet, lest a bureaucrat should slip in low heels. There were feedback cards attached to the two bathrooms she was in charge of, with a number to call if they were not found to be in tip-top condition. Bébé found this insulting. She would have done the best job she could even if there were no feedback cards and no one to call.

At six thirty her shift ended.

Long subway ride back, quick soap down in the dorm's communal shower, take-out falafel or blanched noodles on the dirty stove in the kitchenette, stretching out exhausted on the bunk bed. Most of the women in the dorm were accredited Tunisian guest workers who worked in a textile factory in Saint Denis. At night, Bébé watched them lay down their prayer mats in the same direction, by the sides of their beds. They prayed, some saying the words, some singing beautifully, some with a scarf thrown over their heads, some in a full white shroud that exposed only the face. After prayers, they were garrulous or listless, painting their nails in bright colors or writing letters on onion-skin-thin paper, chatting or bickering, sleeping or singing, a prayer or a pop song Bébé could not tell which, but with them she felt safe.

On Saturdays, Bébé went for her French lessons at the immigrant activity center. She had been promoted to an intermediate course. Of late the pro bono human-rights lawyer had been encouraging her to enroll for a housekeeping diploma or a dressmaking course, whose cost the SCDS would subsidize. But I already know how to clean and to sew, Bébé said to the lawyer. The lawyer explained there would be more possible employment opportunities for her in the future, the more she upgraded her skills certifiably.

Sundays she kept house for the rich old woman.

She endeavored to do every small thing well: selecting the choicest blooms, collating receipts neatly although the old woman never asked to see them, and would round up whatever sum she quoted her to the nearest ten. Being sent out on errands around the well-kept streets of the 8th arrondissement had been Bébé's favorite part of the week, but now on Sundays there was Ibrahim.

BEFORE IBRAHIM, BÉBÉ had never allowed herself to enjoy the city as she walked through it, because she thought it was painfully clear that she was not in Paris for leisure. She knew her place, and should act in accordance with that knowledge. She held her head highest when she was in her maid uniform. Because no one had to guess at who or what she was, she could be.

With Ibrahim, although people stared more at the two of them together, she felt at ease.

He took her to all the things in Paris she would have found embarrassing to go alone to, or perhaps even with another Chinese person. He took her to the base of the Eiffel Tower, though they did not pay to go up. He took her to the Nôtre Dame cathedral, and she asked him why the gargoyles were so ugly. He did not know why. She wanted to tell him that in China there were fierce stone lions outside of houses to scare away evil spirits. Life isn't fair, she would have said if she had the words. Gargoyles must frown, but cherubs get to smile forever. He took her to the Marché aux Puces de St.-Ouen, where she was curious about bearskin rugs with the bear's head still on, Christian tapestries, war medals. He took her to museums. She thought the Louvre was boring, but she was awed by the huge arched skylight windows of the Musée d'Orsay. When she finished browsing all the things on the walls of one of the halls, she circled back to Manet's *Olympia*. I like this, she said to Ibrahim. What do you like about it? he asked. She looked at him as if he were asking a stupid question, and then she looked at the painting again. She turned to him. I like her face, she said.

IBRAHIM INVITED HER to a gig at his workplace one Friday night.

She had not understood what a gig was. He explained it to her.

Bébé showed up at La Java in her swan coat. She refused to give it up to the attendant at the coat check. Ibrahim met her at the counter and seated her at the bar. She soon saw that everyone was in jeans or short skirts, and she felt very silly. She grew embarrassed in her coat, which had a pelty odor she'd tried to hide in free perfume samples from the department store, but she was determined to carry it well. How exciting to be in the midst of a clutch of breezy, boozing Parisians who were all waiting for the performance to begin. When Ibrahim joined her, he passed her a Negroni he'd made. It was deep orange and she'd never tasted anything like it. Bittersweet, she said. He smiled at her and introduced her to Le Tigre. Ouah, Le Tigre said, this your chick? Just a friend, Ibrahim said. Don't worry, love, Le Tigre turned to Bébé, he hasn't brought anyone else here yet. Bébé turned quite red.

A woman with a deep voice and a guitar took to the stage.

Bébé understood little to nothing of the lyrics, a noun here, an adjective there, but she could tap her foot to the beat. Ibrahim slipped her a tiny pill in his palm. She looked to him. He showed her the one on his tongue, dissolving round its edges. She looked at him, unsure. Trust me, he said. Although she was not sure if she believed him, she was happy that he said that, and she put the pill in her mouth. Half an hour later all the lights in the room exploded into slow comet tails. The bass felt like it was coming from inside her body. Frissons, she kept saying, frissons. All the bass lines were flowing out of her chest. She took his hand and put his palm over her heart to let him feel just what she meant. He moved his hand away to her shoulder. She was feeling lighter than she had in years. When the gig was over, she climbed on a table. No one stopped her. They cheered her on. Soft hands braided her hair into two plaits. Someone arranged her arms in a Communist pose. Then they wanted to hear a Chinese revolutionary anthem. She sang for them in a clear alto 我的中国心. How many times had she parroted the song in school in Taishan without considering the words, following the vigorous melody blindly. Only in Paris could she begin to understand the words. Being alive was so often about this sort of foolishness. Why? The beautiful people were calling, Bravo.

Girl, someone shouted, make a baby with me!

A messy-haired man with a camera was pointing a camera at her.

Bébé tried to say to him, You have to ask before you take someone's picture, but the words rolled around hopelessly like marbles in her mouth. She had to find a way to tell him, to tell them all the story that everyone back in her village knew: someone's great-great-grandmother had died under a willow tree after a photograph was made of her for the first time.

But her words were too garbled, and it was too late. The messy-haired man was snapping away before Ibrahim went up to him and pulled him away from her. Ibrahim put an arm around Bébé's shoulder, and she knew that if he was near then everything would be all right.

WHAT BÉBÉ LIKED best about Ibrahim was this: Sometimes she would ask him something, or he would ask her something, and they would laugh or be quiet, for they both recognized there was no way to answer the question. Because they did not have nearly enough language between them, they could see so much more clearly where words were bound to fail. That did not stop them from listening to the question and thinking about the answer with care, each watching the other's face even if nothing would be said out loud.

How did you end up in Paris? he asked.

Why do you have this—? she asked. (She did not know the word for scar.)

What does it feel like for a girl? he asked.

Is life really nothing without problems? she asked.

What was it like where you were from? he asked.

· · ·

HOW ABOUT THE time she pushed a mulberry into her nostril by the river, and she couldn't breathe? She stuck a finger in to try to get it out, but that only lodged the tiny fruit farther up, so she pinched her nose to squish it, blowing out magic purple pulp?

Or earlier—at the dump, poking around for scraps of cloth to fashion a doll with, unraveling a pink cloth swathed around a bundle. Seeing the baby girl within, quite freshly dead, she dropped it. For weeks she saw that tiny bluish face, the curly umbilical cord. Over and over she wished she'd been able to pretend it was just a rag doll so she could wrap it back up before she left, but it was too late.

Or later, when the teacher took her to the shed in the schoolyard and put his hand between her thighs. When she didn't move, he pushed the fabric of her panties to one side, pinching her cunt between his thumb and index finger. First he was hesitant, but when she said nothing, he grew bolder, pressed her between his fingers like he was trying to see if she could be flattened into nothing. She had never touched herself there, not even when she was bathing. Because he was the teacher, she told no one. He did not call upon her in class again, though she always had her hand up. Every time he picked someone else, she wanted to scream: Pick me. You think you know anything about me just because you touched me once? Pick me!

Or the flock of cranes she watched fly over the village one autumn. How did they know where they were going, what if they ended up in the wrong place?

Or the pimply colleague with sweaty palms in a back alley near the factory in Taishan, who had her dead drunk on cheap rice wine. Order whatever you want, he'd said that evening, dinner and drinks are on me tonight. Thanks, she said, the next one's on me. Waking midway through with him already fumbling inside her, his breath stinking of grated ginger and black vinegar, she decided to continue to appear unconscious, because if he knew she was awake, then there would be no way to pretend to him or herself that it had not happened.

Or the assembly line in Shanghai, where all she did for half a year was stitch a logo onto the side of a shoe. She wished she could complete a whole shoe on her own for once. She sang Teresa Teng's "What Do You Have to Say" in her head when she was bored. One time someone else picked up the tune, and she realized she had been singing it aloud. Despite the supervisor's warning to cease and desist over the PA system, the whole group chimed in for the heartfelt final line of the chorus, their collective voice jouncing off the high walls of the factory:

你心里根本没有我
　　把我的爱情还给我

Or every tally mark in Marseilles, and the cold, perfunctory sensation that perhaps she had already been prepared for this—

THEY WERE AT the base of the Eiffel Tower when Ibrahim told her it was built in 1889.

She was shocked, but she was not sure why. He gave her some room to think it over for herself. Now is 1989, she said suddenly, with a forcefulness that surprised him. The tower has stood for a hundred years, he nodded, and it will be here for hundreds of years to come. She counted softly, like she was practicing her French numerals—2089, 2189, 2289. She let herself trail off. Yes, he said, catching the feeling of her meaning, we will not be here. No, she agreed, a little sadly, looking at him. We will not be. She was viewing the gorgeous monstrosity of the tower from below, between its latticed legs, and he was looking at her petite human proportions standing under seven million kilograms of puddled iron.

He asked: What is your real name, Bébé?

But Ibrahim, she said. Is there such thing as a real name?

An Urgent Task
for Top Scientists at
the Kaiser Wilhelm Institute
in Berlin

XV

Everyone wants to know: Were you a Nazi? What sort of man was Hitler? Why did you make those movies? All I ask of you today is to listen with an open mind. Forget everything you think you know about me the instant you hear my name. Take a seat, and let me tell you my story in my own words. Everyone deserves that chance. I, too, have been a victim of circumstance. Doesn't anyone see it from my point of view?

First things first, thank you for coming down to Bavaria to meet me at such short notice. As you know, yesterday was my 101st birthday and we had a big party at the Kaiserin Elisabeth on Lake Starnberg. They were so lovely to sponsor my gathering—the owner is a longtime fan.

No problem—go ahead and tape this conversation.

If I had something to hide, I would not have invited you into my home.

Would you like a cup of tea?

I am glad to be a little better now, and able to receive you in the sitting room. This morning, after reading the papers, I had such a fever I didn't think I would be out of bed anytime soon. My temperature is down, but it still hurts all over. I'll be straightforward. The doctor came by just now. All he gave me were painkillers. Everyone knows that when they do that, it's not a good sign. I don't know how much longer I have, and I'm tired, tired, tired of other people's lies.

They have marked me for long enough. I have paid for them with my reputation, my time. What if I wanted to talk about the things I care about? Filmmaking craft. My career as an actress. How I became a director, what movies I like. Reminisce about old times in Berlin. Weigh in on Hollywood now. Relax and have a real conversation, you know?

No, that's not permissible for Leni Riefenstahl.

The press has never cared to ask me about such topics. No offense, but you reporters are lazy. Relying on stereotypes and templates. Bent on seeing me one way, making my life hell, just because it makes a controversial headline, and people will talk about it.

I am sick of helping you all sell papers. I want to set things straight.

WE WERE CUTTING my birthday cake last night on the Kaiserin's terrace when a message was faxed to the concierge. Thinking it was a greeting card, I had a waiter open and read it out loud in front of all my guests. That was a terrible mistake. You can see for yourself here:

"Frau Leni Riefenstahl is obliged to Zazilia Reinhardt, to no longer make or distribute the following claim or allow the following claim to be made or distributed: 'After the end of the war, Frau Riefenstahl again met all of the gypsies who worked in the film *Tiefland* and nothing had happened to any single one of them.'"

Enclosed was a notice for a court case.

I did not want to cry on my birthday, at my party, but you will agree that this action is vicious and unscrupulous. They want to take a one-hundred-and-one-year-old woman to court for something she said out of goodwill more than half a century ago!

I have no doubt that my taking ill today is a result of the fax yesterday, and the bad press this morning. Are they going to pay my medical bills? What if it gave me a heart attack? Would they be charged with murder?

I have not taken my painkillers though I am in pain.

I want to remain perfectly lucid as I speak with you.

So let me say loud and clear: Who is this Zazilia Reinhardt?

Is she even a real gypsy?

How can they prove she was part of *Tiefland*?

Are they going to freeze-frame and match her face to each and every extra you can see in the larger scenes? I don't think so! And even if she was, why is she speaking up more than fifty years later, if she was so unhappy about what I said, on principle? Or is Frau Reinhardt looking for an out-of-court settlement to set up a nice retirement nest egg for herself, now that she can't play her fiddle on the streets anymore?

Further, my comments were only technical ones.

After the end of the war, I certainly hoped that nothing happened to any of my crew, my actors, my extras—regardless of race and religion, I don't look at that. Gypsies or not, I wanted the best for everyone. I tried to stay in touch, but it was so chaotic, it would have been hard to check in with all of them. I could hardly even take care of myself! I had two hundred dollars left in my mother's savings account and even that was seized from me. Worse, the Allies had stolen my *Tiefland* reels; they thought they could make a quick buck off me. It took me years just to get my footage back. By then they'd lost my assembly cut and I had to edit the entire film from scratch. What's the point of stealing something from someone if you're going to botch the job anyway?

Yes, I'll come back to it—the fax said it was impermissible for me to make such a statement because they had proof that many of the gypsy extras I'd used on *Tiefland* had died in concentration camps after the shoot, and I should be held accountable.

But how could that be my fault, when I did not know that the camps they were living in were *those* sorts of camps?

Well, I was under the impression that they were holding camps for the homeless, or labor camps for the unemployed. The worst thing we ever heard was that certain types of people might be sent off to Madagascar.

I am sorry for the suffering of Zazilia Reinhardt and her friends, but what could I have done? I was not a politician. I was a film director. I was an actress. And that was all so very long ago, why rake up the past? Why don't these people move on and make something of themselves?

UNPLEASANT AS IT is, I'm not entirely surprised.

Open your eyes, this accusation has been designed by certain interest groups to coincide exactly with my one hundred first celebration and all the media attention I've been getting. There were all these press photographers hiding themselves around the lobby of the Hotel Elisabeth when I arrived yesterday. I told them there was no need to hide. I am proud of these wrinkles. I can still pull off heels and a nice dress. Just let me know when you want a picture. I'll be happy to strike a pose, give a good smile for the camera.

Anyway, as I was saying, this Zazilia woman is just a front.

The organization behind her is a human-rights group for gypsies based in Cologne. Have you ever heard of them? Neither have I. Till today, right? With my name involved now, the papers are writing about them. Court case or no court case, they're seeking more attention and donations for their crazy hippie causes.

They've used my *birthday* as a publicity stunt!

They are trying to drive me to the grave, but they do not know just how strong I am. And they have forgotten I have nothing to be afraid of, I am certified innocent. Four times I stood trial after the war. Four times I walked free. I was found not guilty of any crime whatsoever. I can show you the verdicts. So what are these human-rights groups banging on about, if not for some free exposure because no one would be interested in writing about them otherwise?

I'M USED TO accusations and insults. They have taught me so much.

Don't expect the world to be kind to you when everyone is clamoring for their own lost cause. The most difficult part? Hardening your skin to the cruelty of others—but not your soul.

I've come a long way. Now I see it all as a test of fortitude and grace.

Fighting my court case as a young woman back then, I woke early each morning to repeat the words "Nazi slut" out loud. A hundred, two hundred times, whatever it took. Till they had no effect. Just a few syllables of gibberish. You can make yourself get used to almost anything. The hecklers might as well have been shouting "Hey, lady." In court, I did not even dare pronounce the name "Hitler." Reporters will add salt and vinegar to anything. A gossip rag printed that "his name melted on her tongue." Give me a break. You are writing a news report, not a romance novel. And let me ask you something. Have you ever received a rape threat?

No?

I didn't think so.

Have you ever considered that what you write about someone might make her the recipient of rape threats? Every time the papers printed things like "his name melted on her tongue," I received a fresh deluge of hate mail, rape threats.

Justice will not be served until I break your legs and leave you to beg for mercy in a public place. Suck my—you will excuse me—suck my cock as I skin you alive, my sister died in the gas chambers. Let me pound your snatch so you can tell me I'm bigger than Hitler.

Of course, the best part was how self-righteous they were.

Men I did not know were telling me what they would do with my body, because they were seeking redress for the inhuman acts of the Nazis!

In those days I wept, reading such things.

I tried to change addresses every few months so people couldn't reach me. Finally I told each landlord to nail up my mailbox, it was better that way.

These days—water off a duck's back. You can't ruffle these feathers.

XVI

Marlene Dietrich? Why, I have no opinion on her. I'm afraid I don't consider her my contemporary, no.

That angle is old hat, and misleading to say the least. I'd advise you not to write about her in relation to me, I know where you're heading with this—there's already been a stupid article comparing us, calling her behavior "exemplary" and mine "dishonorable," as two possible paths for a German woman living through the same difficult times. Nothing new to me—when you reporters runs out of juice, you'll rehash old favorites.

Let me give you a fresh angle, if you insist.

The essential difference between Marlene and me is not a political one, but an artistic one. She was only an actress. I am a filmmaker. Do you see what I mean? An actress waits around until someone wants her in a movie, until a director tells her to do something. Walk across the room, sit down, turn your head. Shut up and look beautiful.

I can speak only for myself, but that was not what I wanted.

I had my own ideas. I made decisions. I told people what to do.

Marlene and I are often compared, but there is no comparison to be made. She might have been desired, but I was respected. And frankly, if Marlene didn't want to be seen, why would she have installed herself on the Champs-Élysées to be a shut-in? Glamour girls like Marlene were afraid to be seen when they got old, but they were used to the shine of the high life. She died in '92, didn't she? That's a whole ten years ago now. I heard she was an invalid and a hermit for the last fifteen years of her life. That must have been horrible. I am so active, being bedridden alone would have killed me.

NO, NO, YOU'VE got it wrong, I'm younger than Marlene, not older! I was born in 1902. She was born in 1901, but she fibbed about it whenever she could: 1905, 1911, hogwash. Most women are sensitive about their age. I'm not like most women. I'll have your readers know—this is what one hundred one looks like! Good genes for sure, but also what you put into your body. I've never smoked a single cigarette in my life, and I don't like drinking alcohol. It's all paid off, yes, thank you— everyone is always telling me I look fantastic for my age.

The only time I ever lied about it was when I shaved thirty years off for my scuba-diving test. I was seventy-two. The age limit was fifty. Something about it being dangerous for the lungs. No one could tell, and I got my cert. I must be the oldest scuba diver in the world.

I want to get better so I can squeeze in a diving trip for Christmas.

Seychelles, or the Maldives—you should try it sometime. Under-water, you feel so free. It's quiet there. No one is blaming you for any-thing, and there are no walls. You're just swimming into the space ahead of you. I've always been at one with nature. Marlene might have appeared in *Vogue,* but she would be all done up in lipstick, a nice dress, stilettos. When I was on the cover of *Time,* I was in ice boots, tights, alpine skis, with no makeup, going up a mountain!

Marlene was trying to look fashionable.

I was just climbing a mountain.

I DIDN'T KNOW Marlene personally, but we shared a street corner.

Her building entrance was on Hindenburgstraße, parallel to mine. I lived on the fifth floor and she on the third. If I wanted to, I could see into her windows from my roof terrace, but of course I was not that type of woman. I mind my own business.

Marlene was married to Rudi, a producer who had cast her in a short film. Quite a handsome guy, but she still had men outside her marriage. Women, too. Looking out onto the street from my desk, I saw Marlene's valentines loitering on the sidewalk. They would throw pebbles at her window or leave letters in her mailbox, or flowers on top of it. She just let them accumulate! Her husband was the one who brought in the mail and took out the trash.

I thought maybe this was one of those marriages of convenience.

You know, where the man is primarily attracted to men, and the woman to women. That I would have been better able to understand, but I was told that this was not the case. Not to poke my nose into their private matters, but Berlin was a strange place at that time. If I hadn't been born in Berlin, I would never have gone to that city. Munich or Frankfurt might have suited me better. Berlin was too fast. I received heaps of invitations, but I avoided the party circuit. Nightclubs frequented by performers, artists, writers, and musicians. No companion of theirs was seen on an arm twice. Everyone had stopped looking to Caspar David Friedrich's beautiful paintings. They were singing George Grosz's praises, just because he was drawing humans all broken up! I am all for innovation, but I hate trendiness. People who do something differently just to stand out. Like the Dadaists. A theatrical bunch of big babies who did not want to grow up. Hannah Höch was a Dadaist because she did not have talents of her own, needed to stick two or three existing things together and call them art. Worse, along the whole stretch of Ku'damm were men who dressed as women. *Why* anyone would do such a thing was beyond me. Once I was standing next to one of them, and he—or she, or should I say "it"—it reached into its bosom, pulled out a powder puff that it was using to stuff its brassiere, and touched up its nose. Oh, for shame!

Those were the types of people Marlene associated herself with.

Not my crowd, no.

TWICE I'D BUMPED into Marlene outside our neighborhood.

Each time she pretended she had no idea who I was.

This wasn't very nice of her! She must have known I was in the business, since even *I* knew *she* was an aspiring actress. She might have been envious of me at that time. She was just starting out, you know. It's understandable. I didn't hold it against her.

Once I sat behind her in a café on Rankestraße.

I was sketching in my notebook, working on an idea for a film scenario. She was with a bunch of friends, smoking. They were all dressed like they'd just ran away from the circus. She was talking loudly, something about "my beautiful breasts," and asking her friends if theirs had begun to sag, then she swung her pair about in her hands! Needless to say, the entire café was shocked. She behaved as if she did not know that she had attracted everyone's attention, but she must have been lapping it up inside.

The other time we were both guests at the Berlin Press Ball.

The wonderful photographer Alfred Eisenstaedt wanted to make a picture of me, and I had invited Wong May, a Chinese actress visiting Berlin at the time, to join me for the picture.

If I had known that Marlene wanted to be in the picture, too, I would have asked her to join us, but I had not noticed her in the ballroom, until she made a big scene by spilling her drink on Wong May. We were all in shock. Poor Wong May was very upset, but I calmed her down.

Marlene was not sorry at all. She got more and more shameless.

First she kept repositioning that silly pipe-shaped cigarette holder she had to the left and then the right, hamming it up. Then Marlene started telling Eisenstaedt she was a leg model for the new synthetic silk stockings that were going like hotcakes at the Kaufhaus Tietz. If he ever needed legs for his pictures he should write her, these gams could sell anything.

All sorts of unladylike behavior—for just the tiniest bit of limelight!

I did not want to associate myself with Marlene, so I excused myself. Off I went to rejoin my table—I was seated next to the director of the latest film I had been cast in. *The Fate of the House of the Hapsburgs* was about the suicide pact of the Austrian crown prince and his mistress in 1889. I auditioned to play the empress, but the director said I was too young, and too attractive—I was better suited for the mistress, Mary Vetsera. For the role, the director wanted me to "think about history." How does one think about history? I asked. Ripples, he exhorted, think of the ripples! He wanted my every movement, the weight of my footsteps, to carry with it the ripples of future consequences. After all, he concluded, it is because of these two thwarted lovers that Franz Ferdinand became the heir apparent and was assassinated. Thus: the war. Our smallest actions lead to large outcomes, when we cannot yet know it. Think of that when you are brushing your hair!

The director wanted all of us to read a book by Edmund Husserl, *On the Phenomenology of the Consciousness of Internal Time.* He said it was essential reading for the serious actor.

I had never heard of Husserl.

I had heard of the P word in passing, but I did not really know what it meant. The director told me *phänomenologie* was the study of consciousness and its constructions, as experienced from the first-person point of view. The book was so heavy and dusty that every time I moved it I sneezed. I took a peek at the first few pages, saw *erkenntnistheorie* and *ontologie* appear several times, and proceeded to hide it under my bed.

I did not like to read. I liked to be active.

And surely, *internal time* was an attempt by a man to be clever! It has no real or useful meaning. Time is external or it is not at all. Life is for the living. Every morning when I woke I wanted to seize the day. I did not want to be thinking about *phänomenologie*.

I HEARD THE same thing as well—but I doubt if they were lovers for long, if at all. Wong May looked to be a very decent girl. They said Marlene kissed her in full view of everyone in a homosexuals-only club, but Marlene had probably kissed everyone in Berlin once, you know. Did she really go by renal failure, or was it syphilis? Who is to say!

I ran into Wong May round the corner in my neighborhood the day after the Press Ball.

I was coming back from a wardrobe fitting for *The Fate of the House of the Hapsburgs*. My costumes were snug, but I intended to lose five pounds before the shoot began. To motivate myself I wanted the clothes to be taken in a few centimeters all around beforehand. I remember being surprised to see Wong May in this area. It was mostly residential, not for a tourist. I told her I lived on the corner and what a nice coincidence it was to see her around here.

She was wearing a well-cut navy pantsuit with a yellow blouse.

It looked great on her.

I complimented it and asked if she wanted to get a coffee.

I would have loved to find out more about Hollywood, and in turn I could tell her about Berlin. She looked a little flustered. She said she would have loved to, but she was running late for an interview. I helped her to get a cab. We made a plan to meet for tea before she left Berlin.

It was a busy week for both of us working actresses, but we managed to fit tea in.

I think I took her to Konditorei Buchwald—excellent baumkuchen, and a terrace right by the river. I told her about my role as Mary Vetsera, and she told me in London she would play, for the first time, a lead character in a movie. She was excited about that. The movie was called *Piccadilly*. Her character was a dishwasher-turned-dancer called Sho-sho who catches the fancy of the proprietor, to the wrath of his girlfriend. She said she was looking forward to choreographing her own dance sequences for the movie. I told her I had been a modern dancer before making my career switch to acting. She was obviously impressed.

I die at the end of *Piccadilly*, of course, she said, so that everyone else can live happily ever after. What a snooze! I told her my character died in *The Fate of the House of the Hapsburgs*, too, in a suicide pact with the emperor. That's different, she said. Your character chooses to die for love. My character is killed because someone is in love with her and she has to pay for it with her life!

That's the last time I saw Wong May.

I know that after Marlene moved to America they acted in one of Jo's films together, *Shanghai Express*. I always wondered if that would have been a little uncomfortable. Although I take some issue with Marlene's acting—a bit flat if you ask me—I thought that was one of Jo's finest works.

XVII

Two movies changed my life.

One was a German Bergfilm called *Mountain of Destiny*, directed by Arnold Fanck. I was a dancer then, and when I saw that movie I knew I wanted to be an actress.

The other was *Docks of New York*. It was a Hollywood movie, and the first film of Jo's I ever saw. By that time I was an actress, and it made me realize that perhaps I had the eye to be a director. *Docks of New York* was about a roughneck stoker who saves the life of a world-weary prostitute on the Manhattan waterfront. I was drawn deeply to the style. Contrasting surfaces balanced out one another. Smoke and water, light and dark. I was so impressed I went back to see it several times in the span of two weeks, even taking my notebook into the movie theater on the last viewing to scribble notes down.

One of the things that kept me going back was a tiny detail.

Close to the end of the film, there was a subjective shot attributed to Betty Compson.

We see a close-up of a needle and thread in her hand, from her point of view. In the next moment, the same shot is out of focus. On my first viewing, I thought the cinematographer had made a mistake. Then the camera pulls back, and we see that Betty Compson is in tears.

That was why the shot was made blurry.

It sounds insignificant and lasts for only a few seconds on the screen, but I found this to be nothing less than a mark of artistic genius. I could not really explain, even to myself, what I admired so much about it, and so I felt the need to watch it over and over.

WHEN I READ in the papers that the director of *Docks of New York* was coming from L.A. to Berlin to negotiate a film deal with UFA, I marked the date in my calendar. The papers said Josef von Sternberg was Viennese but that he had grown up in New York City. On the day of the meeting, I set off for the studio in a green woolen dress, a coat trimmed with red fox, a matching green felt hat. Another small tip from me to your readers: I take a lot of care with how I dress when I meet an important person for the first time. I pick my clothes according to what I think of him, and how I want him to see me. It sends a message, sets a mood.

Don't be afraid of a little artifice. Use it well.

I inquired from department to department all over the UFA building and thankfully was not turned away—they must have seen Fanck's movies and recognized me as an actress. Finally I found the conference room, but I was told expressly not to disturb Mr. von Sternberg. He was in an important meeting. With whom? I asked. UFA studio executives, the producer Erich Pommer, the novelist Heinrich Mann, and the playwright Carl Zuckmayer, I was told. I could hear their voices from inside the conference room. I was so close to the man who had made *Docks of New York*! Before anyone could stop me, I reached my hand out and rapped on the door. When the door opened, I could barely make out anyone in the room. The cigar smoke was so thick I started to cough. One of them called out: What is the matter?

I would like to speak with Mr. von Sternberg, I said.

The door was slammed in my face. Well, I thought, at least I tried. Then the door opened again. A thinly moustached man stood in the doorframe. He was quite short and his coat was too big for him. He asked: What can we do for you? I would like to speak with Mr. Josef von Sternberg, I said. I've seen *Docks of New York* at least six times. You've seen my movie six times, I remember him repeating my words wryly, and you want to speak with me? So he had come to the door himself. The assistant was apologizing to him and shooing me away.

Von Sternberg stopped him. He took the cigar out of his mouth.

So, he said. What do you like about it?

The subjectivity of the tear-stained shot, I said. I have never seen something like that before.

I could see that he was surprised by my answer.

Not the "heartfelt love story between two underclass urchins," he said, appearing to be quoting reviews, from the officious tone he was putting on, nor the "sumptuous visual decadence that approaches the painterly surface," but the *subjectivity of the tear-stained shot!* He folded his arms and looked at me. I suppose I could lunch with you tomorrow at the Hotel Bristol, he said. Come by at two.

BY ONE O'CLOCK I was at the Hotel Bristol. I was not sure if he would really turn up, but I was prepared to wait. He came down at a quarter to two. I greeted him as Mr. von Sternberg.

Just Jo, he said.

We ordered my recommendation, I recall—tender beef with horseradish. He actually yawned when I told him I was an actress, and was unimpressed when I mentioned Arnold Fanck. That man would be better off as a nature photographer, he said. When I started trying to explain what I liked about *Docks of New York,* he grew more attentive. He might have seemed blasé, I thought, but he was just the same as other men, who liked hearing about themselves!

It's plain to see that your technical solutions are brilliant, I said, just as I had rehearsed all morning, but it is not as simple as that. What I mean to say is, they are made not just for aesthetic principles, but on the grounds of emotion. You leave out a lot. Your camera decides what the viewer's eye will look at, how much of it you will be allowed to look at, from where you will look at it. Of course this is true of every movie, but in most cases it is made to feel incidental, even though it is deliberate. In your case, it is accentuated by a highly personal touch that does not try to pretend it isn't there. Instead, you flaunt it. Also, you do not play out a scene all the way, or to where an emotional climax would typically have been located. I suppose you expect the viewers to complete the scenario with their own imagination.

By the time I had finished my speech, he'd put down his fork.

But my dear fräulein, he said, you are not as guileless as you seem!

I was a little insulted, but I didn't say anything. Men often talked like that in those days. I'd worked with enough of them to know. He told me the reviews had been glowing, but only in the most superficial of ways. He had begun to think that perhaps *Docks of New York* was really a picture that would be appreciated only by directors and cinematographers. He was surprised that I had so intuitively grasped how its technical considerations interacted with its aesthetic ones.

Have you ever assisted a director?

Oh no, I said, I am an actress.

They're not mutually exclusive, he mused, are they?

This had never occurred to me.

Anyway, he said, why don't you audition for my next picture?

He said they had signed the papers that morning. The financing was in place, it was his first talkie, and UFA's first sound film. An adaptation from a Heinrich Mann novel, *Professor Unrat*.

I had not read the novel, but it had a saucy reputation.

Jo said he wanted to call the movie *The Blue Angel*. The novel is more concerned with the point of view of the male protagonist, he said, but I want my movie to focus on Lola Lola. After all, the camera has less fun gazing at a man than it does a woman, whomsoever she shall be.

Before we parted I asked him: *Docks of New York*—is that what New York is like?

No, he said, tipping his hat, but it is exactly what you will wish New York was like.

XVIII

It would not be an exaggeration to say that every young actress in Berlin auditioned for the part of Lola Lola in *The Blue Angel*. They knew Jo was based in Hollywood and were eager to make inroads there. America was too foreign for me. I was not one of those hungry European starlets who wanted to go over and make it big—I've always been a grounded person.

Lola Lola was a barroom singer, a real hussy, who seduced an old professor.

It didn't fit my image at all—I was known for playing sporty, pure-hearted, lively types on the screen, and I wanted to keep it that way. I went for the audition only because Jo had personally invited me. It was the polite thing to do, you know, even if I didn't want the part. I remember wearing a sleeveless cream-colored pleated dress and nude silk stockings to the audition. From the moment I entered the room I tried to avoid Jo's gaze, so I would not be affected by his eyes on me. After that lunch at the Hotel Bristol, I could sense he thought I was special. I liked him, too, but just as a friend. I hoped he didn't get the wrong impression. It was always a headache for me when a man fell for me, and I couldn't reciprocate his feelings.

EACH HOPEFUL WAS given a scenario with a pianist.

We were to sing an English song, "You're the Cream in My Coffee," accompanied on the piano, but the pianist would play it poorly. We were to react to the pianist, who would take it from the top, and we would start singing again. He would flub his notes. We would get mad, chastise him, cross from the back of the piano to the front, whereupon the pianist would begin to play a German song, "Ohne Dich," smoothly this time, and we would sing it.

Dual-language productions were not uncommon.

I had not been involved on one yet, but it meant that each scene was done twice, once in German and once in English. I was lucky I had learned English at school. There were actresses who tried to scrape through without knowing the language, but they were at a disadvantage for such productions. I was nervous because I did not think I was much good at singing. Music's one of the few art forms I don't have a natural gift for. I tried to use my dancer's training by leaning across the piano, with my arm outstretched, when singing "You're the Cream in My Coffee," but it did not feel comfortable. If it did not feel comfortable to me, then it would hardly look right on the camera. When I received the phone call saying I had not been selected for Lola Lola, I was not surprised. The tension between Jo and me was plain to see; it was probably better this way. Now we could get to know each other as equals, since I wouldn't be working with him.

I breathed a sigh of relief and asked who had been cast.

When they said it was Marlene, I felt so happy for her! She was older than me, but she had not received any real roles in a movie yet. I told them she would be a great fit for Lola Lola and wished them all the best. Before the commencement of the shoot I wrote Jo to ask if I could observe him on the shoot. I had given more thought to our lunch conversation, and I was curious about how directors worked.

Certainly, he wrote back.

I visited the set twice. The first was very pleasant.

How Jo positioned his lights made an impression on me. I also got to see how he moved his actors like chess pieces and gave them instructions. The great Emil Jannings, who played the professor, was in a good mood and I got to speak with him.

The second time, I brought my notebook and was asking Jo questions between rehearsals. He was rehearsing the barrel scene with Marlene, where she hikes up her knee and sings, but she was not listening to Jo's cues. She kept looking over in my direction, and I began to feel awkward about being there.

I don't know what's wrong with that broad today, Jo said to me as he puffed on a cigar.

When they resumed, Marlene scratched her armpit vigorously.

I was surprised that she would do such a thing in public. I tried to focus on asking Jo about the position of the lights, but then Marlene tugged her panties down and lifted her leg much higher and wider than she was meant to for the scene, till finally Jo roared: Put down your leg, Marlene, everyone can see your pubic hair!

I was so embarrassed I said good-bye to Jo and fled the set.

The weekend after that incident, I received a telegram from Jo.

He told me to meet him on Lindenstraße so he would not have to pass Hildergardstraße. When I got onto Lindenstraße, I did not see him, but walking down the sidewalk I suddenly heard his voice: In here!

I turned and saw that he was sitting behind the wheel of a car. Hurry, he said, beckoning me in as he checked the rearview mirror. His eyes were bloodshot. I got in and shut the door, worried he was in some sort of trouble.

Marlene's a madwoman, he said as we sped off.

I fastened my seat belt and rolled the window down as Jo began to confide in me.

JO SAID MARLENE endeavored to make him breakfast and dinner even when they were in the midst of a shoot—when of course, you know, the most helpful thing any actress can do for her director is to rehearse her lines and get eight hours of sleep so her skin will look fresh on camera. That would have been my modus operandi.

Instead, Marlene was stewing a vat of beef with vegetables and forcing Jo to finish all of it. It gets worse—Jo told me that Marlene would rouse him in the middle of the night by rubbing her you-know-where on his sleeping hand—till he woke to find his wrist wet. Oh dear, I remember saying to Jo, and he said that wasn't the end of it, for Marlene would goad him: Is Jo-Jo really going to be a spoilsport now?

What's more, Jo told me, an aquiline-nosed woman in a newsboy cap had been tailing them around town. Thinking she was a tabloid photographer, Jo told Marlene to walk on ahead as he stopped to tell the woman to leave them alone or he would smash her camera with his cane. To his surprise the woman stood her ground and told him to return Marlene or she would crush his giblets between her bare fingers. In shock Jo caught up to Marlene. She was peeping around the corner. He told her what had happened, and all Marlene had to say was: Did she really say that? Giggling, she told him that was Ingeborg, a paramedic she'd met in a girlie bar.

The last straw came that very afternoon I met up with him—he and Marlene were crossing Alexanderplatz and an ambulance narrowly missed them. Jo said he was still trying to gather his wits when Marlene exclaimed: Doesn't the ambulance look good on Ingeborg? Maybe she should put on the siren?

Jo's knuckles were white on the steering wheel as he related all of this to me. I'm going to have a nervous breakdown, he said, tapping the gas pedal. You know how hard it is to shoot a movie, all that notwithstanding. And I can hardly tell the men about my problems. They would just make a joke of it. It would lose me respect on set, or someone would pass it on to someone and his wife would pass it on to my wife. You know I had thought this would have been a quiet affair since both Marlene and I are married.

At least you know you've cast Lola Lola right, I said.

He brightened up a little. That's big of you, he said.

After that, I remember clearly that we went to the river and rented a canoe. Jo rowed us out. All around in the Sunday sun were young couples, and families with small children. He seemed calmer now that he'd shared his troubles. Rowing smoothly, he said: So you would like to be a director now?

Caught off guard, I squeaked: Perhaps, who knows?

Who knows? he said. *You* know whether you have it in you.

He straightened his oversized jacket, cleared his throat, and put on a magisterial tone.

Let us not mince our words in this decisive matter, he said. Art is not like baking apples or chopping firewood.

He said that an artist must apprehend the primal nuances of his or her medium, and that cinema is time on the axis of sight. Jo told me that the best films were not those that looked the most real—then we filmmakers would be mere stenographers. Nor were the best films the most lavish, or the most absurd. Those were too clean a break from reality. They called too much attention to the artist and the object for the viewer to really see. Throughout my career, I thought back often to this afternoon, and Jo's generosity in sharing his wisdom with me.

Take the right risks, he said, to contrive a meeting with the committed viewer in the eye of the storm. Pull her into your pale, he said, make her recognize she is in the act of seeing. Honor her captivity, he said. Make a silent pact with her. The best films are those that create a hypnagogic state for the viewer, so she can be thinking through seeing, in dreams awake. I remember being so enthralled by his words, and Jo must have been so caught up with speaking them, that neither of us had noticed that one of our paddles was floating away from us. Unbuttoning his jacket, he reached out to retrieve it.

Jo, I asked him. Why do you wear your jackets so oversized?

Everyone notices that, he said as he rowed us back to shore, but no one has thought to ask. I wear them too large, Jo said, to remind myself that there is always room to grow into becoming the director I want to be.

XIX

What I learned from Jo: if you are an original, you might as well compete only with yourself. Whatever I did, whether it was a fiction film or a documentary, people could smell my originality, and it would set off copycats. Even when I switched from filmmaking to photography after the war, when it was too hard to find investors for my movies, my photographs of African primitives in their natural state were acclaimed right away.

Let me say here say how much I love Africa.

Have you seen my photography?

Here, feel free to refresh your memory, I brought out the coffee-table editions.

Black skin is *more* beautiful than white skin. Like Rodin in black marble. When a black man is naked, I never notice it. I don't know if you remember, but my nature photography of these Nubians set off a storm in the seventies. Not only in art, mind you, but tourism! Africa was *in*. Well-heeled adventurers organizing their trips to the safari started booking tours not only to shoot some big game, but to take their own photographs of the Kordofan tribespeople. This changed the lives of the Nubians completely. When I first visited, they did not even know what money or a camera was. Now they could receive large tips just by stopping to smile for a picture. I am glad I got to know them before they became aware of the camera. They were not posing for me then. I was just capturing their way of life.

What problem? We got along fabulously.

I DID WHAT my instincts told me to.

People were so impressed that I was a woman. Don't be impressed that I am a woman, I told them. Be impressed that my work broke ground I didn't even know I was breaking.

Look, I appreciate what you are saying, but I am not "the first female filmmaker."

I am a filmmaker.

This is what I have been saying from the start.

It is 2003 now, and I am still saying the same thing.

Put it this way, it doesn't make me happy or unhappy. That would be short-sighted and vain. What I have come to understand is that people will find meaning in your story, in their own way, regardless of the meaning you have inscribed, and that with time, meaning can change.

Even by the late sixties and early seventies, things were evolving.

Some American poststructural film theorists wrote to me.

They'd watched *Tiefland* and termed it a "psychobiography."

What is that? I asked.

Watching *Tiefland*, they said the symbolism encoded by my psychological state was obvious. The Nazi state was the greedy Marquis and Hitler was the lone wolf menacing the village. As Martha, the gypsy dancer wooed and coerced by the Marquis, I was caught between two opposing forces. At heart, I wanted to be with the shepherd and his sheep, who represented the common people of Germany. Wow, I thought to myself, these academics sound so loony! I mean, that's a lot to speculate on—concerning a time you know nothing about, a person you know nothing about—from one film. I am sorry to disappoint you, I wrote back, but I do not want to lie. Your interpretation is riveting, but it is not what I intended. I did not intend any particular meaning, because that would be a limitation. Meaning is individual, range bound. But beauty in form is total. The cinematic language is universal.

They found my words so impactful that they wanted to fly me over for some lectures. There, they wrote, we would be able to discuss my work in its full context, outside the blanket notoriety and willful ignorance dogging any objective discussion of my films. That sounds splendid, I agreed. Everything was coming along so nicely—I was getting quite friendly with the coordinator, business-class airfare was arranged—till they went to the head of the film department for his sign-off. The coordinator told me afterward exactly what he said:

If I met that woman, I would cut her nipples off.

. . .

BLESS YOUR HEART—yes—I was just as shocked by how inappropriate this statement was!

Exactly. He was free to reject my guest lecture, to flay my movies, and even to judge my character, but did he have the right to say he would cut my nipples off if he saw me? If I were a man, was there any chance he would say something like this?

But no, that's where you're wrong—it's not just "misogyny." It's not just "the things men say." I am sorry to say this, but women can be far more vicious. They only hide their tracks better. For example, it was very chic and calculated what that Susan Sontag did.

You've read "Fascinating Fascism," where she bashes my work and discredits me, yes?

Going from my films and photography to sadomasochism and fascism in one essay. I can see why people would want to read that. She is good at mixing and matching topics. And she has such a way with words, she can throw together a few things that have nothing to do with each other, tie it all together with a big ribbon, and make you believe.

When in fact, *she* is exactly what she says I am: an insincere, attention-seeking liar!

And I can actually prove it, in print, her two-faced games.

Now, you say you've read "Fascinating Fascism."

But the real question is, have you read "On Style"?

No? You're in for a surprise. In this earlier essay, she defends me, *Olympia,* and even *Triumph of the Will.* See for yourself—her collected essays. Take note, "Fascinating Fascism" was published in 1975, "On Style" in 1966.

Here—

My favorite part, highlighted.

This bit, where she compares me with Homer and Shakespeare. What does she say?

"The greatest artists attain a sublime neutrality."

. . .

THAT'S WHAT SUSAN SONTAG wrote about me. Not so righteous and angelic now, is she? Over the years I began to understand. It was all opportunism for her, wasn't it? In 1966, when the rest of the world hated me, it was daring for her to defend me. In 1975, when everyone was coming around to me, why not flip the tables? Start a witch hunt with a zappy title, have it published in a magazine in New York, get some street cred for stirring up a shit storm. Next to Sontag's hypocrisy, "If I met that woman, I would cut her nipples off" seems direct and honest. That's what men are good for. Women? I shudder. Sontag's personal attack hurt for a long time, but it all made more sense to me when I found out that she was an aspiring filmmaker.

You didn't know that either, did you?

Of course you didn't, she's tried so hard to bury them.

When the twenty-day Yom Kippur War broke out, little Miss Susan hopped on a plane, landed in Israel, and started rolling a camera—yes, that's what she thinks a movie is! That was her third movie. What does a movie like that do for anyone, I ask you? What does it prove? That an American intellectual has enough ignorance to pull off a stunt like that? Her first movie was even worse. Set in Sweden so it could be an Ingmar Bergman rip-off, everyone ends up in bed with everyone else— either she has a dirty mind or she has no idea how to end her story.

When I saw her films, immediately I understood why she had written those nasty words about me. Sontag says I am "no thinker." Yes, but I never pretended I was one. I was happy just making my films.

As to *her* films—

You know what? I shan't do to her what she did to me.

I'm going to take the higher ground here, one woman to another.

IN ANY CASE, I am used to people, men and women alike, being jealous of me. From the outside, before it all came crashing down, it might have looked like I was immensely lucky, that I had boundless resources at my disposal to shoot big-budget films that no one else did, but I fought tooth and nail every inch of the way.

There she goes, Goebbels would say, Leni's being a woman. A crisis a day. A ball of nerves. Her health is poor. She is addicted to painkillers. Of course a man with a clubfoot will want to put down a successful woman who has rejected him! Please have this in print: Joseph Goebbels fondled my breasts at the opera. It was a Wagner premiere. We were in the box with his wife. I never said anything to anyone because I was afraid that no one would believe me, or that he would punish me for it. Success is lonely, in particular for a woman of my time.

There were so few of us, and no one saw us for what we were.

People said I was an egomaniac for casting and directing myself, but that was not so unusual. Look at Charlie Chaplin or Orson Welles then. Look at John Cassavetes or Woody Allen now. People don't call them egomaniacs. They call them geniuses.

Being a woman is a very complicated thing.

During my postwar trial, my lawyer told me to soften my courtroom demeanor. Listen, Leni, he said, it doesn't matter if you really knew nothing about the camps, if you knew something, if you knew everything. I believe that a large part of whether we win or lose the case is hinged on whether you can act like a woman. Dedicated and talented, yes, but also vulnerable and helpless. If you were a man, he said, do you think anyone would believe for a second that you did not know anything about politics, that you were simply an artist obsessed with beauty? You have to show to them that you are a woman.

He did not know that as a woman, you are always acting as a woman!

BEFORE I ANSWER that I should clarify: what is your definition of *feminism?*

I can't, as you say, "identify" or "not identify" with that. You see, when I was growing up, when I was making work, there was none of this "feminism." So I think it would be dishonest of me to jump on the bandwagon. It's true, though—in recent years, young women have reached out to me of their own accord to say that I am a role model in my own right. They write to me about "glass ceilings" and "smashing patriarchy." But I tell them in good faith, as I am telling you now, that I do not identify with stances. I am just a woman who works. If they find my life inspiring, that is very touching. You see, every tide turns. Fifty years ago, rape threats. In this new millennium, feminist inspiration!

It is just the passage of time. I have remained constant.

This, if nothing else, is what I would like people to understand.

WELL. IT'S IRONIC you would ask this question right after your last one, don't you think? No, that's all right, you don't have to backtrack, but let's at least do away with the euphemisms. If you want to ask me that question, just say it like it is: did I ever engage in sexual relations with Adolf Hitler?

Tell me, is sex really the most intimate thing that can happen between two people?

What if I told you the most intimate thing he ever did to me was to support my talent? When we first met, he told me he saw my potential, and that he would place his resources at my disposal. Do you know how much that meant to a woman with a dream back then?

Men *were*. Women behaved. Men did things, women watched.

I wanted to do things, too, but I was not born into money. My father had a small business making bathroom pipes and toilet bowls. My mother was a housewife. I was not the wife of an aristocrat, or the girlfriend of a banker. If I wanted to make things happen, I needed someone to share my vision and believe in me.

That's intimacy.

MARLENE LIKED TO say that Hitler had a thing for her, but she meant that only in a superficial sense. And I have to jump in to say that for the record, even on the surface, I don't think that could be true. If you knew him at all, you'd know that he did not like vamps. He thought Vivien Leigh was okay, but Louise Brooks was too modern. Of course, the funny thing is that while Marlene would be trying to *start up* rumors that Hitler had the hots for her, I could hardly *put out* those flames wherever I went.

In America they called me his mistress.

To be very honest, I was not his type, and he was not mine.

My kind of guy: well-built and clean-cut. I had quite a number of those. A tennis champion, a weight-lifting cameraman, a Wehrmacht general who won the Iron Cross. A perfectly formed boy I found wandering the foothills of the Acropolis, who looked just like one of the Greek statues. We hired him to appear in the opening sequence of *Olympia*, even though he was neither Greek nor German, but the son of Russian farmers. Also during the filming of *Olympia*: the American sprinter who won the four-hundred-meter decathlon. He walked off the prize podium with his gold medal and came toward me in the spectator stand. When I leaned forward to congratulate him, he kissed me on the lips in full view of the cameras!

So if you look at my track record, you will see that it was practically impossible for Hitler and I to have been lovers. As for him, he preferred homely, unassuming plain Janes who remained in the background, who were not too attractive.

Look at Eva Braun, right?

THE LAST TIME I ever saw Hitler?

Toward the end of the war.

He made a surprising request of me then.

I was in Kitzbühel with bladder colic, on medical leave from shooting *Tiefland*. I thought he would chastise me for budget overruns or hurry my production schedule, but the first thing he did was to give me his personal homeopath's calling card.

Leni, he said, take better care of your health.

Then he called for some tea. No coffee, no alcohol. Tea and mineral water. That's what he liked.

He told me he was tired, and looking for a political successor. Nobody was quite right, but he would leave it up for the Party to decide. After the war, he said, come visit me at the Berghof, and we can cowrite screenplays. He smiled at me. I did not dare to ask if he was joking. He heaped on many teaspoons of sugar and grew preoccupied with swirling his teacup to dissolve it without using the spoon. He took a sip and looked up at me. Leni, he said. Will you do me a favor?

Yes, I said, because who says no to him?

I remember feeling nervous—I did not know what sort of favor this was.

Once you have finished your movie, he said, please contact the top scientists at the Kaiser Wilhelm Institute in Berlin. I've been meaning to discuss with them a most important matter, but I have not had the time to do so. It could take years to perfect, he said, and we have no time to lose. I want the best brains in Germany to start on this right away.

I swallowed and listened carefully.

With scientists involved, I feared the worst. It must have something to do with weapons for the war. He put down his teacup and went on. Silver nitrate is not good enough, he said, it is perishable. We are losing so many images from our time, he said. How would everyone be able to see what we have created in the future?

I did not understand what he was talking about.

I asked him for a clarification. They were the last words I would hear him speak to me.

I am talking about the mutability of film stock, he said. Surely, our scientists can invent for mankind a film stock of the finest metal? An invincible alloy, which cannot be altered by time or weather?

In the middle of a war, I could not believe that was what he was asking of me.

Is it wrong for me to admit that I was moved by his request?

That even now, telling it to you, I'm getting the chills?

XX

Now we are in the age of digital video, but I see advertisements on the TV that are more artful than the movies. Has the digital erased time? A viewer can play, pause, rewind, and fast-forward at the touch of a finger. Filmmakers can see the shot on a screen as they are shooting or move through footage without taking time for it to unspool in reverse.

If you don't have a feel for time, how can you make a movie?

In movies now, the sad thing is when you see that the camera is moving, but there is no meaning to its movement. You see this a lot in blockbusters. The camera is completely arbitrary. In our time, there was no distinction between an art film and a blockbuster.

Just look at my movies. *Art blockbusters!* They won prizes, but they also filled cinemas and made lots of money.

I prefer Hollywood movies now, without question. I'm not sure what happened across Europe after the war, everything became so ugly. I do not understand that whole genre of independent films. Italian neorealism is dreary. People go to the movies to be bewitched, not bored silly. If anyone wanted to watch something like that, wouldn't they be better off looking out the window or taking a walk in the park? The French New Wave was made up of a bunch of whiny boys who are too intellectual. Without the fanciful things they say, the images they make do not hold up. If I could say something to them, it would be that art is not philosophy. Art is art!

There are a few filmmakers in Hollywood today with ambitions that are in line with what I had been trying to achieve. I like Oliver Stone, Francis Ford Coppola. I sense kindred spirits in Steven Spielberg, George Lucas, James Cameron. We know how to use scale. We know how to make a viewer swoon. We have a feel for the epic.

Women are still lagging behind, and I can't see why.

If I was already making great movies sixty or seventy years ago, more women should have stepped up by now. Of those that have made a name for themselves, I confess I can't understand some of the work they make. I tried to watch Chantal Akerman's films, but nothing is happening in them! Agnès Varda and Catherine Breillat make me dizzy. Claire Denis is not so bad, but all these Frenchwomen suffer from the same problem. They think too much. A movie is for feeling, not thinking. Sofia Coppola's *The Virgin Suicides* I enjoyed, she knows just what she is going for visually. But so soft, so delicate! I know she is trying to do things differently from the men, but is this really the only way to do it? Seven teenage sisters running around in flowing frocks like it's a *Vanity Fair* fashion shoot?

If I were making movies today, I could definitely see myself making fantastical thrillers like *Jurassic Park*, space operas like *Star Wars*, romantic natural-disaster dramas like *Titanic*. I love Leonardo DiCaprio, he is so pure and handsome! I would have cast Leo in one of my movies in a heartbeat, he is 100 percent my type. I wept when he froze to death in the water in *Titanic*. And why couldn't Kate Winslet share the wooden door with him? I mean her face is pretty, but maybe she was too heavy? If I had been directing, I would have had them lie one on top of the other. I like happy endings.

HOLLYWOOD GAVE ME a call over the summer.

Please keep this confidential—

Jodie Foster wants to make a movie out of my life, and she would like to play me!

Well, I have to consider. My reputation would be at stake.

I am sure that Jodie Foster is a lovely lady, I said to the execs, but I am not sure she is the most suitable actress to play me.

Ah, they said, was I worried about authenticity? Was I thinking of a German actress?

Typical. They had misunderstood me.

No, I told them, I was thinking of Sharon Stone.

When I said that, there was dead silence over the line. I'm guessing that if Jodie Foster is producing the movie herself, then it is not going to be possible for Sharon Stone to play me in Jodie's production. Jodie wants the role for herself, of course—it'd be a great part to sink her teeth into, Oscar-worthy. I don't blame her.

I DON'T MEAN to be rude, but "What would you have done differently?" is a stupid question for you to ask me, in my context.

Well, either it is stupid or you are angling for some kind of apology from me.

I'm not going down that path.

What I will say is that for all that I have been through, I am glad I was born in 1902, and not now, when all forms of art seem to be practiced at a distance. I had distance from my subjects when shooting them, but I have never had distance from my craft.

Nothing in the world feels closer to me.

These days, to be an artist seems to be about making some theoretical statement, showing that you do not care about anything! I should feel very sad if art goes down that route. I mean, I am acquainted with Andy Warhol, but to be honest his work leaves me cold. If you are sincere and serious about your work these days, people will laugh at you!

I am too warm for irony. Mine is the struggle of the pure artist.

That might be unfashionable these days—it doesn't bother me.

When I said I was not interested in what is real, only in what is beautiful, people said, "You see, either way she is a monster!" But the true Romantics understand what I mean. For example, Jean Cocteau tried to have *Tiefland* screened at Cannes. He was the head of the festival in 1954. The whole committee vetoed him, but bless his heart for trying. And when the Venice Biennale wanted to rescreen my films as a fringe program in 1959, I agreed at once. I had such fond memories of Venice—I was in the main competition in 1937, and I won the top prize for *Olympia*, beating out Walt Disney and Marcel Carné.

It's true, I was the first woman ever to be recognized at a film festival. I paved the way for all of them, Chantal and Agnès and Catherine and Claire and Sofia.

It is important, especially for women, not to shy away from owning our achievements, even when the going gets tough—I had been booed off carpets, shown middle fingers, asked to leave restaurants. It takes fortitude to keep showing up. If I never gave up, I don't see why any young filmmaker today should, either. They'll weep and fret over one bad comment in an internet newspaper! Chin up, I say. If art is in your bones, no one can take that away from you. Fight on. It's not all about trophies and recognition—being able to say you've remained true to yourself is an artist's biggest achievement.

LET ME TELL you about the time I went back to Venice.

I've never discussed returning to Venice in '59—I used to think it was a shameful memory, but considering it now, I've every reason to be as proud of that trip as I was of '37, collecting my Golden Lion. People were calling me a genius back then. "Golden Lion for the golden girl" and all of that. Everyone wanted to take my picture, I gave out hundreds of interviews, guests of honor requested to dine at my table. All my *Olympia* screenings were sold out. People queued outside for a chance at rush tickets. When I stepped into the cinema, the audience would leap to their feet and give me a standing ovation.

In Venice the second time, of course, everything had changed.

The war had been over for almost fifteen years, but people never let you forget. I looked at my press call sheet and there was only one interview, but at least it was for TV. We did it in a quiet corner of the hotel lobby, and I'd mentioned beforehand that I would answer only questions that were not political in nature. Everything went well until a well-dressed young man in sunglasses came in with a placard and stood in the background.

Tracking shots are a question of morality.

He had written it in German, French, Italian, and English.

He sat a few tables behind me, in the eye line of the camera.

I was not sure what exactly he was trying to say, but I knew he was saying something bad about my movies, about me. I pulled the line producer over. Could we please get him out of here? She went over to have a word with him. When she came back, she said to me: He is from *Cahiers du Cinéma* and he says that if you are not guilty, there is no reason to think that he is saying anything about you. The cameras were still rolling. I asked the crew if we could change an angle or crop him out of frame, but I soon realized that they were deliberately framing him in the shot. As a director I understood: it made for more exciting footage.

In that moment I began to regret the festival.

It was very well that they were screening my work, but I should have stayed home. A familiar pain began to bite at the back of my hip. I used to have very bad bladder colic. It was brought on by stressful situations. I thought of asking the production crew for aspirin, but if they caught me popping pills on camera, it would look bad on TV.

I took a deep breath and went on.

The interviewer was saying: Would you say that your obsession with finding form is very German? I got very nervous. This question could be mocking me, my work. I did not know how to answer. Right then an old man took a seat between my seat and the young man with the placard. Opening up his newspaper, the old man obscured the young man's sign. I was relieved. I could speak properly again. When the interview was over, the old man rose, and I saw that it was Jo von Sternberg. It had been no accident that he had positioned his body between the punk and me.

Seeing that I had finally recognized him, he tipped his hat.

I had not seen Jo in decades. He had aged terribly. I was fifty-seven then, so Jo must have been in his sixties, but he looked much older. All his hair had gone completely white, and he was so thin. I noticed that the suit he was wearing was no longer oversized. It was tailored to fit.

I wanted to run over to say hello, but I stopped myself.

An old acquaintance had recently thrown her shoe at me at the Berlin Hauptbahnhof, and when I visited a production at the newly reopened UFA, where they were making an adaptation of one of my early movies, an actor I knew from before said he would not work until I left the set. Excuse me, I said, you are making an adaptation of my work, and you have not even paid for the copyright! He ignored me completely, and I was ushered out by security. Anyway, to be on the safe side, I had grown used to seeing if an old friend would welcome or reject me before I approached them. It was less embarrassing this way.

Jo was walking over.

He used to move with such a bold swagger, you'd have cleared out
of his way even if you didn't know who he was, but he was coming
toward me in small, uncertain steps. He had the same mahogany cane
he'd carried around for show all those years ago, but now the weight
he leaned on it was real. It was painful for me to watch him. Reaching
me, he did not ask how I had been. He kissed me on both cheeks and
said: Coffee?

WE ORDERED ICED lattes in a café—I recall it to be a very hot day.
Jo told me he had a new film in the official selection. *Anatahan* was the
first movie he'd made in many years. It was not slated for the main
competition—nor was mine, but in my case I was presenting old work,
whereas his was a premiere. We did not discuss that of course; I did not
want to hurt his feelings.

Jo said he'd fulfilled his lifelong dream of making a film in Japan,
in Japanese, with an all-Japanese cast. He'd been quite pleased with
his final cut but grew worried when no one else seemed to care for it.
Distributors and festivals had not bitten, so he spent some time recut-
ting the film, adding his own voice-over narration in English to explain
the Japanese culture and rituals, till the last iteration was accepted by
Venice this year. One can only hope their decision wasn't motivated by
sympathy, he said.

I understood what he meant: he wouldn't have known where to
hide his face if his comeback film didn't have a premiere at a decent
festival. I'd have felt the same, but I was also surprised that the great
Josef von Sternberg had been cowed into edits for fear of being passed
over. He told me he'd been asked by a French critic this morning at the
hotel: Monsieur von Sternberg, why did you go to the Far East to build
a studio set to shoot your movie, when you could have constructed an
identical set in a Hollywood back lot?

I told him: Because I am an artist.

He laughed and wrote it down.

You are very quotable, he said.

After he left, I thought: I am not an artist, I am a con.

Why? I asked Jo. I don't think you're a con. Not at all.

He smiled at me and lit a cigarette with a gold lighter without answering. Jo was so different from how I remembered him to be. I knew him to be full of conviction and panache, yes, you could say he was arrogant, but he was so dedicated to his vision, such a perfectionist in his approach, that you would forgive him the bluster. Seated across from me in that café, not only was he quiet, hesitant—he looked defeated. I had to ask him what his film was about. It was based on a true story that had happened during the war, he told me. After losing a maritime battle, twelve Japanese seamen are stranded on an island in the Pacific Ocean. The island's only other inhabitants are the overseer of an abandoned plantation and an attractive young woman. Everything is in good order to begin with, but soon it all descends into a struggle for power and the woman.

Men are brutes because they are so predictable, I remember Jo declaring. I would have made a fantastic woman, he said. Then I would not have wanted to be a good director. I would have wanted to be a great actress. For a moment I saw his old flamboyance. Then our drinks came and Jo hunched over as he told me the Japanese reviews had lambasted his direction as stilted, his cast's acting as amateurish, his world view as exotic.

Jo, I burst out. Since when have you cared for criticism!

He seemed surprised that I'd raised my voice. Look, I said, have you noticed to whom you're whining? He looked at me, saying nothing. If I'd taken all the bad press to heart, I went on, I'd have hung myself years ago. Sobering up, he put his coffee down and asked quietly: Do you ever wonder what would have happened if I'd cast you instead of Marlene as Lola Lola in *The Blue Angel?*

No, I said to him. It has never crossed my mind.

Not once? he said, a touch playful. Might have saved you a whole lot of trouble.

I could never have been Lola Lola, I said. And are you still in touch with Marlene?

He reached into his pocket and took out the gold lighter. All that's left, he said, passing it to me. I turned it over in my hand and read the inscription: TO MY CREATOR, FROM HIS CREATION. I gave it back and he flicked it open, passing a finger through the cold blue of the flame.

I've faced up to it, Jo said, it's true. After we parted ways, it was all downhill from there. The seven movies they made together were his best, he admitted, but undoubtedly, they were Marlene's best, too. With him, she had been an actress. Now, she was only an icon.

I had not thought of that before, and isn't it true?

She went on making movies, I remember Jo saying, but it wasn't the same. I could see it, critics wrote about it, she knew it. A Paramount cinematographer told me that during a take, Marlene trailed off midway through her lines to whisper: Where are you, Jo?

They didn't light her the way I did, he said. They didn't shoot her the way I did. They couldn't see her the way I did.

JO TOLD ME with a sad sort of smirk that he'd heard that Marlene had become the first and only actress in all of Hollywood to apply for a union technician card, just so she could light herself. While acting, she kept an eye on the lighting configuration by way of a huge mirror on the other side of the set, making adjustments till the perfect butterfly shadow appeared under her nose and above her lips. She ordered her own lights to mimic his setup, tried working with his cinematographer, but they couldn't achieve the same effect. Jo said he wanted to believe it was technical, too—that he needed to believe it more than she did. I tried to shoot every other woman the way I shot her, he said. They were no less beautiful, and some were far better actresses. But it never worked again, you know? They just weren't Marlene.

ANATAHAN WAS SCREENING in the afternoon, so I thought it was on Jo's schedule, but when the hour neared he suggested we go to the Piazza San Marco.

I don't want to see it, he said, and I don't want you to see it.

If you didn't want to see it, I remember asking, why are you here?

He turned to me with a rueful smile and shrugged.

At the Piazza San Marco, Jo bought me a green cashmere scarf. I still have it; I wear it in the winter. Then we ate the most delicious gnocchi I ever had in my life, served with a butter sage sauce in a tiny trattoria. We got lost in the alleys and ended up by the canal. One of the touristy gondolas with their gondoliers in striped shirts passed by, and I remarked that I'd never been on one. Leni Riefenstahl, Jo said, you won the Golden Lion in Venice, but you've never been on a gondola? He flagged it down. Jo steadied me, making sure I got in safe before he hopped on with the help of his cane. Immediately our gondolier assumed we were a retired German couple on holiday, and asked us in a mix of German and Italian how many years we had been married.

So, Jo said as he took my hand, it's coming to thirty years now.

And children?

None, Jo said.

I remember what the gondolier said: None? Then you must have big love, or big career.

Both, Jo said.

Both! The gondolier said.

I grinned at Jo as we glided through the backwaters of Venice.

IN THE EVENING there was a screening of *Olympia*.

We parted early as I wanted to take a shower, put on my makeup, and change into the dress I'd bought for the screening. It had some beadwork at the shoulders, and a matching shawl.

I was a little embarrassed to want to attend my own screening, since Jo had not gone to his. I told him he didn't have to come with me, but he insisted he would like to. We agreed to meet at the hotel lobby. When I went downstairs, I saw Jo waiting for me in a tuxedo, with his thin white hair neatly slicked back. As I got closer, I noticed one of the programmers from the festival. She looked very apologetic as she told me that in order to assuage protestors, they'd had to cancel my pre-screening introduction, and my postscreening Q&A. At least we didn't have to ax the entire thing, she said. I tried to hide my disappointment, especially in front of Jo. She said I could skip the screening if I felt more comfortable with that, but the truth was that I had been waiting to see *Olympia* on the big screen. Who knew when I'd get the chance again?

Jo saw my face and said to the programmer: We'll enter from the side, and sit in the back. The programmer said that would be okay, and she apologized again. There was a festival car waiting up front, she said, but it might be too conspicuous if we arrived in that vehicle—

Jo offered me his elbow.

It's a short stroll away, he remarked, who needs a car?

THE CINEMA WAS small, but even so, it was more than half empty. Though no one knew I was there, I felt quite ashamed. I was used to walking in on a red carpet, being greeted by a full house. Not an empty seat in the theater, cinephiles outside begging to take a ticket off someone's hands for twice the price. Maybe the protestors had frightened everyone off, or it was the time slot, it must have been programmed against one of the popular hotshots who was screening a new movie at the same time at a bigger venue. Sometimes you can't compete with all of that. I've learned to let go over the years. You have just got to be grateful that someone wants to show your old work on a big screen in its original format, as it should rightfully be seen, in a proper cinema. My epic films are not for small TVs and home stereos. They are meant to be experienced as a world that can envelope your senses fully.

This is why I love the movies, they sweep you away.

Olympia was starting.

Suddenly I was excited again, my palms soft with sweat. Frame by frame, it was just as beautiful as I remembered it to be, and it struck me that the best and most unknowable parts of ourselves are recorded in our work, and why should anything else matter?

Humans are pack creatures.

When someone booed for no reason at the mesmerizing pole-vault sequence, a few others echoed back. I became afraid—what if the booing grew louder and did not stop? What if everyone walked out and I was the only one left in here? What if they noticed me, and started throwing things at me, calling me awful names? In the dark Jo took my hand and squeezed it. I was just waiting for the part where Jesse Owens wins the one hundred meters. Anyone with eyes can see that I am not a racist. There I was documenting a black man winning the race for the whole world to see. How magnificently I've captured his victory. True enough, someone began to clap as Jesse Owens reached the finish line, and I was glad for that.

It was over so quickly. I could have stayed in there for hours.

As the credits rolled and the exit lights came on, there was a brief smattering of applause, and for a moment I wanted to stand up right where I was and say hello, just to wave, you know, and thank them for coming. But the applause was immediately extinguished when a voice shouted: *Fanculo al fascismo! Mai perdonare, mai dimenticare!*

Jo threw his jacket over me, and we waited in our seats as people filed out of the cinema.

I couldn't see anything through the dark wool, but my sense of sound was heightened. I heard every last footstep as my credits rolled. The film was over, but I wanted to tell them to come back, please come back. How many times will I have to say it? I have never been a Nazi. I was just an artist working in a certain place at a certain time. I am the scapegoat because it is easier to take your rage out on a woman, instead of the system. Why has that long shadow been cast over the rest of my life? Don't think I haven't suffered. Every last thing I loved has been taken from me. Do you know I never got to make another movie after *Tiefland*? I tried so hard, but all my projects after the war were blocked. Maybe that doesn't sound like much to you, but filmmaking was what I lived for. I would never again call "Action!" and hear the clack of a slate, assistant directors shouting for everyone to clear my shot as they scurried away before the camera rolled. I would never again hear the thunder of applause in a movie palace filled to maximum capacity, and rise to receive it with no weight on my shoulders. On the screen, everything is perfectible and nothing hurts. Life is just the opposite. Pockmarked, full of mistakes. You can't call for a reshoot to iron out your slipups, or edit them out of the final story. No, you have to live with everything. Can you understand, for a perfectionist, how rotten that is?

Leni, I heard Jo's voice.

Breathing deeply through the lining of his jacket to reduce the drumming in my ears, I recall pretending it was a fresh towel over my face—an old calmative from childhood. On hot summer days, my mother would wet them with thyme water and tie them around my neck to cool me off from an afternoon's play. That's enough now, she used to say, you are so active you should have been born a boy. I told her I liked being a girl. Of course you do, she said. I prayed for you to be born a girl, how many times have I told you?

Countless times she'd told me.

Did you know my mother had wanted to be an actress?

But that was as far as she got—she was afraid.

Does it ever change? What are women afraid of these days?

Nothing, and everything—

That they're too plain, too dumb, too fat, too thin. That it isn't the right time, the right place, the right thing. That one day they'll try for something they really want—then hear: No.

It'll be different for you, my mother would say to me. You shan't be just like everyone else. You'll go far, won't you, my darling girl?

Leni, I heard Jo say to me in the theater. There's no one left, it's safe. Let's go.

I remember forcing back my tears under his jacket: I was not going to cry. Not when I got everything I wished for.

Everyone knows my name. My movies, my pictures, they've stood the test of time. Even my haters can't say my work isn't beautiful. The last thing I am is ordinary. I can't turn back time, but in the ways I knew how, I must have made someone proud. I must have done some good in this world, too.

I did not cry then.

I am not going to cry now.

Marlon Brando
Lays an Egg
as News of Pearl Harbor
Reaches a Chicken Coop
in New York

十四

For years Anna May's line was stone cold. Hon, my job is to be real with you, her agent said. You're fifty-five, you're Asian American, you're a woman. Chin up. Ciao-ciao.

Her dry spell continued into 1960. Even before the end of the war, Oriental-tinged classics had passed firmly out of style. In the decade and a half since, sci-fi, youth rebellion, and noir thrillers were in demand, though of late the picture houses were emptier than ever. TV sitcoms kept everyone home, glued to the small screen. *I Love Lucy* was huge. All everyone wanted to talk about was marketing. Even as Anna May slid precariously from B pictures to Poverty Row studios, when approached to front a Colgate-Palmolive toothpaste campaign for a whopping wage, she had turned it down without thinking twice. The proposed TV spot was centered around the absurd visual of Anna May in a cheongsam sporting a Fu Manchu-esque toothpaste moustache, giving a wide grin to the camera as she held up the tube.

What does Fu Manchu have to do with toothpaste, Anna May had asked the ad man.

Nothing, the ad man had said.

Seeing what endorsements did for her B-list peers opened Anna May's eyes. Betty Furness's popularity soared for the next ten years, after she became the spokeswoman for Westinghouse appliances. She'd made more money with a string of two-minute refrigerator ads than she had her entire career playing hillbilly supporting parts. They were even terming Betty a "consumer advocate" these days. No one had any idea what that meant.

ANNA MAY'S AGENT still grumbled about her rejecting the tooth-paste spot. Would've been much easier to sell you for TV work if you'd

accepted that ad, her agent would say. We've pretty much missed the
boat now.

I'm not some product endorser, she protested, I'm a film actress.

Principles are lovely, her agent said, but we've entered a new age.
Why can't you be both? They're not mutually exclusive, and I want us
to do right by you.

Privately Anna May had to wonder—did she really have principles, or was it that it was Colgate? If Lanvin had come calling, would
she have turned it down just the same? In any case Anna May did not
regret passing on the ad, but she would have given anything to get one
of those evil Chinese vixen roles in a sumptuous production again.
Why is it that the screen Chinese is nearly always the villain? she'd
commented to *Film Weekly* as a young actress. And so crude a villain.
Murderous, treacherous, a snake in the grass. We are not like that. How
should we be, with a civilization that is so many times older than that
of the West? Protesting the ills of stereotyping, she had been far too
busy ferreting about for good-girl lead roles back then to revel in being
the bad girl. She'd never quite seen it this way till just a few years ago,
when she bumped into an over-the-hill B-lister at a gas station.

I'm just going to come right out and say it, the B-lister said. You got
the best parts.

I got the best parts? Anna May almost choked.

Never rode into the sunset with anyone, the B-lister was saying.
Someone pulls a gun on you? You twist a dagger into them. You had
the sexiest costumes, the sassiest lines. No kissing anyone up, you
kissed them *off*.

LAST WEEK, A phone call from her agent: Do you know Lana Turner?
Yes, Anna May said.

They're interested in having you play her housemaid.

The maid's name was Tawny. Anna May waited for herself to hang
up the phone. Instead she heard herself say: When do we start?

Her agent filled her in on the details, telling her not to worry, he
had her long absence from the screen covered. He read her the press
statement he'd prepared: Anna May Wong returns to big screen with

Lana Turner for *Portrait in Black* after spiritual hiatus. The veteran performer, best remembered for her roles as Hui Fei in *Shanghai Express* and Princess Ling Moy in the *Daughter of Fu Manchu,* has been cultivating bonsai in the Palisades and taking a break from the industry but is now ready to jump back in and make a splash.

Anna May was cringing on the other end of the line.

I don't know, she managed to say. Tawny's just a maid.

Hey bean, her agent said. Don't shortchange yourself now. Look where playing a maid in *Gone with the Wind* got Hattie McDaniel, eyes on the prize!

EVEN AS HER own career tanked, Anna May followed the movies religiously—1960 had been a fabulous year so far. She'd seen *Psycho, Hiroshima Mon Amour, La Dolce Vita, L'Avventura, The 400 Blows, Some Like It Hot, Breathless.*

Things were changing.

Whole movies could be shot on location with handheld cameras without scripts; there was no need for perfect lines played to cameras on sticks and huge sets in studio lots. In Hollywood, it was no longer illegal for a white character to kiss a brown or black or yellow one— the Motion Picture Production Code had been abolished, as if it should never have been there in the first place. Anna May still had a special place for Chaplin in her heart, but her new favorite performer was Marlon Brando. While everyone else projected their performance toward the camera or an imagined audience on the director's cue, he simply waited till he felt like doing something: mumble a line, smile, touch his costar.

If Brando did not feel it, he did nothing, said nothing.

How Anna May treasured that anecdote told by Brando's acting teacher, Stella Adler: In her West Village workshop in New York, Miss Adler had told the class that they were all chickens. In their chicken coop was a radio. Over the radio comes news of the bombing of Pearl Harbor.

React as chickens.

Bwak buk buk buk all the other students clucked madly, hopping around the auditorium, knocking into each other as they flapped their wings. One girl, who would later become a successful Broadway star, acted quiet and fearful. Across the room, in a corner, the boy who would be Brando folded up his wings and squatted down.

He laid an egg.

THE ONLY MOVIE anyone ever remembered Anna May in was *Shanghai Express,* a fact that would inadvertently be put to her in this manner: What was it like working with Marlene Dietrich?

In the beginning she worried that no matter her response, it would come off sounding insincere or bitter, even if she meant otherwise. But over the years Anna May saw that everyone carried with them their own fantastical impression of Marlene, skimmed off the cream of her diva public image: studio features, glossy covers, industry scandals, gossip columns. When Marlene played a glamorous singer in Billy Wilder's *A Foreign Affair* in the forties, her costar Jean Arthur made a ruckus accusing the director of playing favorites. The tabloids had published an account of Jean driving to Billy's house to confront him with: Marlene told you to burn my close-up, didn't she? Slated to appear in Hitchcock's *Stage Fright* in 1950, Marlene was rumored to have issued an ultimatum as regards her participation: No Dior, no Dietrich!

And so the answer Anna May gave did not matter, not in the least.

What was it like working with Marlene Dietrich? She'd come to smile sagely on these occasions. Just like everything you'd think it would be.

Anna May tried to avoid taking the route that would pass the large billboard of Marlene's face advertising her year-end gig with the Riviera. It had sprung up in the fall of '60. Vegas was booming if you were the right type of performer. One-upmanship was the sport of the day as Italian, Russian, and Jewish mobsters building up one casino resort after another tried to outdo one another on the strip: camel murals, wave pools, futuristic dance clubs, Old West steakhouses. By all accounts, they were generous paymasters when filling out their entertainment rosters, connoisseurs with real taste who knew what they were paying for. Nat King Cole, Liberace, and Mae West were earning the fattest paychecks anyone had ever seen. Even Hollywood couldn't compare. The papers said Marlene commanded at least sixty thousand dollars a week. Her 1960 show with the Riviera was part of a world tour including Germany, Israel, and France. She'd made the news when she became the only performer in Tel Aviv allowed to sing in German since the war. After Marlene's Vegas opening night was announced, that symmetrical face, which through the years so reminded Anna May of her own failure, began turning up all over town.

Billboards and newsstands were to be expected, and those she could ride or walk by with averted eyes, but the glossy poster tacked to a supermarket bulletin board in Anna May's neighborhood in the Palisades took her wholly by surprise. Hugging a bag of produce to her chest, Anna May stared at the tight, sequined dress, the triple-strand pearl choker, and the pout effected to look like the mouth had just blown a kiss. The cheekbones were as high as they'd ever been, the blond hair more platinum than before, across the forehead not a single discernible wrinkle. All in all, the face came across as invulnerable rather than beautiful.

Attack of the airbrush, or immoderate coats of foundation?

Anna May didn't mean to condescend, not when she knew she was so much worse for the wear. She should not like to imagine her own face on a poster. The last time a picture of hers was printed in the papers, it was a couple years back—for a drunk-driving incident. The level of toxicity in Anna May's blood was so high they had to give her an emergency blood transfusion. There was no one at her bedside when she came to. She was used to living alone, and had come to value deeply her independence over the years, where there was no need to acquiesce to anyone about anything, but for one of the few times in her life, Anna May thought: At the bottom of it all, this is why people marry and have kids. To have someone to wake up to on a hospital bed. When the doctor came around, she wanted to know: Could I have died?

Ma'am, the doctor said, you were basically dead.

She'd been clean for almost a year now, but her body had not recovered from the long years of abuse, forget about her face. Every week Anna May went to an expensive clinic to pump excess liquid out of her belly. The liver damage was irreversible, and she now followed a strict diet. All this "clean eating" was tasteless. Between sessions, she was careful to wear loose clothing, lest anyone cotton on to what did rather resemble a baby bump.

AND YET MARLENE at sixty looked just as assured as she had ever been at thirty. It'd been a long time. Anna May removed the thumb-tacks holding the poster up and slid it into her paper bag. As she was leaving the store, she was stopped by security. In the office she handed over the poster in silence, too embarrassed for words.

The guard admitted that he, too, was a Dietrich fan.

He wanted to see her show, but tickets were expensive, he said, and Vegas was something else. You really have to dress up for that town, he added, but once you're inside, the buffets are practically free!

Although it was just a couple hours' drive, Anna May had never been to Vegas, and she could only nod lamely. Pointless to tell him she was also an actress, much less begin to explain the tiniest of chival-rous inanities: that it'd felt wrong to see the face of an old friend tacked up between a posting for Swami's Self-Actualization Fellowship (Free Revitalizing Mood Crystal + Forty-Day Results Guaranteed Or Your Money Back!) and a lost white-and-tan Pomeranian named Pebbie (fourteen years of age, pink-nosed, bowlegged).

When Anna May got home from the grocery store, she called up the Riviera and booked a single ticket to Marlene's show. It had still been months away then, and was no cause for concern. But now that the day of the show had arrived, she was surprised to feel jumpy about seeing Marlene again. For any number of years after *Shanghai Express*, they'd bumped into each other, with predictable regularity, at the usual socials. Any time Anna May guessed that Marlene might be at a certain event, she fussed over her appearance, for fear of looking underdressed—or worse, overdressed—though she knew she'd barely exchange with Marlene a concise nod, a polite greeting. Both made it a point to keep that distance.

As the years went by, either Anna May's invitations to premieres and parties began drying up, or she stopped accepting them. Honestly, she could not say for certain which it was. And once she grew used to a quieter life, she found it hard to believe that she'd rolled around for so many years pretending she belonged in designer dresses she couldn't afford.

It had been some time since Anna May had to care about whether this evening bag went with that pair of shoes. She changed out of heels and into sensible flats before she left her apartment in a burgundy silk Chinese gown. Checking her appearance, she found it passable. It was a good thing she was tall and could still cut a fair figure. Getting into her old blue Chevy coupe, she made sure in her rearview mirror that she'd covered up all the liver spots on her cheeks. Before turning out toward the freeway, she stopped at a florist's, dithering between roses and lilies. Lilies were probably still Marlene's favorite, but perhaps it was more impersonal, then, to buy her roses?

The lilies were pricier than Anna May expected, but Vegas glowed from the freeway exit, and she was getting excited about seeing Marlene again. Everything was gigantic and lit up in neon: a winking cowboy, a rotating star, a sultan with arms akimbo, a lady's silver slipper with a yellow bow. Reaching the Riviera, Anna May gave her coupe to the valet as a muscly, tail-finned Cadillac rolled past. The Riviera was one of the few casinos on the strip with a high-rise hotel tower. Looking out to the poolside, she saw women who'd thought to pair their two-piece swimsuits with three-inch heels. As she went through the air-conditioned lobby, solicitous staff directed ticketed guests away from the gambling lounges to the Versailles Room, where Marlene would be performing.

Every seat was filled, and the crowd was buzzing.

The emerald earrings of the woman next to Anna May were so pendulous and heavy, they looked like they were about to tear right through her earlobes. Evidently, they were meant to match the bright-green cling wrap she was wearing on her body, which appeared to be adhered at her shoulder to the armpit of a man in a fez.

As the lights dimmed, a hush settled.

In the dark, Anna May could still recognize that unmistakable voice saying hello into a microphone. Marlene said hello as if they were the longest two syllables in the world. When the spotlight hit her, she was standing center stage, shimmying a shoulder in her much-publicized swansdown coat. The audience cheered. The coat wiggled down a notch and Marlene sighed into the microphone: Good evening, Vegas, there's no other city in the world like you, is there?

Her voice was deeper now.

Her eyes were sleepier and her mouth thinner, but Anna May had already noticed those details from following Marlene's career through the years. Age had hardly slowed her down—she'd last seen Marlene on the big screen in Orson Welles's *Touch of Evil*. Marlene played a brothel madam in Mexico, and Anna May could recall the look in her eyes as she delivered that killer line: You have no future. It's all used up. Welles was one of those directors Anna May wished to work with, but if it had yet to happen for her by now, she knew it was likely to remain a dream.

Catcalls from the floor, as Marlene's coat came off in one flamboyant movement. Seeing what she had on beneath, Anna May had to smile. In a tight dress of nude mesh, Marlene raised an eyebrow at the room. Strategically placed Swarovski crystals covered her bits, and it was obvious that she was not wearing a bra. Marlene's singing voice had slid back from her spoken mid-Atlantic accent, that sardonic German edge was back as she breezed through her set list. Midway she changed into an all-white men's tuxedo suit and a top hat. The way Marlene used to wear menswear had been so natural, contrarian, and new. Heads turned not for the fact that she was in a finely cut pant and chunky-heeled oxfords; they turned to see just how a woman who was utterly herself walked into a room.

Now it all looked like props to Anna May.

Marlene was singing "I've Grown Accustomed to Her Face" and winking knowingly to the crowd:

I'm very grateful she's a woman and so easy to forget
rather like a habit one can always break and yet—

The lady onstage was a savvy businessperson, clever at peddling her own nostalgia before it ran out. Of course, the audience was still hungry for her pantomime. Between songs Marlene tossed in the occasional dirty joke. It made Anna May twitch to imagine Marlene saying night after night: What does one saggy boob say to the other saggy boob? The audience, already cracking up, even before she delivered the punch line: If we don't get some support, people will think we're nuts! That was what the Riviera had written Marlene such a big check for, what people drove out to see: not Marlene, but how much Marlene had aged. For the finale Marlene came out in tiny black shorts, dressed in a circus ringmaster's topcoat and tails, with a whip in hand, as young showgirls in animal costumes revolved around her in cages.

She disappeared after the encore, throwing kisses at the crowd.

As the lights came back on, Anna May wasn't sure what to do next. She hadn't gone through her connections to set up a backstage invite in advance, and in fact she was no longer certain if she wanted to greet Marlene face-to-face. The crowd was on their feet, spilling out into the casino. Anna May stood to go, too, leaving the bunch of lilies behind on her seat. Before she made it out of the Versailles Room, an usher rushed up to her with the bouquet. Ma'am, he said, you forgot this. Stage door's to the left of the box office, he added helpfully, you won't miss it.

A LONG LINE snaked around the corner.

Anna May loitered around, unwilling to join up, but not quite yet ready to leave. The queue was dotted with lilies, too, some bouquets much larger than hers. Marlene emerged from the doors far sooner than anyone expected, flanked by security. It was just fifteen or twenty minutes after the last curtain call, but she was looking fresh in a pleated taffeta dress and two-toned Chanel heels. Her strut seemed less steady than before, but she really knew how to move in couture. Onstage, at a safe distance, it had been easy to dismiss: she was turning old tricks. Less than ten feet away now, everything was cantilevering toward Marlene, and it was impossible to discount her presence. Anna May turned away, desperate to leave unnoticed, signaling silently for a valet's attention so she could get her car and go.

Anna? She heard it from behind her.

Marlene still said it with two hard As.

She turned to see Marlene striding forward, reaching out to catch her by the elbow, and leaning in to kiss her on both cheeks as security held off the fans waiting in line. The lilies were crushed between them. Shrugging off a sheepish laugh, Anna May offered them up to Marlene. Their fingers touched briefly as the lilies changed hands, resting in Marlene's arms for just a beat before they were conducted away to a minder. Marlene had turned briskly to an assistant: Why wasn't Miss Wong shown to the greenroom?

Oh, Anna May said, I didn't tell anyone I was here. I bought my own ticket.

Pardon? Marlene said it the French way. You should've just had your manager write mine for a VIP seat, Marlene scolded as she pulled her into her posse. What do we keep those bloodsuckers around for? Already Marlene was introducing her to the pianist, the publicist, a bevy of backup dancers, and a laddish young man who was referred to as a "friend of the family." Anna May couldn't be sure, but she took this to mean the mob. He was in a perfectly pressed pinstripe suit and half-tinted glasses he kept on indoors.

Let's go, Marlene said. After party.

Clicking her fingers, she began to walk down the line, signing autographs at random and receiving bouquets expertly without breaking the staccato rhythm of her stride, as they all fitted themselves into a stretch limousine that had pulled up silently on the side. Their big ride dropped them off outside a Polynesian bar. A white girl in a grass skirt showed them to a private section cordoned off with a frangipani chain. They reclined on rattan sofas and futons. Anna May failed to see why Marlene would rope her into this if she was going to be busy horsing around with the "friend of the family"—Marlene was pressed up against the youngster as he explained that the giant tiki moai statues out front flanking the little wooden bridge of this bar were fakes, whereas the one in his Malibu garden had been shipped from Easter Island itself. The grass-skirted waitress was back to take orders for "Original Drinks from the Far Islands."

Anna May said she would pass.

At this, Marlene appeared to remember that Anna May was present. That's not permitted, she called out, let me put in an order for Miss Wong. She scanned the menu. Easy, she said, flashing Anna May a smile, the Savage Island Pearl Cocktail. As the menu went around the table, someone pointed out that there was a Genghis Khan steak. Breakfast of champions, Marlene said, and everyone laughed. The drinks arrived in no time, each with its own tropical presentation. Check out these teeny-weeny umbrellas, someone cooed, don't they make you feel like you're on instant vacation? They raised their drinks, and someone proposed a toast to Marlene. Not forgetting the Riviera, Marlene added, nodding around her posse to acknowledge the relevant people, my musicians, my dancers—and the most amazing Asian American actress of our time. Heads turned quizzically toward Anna May, and she felt uncomfortable. She wanted to say it wasn't so difficult to be the most amazing Asian American actress of your time when you were the only one, but of course the toast wasn't really about her. Everyone was already clinking glasses and uttering cheers, bottoms up!

Anna May's glass met Marlene's across the low rattan table and she lifted the cocktail to her lips. She knew Marlene was watching now, to make sure she drank. As soon as Anna May downed her cocktail, Marlene moved on. For a while she observed Marlene put away drink after drink, person after person. When the light caught Marlene's face, Anna May noticed that she'd taped back the skin around her eyes so it would look tighter.

A young woman sidled up to Anna May.

I'm so getting statement bangs like yours, she said. What's your name again?

Anna May had not even answered this before the young woman parachuted into her own bio: part Italian, she'd studied drama under so-and-so, more Meisner, less Stanislavski, also had she mentioned she was the niece of such-and-such, you know, the notable screenwriter? Probably she was totally the inspiration for Ann in *Roman Holiday*, because she'd fallen asleep on a park bench once after smoking a roach, and her uncle had found her—Anna May waited patiently for the young woman to finish, till she began to see that the story had no end.

Excuse me, Anna May squeezed in finally, I have to go.

Ah, the young woman said. Where're you off to?

I'm off, Anna May stalled, to the bathroom.

She wanted to say good-bye to Marlene, but that woman was nowhere to be found. So be it, she did not have it in her to endure any more small talk with this gang. In the bathroom she went into a cubicle and put two fingers down her throat to force up the whiskey from her stomach. When she was done, she checked that no one else was out-side before she stepped out. Washing her hands at the sink and already looking forward to being home, Anna May noticed a cubicle door creak open slowly from behind her. It was Marlene, huddled over the top of the toilet's closed seat cover, hands bracing herself against the cubicle's walls. Her left ankle was huge and swollen. Her Chanel heels and a pair of compression stockings lay on the floor. Marlene looked like she was trying to force her grimace into a smile as she said: Would you be a dear and get me some ice?

I'll go get help, Anna May said, but Marlene shook her head.

No, Anna, she said firmly. Just some ice, please.

MARLENE HAD MISSED a step and taken a fall right before the show, but she did not want to cancel the performance. Twenty grand a night, Marlene said. She'd injected her legs with a champion blend of cortisone and morphine, felt invincible, and gone right on with the program, but those drugs must be wearing off right about now.

Anna May locked the door to the bathroom from the inside before Marlene agreed to come out of the stall. You're sure? Marlene called out. Yes, Anna May said, rattling the door to show her. Marlene unzipped her dress, then began to remove a flesh-colored latex suit wrapping and contouring her body from neck to ankle. Anna May had not even noticed it was there. My support system, Marlene joked. Helping Marlene out of the suit, Anna May was surprised at how loose Marlene's flesh was to the touch. The veins in both her calves were blue, even the uninjured calf. There was hardly any pulse in them as Anna May tied the ice to Marlene's shin in her shawl.

She asked: How did you walk out of the dressing room?

Willpower, Marlene quipped. I'm German, remember? She fiddled for a cigarette in her bag. Do you think there's a smoke alarm in here? Before Anna May could check, Marlene had lit up. Want one?

Anna May shook her head.

You should get that checked out, she said.

Doctors, Marlene scoffed. Professional wet blankets! Why should we pay them to tell us what we can't do? She sat down on the bathroom floor, leaning against the wall and exhaling a huge puff of cigarette smoke. You know what they said? Double amputation in the near future, if I didn't get treated right away. It's been a year. Look, I'm still here and perfectly able-bodied, aren't I?

Hold up, Anna May said, sitting beside her and rearranging the sliding ice compress. Amputation?

The only sensible thing to do, Marlene went on airily, ignoring her, was to redesign my wardrobe. Ten pairs of custom-made boots in graded sizes, to accommodate the swelling. Even without the fall, they bloat up to a full inch all around when I'm on my feet for too long. I change in and out of the larger sizes as the show progresses, but the audience notices nothing, right?

Right, Anna May said, but why can't you be seated?

Anna, Marlene said. People pay to have me onstage! The least I can do is be upright. My next tour stop is Cannes, thirty grand for three shows. I gave them a discount in Germany, but a girl in a mullet—already you can see she's not going to go far in life—spat in my face. I'm never going back. Marlene pushed a smoke ring out of her mouth. You know, she said slowly, I kept that old apartment. Always thought I'd go home to Berlin. To retire—or die, for that matter. They watched the smoke ring hang in the still air. You're not going to die, Anna May said firmly, and it doesn't look like you're about to retire. The shape of the smoke was coming apart by the time Anna May realized she knew just which apartment Marlene was talking about. In any case, she went on, you're probably going to live forever. Marlene made a face at her, as if to say such maudlin consolations weren't necessary between them. No, really, Anna May said. How should I put it? I saw your face on a mug in a gift shop in the Palisades.

Well, Marlene said, I don't know whether to laugh or to cry.

They sat in comfortable silence as Marlene finished her cigarette.

How's your leg doing? Anna May asked.

Better, Marlene said. Everything's nice and numb now.

We'd better get you back outside, Anna May said, everyone must be wondering where you are. No no, Marlene said. Take me back to the Riviera, please. And not in the limo waiting in the parking lot, she added quickly, then they'll know I've left. Anna May was trying to understand what Marlene meant. The after parties, Marlene said, they're in my contract.

For a moment she was quiet, and Anna May felt sorry for her. But Marlene had already begun to busy herself, shaking out two crumpled Hermès silk scarves with a flourish. Come, she said, signaling to Anna May. When Anna May didn't move, Marlene inched forward to wrap the scarf first around the crown of her head, then over her mouth, nose, and cheeks. The two silk ends she brought to the back of Anna May's head and tied a dead knot. I always keep one or two handy, Marlene said, they're very helpful.

This is ridiculous, Anna May said. Anyway, I don't get spotted anymore.

With a face like that? Marlene said. Rubbish! Can you breathe in there?

THEY SLIPPED OUT through the back of the club in their makeshift silk masks, Marlene gripping Anna May's arm to steady herself as they hailed a cab. In the cab they kept silent, but Anna May's shroud had begun to slide down her nose, and she fidgeted to keep it in place.

Everything okay back there? the cabbie asked. He was a young Latino in a rumpled T-shirt. Yes, Marlene called out, we're perfectly fine. The words came out muffled. Marlene turned to Anna May to readjust the scarf. The cabbie looked uncomfortable as he eyed them in the rearview mirror. What's with the hankies, he said, you sick or something?

At this Anna May burst out laughing.

She began to untie the scarf, even though Marlene was shaking her head vehemently. My friend here is a hypochondriac, Anna May said to the cabbie. I'm sorry? the cabbie said. She's afraid of cooties, Anna May said. Marlene pinched her. Ow, Anna May said. Are you okay, ma'am? The cabbie seemed very confused. Look, ladies, he said, you're not taking me for a ride, are you? Some skank already ran off on me without paying this evening. If that's what you two're thinking, I'm going to have to let you off right here, right now.

He pulled up the hand brake.

They were on a street corner with a cheap-looking motel, lit up by a large horseshoe. Even though Marlene's face was swaddled securely in silk, Anna May could read the indignation all over it. Rifling through her purse, Marlene brandished a big fifty-dollar bill. Look, sonny, Marlene said, peeling back the silk around her mouth to speak sharp and clear. This here's more than ten times the fare. Yours to keep, if you shut your trap the rest of the way back. The cabbie took the bill from

Marlene, checking for the watermark. He let out a low whistle. You ain't shitting, he said. Nope, Marlene agreed, I'm worth my weight in gold.

They rode in silence till the cab passed a nondescript late-night diner. Pull over, Marlene said. Make a detour. What is it? Anna May asked. Ninety-nine-cent shrimp cocktails, Marlene said importantly, pointing to the flashing neon sign outside. Anna May suggested it would be easier to get something to eat back at the Riviera. Of course, Marlene said, but what would be the fun in that?

Marlene drew out another fifty-dollar bill.

I want you to go in there, she said to the cabbie, and get two shrimp cocktails. Three, she added, if you'd like one as well. She gave him another fifty-dollar bill to pay for the shrimp cocktails. Tell them for fifty dollars you want it for here, she said, but to go. He looked nonplussed. For here but to go, Marlene explained as if it were obvious, you're paying good money to take the works with you—glass, spoon, and all. He thought for a moment, eyes on the fifty. Ma'am, he said, I'll try my best. Then he turned to them seriously. Ma'am, he said. You're not going to carjack me, are you? Sweetheart, Marlene said, honestly I don't know where you get your ideas from!

He left them in the cab.

Marlene leaned over Anna May to roll down the window. Hey, she called out, see if you can pinch a bottle of hot sauce on the way out! The cabbie signaled A-OK, and Marlene bobbed her head at him, the offhand nod of a woman who was used to getting whatever she wanted wherever she went. So, Anna May said, I guess some things never change.

What? Marlene wanted to know.

You know what I mean, Anna May said.

You say that like it's a bad thing, Marlene said. She turned to her and smiled. Have I told you how happy I am to see you, Anna?

SIGHTING THE CABBIE'S silhouette walking back toward them balancing three cocktail glasses between his two hands, Marlene let out a whoop. Anna May reached across to open the front door so he could come back in. Señoritas, he bowed as he passed them their shrimp cocktails and cutlery. He dipped his hand into his back pocket and presented a bottle of hot sauce. Excellent, Marlene exclaimed, ripping off her scarf and pecking him on the cheek, I knew we could count on you! Stunned, he relaxed into his seat. Knicked the hot sauce, he mumbled thickly. No one saw, I don't think. Done dousing her cocktail, Marlene turned to Anna May: Want some? Just a bit, Anna May said, as Marlene let loose a whole volley by accident. Oops, she said. As they rolled out of the parking lot over a hump, Marlene screeched and dripped gravy all over the backseat.

The cabbie was tuning through radio channels.

He stopped on Connie Francis's "Who's Sorry Now?"

Anna May had always thought that Connie Francis was daytime pop, but listening to this song past midnight in the back of a Yellow Cab, shrimp cocktail in hand, beside an old friend who was singing along with full-throated gusto, she wasn't so sure. Then the song ended, and the station program segued into a late-night talk show. They were quiet for a while, until the cabbie began to hum "Cuando Calienta el Sol" over the radio's indistinct banter, tapping his fingers on the steering wheel. When Marlene came in at the chorus in what was clearly phonetic Spanish, the cabbie joined in with native facility. He had a beautiful baritone. Starting tentatively, his voice grew stronger, and Anna May heard Marlene pulling back to harmonize with him.

The cabbie was in top form.

This was the real show, Anna May thought, leaning back in the cab. There are never any tickets to the real show. Marlene's eyes were shut tight as they hit the final verse, and the cabbie had lifted his hands off the steering wheel, *mi delirio, me estremezco, oh oh oh!* Anna May drank in every last consonant until an empty echo rippled through the moving vehicle. All that was left now was the engine's muted hum, and the laugh track on the radio. Anna May didn't know what to say, so she put her hand on Marlene's knee. But Marlene was noisily spooning up the last of her shrimp cocktail, scraping the bottom of the glass, and if Anna May knew her at all, Marlene was doing it just to undercut the emotion of the moment, the way the best directors followed a heavy scene with a light one, or vice versa. True enough, when she was done, she turned to Anna May with a sly, smug look. Tell me, Anna, Marlene said, delivering the line like it was stock dialogue from a drive-in movie and she was some sort of teen idol, tell me this isn't the best ninety-nine-cent shrimp cocktail you've ever had?

As per Marlene's instructions, the cabbie dropped them off at the Riviera's service entrance so they could sneak in from the back. Empty cocktail glasses clinked in the backseat. I'm sorry I didn't recognize you earlier, he said reverentially, bidding them farewell.

That's no problem at all, Marlene said magnanimously.

Before you go, could you please, he blushed, sign an autograph for me, Miss West?

ANNA MAY WAS laughing so hard she had to stop and bend over as they made their way through the corridor of the service entrance. You be the judge, Anna! That minx is at least ten years older than me, Marlene was fuming, and a whole head shorter. Do I look anything like Mae West? Not to mention the bucked teeth, Marlene added sourly, and those farm-girl tits. Don't get me wrong—I like Mae, but young people these days have shit for brains!

Anna May had sunk down to the carpeted corridor floor.

Get back up this instant, Marlene said, hooking Anna May's arm in hers, where are your manners! Anna May let Marlene pull her up, but a few steps later she'd burst out laughing again. For all her bravado, Marlene had not said anything to the cabbie about his grave mistake. Silently she'd taken his pen and written M, then A in block letters on the bill of his baseball cap, before hesitating and passing it back.

Ma, Anna May said weakly, Ma.

You're cruel, Marlene pouted, but she was trying not to laugh, too.

Arm in arm they careened down the service hall, passing gigantic carts of unlaundered sheets. Can you smell it? Marlene said loudly, sniffing the air. Makeup sex, breakup sex, Christian sex, heathen sex—

A chambermaid down the hallway turned back, and Anna May nudged Marlene. Marlene winced. Her leg must be hurting, Anna May had forgotten all about that. Shut your mouth and lean on me, Anna May said as they found the elevator. Marlene was heavier than she had expected and it was difficult to prop her up, but they managed to make their way back to the guest wing and into Marlene's corner suite after crisscrossing service corridors.

We made it, Anna!

Anna May looked around the suite. Bouquets of lilies on the dresser, who knew where hers had gone? It was just another bunch of flowers. Several pairs of boots were lined up against the wall. If Marlene hadn't mentioned their half-size variations, Anna May would have thought they were identical spares. Marlene made straight for the telephone to check through her voice messages. There was just one from her manager, who wanted to know if she was still at the after party.

Nothing from *him*, Marlene said. He doesn't even care!

She looked over at Anna May, as if expecting her to ask: Who?

Anna May was not about to be drawn into any of this. It took her no effort to step away, saying: Let me go run you a warm bath. She saw Marlene's face fall as she walked away, but there was nothing she could or should do about that. In the bathroom, waiting for the tub to fill up, Anna May recapped a tube of lipstick on the vanity counter. Beside it was a squarish hairbrush with wire bristles filled with linty blond hair, and a half-used travel-sized bottle of expensive-looking hand lotion. Anna May worked the rich cream into her fingers. When she got back to the room, Marlene had fallen asleep. Walking in on her like this was a nice secret to keep. To know that this face could look susceptible and unknowing, too, parted lips breathing in and out with a slight wheeze. She tapped Marlene on the shoulder, waking her gently.

The bathwater will get cold, Anna May said.

Marlene frowned as her eyes readjusted to the light, and then she jumped right back into action. Shall we go down to the Hickory for porterhouse steaks, Anna? There's an open-flame grill in the middle of the restaurant, and you can watch your meat being done. Plus it's all on the house, I pay for nothing in the Riviera. Those gangsters really know how to treat you like a lady.

It's way past midnight, Anna May said.

I'll make us some coffee, Marlene said, and we can head over to the blackjack lounge or the slot machines. I haven't much luck at slots but blackjack? I never lose if I'm playing a heart hand. And the croupiers— twins—so cute! I've been working on them.

It's late, Anna May said, I think I should go.

You could stay the night, Marlene said, nodding toward the luxurious room.

I'm getting too old for sleepovers, Anna May said, and so are you.

Pooh, Marlene said, waving a hand, speak for yourself! We could have room service for breakfast, she added, they make the best pancakes, and they iron the newspapers. How about that?

Marlene was getting carried away, and it was all too clear now: her wants were not needs, they had always been whims. Thirty years ago, Anna May might have stayed—and although she was not surprised by any of this, she was disappointed that Marlene had not even noticed any change whatsoever in her mood, and was still going on. This suite is *huge*, she was saying, I told them I had no need for something so large, but they insisted—

Don't you ever get tired of yourself? Anna May asked.

Marlene stared unblinkingly back at her, but Anna May could see from her eyes that she was hurt. It was too late to take the words back, and she did not want to pretend she was sorry. Uncharacteristically, Marlene seemed to have nothing to say. Her hot-ironed curls were coming loose. I'm going to go, Anna May said, okay? Without waiting for an answer she slipped out of Marlene's suite, hearing the heavy door click shut behind her as she made her way down the carpeted corridor.

WAITING FOR THE valet to get back to the driveway with her car, Anna May was glad she would be out of Vegas soon. Nothing on the strip felt real, she thought, everything was made to seem like it was something else. Across the road a big sign for cheap Indian jewelry was flashing, 50 PERCENT OFF. Someone lit a cigarette beside her on the Riviera's driveway, and she was about to move away from the smoke when she realized it was Marlene. She'd thrown on a gabardine coat and dark glasses and was leaning her weight on a hotel umbrella for support. Anna May was surprised Marlene had come down, but she gave her a cool smile. I forgot to thank you, Marlene began, and who knows when I'll see you again. In another ten years I could be a double amputee, she joked, taking a drag, but there's probably a market for *that.* But really now, she turned to face Anna May more directly, thank you. I don't know what I'd have done without you.

Knowing you, Anna May said lightly, you'd have found a way.

She couldn't see Marlene's eyes behind her dark glasses.

Yes, Marlene said. But tonight was kind of fun, wasn't it?

Sure, Anna May said noncommittally. The valet was pulling up in her beat-up blue coupe. It was nothing like Marlene's chauffeured limo, and Anna May was glad to note that she didn't care, and wasn't embarrassed, that Marlene was seeing this. My car's here, she said to Marlene as the valet got out and held the door open. Marlene ground her cigarette out under her heel and stepped toward Anna May. They embraced formally, touching cheek to cheek. Between Jo and you, Marlene murmured, *Shanghai Express* was my best picture. Don't you agree? There was nothing to agree with, Anna May thought. We never kept in touch, Marlene said as they came apart. She removed her dark glasses, and her eyes were uncertain, just this once. You don't hate me, do you?

No, Anna May said carefully. What would I hate you for?

You know, Marlene said. We could have given them something to talk about.

An old look began to pass between them. First it was real. Then it became a look only two actresses could have shared. She was starting to open herself up, to let the way Marlene was looking at her affect the way she looked back. The valet stood at the car door. Her engine was running. If she didn't go now, she might never leave. Take care of the legs, Anna May said as she leaned in to kiss the fine wrinkles crinkling the ends of Marlene's eyes. That glamorous goose had piled on two layers of false lashes and they tickled her lips at their ends.

Good-bye, Shanghai Lily, she said.

Anna May did not look back as she slid into the driver's seat. The valet shut the door with just the right amount of effort to make it catch briskly, without slamming. Discreetly, as she drove off, she watched the small shape of Marlene recede in the rearview mirror. Marlene was putting her dark glasses back on, but she did not step back into the hotel right away. That might have meant little to nothing, but for Anna May it was enough: this woman, standing on a porch, watching her leave. It was not until Anna May rounded the bend of the driveway that she saw Marlene pull her coat more tightly around her and limp inside with the help of the umbrella, as the bellboy opened the heavy glass door with a smart salute.

COMING TO THREE in the morning, the asphalt grids of any given city are thick with the warm shadows of the day gone by. Riding through her town, Anna May rolled down the window. I love you better by night, she thought. L.A. never looked more beautiful than when it was empty. The tall palm trees on either side of the long boulevard were planted in such straight lines their dark silhouettes looked like a desert mirage with no beginning and no end. Passing the quiet streets, she smiled to no one, for no reason she could think of. She slowed to a halt at a red light, waiting patiently for the pedestrian sign to be done with its urgent blinking, although nobody was there to cross the road. She put all ten fingers to her nose and inhaled. Marlene's hand cream had dried down to something sweet and dirty, like old money and lavender sprigs left forgotten inside a calfskin satchel. When the light turned green, Anna May floored the accelerator. Picking up speed down the long road, she leaned out to feel the night breeze cut against her cheek, bangs blowing in every which direction as she swept them out of her eyes and raced back home.

Shanghai Express was banned in China for its political window dressing and the implicit suggestion that law and order were ineffectual: the film is set during the Nationalist-Communist civil war, and the titular Shanghai–Peking express train is held up by a band of bandits. There was even an arrest warrant issued for the degenerate foreigner Josef von Sternberg should he disembark on Chinese soil, for his continual insistence on insulting lines like "Time and life have little value in China" in his screenplay, and for the fundamental immorality of having a pair of prostitutes travel together.

When Anna May rode the real Shanghai express train in 1936, four years after making the film, she rode it alone. The voyage east had been suggested to Anna May by her agent, after the *Good Earth* casting fiasco with MGM.

Brood, her agent instructed, but brood photogenically.

Pack your high-collared silk dresses with the frog buttons, he advised. Send me pictures so I can field them out. Ink calligraphy, fan dancing, whatever, the works. Give me some variety. We'll send over a small documentary crew when you visit your ancestral village. There's bound to be some good footage there.

MGM had done extensive screen tests with Anna May in the spring of 1936 for the lead role of O-lan. *The Good Earth* was all set to be the first Hollywood production whose lead character was an Asian woman, played by an actual Asian woman. O-lan was not a strumpet or a villain, she was a real character, a strong-willed peasant tending to her harvests. Anna May had read the Pearl S. Buck novel even before it won the Pulitzer and brought to the screen test her personal copy. She'd reread it assiduously, highlighting all the parts about O-lan, and was already developing her mannerisms for the role when it was publicly announced that the part was going to Luise Rainer.

There must be a mistake, Anna May said to her agent. She'd even met with the head of the MGM costume department to give him ideas on authentic Chinese dress. He'd borrowed some of her cheongsams and made sketches based on old family pictures she'd shared with him.

Her agent showed her MGM's screen test notes:

> Too Chinese to play a Chinese. Does not fit my conception of what Chinese people look like. Recommend to use as atmosphere and not principal characters.

They want to know if you'll do another audition, her agent said. For the side character, Lotus Flower. Anna May started to laugh. Have you read the book? Anna May asked. Her agent said no. Lotus Flower is the villain, Anna May said. Luise Rainer is O-lan, Paul Muni is Wang, Charley Grapewin is Old Father, Jessie Ralph is Cuckoo—I can't possibly be the only real Chinese, playing the bad person—

I'm with you, her agent said, but let's not be hasty. It's a high-profile project. If you turn this down and shoot your mouth off about it, you could get a bad rep, fewer callbacks. Sleep on it. I'll ring you tomorrow. All night Anna May fantasized about firing her agent, but when he called her in the morning, she told him to schedule her in for an audition. She'd been so invested in the project, it was hard to give it up completely. In any case, she tried to rationalize it to herself, it was still a movie about Asians, and that was worth her while, wasn't it?

Atta girl, her agent said. That's the spirit.

Lotus Flower was a devious girl who tried to steal Wang, the honest farmer, away from O-lan, his honorable wife. For the audition Anna May was to "interpret an Oriental striptease." A week later, her agent called. MGM was going with Tilly Losch for the role of Lotus Flower. In terms of her acting, they liked Anna May's audition, but they thought that at thirty-one, she might be too old to play a young seductress. Also, there were some concerns that she would stick out like a sore thumb, since the rest of the cast would be in yellowface.

A reporter asked: Are you disappointed about *The Good Earth*?

How could I possibly be, Anna May said, when I'm too Chinese to play a Chinese?

For a week she forgot to eat, just lay on the couch with a couple of whiskey bottles within reach, phone off the hook, till she had to go answer the doorbell because it wouldn't stop ringing. It was her agent. He shook his head when he saw her. She let him in as she tried to decide if she was touched that he'd come to her door. Clean yourself up, he said grimly. I've booked you tickets to Shanghai. Shanghai? She laughed. What would I do there? He was junking her bottles and throwing her windows open. Take it as a break, he said. I don't need a break, she shrugged, swaying on her bare feet. Anna, he said. You need something in your life. No, she disagreed, I need nothing. Go put your face on, he said, I'll buy you lunch. Over paninis he told her to stay sober, take in new sights, keep a travel journal. As the food hit her stomach, she began to feel sick. I've wrangled some column space from the *L.A. Times*, he said. Pitched it as your China diary, a weekly dispatch. I'll hook you up with the editor later. We want to call it "Orientally Yours."

Ha-ha, she said.

You can thank me later, he said.

EN ROUTE TO SHANGHAI, Anna May had a stopover in Hong Kong, where a meet-and-greet with the press had been arranged for her. She turned from reporter to reporter, but they all had the one question for her, namely: why wasn't she married?

The microphone was thrust in her face.

I am wedded to my art, she said.

She read the English edition of the morning papers on board the cruise liner the next morning. It was printed that Anna May Wong was engaged to a wealthy European businessman named Art. Worse, they'd dug up the Eric Maschwitz business, even reproducing the lyrics to "These Foolish Things." This popular jazz standard was allegedly written for Wong after the pair committed multiple instances of adultery in London, the papers read. But even then, Maschwitz attempted to suppress his mistress's Asian identity by describing Wong's smile as "the smile of Garbo." Reader, can this be called love? Or should it more accurately be termed lust and shame? ANNA MAY WONG LOSES FACE FOR CHINA YET AGAIN.

It was a done deal.

Anything she did, public or private, could be hung by its thumbs and chalked up to that pet line of the Chinese press. But quite laudably, they were otherwise alive to the same sentiment as she—before things ended between them, when Anna May saw her man after "These Foolish Things" was released, she'd asked: "The smile of Garbo"?

He could not for the life of him understand what she was going on about. It's just a metaphor, love, he'd said. You're what's real, why are you upset?

A white songwriter is in love with a Chinese woman, has made frenzied love to her ten times in three days. Driven mad with passion when they are apart he writes a song about her. Lyrics flow out of him onto paper, black coffee is spilled on the piano. But he does not believe for a second that her lips can hold up the symbolic pizzazz of a jazz classic, and so defaults to the generic singularity of Garbo's Caucasian mouth to carry the bluesy melody. Anna May was afraid she was only ever going to be someone's side character, in real life or in the movies. It's just a metaphor, love.

Arriving in Shanghai, Anna May saw her pictures in the papers, but she could not read the Chinese headlines. She brought them over to the hotel reception to ask what they said. Ma'am would like to know what the papers say, the concierge repeated back to her uncertainly. Yes, she said. He swallowed. This one says you are a race traitor, he started, then stopped, not daring to meet her eye.

And? She prompted him to go on.

And—an arse-kissing American lapdog, he continued, looking up at her to see if he should go on. She nodded. An arse-kissing American lapdog with an abominable accent, he said, who can't even speak a squeak of Mandarin.

Rifling through the other papers she asked: Do they all say the same thing?

No, ma'am, the concierge said. This one asks why you are still single at this age. And this one says you look better on the screen than you do in real life, where you remind the reporter of a faded old bag.

· · ·

WHEN ANNA MAY headed north to visit Taishan, her ancestral home-town, the villagers formed a line to see her, not out of goodwill but curiosity. That shameless look on her toady face, she heard someone hiss in Cantonese. She thinks she's better than any of us! She's asking to be kicked!

Where were the tea drinkers and philosophers she'd dreamed of?

China was not in any way like the country she'd built up for herself. Now she saw clearly that the last thing it could be for her was a spiritual homeland. How harebrained that far-fetched scheme had been, and who was her father to have suggested it? What did he know about China, when he had been born in Sacramento?

The problem, she used to think, was L.A.

But now, finally, in a place where everyone was said to be the same as she, she was more out of place than ever. She had nothing in common with them but the color of their skin. It was exactly the same difference here: still they heckled her and called her names. The problem was neither L.A. nor Shanghai, she thought. The problem has always been me.

Contributing to MGM's decision to bypass Anna May for *The Good Earth* was something Pearl Buck had said. She'd expressly described O-lan's character to the studio as "not a slangy Anna May Wong type." When Anna May found out about this, she wanted to meet with this puffed-up novelist so she could slap the hot air out of her—a white woman writing about a Chinese woman had called her a type, purporting to know better what a Chinese village woman was like!

Yet as she moved through Taishan, Anna May was first ashamed, and later amused, even at her own expense, to admit she could see what Pearl Buck meant. The Chinese peasant folk had a guileless honesty to their bodies, a robust strength in their faces. Anna May was much too self-aware to resemble them in any way, and was it any wonder that Pearl Buck knew better? Having lived most of her life in China, Pearl Buck spoke various Chinese dialects, read and wrote in classical Chinese, translated Tang dynasty poems. She'd even survived the Boxer Rebellion and the Nanking uprising. Anna May had grown up on Chaplin flicks and Fitzgerald stories, trying to look like Clara Bow and sound like Baby Esther. Who was she to play O-lan? They couldn't cast me not because I was *too Chinese,* Anna May explained to herself, but because I was *too cosmopolitan!*

At the 1938 Academy Awards, Luise Rainer would go on to win the Best Actress Oscar for her convincing and compelling portrayal of O-lan.

SHANGHAI'S MOST EXCLUSIVE enclaves could easily be mistaken for Paris or London or New York. Furs, fashions, foods were up-to-the-minute, and the merrymaking never ended. Even if the press were baleful and unkind, Anna May was still invited to dine out with the local and expatriate elite night after night. Over dinner in a fine French restaurant booked by a popular Cantonese songstress who was wedded to the city's Belgian ambassador, a retired Chinese journalist said to her in clipped, British-accented English: Excuse my frankness, but you're quite charming in person—you're not nearly as obnoxious as I thought you would be!

He had been the chief film critic of the biggest English newspaper in Shanghai, and confessed that he'd written a scathing review of *Piccadilly* some ten years ago.

It was not because she was a Chinese girl who wore a cloche hat and knew how to jive to jazz, he said, they had plenty of new women in Shanghai who dressed and danced just like her character, Shosho. It was not even that she was a Chinese girl in the film, but Shosho was a Japanese name; perhaps that oversight was out of her control. But why was it that Shosho did a "Chinese dance" in a "Chinese costume"—when her dance and costume were obviously Siamese! It was a spectacular sequence, but Anna May couldn't blame him for feeling outraged when he'd read her eager declarations in press interviews that she'd choreographed the dance herself, from some Far Eastern travel pictures she found in a shop in the Pacific Palisades.

A few guests turned toward Anna May, waiting to see what she had to say.

She was not sure, in the moment, that she understood him, and capitulated quickly to her stock response: To be a nonwhite actress in

Hollywood is to be a puppet playing by rules that are the opposite of your own beliefs. I was so tired of the roles I had to play, but if I didn't do what I was asked, I would be out of a job, and the role would still go to someone else who would be made to do the same thing anyway—

Here he interrupted her.

Even if you could not learn a Chinese dance for the role, Miss Wong, you could have just danced the Charleston or the polka. That would have been less deceitful, and I would have had no complaint.

It's just a dance, Anna May said, but as soon as the words left her mouth, she tasted the bitterness of having to smile and teach Lon Chaney and Renee Adoree how to use chopsticks when they were all acting together in *Mr. Wu*. Without naming names, she'd lamented to the press that MGM was not looking for Chinese, they were looking for *MGM-Chinese*, who knew next to nothing of the cultures they were portraying, were only mining them for a visual impression at the expense of authentic expression!

So it is not that we find you too daring, Miss Wong, the reporter was saying in a summative fashion, but that we find you quite derivative. You have found success in Hollywood not just for your talent, but your willingness to exploit Western fancy. Can't you smell your own hypocrisy? You speak out strongly against the prejudice you face in Hollywood, when the white devils do it to you. But as soon as you, an Asian American, are given the opportunity, you have no problems at all poaching from Asians who are not American. Worst of all, you think you are doing us a big favor with your false representations on the imperialist screen. In your own actions, you replicate the same bigotry you decry.

THE OTHER GUESTS at the table were trying to pretend that they were not listening in, but their forks and knives had stopped moving as they surveyed the dustup. Anna May floundered for something she could grab on to and fend him off with. She had no role models. Was pragmatism really a sin when the end of the stick she had been given was so short to begin with?

She could hardly put her hand around it.

The *Good Earth* snub was such a crying shame, she thought it afforded her the everlasting self-respect of suffering injustice with dignity. She had been determined to move through the ugly double standards of the industry with integrity, but why was this stranger telling her that not only was she far from the graceful martyr she thought herself to be, she was part of the problem?

Could anyone blame Hattie McDaniel for playing only maid roles?

And let us not forget the curious case of Hollywood's first sex symbol: Sessue Hayakawa had been a pre-Code headlining superstar, rivaling Charlie Chaplin and Douglas Fairbanks. Stepping out of his limousine in front of a theater in 1915, Sessue grimaced at a puddle. At once, dozens of white female fans fell over one another to spread their fur coats at his feet. His popularity upset many American men, who wrote disparaging letters to the studios. Sessue himself protested being typecast as an exotic man of sexual prowess, turning down the glamorous lead role in Paramount's blockbuster extravaganza *The Sheikh* in 1921. The lead role of *The Sheikh* was passed on to the then-unknown Rudolph Valentino, who became an overnight sensation, while Sessue was quickly downgraded following Hays Code prohibitions. Soon, the types of roles Sessue usually played were given instead to Euro-American actors, so as to assuage the menaced virility of white male viewers.

When Anna May and Sessue worked together on *Daughter of the Dragon*, he confided in her his one ambition: To play a hero. He was older then, but still handsome. He had a supporting part as a Scotland Yard sleuth in *Daughter of the Dragon*. It was a small role, but at least this time he wasn't a sadistic, cruel villain. That was left to Anna May, and Warner Oland, who played Fu Manchu, as usual. Anna May played his daughter, Ling Moy, an Oriental princess turned evil for vengeance, who spoke her lines in perfect English but had to refer to herself at every point in the third person: Ling Moy will do this, Ling Moy wants that, Ling Moy swears she will restore glory to the Fu ancestral tablet!

No matter what they make you do, Sessue said, think of it as jujitsu.

Jujitsu?

Sessue smiled. He hoped this wouldn't sound like Oriental flimflam, he told her, but he was, in fact, descended from a line of samurai back in Japan. Jujitsu was the gentle way, a weaponless defense developed by an Edo pacifist. Your opponent might be much bigger or stronger, he said, but you would be able to defeat him. Not by brute force or size, but by using his body weight against him. The smallest movement, the largest impact. Instead of resisting his force, yield—then use his movement to throw him.

We don't need a hundred lines, Anna May, he said. Steal the scene.

EVERYONE AROUND THE dinner table was staring, waiting to see what would happen next. They were no longer trying for discretion. Anna May had made no verbal response to the journalist's condemnation, but tears were running down her face. My apologies, Miss Wong, the journalist sputtered, offering her the dinner napkin he had already wiped his mouth on, I was only sparring with you.

She sat there without cleaning the tears beginning to streak her makeup, keeping her eyes at a fixed point before her, on a platter of imported cheese and terrine. The hostess songstress cleared her throat. Would anyone like to take a look at the dessert menu? No one dared to answer. The air was tense, but in fact Anna May was completely calm inside. Sitting there without moving, hardly blinking, she was working through all of it, waiting for the right moment to start. It was taking some time for the frustration and insecurity that had turned into embarrassment and anxiety to pass through into quiet rage, but she would not begin until she was ready. She could feel it building up in the middle of her chest. When it swelled and reached the back of her throat, she held it down and snapped her purse open. She counted aloud some banknotes for dinner, inquired as to an appropriate tip amount, looked around the petrified table, nodded at the host to answer. It's on me, the woman stammered twice, first in Cantonese and then in English. Thanks, Anna May said, but I'd prefer not to owe anyone anything. No answer came, so she dropped a big bill onto her plate of half-eaten food, clicked her fingers, and called a waiter for her furs.

Cutlery plinked as she rose from her seat majestically.

She turned to the journalist.

An actress's authenticity is not in her life, she said, it is in her performance. Now did I dance well, or did I not?

She could feel the electrified gaze of the whole table on her as she took her time slipping into the mink coat the waiter held out for her. The journalist seemed to have run out of words. Simply, he watched. She exited the restaurant without looking back. Outside, she took a deep breath. The Shanghainese air was briny. Her heart raced from the pure rush of performance, and her body felt lighter than it had in years.

She broke into a jog.

Low heels sounding a sharp staccato against the uneven pavement, Anna May ran through the unfamiliar city, weaving through Chinese faces till she stopped short, out of breath, in the middle of a busy street, and turned abruptly, as if to look for someone over her shoulder, though she knew she was alone and expected nothing less. An anonymous face in the crowd who knew neither where she was nor whence she was headed—at least until she was next obliged to find her bearings—she was free.

十七

In the village of Taishan there still stands a willow tree, marked by a torn sash tied about its trunk. Once the sash would have been red. But the red had long faded to pink, and even the pink was bleached white by the sun. When the documentary crew met up with Anna May in her ancestral village during her 1936 visit, one of the shots they wanted to nail was of her stumbling upon a willow tree with a red sash, seemingly by pure happenstance, under which she would then sit as she revealed to viewers the story her father had repeated so often to her when she was a child, about the old woman and the new camera.

The location scout scoured the village.

He found no such tree, but there was a particularly picturesque willow with a bendy trunk, not so far from the river. He pointed it out to the producer, who agreed it was ideal and procured a red sash, which they tied around it. They wanted to shoot cutaways of Anna May walking up to it as she exclaimed: Look! This must be the willow tree. Anna May was reluctant in the beginning, but they managed to convince her that it would make great content for broadcast; they hadn't sailed all the way over to China just to capture peasant children playing with water buffalo by the river. She did the shot in one take, and they gave her a stool to sit on as the cameras rolled for her narration.

THERE WAS ONCE an old woman in the village who lived alone in a shack under a willow tree. The rest of her family had moved to the city and done well for themselves: first they pulled rickshaws, then they sold noodles, and when finally they saved enough for a rice mortar, they made a good living as rice merchants.

When her oldest grandson returned to the village for a short visit, the entire village was eager to ingratiate themselves with him, for he came with a small black object, no larger than his two hands, that was said to be able to transfer scenes and figures from real life onto a flat surface. Hung around his neck on a leather strap, it had an open top fitted on the inside with mirrors, various knobs on the hard casing outside, and two glass eyes. What unchaste malevolence from which white bone spirit had allowed such deception?

It's called a photograph, the city grandson explained.

His village grandmother regarded the object dubiously, asking: But how does it work?

He went down on one knee and tried to explain to her light, emulsion, negatives, and positives. She waved a hand at him. Every time that thing does that a part of your soul is stolen, she said. How else could our faces appear on a scrap of paper?

He laughed at her feudal superstition, cajoling her for a picture as he brought out a chair covered with a red cloth and seated her at a nice angle under the willow tree. She grumbled about young upstarts these days but went along with it—he was the oldest grandson, and she would have done anything to please him. He positioned her with artistic flair, raising her chin slightly, unloosing the tight fists she'd made of her hands and placed over her knees.

Don't move, he called out.

The flash went off. His grandmother blinked.

Then she groaned and toppled over.

When the young man reached her, she was dead.

IN REMEMBRANCE OF the old woman whose poor soul was swallowed whole by the new camera, Anna May's father would end the story each time, a red sash was tied around the willow tree in Taishan.

What do you think I am, a baby? Anna May said each time her father told her the tale. I am not going to fall for a story as silly as that.

Suit yourself, her father said. Just don't say I didn't warn you.

What happens if you lose part of your soul?

He smiled at her, smoothing her hair back as he said: Don't you think it would be best if you never had to find out?

. . .

ON THE DAY that Anna May finally decided to chance a visit to the photo studio, she wore a charmeuse dress that had been left uncollected by a customer at Wong Sam Sing's Chinese Hand Laundry. Taking the hem up and the waist in, she'd altered it in a childish stitch, trying to make it fit her as best she could. The photographer's studio was filled with portraits, silver gelatin prints and photographic plates of his clients. Anna May observed them on tiptoe before she was called to the backdrop. Looking at the photographer and the camera aimed at her like a gun, her knees went soft. To be an actress, she would give anything. Even if it robbed her, there was no room for fear of the camera. One day, she swore, it would all be worth it. Her eyes were beginning to water. She tried to hold them wide open to round them out, so her pupils would appear larger, her single eyelids more contoured.

Relax, the photographer said.

She smiled.

The flash was blinding.

十八

Tawny the housemaid was Anna May's final role in a movie. She wears a stiff black uniform and keeps a clean house. Another character in the film tells her: You oughta save your wise words for a fortune cookie! Whenever she appears in a scene, the background music switches zealously to East Asian instrumental strings, just in case the viewer has not noticed that a Chinese woman is on the screen.

When Anna May passed on in the spring of 1961 from pulmonary failure brought on by liver cirrhosis, all the papers recycled that exquisite folk proverb in their obituaries, passed on to the statuesque Chinese actress by her laundryman father:

Every time your picture is taken, you lose part of your soul.

It was Rudi, reading papers in the kitchen of his chicken ranch in the San Fernando Valley—purchased for him by Marlene as a retirement home and project—who saw the notice. They'd printed one of the publicity stills from *Shanghai Express* to accompany the obituary, the one with Anna May in a heavy brocade gown next to Marlene in a dress of glossy black feathers.

Marlene had "just popped by" the ranch in a tight skirt and ankle boots, with enough filet mignon to feed a battalion. She'd rounded off her North American performances and was about to set off on her French tour. She wanted to make sure he was well fed while she was gone. The meat had already been presliced into half-inch-thick strips for steak. She chucked the whole lot of them into the freezer.

All Tami's got to do is thaw them and put them on a greased pan, Marlene said. Not more than two and a half minutes each side. Idiot-proof, isn't it? Where is she anyway?

Marlene did not know that Tamara had fled to the chicken coops just to avoid her, and that whenever Marlene left the ranch, Rudi threw out every last thing she brought. Now she was tasting the filter coffee Tamara had prepared. This drain water is what you drink? Marlene made a face. I just splurged on the most gorgeous espresso machine, the latest Faema with an electromagnetic pump, a real beast. You've got to come over and try it sometime.

She threw Tamara's coffee down the sink and put the kettle on.

As they waited for the water to boil, Rudi folded the paper in half and showed it to her. Taking the paper from him, what Marlene saw first was the *Shanghai Express* publicity still. She'd always liked that picture. They looked so good together—Jo really knew how to dress women. Then she saw the obituary notice. A heart attack, liver problems.

Instinctively, she turned away, busying herself with the coffee beans and the bean grinder. She hadn't mentioned to Rudi that she'd seen Anna May just a few months back, before the year had ended. Had Anna May been ill then? She'd said nothing, looked fine as ever. Older, sure, but that face, that figure? She could upstage anyone in a scene at any time. To think they were just two bits of calico looking for a big break when they first met. She heard Rudi say: Wasn't she one of your special friends?

Oh, Marlene said. I would hardly call it *that*—

What would you call it?

Walking away from Marlene toward her car, Anna May had looked to be in such good shape. That woman was always making a late entrance and an early exit. No, Anna May had not been a special friend. She was the one who'd got away.

Marlene swallowed.

Come now, she said to Rudi, trying to distract herself by teasing him. Are you jealous?

He laughed. Jealous?

Don't think you know it all, she said, pushing away the paper and trying to sound playful. Like I always said, sentimental love is better with a man, but romantic love is better with a woman.

And? he prompted.

And I am a sentimental person, she said. I love women, she added. I just can't live with them.

But, Mutti, Rudi said, not unkindly. Who could you live with?

She was not sure how he meant it and so pretended not to hear him. Surely the water for the coffee was ready. Marlene strode over to the stove top with a slight limp. Her leg was hurting again, but she did not want Rudi to worry. She rinsed out the filter paper and filled it with freshly ground coffee, pouring scalding-hot water over the cone in a steady spiral. Breathing in the bloom, she turned back to Rudi, to see if he was still looking at her. She was glad that he was, and to keep his eyes on her she said: What? Her voice came out husky, but he would not know why. What are you looking at, she repeated, egging him on.

Your legs, he joked. What else?

How well he knew her, didn't he know just what to say! She let herself cheer up at once. Back in her element, Marlene pursed her lips and narrowed her eyes, smiling at him as if he were a man she'd just met, not the stoic who had sheltered in her shadow for decades, whom she came over to play house with whenever she was burned out from everything else she'd orchestrated to happen around her.

Darling, she said, the legs aren't so beautiful. I just know what to do with them.

The Most Handsome
Bureaucrat in
North-Rhine Westphalia

13

Chop up my body when I die, Marlene said to the Chinese maid, so you can get it out of my apartment unnoticed. It's possible, I should think, with a good boning knife. Double-line my Louis Vuitton trunk with trash bags, the one with dinky trolley wheels. No body bags or stretchers. Take the service entrance. Make multiple trips.

I'll never forgive you if a picture gets out.

Did you see that picture of Garbo in the papers?

Ugly, ugly, ugly—and her hair so long!

The newspapers say it's liver cancer. Smelly pee suits her. Watching the sugar bowl like a hawk, so her maid couldn't pinch even one cube! I'm so much nicer to you, aren't I, choupette? By the way, that woman had *huge* feet. She tried to avoid wide shots in all her movies.

They got her, dammit.

All those years of hiding for nothing.

They got her good.

WHEN MARLENE'S TIME finally came, hordes of fans followed her Parisian funeral procession along the streets of the 8th arrondissement to her favorite church, La Madeleine. Some came turned out in coattails like Madeleine de Beaupre in *Desire*, others festooned themselves with cheap black feather boas in honor of *Shanghai Express*'s Lily.

Had she elected to bed down with Molière, Balzac, and company for the burial proper, Père Lachaise would have gladly transferred some anonymous bones over to the ossuary to make room for the shell of her body, but Marlene chose to be laid to rest in the nondescript, unpretentious Friedhof III cemetery in suburban Schöneberg, near the house she was born in. She had not been back to Berlin in more than thirty years, not since her last cabaret performance at Titania Palast in

1960. Her body was freighted from Paris to Berlin in a lead-lined coffin, draped first in the French tricolor, then the American Stars 'n' Stripes. The German Schwarz-Rot-Gold was nowhere in sight.

Marlene had a long-running joke about her funeral service.

If she had it her way, the church doors would be minded by a beefcake bouncer, armed with an annotated list of her guests-in-mourning, and a basket of mixed carnations. The list would be divvied up into two columns: those who had Made It, and those who had Not Made It. A red carnation would be handed to the former, a white one to the latter. Between pews her guests would suss out each other's color-coded carnations: *You* bedded Marlene and *I* didn't? Ensue fervid catfight or fisticuff to the elegiac score of Bach's fugue in D minor, as the good pastor harangues: Blessed indeed, says the Spirit, that they may rest from their labors, for their deeds follow them! She laid it out once to Jean Cocteau, and he'd wanted to turn it into an absurdist play. Only after you're dead, love, he said, so I don't have to pay for the rights. In practice, of course, the city officials of Berlin were too humdrum for anything quite so lively, and Marlene might have been disappointed to know that at a simple graveside service, after her coffin was lifted out of an open black Cadillac, a Lutheran minister read the stock Twenty-third Psalm as she was lowered into the ground, and that was that.

Postburial a small scuffle did break out between a troupe of transvestites in secondhand organdy gowns holding up xeroxed posters of Marlene as Lola Lola in *The Blue Angel* and a band of jackbooted neo-Nazi skinheads who were attempting to sling feces onto her gravestone. Before the police were alerted, the transvestites had already driven back the skinheads, and after everyone left, they played Cher's "If I Could Turn Back Time" on a boom box to send off their dead queen, returned to the earth on a balmy May day as spring turned to summer.

But May 6, 1992, was still two and a half years away, and for now the maid was trying to shush Marlene as she expounded on various creative and gruesome ways her body could be disposed of on the sly. Please, Madame, the maid said as she prepared to clean Marlene. Bad luck to say such things! She placed her two palms together and shook them toward the ceiling.

Then the bath towels came toward Marlene, and she struggled to get free.

I don't need a wipe down, Marlene said, I just need more perfume. I want the whole church to smell fresh and green as a Saint Laurent fougère when they're praying over me. Marlene spritzed the air around her generously, like her flacon of branded fragrance was a spray can of air freshener. There, she said. Nice again. The maid pointed hesitantly to a damp shape on the sheepskin spreading out from under Marlene. What? Marlene demanded right away. What's that, she said, but now she felt the sticky wetness of pee on the backs of her thighs.

Marlene resolutely ignored the maid, keeping her eyes fixed on the TV till the maid left the room. *Oprah* was on. Marlene turned the volume up. She could feel the sodden maxi pad silhouetted against her thighs like a rancid, tumescent tongue. For a long time Marlene had been wearing sanitary pads daily to manage the dribbles of her incontinence, discarding them under the bed wrapped up in pages torn from *Vogue*. Listen, Oprah was saying, you can have it all. You just can't have it all *at once*. The squeak of unoiled metal made Marlene jump. She turned to see the maid pushing in the disused wheelchair, usually folded into a spidery alcove of the kitchen. Put that back right where you found it, Marlene shouted over the TV, I am not going to sit on that dummy! Marlene began throwing whatever she could get her hands on in the wheelchair's direction. A fork. She saw the maid ducking. Her peace prize medallion. Hey—hey, I got you, Oprah boomed on the TV. Lots of people wanna ride with you in the limo. But what you want is someone who'll take the bus with you when the limo breaks down.

Liberated from their weighted placeholder, the cut-out obituaries of friends, enemies, lovers, peers floated off the table like black-and-white confetti.

She tried to clear her head.

Look now, Marlene said to the maid. Let's be reasonable. First, turn off the TV, I love Oprah, but her voice is so loud, she needs to go easy. Stow that contraption, only invalids have any use for it. Chuck the basin, too. We'll walk to the bathroom like civilized people. I'm going to have a proper bath.

With Marlene leaning all her weight on the maid, they reached the bathroom on foot together. Marlene began to wheeze as they were nearing it, and the maid carried her over the threshold, setting her down on the toilet bowl.

The maid flipped the lights on.

Marlene had forgotten about the full-length mirror, from which a ghoulish old woman gaped back at her. She turned away as soon as she could, but not quickly enough. The maid ran the bathwater and helped Marlene disrobe. The legs that slid out from under the silk chemise were so thin and misshapen. What a hoot that they had once been insured by Lloyd's of London via Paramount for a million dollars. Everything became a fantastic joke if you could afford to hang around long enough for the punch line. The maid was about to help remove her bloomers when Marlene remembered the waterlogged pad between her legs.

Give me a minute, she said to the maid. Step out.

Madame, the maid said, I can help you, anything.

Privacy, Marlene said. Something you don't understand. Don't come in till I call for you. After making sure the maid shut the door behind her, Marlene removed her panties, fishing a line of toilet paper to wrap the pad up with. There was no bin in the bathroom, so the damp wad she tucked away as best she could behind a water pipe.

Ready, Marlene called.

The maid knocked and reentered. Checking that the temperature of the bathwater was comfortably warm, she lowered Marlene down into it slowly by the armpits. When Marlene was settled, the maid took the bath sponge to her, gently glossing over breasts and groin.

I'll never get clean this way, Marlene complained. Scrub harder!

Back in the room, Marlene sniffed the fresh scent of soap in a line down her forearm and rearranged her legs under the blanket as the maid toweled her dry. Some of Marlene's pubic hair, still a dark dirty blond, fell out. The maid was bashful, moving the towel quickly to disperse the hair. Marlene caught her eye and laughed. Oh you prude, Marlene said. We need some music, put on the Piaf LP!

.   .   .

A PROPER BATH, not a wipe down or a sponging in bed, but a real one with soap bubbles in a tub, was quite an occasion. Her onetime beau's unyielding voice filled out the dark corners of the apartment as the maid picked out fresh clothes for Marlene. The soiled sheepskin was no longer on the bed. Marlene felt plain without it. She saw it folded discreetly into a dry cleaner's bag in the doorway, as the maid came over with a selection of nightgowns and underthings. Marlene picked out what she wanted to be dressed in: mauve panties, a silk dressing gown. To top it off, a decorative antique Japanese kimono presented to her when she performed her cabaret years ago in Tokyo. The musicians had been late, and Marlene was so incensed she'd tried to push the kimono back into the hands of the apologetic organizer, who bowed so low his nose was almost touching his knees, as she proclaimed: Take back your bathrobes! None of you are to be trusted, I have not forgotten Pearl Harbor!

A trumpet solo. Edith was singing "La Vie en Rose" over the record player.

If you die, Marlene had said tearfully to Edith when she was very ill, I'll never sing "La Vie en Rose" at my shows again.

Edith died. Marlene went on singing "La Vie en Rose."

It was an audience favorite; Edith would have understood.

In the first place, Marlene had never really liked performing cabaret, but it paid so well, and she was in demand on the stage. It was the sixties, and the movies were overrun with skittish gamines like Audrey Hepburn. Roles for the screen still came Marlene's way, but they were small supporting parts, and she had zero interest in playing some ingenue's mother. What had any of them done to deserve her? At least on the stage it was still her show—people came out to see Marlene alone. She'd perfected her routines on her USO tours in the forties, having signed up as an entertainer for war morale with the Office of Strategic Services. Departing for "Destination Unknown" in the spring of 1944 with a fifty-five-pound luggage allowance, she managed to pack tropical uniforms, gray flannel men's trousers, combat boots, transparent Vinilite slippers, lingerie, one silk-lined Mainbocher cashmere jumper, one strapless brocade gown, and two long sequined dresses, one in white and the other in gold. Practical as ever, she carried with her three months' supply of cosmetics, labeled clearly in block letters using her nail polish, so she could put her face on by torchlight. North Africa was where she'd cut her teeth, entertaining GIs waiting to do battle along the Mediterranean with Rommel's Afrika Korps in Sirte and Tobruk. Their favorites were "No Love No Nothing," "Anny Doesn't Live Here Anymore," "The Boys in the Backroom," and of course, "Lili Marleen." With these performances she learned how to pitch her voice, time her laughs, and deal with hecklers. Marlene liked to open her USO shows hidden in the audience. Whenever she made her way onstage and began changing from a GI uniform to one of her sequined dresses in front of a thousand sex-starved active-duty GIs, they roared.

She would never forget that sound.

It wasn't long before she was one of the boys. She liked that about herself, and the boys seemed to like that about her, too. Luncheon meat spread thickly over malted milk biscuits with the back of a pull-ring can in Sirte. Nothing but K-rations for two weeks in the Ardennes, melting snow in a helmet to wash her face. Her only luxury was a special bar of soap for the hair that would lather in hardly any water. Marlene had no airs as she chatted with the GIs, warmed her frostbitten hands over a fire, listened to their stories. Her vinegar douche kit saw plenty of use. There was a sweetness Marlene sensed in each and every GI. They were so grateful for anything, even a film actress coming to see them, when they were the ones putting their bodies on the line of active resistance to earn everyone else at home their oblivious right to passive freedom. To Marlene, singing for them and bedding down with them hardly felt like enough. During a broadcast for the Armed Forces Network she forgot herself, launching into rapid-fire German and addressing Axis servicemen, when she was meant to be speaking in English to Allied soldiers: *Jungs! Opfert euch nicht! Der Krieg ist doch Scheiße, Hitler ist ein Idiot!* Sent back to L.A. on sick leave upon contracting pneumonia, Marlene was asked by the press when she would be returning to the movies. After being out there, she said, I don't know if I could concentrate now on keeping every eyelash right like you have to do here, you know?

.   .   .

THE ONLY CABARET Marlene had ever been nervous about performing was a Berlin show in the summer of 1960. It was her first time back in Germany since the war ended. She'd marched in on the side of the victorious Allies in 1945, and her fellow Germans must have been out to settle a score. Ticket sales in Cologne were dire, and Essen had canceled. The five days in Berlin were whittled down to three. Her manager was keeping tabs on the letters to the editor sent in to German papers ahead of her tour:

> Aren't you ashamed to set foot on German soil as a common, filthy traitor? You should be lynched as the most odious of war criminals. Signed, for all my German brothers and sisters.

> Artists like Marlene Dietrich and Thomas Mann knew that their homeland had fallen into the hands of a band of criminals. Should they have remained silent, just because they were Germans? Was Marlene perhaps not a better German for demonstrating that there were *other* Germans? Who showed more character: Marlene, who resisted all the lures of an admiring Hitler and went into battle without compromise against criminal Nazi Germany, or we, who bowed before the Nazi cross?

> It would perhaps be better for Marlene and for us if she stayed where she is. It would save her a lot of trouble and make it easier for us to forget the ardent enemy of the Germans, and to keep in memory only the great actress.

> Honored Madame, where do you get the nerve to put on a show in Berlin after your behavior during wartime? We recall like it was yesterday the shameful images of you dressed up in an American soldier's uniform, boosted up into the air by your ankles to kiss Allied sailors returning from decimating our brave naval warships. We wish you a correspondingly friendly reception readied by the German public.

Darling, I worry only about the eggs, Marlene had joked with the press in New York before boarding her flight. Eggs leave such awful gooey streaks! The American journalists laughed as she grazed the soft white feathers of the lapel with her fingers. You see I have the only swansdown coat in the world, she went on, milking it, and if an egg ever hits it, I don't know what I'll do. You couldn't clean it in a million years.

Marlene, right after the German tour, you go on to Israel. Then you'll be back in Vegas, before moving on to France. What is the hidden message behind the sequence of countries in your tour schedule?

If I wanted to say anything, Marlene said, I would have said it directly. That is what has landed me in hot soup with my people.

Marlene, do you think the opposition to you in Germany is a repressive expression of collective guilt?

I abhorred the Nazis, Marlene said, that is a fact. But I never once abhorred the country. I leave the rest up to the people to decide.

Marlene, do you identify more as German or American?

At the best of times, Marlene said, categorical limitations should be difficult to determine, in nationality as in gender. Why, please, should a table be male in German, female in French, and castrated in English?

Making ceremonious banter with American journalists in New York was vastly different from seeing Berlin like a tin toy city from overhead. As the plane circled Tempelhof airport, she felt woolly in the throat. So many years away, and Berlin had looked like the end of the world in 1945. Growing up in Schöneberg she knew Berlin was in her future. One day she would be old enough to cross the canal. Just a stone's throw from where their house stood was the fastest city in the world. She'd heard about the massive underground railway, the girls in drop-waist dresses who guzzled lager in dance halls and the boys in tweed berets who took their hands, the opera houses with painted ceilings, attended by women with rose-gold lorgnettes that could magnify the players onstage by a factor of three!

It was only a matter of time.

Seeing a whole bunch of Germans carrying large welcome cards waiting at the terminal in Tempelhof, Marlene was pleasantly surprised, but when she got closer, she saw what the signs said: MARLENE GO HOME! How efficacious, how economical, how wholly German

it was of them to have the signs read MARLENE GO HOME instead of
MARLENE GO BACK TO AMERICA! Her minder tried to shield and bundle her into the waiting limousine.

Marlene, what do you have to say about this greeting?

Is it true that you once said you would kill Hitler with your pussy?

She had to laugh as she ducked into her car. How had they got wind
of that? It had been a serious-frivolous remark she half remembered
making to goad the important men at a champagne brunch on the Riviera into some form of action or reflection. The war had not yet begun,
no one was even taking the threat of it seriously back then; rather, they
were trying to get into her pants.

Marlene, what is in your purse?

The frivolity of this question was refreshing, although the actual
answer was banal: other than her passport, the customized Hermès
mini held an assortment of strong painkillers for her bad leg. She
wanted to know: Why do you ask?

Because it is so tiny.

My costume, she quipped, as the door was shut and her ride
drove off.

Later that evening, the opening applause at Titania Palast in Berlin
was lukewarm, and Marlene did away with her signature drawn-out
"Hel-lo." With no fanfare, she opened with "Falling in Love Again." Her
vocal range had always been quite narrow, but she knew how to maxi-
mize it by singing *sprechgesang* style and performing popular oldies that
were low on technical difficulty but loaded up with misty-eyed nostalgia. Next up was a ditty she'd learned from a butch singer in a girl-on-
girl Damenklub all the way back in the twenties, "Kleptomaniacs":

> *Perhaps it sounds pathetic, but we find it quite magnetic*
> *Though our palms and pants get wettish, it is nothing but a fetish.*

Then of course "Lola Lola."

She saw in her head the audience picturing her as naughty Lola in
The Blue Angel, leg hitched up on a barrel. On the day she shot the barrel
scene, that cross-eyed sycophant Leni Riefenstahl had visited the set

and hovered around Jo with "craft questions." Marlene hated anyone who wasted someone else's time, and on a shoot, individual time was collective. Worst of all, Jo, whom everyone knew as a cutthroat tyrant, was patiently answering her vapid questions like an affable puppy, allowing her to look through the viewfinder as they discussed focus racking. Deviously Marlene began to scratch her armpit. When that did not make enough of an impression on Jo, she raised her leg higher and higher on the barrel, till finally Jo shouted at her from behind the camera: Put down your leg, Marlene, everyone can see your pubic hair! It worked wonderfully. The fishface was so scandalized she bade Jo goodbye, making some sanctimonious remark about "not distracting him from his lead actress." Bitch, please, *na klar*!

She began to feel the audience relaxing into her as she finished "La Vie en Rose," and when she got to the rousing "All Alone in a Big City," she made sure to credit the song to Wachsmann and Kolpe, dedicating her performance to them. Their Jewish last names had been erased from the annals of pop culture since 1933, a ruling that had not yet been revised; there were more urgent reparation issues for the new constitutions to grapple with. As the last bars faded out under the pianist's pedal, Marlene angled her face away from the microphone, lifting her cheekbones to catch the light. "Lili Marleen" came next, and she wanted to be ready for that. Everyone knew this was the classic she sang to American and French servicemen in English as they battled German contingents. Now here is a song that is very close to my heart, she said, sounding more confident than she felt. I sang it during the war. I sang it for three long years, all through Africa, Sicily, Italy, to Alaska, Greenland, Iceland, to England, through France, through Belgium—to Germany. She nodded at her pianist, and as the opening bars of "Lili Marleen" came on, she took a deep breath before she began to sing the German version:

Vor der Kaserne, vor dem grossen Tor
Stand eine Laterne, und steht sie noch davor.

It was very quiet as she went through the first stanza. At the chorus, she dropped her voice and bowed her head to the audience. It would be their choice to hold her up or leave her hanging. *Wie einst Lili Marleen,* she heard the words coming back. The audience was singing it to her.

She was home.

ELEVEN CURTAIN CALLS and two encores later at Titania Palast, Marlene locked herself in her dressing room, injecting her legs with cortisone and stuffing them back into their boots before hopping into her ride back to the hotel lounge for her Berlin after party. When she stepped out of the limousine toward the Park Hotel, there was a small crowd awaiting her, and Marlene was approached by a girl in a mullet haircut who tugged on the sleeve of her swansdown coat. She disliked it when people pulled on her, but she was in a buoyant enough mood so she turned around, ready to sign an autograph. The girl spat in her face.

The spit was warm on Marlene's cheek.

Her minder gasped, rummaging through her purse for tissue.

It is just as well Marlene Dietrich is an actress, the girl snarled loudly for everyone to hear, for she is a class hypocrite! She asks of the people, Where were you when the time came to resist the Nazis? And where was she? Living it up in America!

Do you want me to call the police, Marlene's assistant whispered as they walked on. Marlene shook her head.

If I were a rich and famous actress, I, too, would have put my feet up in a Hollywood mansion, the girl went on. But unlike the whore, I would not have made it seem like everyone had a choice in the matter. I would not have traded in my passport to suck American dick, I would not have made singing for Allied soldiers seem like a life's work, I would not have posed for *Vogue* in a GI uniform, as if war were a fashion statement, and I would not have proclaimed loudly that Germany begat her just deserts! Go back to America, two-faced cunt!

14

When Ibrahim asked Bébé to accompany him on a weekend trip to the Baltic Sea, she said okay. She had never been to the beach before. Because Bébé did not know how Europe was shaped or scaled, she was surprised when Ibrahim told her they would be on a train for eight hours.

So far?

We are passing from one country into another, he drew it out for her, France into Germany. They would take the sleeper train on Friday and arrive in Travemünde, an islet on the tip of Germany, at dawn on Saturday. On Saturday evening they would take the sleeper train again, arriving back in Paris early on Sunday. Are there not beaches nearer Paris, she asked. Yes, he said, but Travemünde was where his mother was buried. Sorry, she said. He told her it was an accident that had happened ten years ago, and he was no longer sorry, but every summer he visited to tidy up the grave. Bébé wanted to tell Ibrahim about the powdery smell of joss sticks and the burning of silver-leafed paper at the graves of ancestors she'd never met on the fifteenth day after the spring equinox, but she did not know how to explain it to him. I don't even know these people, she remembered saying to her mother behind her father's back. Don't talk like that, her mother said. If not for them, there wouldn't be you. Isn't that a way of knowing a person, too?

The train would leave from Gare de l'Est. From Paris they would pass Cologne, Hamburg, Lübeck. They met at the platform. Ibrahim was in a gray hoodie, and Bébé was in her swansdown coat. He laughed when he saw her. Ah, she blushed. You know, he said, as they bought hot coffee and cheap oily madeleines at the station canteen and boarded the train early, I can't understand anything about you. She wanted to know if that was a good thing or a bad thing. He said it was neither. Some things are just what they are, he said, as the train pulled out of the station.

. . .

BY THE TIME they got to Travemünde, the sun was coming up.

Ibrahim was still asleep when Bébé woke. She had a crick in her neck but felt well rested. Looking around, she noticed that at this point in the train's journey most of the other seats were empty. It had been a long time since she'd fallen asleep in a place that held fewer than ten people around her. Bébé watched Ibrahim breathe through his nose, his mouth pressed neatly together in his sleep. One of his hands was curled up into a fist that he tucked toward his chin like a baby. In the beginning the feeling inside her was neutral, then it turned soft and warm, but the longer she observed him, the more she was unable to shake off an imprecise nausea at having nothing in common with this stranger in the seat opposite hers. She could hardly stand sharing this space with him any longer. Her hands grew hot and they would not cool, even when she pressed her palms against the window, where they left an ugly, colorless smudge. When he stirred, her skin crawled. Then he opened his eyes and smiled up at her sleepily, and she was sure they knew each other again.

Day is new, she said, pointing at the light outside.

So are you, he said.

Ibrahim seemed to be in high spirits as they left the train station. He picked out an elegant café for them to breakfast in. The waiter wanted to take her coat, and this time she knew to let him. He seated her, laying a napkin across her lap. Everyone else in the café, other than them, was white. When she opened the menu and saw the prices, she kicked Ibrahim's foot lightly under the table, and said as softly as she could: Maybe somewhere else?

Don't worry, Ibrahim said, it's my treat.

No, Bébé said.

Hey, he said, touching her hand across the table, this is my part of the world. At this she relented. She understood homestead hospitality. Where would she take him if they were in Shanghai? There must be nice places there, too, just like this. He chose eggs in green sauce, she raspberry-quark pancakes. He ordered mineral water, freshly squeezed

orange juice, and coffee. Having three different drinks to accompany
one meal was extravagant, but the order had been made and she
resolved to enjoy it. In the beginning, she found it stressful to be served
by a white waiter, but she quickly learned to ignore his presence as a
person, merely making room for the function of his gestures. Without
a doubt it was the nicest meal she'd ever had, but she was unsure if she
would like to do it again.

She was relieved that Ibrahim left a big tip.

Outside, the morning air was cool and wet. Perked up by breakfast,
they walked over to the cemetery. Bébé had never visited the grave of
someone she was not related to.

Are you sure your mother will be okay, she asked, with me?

I think she might even be happy about it, Ibrahim said.

The cemetery was quaint and quiet. Bébé's mother was still alive,
and she had never missed her in any real way. I am a colder person
than anyone can know, she thought. They made two lefts, then a right,
toward the end of the compound. There was no gravestone where Ibrahim stopped, only a hole in the ground. He backtracked and recircled
the cemetery. The only sound in the cemetery came from a quarrel of
common brown sparrows. Their chirruping call was one note, with
no melody—just a cry, not a song. Ibrahim went toward the shed of
an office they'd passed on their way in, and Bébé waited for him outside. His face was bloodless when he came back out. He was so pale she
wanted to ask him to sit down. Let's go, Ibrahim said. His voice was
trembling. He yanked her by the forearm and they left the cemetery.

THE SEA WAS not blue, as Bébé had always imagined it to be.

It was gray.

There had been a ten-year lease on Ibrahim's mother's grave at the
cemetery, and the option for renewal, or an upgrade to any of the three
other tiers—twenty-five years; fifty years; in perpetuity—alongside a
discounted down payment offer, mailed to a Mr. Müller here in Travemünde, had not been exercised within the six-month grace period.
When the ground thawed, they'd dug up what was left of the unre-
newed graves, cremated them, and scattered all the ashes in the sea,

same as they did every spring. At the end of the day, it was still a business. Burning the dead is an act of mutilation in my mother's religion, Ibrahim said to the caretaker, it is strictly forbidden. Please accept my deepest apologies, the caretaker said. It was nothing personal.

Ibrahim explained all of this to Bébé in an even tone, without crying or hesitating, but when he was done talking, he stood up and said he would like to go for a swim. It's cold, she said. Yes, he agreed, you should stay right here. Okay, she said, watching him strip off his clothes. As he turned to go toward the water, she called out: Wait. He turned back.

I come with you, she said.

It's too cold, he said.

Still, she said, I come.

The water was not as cold as Bébé expected. She held her fingers outstretched, letting the sea sluice through. Aside from the long-dissolved ashes of Ibrahim's mother, she wondered how many other strangers' remains she was bathing in. As they moved deeper, she put her arms around his neck, and the backs of her legs over his hips. She could feel her nipples slide up and down against Ibrahim's skin as the waves nudged them back and forth. Looking back at the Travemünde shore Bébé could still see their clothes in a pile on the sand.

Nearby, there was a family with a russet hound. The hound nosed behind the child, who was raising an airplane-shaped kite in the vacillating breeze—it took to the wind, and the child let out a long happy shriek. Farther off, there was a handful of middle-aged couples strolling around the beach, and on the farther end of the beach, despite the chilly weather, a naked blond man was taking a dip in the shallows. Bébé noticed that Ibrahim was still moving forward, away from shore, even though the water was over their shoulders. She tightened her arms around him.

Ibrahim, she asked. Are your feet touching ground?

Yes, he said.

Bébé let a hand slip from Ibrahim's neck, and reached between his legs. In Paris, they had never even held hands when they were out, or embraced in parting. She rested her cheek against his so they would not have to look at each other, and when he was all warmed up, she tried to bring him into her body. Instead, he pressed a finger to her clit, playing with her till she pushed her face into his neck. She had not been with anyone since Marseilles. Everything that had ever taken place with her body, in Marseilles, Shanghai, or Taishan, had nothing to do with her. It had taken a long time, but now she was very clear about this. Occasionally in the dorm in St. Denis she touched herself at night, under the covers, when the Tunisian women were singing in prayer. She'd grown more than accustomed to their strong voices. It was a sound Bébé had come to love. Under the soft cover of their song she could bring herself to climax with her eyes wide open, without her breath shorting. Now she wanted Ibrahim to know she was giving something of herself, but there was nothing she could find inside. He did not seem to mind.

Buoyed by the undertow, they strained one against the other, the sliver of heat generated between their bodies conducted right away into the vastness of the water. When she was a girl, she thought that rivers, seas, and oceans were blue. Also, mountains at their apex must be a perfectly sharp point, and when there was an earthquake, the land was trying to walk away from itself. She felt weightless and numb when she came. Both her hands around his shoulders, she pulled him close. Bébé felt Ibrahim treading water. I'm sorry, she said. No, he said, that's the last thing I want from you. Everyone is always sorry for me, he said, his voice catching. Why can't you be the exception? The water was lapping close to her chin. Bébé, he whispered. What is your real name?

If I tell you, she said, can we go back to shore?

The current pushed them back lightly, then more aggressively forward, and lightly back again. Very softly she heard him say: Yes.

My real name is Bèibèi, she said.

He smiled at her sadly.

You won't ever tell me, he said, will you?

Looking at his face, she felt certain that this was the closest she would ever get to another human being. That was so far off from where she would like to be, it made her feel like crying. There must be a way to make him understand. She opened her mouth again, but he shook his head and touched his forehead to hers.

It's okay, he said.

. . .

BACK ON THE beach they put their clothes on and lay down in the sand. The sun was out strong, and Ibrahim seemed much calmer now. He propped himself on the backs of his elbows, looking down the shore. Close to the naked blond man, who had now assumed a meditative pose by the shoreline, there were two policemen in uniform manning a small outpost. One of them was standing outside the hut with a cigarette. Behind the outpost was a line of poles linked up by a red-and-white plastic chain. Some twenty feet behind the red-and-white poles was a HALT sign, followed by a tall wire-mesh fence. Beyond the fence were watchtowers spaced out at regular intervals with uniformed guards in them, and behind that, patrol dogs moving in a businesslike fashion. These barriers had been up ever since Germany was divvied up by the Allies into the Federal Republic of Germany and the German Democratic Republic in 1949. The beach on Travemünde was where the northernmost tip of the FDR met the GDR before it opened out into the sea. Across the gulf of the Baltic Sea were Sweden and Denmark. Every now and then in the past three decades, Swedish or Danish fishermen and coastal guards would encounter a couple of bloated East German bodies, sometimes half eaten by crabs, washed up on their shores. It was a foolhardy plan, but they must have been attempting to circumnavigate the inner German border by swimming to their freedom. Were things that bad there?

What are you looking at? Bébé asked Ibrahim.

Ibrahim told her that behind the red-and-white poles was East Germany. He drew a vague map for her in the sand. It showed a landmass divided in two by a zigzag. As an afterthought, he added an *x* in the middle of the right portion of the diagram. We are in West Germany (he pointed to the left side of the zigzag). Across the water (he shadowed the sea in with a finger) is Sweden. You can't really see from here, but Denmark's on one side, and Poland on the other.

And?

And there they are not free.

There?

East Germany. Aside from West Berlin, of course. He pointed to the *x* on the map in the sand. There's a wall.

A wall?

The Berlin Wall.

Who made this wall? Bébé asked.

Ibrahim sat up. We did, he said after a long pause, as if he had just realized that it was true. We built the wall ourselves.

Why?

Because—

But he did not know what to say to her. He shrugged. She nodded. He lay down, spreading his limbs in the sand. He turned away from her, searching himself for an answer. Nothing came, so he flipped onto his back and sighed, resigned to borrowing. Because there is no story of civilization, he settled upon a half-recalled quotation in German, that is not also a story of barbarism. He tried to make a circle with his thumb and index finger to lasso the shape of the sun in the sky. They had no sunscreen, and the tops of Bébé's shoulders were already starting to redden. Her back was so slender, it reminded Ibrahim of a kitten you could pick up in one hand by the wisp of its neck.

She was studying his cassette tapes.

He'd brought along his Smiths collection for the trip, all four of their studio albums and the one live recording. When she saw that he was looking at her, she said: Choose song, for me.

He reached for the orange tape, marked *Strangeways, Here We Come.* It was the last studio album the Smiths made before they broke up. He slid an earphone into her ear as he played "A Rush and a Push and the Land Is Ours." A flock of shorebirds flew by, steady and low. He sang along intermittently in English. She ran a sandy finger along his cheek. Do you want me to tell you what the song says? he asked. No, she said confidently, leaning on his shoulder and shutting her eyes.

THE SUN WAS noticeably lower when Bébé woke.

Briefly she closed her eyes again, observing that the color behind her lids was a warm blood red. She opened them: blue sky. She saw Ibrahim walking along the beach, near the line of red-and-white poles.

At this distance he seemed so small. She propped herself up on her elbows, watched his back recede, and thought about whether she was in love with him. A large white cloud passed overhead. Her eyes followed its shadow as it skated over the sand and disappeared into the water and she decided that she was not. *Je t'aime, je t'aime,* she used to practice to herself in the mirror at the Ministry, when no one was in the bathroom. The bathroom had a good echo. She practiced it not because she thought she would one day have reason to say "I love you" in Paris, but the very opposite, because she knew she would never get to use it.

She turned back when she heard shouts.

The policemen appeared to be yelling at Ibrahim. She saw him skip over the red-and-white chain, breaking into a jog past the HALT sign, triggering a trip wire with a yellow flare. More shouting now, through a loudspeaker, from the watchtower on the other side. The policemen on this side ran all the way up to the red-and-white line, calling out to Ibrahim, but they followed no farther. Ibrahim stopped short at the fence and began to scale it. Everything was happening so quickly. Bébé stood up and called out his name once, then a second time, as loudly as she could, with the force of her whole body. Turning in her direction he shouted something. She could not hear him, but she saw his mouth moving. The dogs were barking behind the second fence. Ibrahim did not look back again. At the top of the fence he jumped over. Bebe watched him land in the sand on the other side, pick himself up, and go on running.

He was reaching the watchtowers.

The voice over the loudspeaker was very powerful now.

Drei, she heard. *Zwei!*

Eins, she heard, and then gunshots.

15

What did the deceased shout to you before he crossed the line? the German police asked Bébé over and over, in their German-accented high school French. I don't know, she said over and over in her Chinese-accented basic-intermediate French. I don't know.

What Ibrahim shouted across the beach to Bébé was brought to light by the nude swimmer who witnessed the episode. He testified in his report: The boy shouted to the girl in English: *We'll always have Paris.* What is the meaning of *We'll always have Paris*? the police asked Bébé. The words they were asking her about were not even in a language she knew. They told her it was English. She said she knew no English. When one of the police officers translated *We'll always have Paris* into French for her, she started to cry.

Why are you crying?

I would probably have cried no matter what the meaning was, she thought soberly. She did not have the French for that. She had not eaten or slept in more than twenty-four hours.

What was the Turk doing?

He not doing anything.

What did he have to do with the GDR?

What is GDR?

Don't bullshit me, girl.

(Silence.)

East Germany (makes a strip with his hands). West Germany (makes an adjacent strip with his hands).

I don't know, I am in Paris.

What are you doing in Paris?

I am cleaner, I am maid.

What were you doing in Travemünde?

We go to dead people place and the beach.

Are you a Communist?

No.

Haven't all Chinese pledged allegiance to the Communist Party of China?

Only one Party, no to choose.

So you are a Communist?

(Silence.)

Were you trying to organize with Communist factions in the GDR?

I not knowing what you are talking.

Did you plan this together?

No planning.

Were you planning a violent act?

You checking already the bag. Nothing inside.

Was this politically motivated?

What?

Why did you and he go for a swim?

His mother in the sea.

His mother? The sea?

His mother. The sea.

Were you and the deceased lovers?

How is this love that you mean?

16

The Lübeck municipal police had Bébé in their custody for twenty-four hours. She was passed on to the Hamburg police, who held her for a few days before the federal department decided it was more prudent for Hamburg to escort her down to Bonn instead of having to send a functionary from the Ministry of Home Affairs up to Hamburg.

The foreign liaison officer assigned to deal with Bébé in Bonn had once been voted the Most Handsome Bureaucrat in North-Rhine Westphalia at a municipal social, where he was made to wear a colorful paper sash crafted by the secretaries. He was blessed, indeed, with a well-shaped nose, hazel blond hair with a neat side part, and a congenital fondness for conjunctive adverbs, with an especial weakness for "hence" and "nevertheless." Unlike the policemen, he was not in a uniform, but in a well-pressed suit, and his French was smooth. Thank you for complying with this interview, he said when they met, and assisting in our investigation. This all lent Bébé the impression that he would be inclined to help her. When she told him she was the maid of an actress in Paris, he even smiled at her and appeared to write it down. I appreciate your kind feedback, he said at the close of the session. Consequently, we will be looking into your matter, and sharing our findings as soon as we can.

He held the door open for her.

She hesitated.

Ladies first, he said.

Bébé would not have known the extent of the bureaucrat's efficiency. Even before meeting with her, he'd taken the initiative to fill out the outcome box in his neat handwriting: Best suited for immediate deportation. The meeting was mere protocol, an administrative formality before the paperwork could be processed. It was not a matter of his believing or disbelieving her. That was beside the point. His job was

merely to establish the most administratively expedient and diplo-
matically strategic means of handling each situation that came his way.

The Most Handsome Bureaucrat in North-Rhine Westphalia was
also the one who clarified the provenance of that curious line, *We'll
always have Paris.* Both his subordinates and superiors were irritated that
it was he who had the answer to this riddle. I have to admit, he said,
looking quite pleased, I'm surprised! Surely I can't be the only one who
happens to know this? It's a famous line from a Hollywood classic.

What movie?

Casablanca.

When was it made?

In the early forties.

The context of the line?

Humphrey Bogart says it to Ingrid Bergman as she leaves. He's
passed her his precious exit visas so as to facilitate her safe departure
from the city henceforth, away from Nazi collaborators.

A political film?

American propaganda in its time, but an epic romance now.

THERE WOULD BE no formal charges pressed against Bébé with
regard to the incident, though her case was officially stamped with
"public nuisance." No one wanted to mention Ibrahim, or the fact that
the real criminal charge here might have been manslaughter committed by East German police against a West German citizen. Both states
hardly wanted relations to sour further. At an early meeting, the Most
Handsome Bureaucrat in North-Rhine Westphalia had raised the possibility of using the tragic aspect of the incident as a creative catalyst
to call for reunification. The ambiguity herein can be played to our
advantage, he proposed. We have only to frame the incident correctly
for the media, hence influencing the groundswell of public opinion.

Have you gone out of your mind? his boss said quite abruptly.

Sir, he said, looking hurt. I'm sorry?

Did it escape you, his boss said, that the deceased minor is a Turk?

Ah, the Most Handsome Bureaucrat in North-Rhine Westphalia

rose to the occasion, in fact you are mistaken. He is German, I made sure to check. His mother was Turkish, but his father is German, and we emphasize of course the father and his youthful age—

Both sides will be at our throats, his boss said. Racists, one side yelps. Mongrels, the other hits back. I certainly will not be caught dead in the crossfire. Pun unintended, he added quickly. You see how dangerous words can be? These days a man can hardly speak two sentences before he is attacked for being this, or that. No one knows what they're talking about, but everyone wants to be heard. We should hold our breaths and pray for this incident to sink with no trace. We engage only in undertakings whose outcomes we can be certain of, his boss remarked in closing. The moral pose of leadership is maintained via foregone conclusions.

The Chinese girl was an incongruous part of the state narrative; what was left were the logistics. It would have been most economical for them to send her on to France, and have their neighbors do as they saw fit, since she had cited Paris as her last port of call, regardless of whether her attempts at personal biography were true ("prone to fancy," the Most Handsome Bureaucrat in North-Rhine Westphalia noted circumspectly under character assessment), but they had so recently tussled over a whole boatful of Lebanese refugees, and France had ended up bearing the cost of that. There was no point in pinching pennies over one Chinese girl, and in any case, it would require even more paperwork to have her sent to France.

It was cleaner for everyone to repatriate her directly to China.

His boss signed off on the deportation recommendation, and the Most Handsome Bureaucrat in North-Rhine Westphalia made a photocopy of the approved memo. Filing it away neatly, he leaned back in his swivel chair and took a quick moment to admire his empty in-box, which would soon be full again. C'est la vie.

17

The shackles were not removed from Bébé's wrists except during mealtime, and those around her feet were not removed at all. Her shoelaces were confiscated, though they'd returned the swan coat, the Smiths tapes, and the Walkman. She did not understand why they removed her laces, her shoes looked so strange without them. The last to board the plane from the back door, she was escorted to an empty row at the very end of the cabin.

The flight attendants were tall and attractive, in navy-blue uniforms. Bébé had never imagined she would one day be a passenger on an airplane. She had only seen them in the sky, and marveled that they did not fall down when they must be so heavy. She tried to count the hours but fell asleep midway. Wrists clamped together, she shimmied the window shade up with her fingers. They were up in the sky, and the clouds were so fluffy. The land below was incredibly far away. They must already have passed Paris. Hot meals were served on tiny trays. Each time they unlocked her handcuffs for the meal, a stewardess sat beside her to keep watch, and she ate as slowly as she could. As the plane commenced its descent and the air pressure in her ears began to pop, Bébé gazed out at the huge landmass growing closer. That could only be China, she thought, with an unmistakable tug of pride.

She wanted to see the Great Wall from above—in school they had been told that it was the only man-made object in the whole world that was visible from the moon. Sadly, she couldn't seem to find it, but tried her best to feel glad to be home. It must not have worked, for when the runway jumped into view she hoped the plane would crash, so there would be no need to begin again. Then she took it back because that would not be fair to everyone else on board. The wheels greased the ground lightly in a smooth landing, as a pleasant voice over the PA system welcomed them to Shanghai and announced the local time.

Ground staff from the airline, a graying brunette with a stern brow, came up to collect Bébé from the cabin crew. Finally both cuffs were unlocked, and she stretched her ankles. Her shoe fell off.

May I, she said in French as she pointed to her laceless shoes, something to keep it together?

Right, the ground staff said in Mandarin. Let me look around.

Bébé noted the white woman's strong Beijing accent—nothing could really surprise her anymore. The ground staff came back with a handful of cable ties. They'll have to do for now, she said to Bébé, better this than nothing. Better this, Bébé echoed, than nothing. Mandarin on her tongue was easy, intimate as breathing. When she finished lacing her shoes up, she was ready to step off the plane. Before she was brought to immigration, she asked to use the bathroom. When Bébé saw the squat toilets, she almost laughed out loud: she'd forgotten they existed. Sidestepping the pail with the scoop of water meant to act as a manual flush, and the besmirching stool that had fallen out of bounds of the latrine's canal, she held up the end of her coat daintily, careful not to soil it. Back in the hall, she was dumbfounded by the sight of Chinese people in large numbers again. The ground staff cut through to the front of the line and had a few words in private with the frizzy-haired Chinese officer sitting behind a counter, who did not bat an eyelid as the situation was explained. Bébé was handed a provisional document. Even if you were using a fake name in Europe, the ground staff said, please put down your real name here. She filled it out. The immigration officer stamped it with a firm hand, already looking past her disinterestedly to call out: Next!

I did not even get to tell my story in my own words, Bébé thought as she walked away. PROGRESS AND LEAP FORWARD TOGETHER read the slogan hung at the far end of the arrival hall, white characters on a red banner. Under the banner was a money changer. She approached him with whatever was in her purse. She guessed that he quoted her a poor rate, but having no point of comparison, she did not feel like she could ask him for a more equitable exchange, and so accepted whatever amount of yuan he handed over to her, without bargaining or counting the notes.

.   .   .

AFTER CHANGING BUSES three times, once at the main station and then at increasingly smaller transit stops, Bébé reached the lane house on the western tip of Wujiaochang two and a half hours later. The sun was setting as she climbed the old steps to the third level, where she'd rented a room with a few other colleagues from the factory. Running her hand along the staircase railing, she sensed that she'd returned out of curiosity rather than familiarity. The unit was vacant, and she could not say that she was sad to find the place empty. In fact, if she'd found the other girls here, she would not have known what to say to them.

One floor down, she could smell fragrant garlic being sautéed in the kitchen on the stairwell. It was dinnertime. Looking for someone? an old woman asked as she flicked salted fish this way and that. Bébé shook her head. She doesn't live here anymore, she said as she passed the old woman and went on her way.

There had been a red-braised beef noodle shop with a faded awning Bébé frequented near the sports stadium, where she sometimes went with her colleagues to watch free baseball games on weekends. The other girls would cheer their favorite players on, calling out their jersey numbers. Once, the visiting team scored a home run, and the ball hit Bébé's shoulder. She admired the bruise on her flesh for a week. Every day it presented a slightly different shade. Near the stadium was a single-screen cinema where they treated themselves to a movie on occasion, and a short bicycle ride from the cinema was a university.

Not much had changed on that alley.

A billiard hall had sprung up, and some boys were showing off their tricks. The noodle shop was still there, clear plastic flaps demarcating its entrance. When she stepped in, there was still no menu. Taking a seat, she called out her order without having to ask what they served. When the noodles arrived, they tasted the same as they ever had. A hint of cumin and cinnamon in the tomato-and-beef broth, the noodle dough pulled by hand. Ravenous, she ordered a second bowl, just broth and noodles this time. It was cheaper without the meat. Drinking the soup down to the last drop, she then paid and left. There was nowhere to go. Passing the cinema on the street, she went in. The garrulous ticket boy, who looked about her age, informed her that the last screening of the evening had just begun, Hou Hsiao-Hsien's *Daugh-*

ter of the Nile. It was a Taiwanese film, he added clandestinely, for which reason it was not widely screened in Shanghai, but they worked with someone who circumvented the system.

Are you from Fudan, too? We get a student discount.

I'm majoring in life, she said, in a deliberately rustic accent.

The boy blinked. She handed him the full price for the ticket, even though she did not know what she would do once her money ran out.

IN *DAUGHTER OF THE NILE*, a listless Taiwanese girl sporting a fashionable perm goes to night school and waitresses at Kentucky Fried Chicken in the heart of Taipei, even as she tries to keep her family together. Hsiao-yang rides a scooter in shades, listens to American pop on the jukebox in a nightclub her brother owns, and even gets a whole cream cake for her birthday, but her friends are leaving Taipei soon, and the older boy she likes is involved with the wrong people. She finds solace in a pet puppy, and the cutesy Japanese *shōjo manga* she is reading in Chinese, *Crest of the Royal Family*, whose lead character is Carol, a rich American teenager studying Egyptology in Cairo, where she falls in love with Memphis, a teen pharaoh she awakens from the dead.

Bébé sank low into her seat after the movie to see if she could sleep the night in the cinema, but a hunchbacked woman with a broom came in and swept her out. The boy who had been manning the ticket stand was smoking on the steps.

Some coat, he said, nodding over at her. Imported?

She ignored that and asked: Got a cigarette?

He offered her his pack and asked how she found the film.

I'd really like some of that fried chicken, she said.

He seemed surprised by her answer, but it made him smile. Yeah, he said. Too bad there's no Kentucky Fried Chicken here, huh?

Well, she said, there's no Kentucky Fried Chicken in Paris either.

Sure, he said, not taking her seriously. A whole bunch of my classmates took the train from Shanghai to Beijing just to visit KFC, he scoffed. "Unity-building class trip," they called it. Don't people have anything better to do with their time?

Wait, she said. There's one in Beijing?

First one in all of China, he said, everyone knows that, no?

For some reason, she said, taking a long drag on her cigarette, I'm the sort of girl who's always the last to know. Her gaze was far off as she blew smoke into the night breeze. So, she asked lightly, how was the chicken?

They couldn't stop talking about it, he said. They said fast food is a kind of freedom.

She burst out laughing.

What? he said.

I don't know, she said with a shrug.

He studied her for a moment before asking: What is your name?

My name is Bèibèi, she said, and then she started to laugh again.

What's so funny, he wanted to know.

Nothing, she said. Can I have another cigarette?

18

Marlene's new maid was Algerian, from a maid agency. The refugee pilot program had been put on hold as the pro bono lawyer reconsidered her life goals, decompressing over Swedish deep-tissue massages at the behest and expense of Papan.

The Algerian kept a clean house and made no complaints clearing Marlene's waste, but she cleaned as many as ten houses on a daily basis, and was not one to dawdle and sit by the TV with Marlene, or run out and buy pastries for her.

Madame, the maid said pridefully. Some of us are on a schedule.

Marlene never had a nice word for the maid after that, picking on everything from the way she folded the blanket to the sound of the vacuum. In turn the maid was ungentle and curt. Every time Marlene reached for her piss pitcher she almost knocked it over, because the Algerian maid never thought to place it with the handle turned out, the way the Chinese maid used to. Marlene's skin itched terribly now that she'd grown used to having moisturizer rubbed into her back, her armpits stank of rotting flowers more than ever, her nails were so long she broke them off with her letter opener. No more their weekly clipping, and she'd forgotten how she used to get by, biting magnifying glass between teeth as she tried to trim her nails without lopping off the tips of her fingers.

IT HAD BEEN weeks, too, since Bogie last called.

The first week Marlene kept up with putting her face on. The second week, she took the phone off the hook. You won't be calling? More like I won't let you. The third week she put the telephone back on the hook again, sprayed perfume under her arms. The fourth week she told herself not to be stupid, she'd known this from the start, how else would it have ended, when he was eighteen, and there was so much life out there, waiting to be lived? When you were eighty-eight and you lived alone, you had to cut your losses as swiftly as you could. Why should she miss a Chinese maid who had hardly a hundred words of French on her, or a German schoolboy harassing her on the phone with poetry?

Marlene was furious now, but there was no one to take it out on besides the TV.

She counted to a hundred as she flipped channels, and when she lost count, she picked up her mother-of-pearl binoculars, focusing them on the framed portraits hanging on the wall across the room.

Most of the people photographed were dead, but from her bed now, she could see them smiling, posing, drinking, dancing. Let there be no doubt: she was beautiful. Marlene's favorite pictures were the candid shots where life had been interrupted in motion. Dolores del Río turning to whisper in her ear as they stood before a Frida Kahlo self-portrait in a gallery. Sharing fruitcake on paper plates with John Wayne, he in an undershirt and white suspenders, looking away from the camera, she in a crisp white men's shirt and black pants with brows raised, mouth caught chewing. Jo and her smoking in a fancy restaurant.

Marlene had looked over this picture of herself with Jo any number of times, but only now did she notice that the cigarette in his mouth was, in fact, unlit. She zoomed out, and in again. Jo had a matchstick at the ready in his right hand, and an open matchbook in his left. He was about to strike a flame just as the picture was made. Although she understood, Marlene found it difficult to accept that Jo must have put a match to the cigarette and gone on to finish it right in front of her at the restaurant years ago, but in this photograph, its unlit counterpart would remain forever pristine.

DINNER WAS A can of split-pea soup on her stove. Too thick, and terribly salty. There was no water within reach to dilute it, so she ate it like a spread over crackers. Some skinny misfit with messy hair was skulking about on TV. Marlene did not quite understand Winona Ryder and Chloë Sevigny, this whole new breed of actresses who prided themselves on looking malnourished and disheveled. The century was regressing as it reached the millennium. Growing drowsy by nine, she left the TV running at a low purr, dialed down her bedside lamp, and reread Hemingway till she dozed off. She'd called him Papa; he'd called her Kraut. Over the years, before he killed himself, Papa and Kraut agreed that they would have married each other if they weren't already married to other people, but both knew that neither would have said such a thing if either had been single. Close to midnight, French news stations interrupted a late-night comedy to broadcast live footage of hordes of East Berliners passing through the Wall into West Berlin. When Marlene woke at six, reaching for the half-full Limoges pitcher bleary-eyed, she saw young punks holding hands and dancing on the Berlin Wall. She had slept through something momentous. Her hand shook as she replaced the pitcher under her bed. Striking the side of the frame, the pitcher broke.

Later that morning, when the Algerian maid came in, the dank odor of urea was very strong. Marlene was sitting up straight in bed. The TV was still on. Look, Marlene said to her, eyes glassy and blood-shot. The Berlin Wall has fallen.

The maid nodded and got to cleaning. Whatever was on TV had nothing to do with her. Seeing the broken pitcher, she asked: Madame, might you need a new bedpan?

The words reached Marlene from far away.

A bedpan? Marlene repeated slowly. The maid stood by. Do you know where my pitcher is from? Marlene demanded. Do you know that only porcelain of a certain quality can be stamped Limoges? Her voice was growing louder and louder. *Where are my lilies?* Get out. Get out of my sight!

19

Bèibèi bought a hard-seat express ticket from Shanghai to Beijing. There was an old man in her seat when she boarded the train. She showed him her ticket. He stared back defiantly. She stood the six hours to Beijing, listening to the Smiths till the Walkman's batteries went flat. When the man standing beside her yawned, his mouth smelled of gasoline, and she held her breath till he was done. As the train pulled in to Beijing, everyone rushed to exit before the doors opened, jostling up against one another. She waited for the other travelers to vacate the train before stepping out.

There was a friendly ink-brush portrait painter on the platform.

What a beautiful coat on a beautiful girl, he exclaimed when Bèibèi was passing him by, would you be so kind as to stay still for a minute or two? In fact the coat was very dirty by now, more cygnet gray than swan white, but she supposed no one here could tell the difference. Tan-skinned cross-country laborers lugged their belongings in red-white-and-blue market bags, and a ways ahead a pair of lovers was parting. The boy was in tears. The girl wore her hair in pigtails. The painter announced he was done. He showed her the sketch. The face hardly looked like Bèibèi's, but she had to wonder if the sadness in its eyes was true to life. For a quick sketch, it had its merits. She smiled at him, turning to go.

Hey! he said. Eighty yuan.

Eighty yuan? She was confused.

A man's got to eat, the painter said. I can't be sitting around making portraits for free all day, can I?

But I didn't ask you to make a portrait of me.

Look, miss. You stopped, you posed.

Bèibèi began to walk away. He shouted after her as he tore up the rice paper with her likeness: What's eighty yuan anyway to a slut like you who'll put out for a coat like that?

· · ·

WANGFUJING WAS EASY to get to, it was in the city center. People thronged the boulevard. Kentucky Fried Chicken gleamed like a temple, fronted by a life-sized statue of a four-eyed foreigner in a cream-colored suit with a beribboned bow tie. He was all smiles. Bèibèi crossed the street toward the statue. Provincial geriatrics squinted in the sun as they headed in the opposite direction, toward Tiananmen Square and the mausoleum, to pay their respects to the Chairman. Passing an electronics shop on the thoroughfare, Bèibèi ducked into it, purchasing shiny new batteries for the Walkman. She put on the earphones and looked through the tapes for the orange one, *Strangeways, Here We Come.* The first track was her song. She might not have known the meaning of the words, but by now she knew exactly what sound came after which note, could have sung the whole song out loud by ear if she wanted to.

In KFC Bèibèi joined the queue.

The patrons in here were not like the people in the square, sun-beaten faces upturned with slack-jawed amazement at every building without discernment, thick-waisted men and women in drab olive jackets with large shiny buttons. They were trendy teenagers chatting over Cokes and fries. How they had surmised these fashions it was hard to say, when all manner of foreign influence had been banned here. Girls sported hoop earrings against soft-permed hair. One boy was in blue jeans. He'd tucked in his shirt in the back so the brand label, red stamped on a brown leather patch, might be noticed. KFC was a place to see and be seen. It was far from the homely grime of cheap eateries with huge portions, where you would be elbow to knee with a troop of drunk laborers in the corner asking for extra rice, swearing their mouths off. Nor was it like the formal restaurants with starched tablecloths and electric candelabras you could go to if you had money. Those were stifling, too quiet, and you would have to worry if you were using the cutlery the right way. At KFC you paid up front and sat yourself wherever you pleased, amid pleather booths, plastic tables, full-length windows. KFC was casual, anonymous, and you got to choose what you wanted for yourself. Bèibèi reached the front of the line.

I would like a box of fried chicken.

Would you like to make that a meal?

Yes, she said to the cashier, as she looked through her money envelope. She was down to her last bills. And would you like to upsize the Coca-Cola, the cashier pressed on, and the side of mashed potatoes?

Yes, Bèibèi said. The biggest, please.

BÈIBÈI FOUND AN empty counter seat by the window.

The previous customer's tray was still on the table, and there were remnants of fried chicken. Thin, dark bones, eaten very clean. In a jiffy, a girl in a uniform came to clear the table with a spray nozzle and a dishcloth, just like in the Hou Hsiao-Hsien movie.

Thanks, Bèibèi said. The girl gave her a suspicious look and did not respond. Bèibèi set her meal tray before herself. Everyone else in KFC was eating in a pair or a group. She was the only person in the establishment who was alone. She felt very sophisticated as she slipped the swan coat off her shoulders, draped it over the back of her chair, stuck the striped straw into her paper cup of Coke, and sipped gently, careful not to make a slurping sound. She crossed her legs.

The fried chicken was piping hot. She bit into a drumstick.

On the outside, it was browned to perfection, and the marinade was like nothing else she had tasted. Inside, the hunks of white chicken flesh were succulent. What else did they eat in America?

Looking out of the only KFC in China, she could picture the guards milling around the perimeter, and the Chairman's rosy cheeks glowing down from his enormous portrait in the afternoon sun at Tiananmen Square. That prominent mole on his chin, which made him look so learned and stately, would have been unflattering on a man of less character. Thinking of the Chairman, Bèibèi sat up straighter. She wiped her lips on the napkin, squeezed all the ketchup out of its sachet, and started on the chicken wing. She had been taught in school that the Chairman could hear her thoughts, so she'd best be an upstanding little comrade at all times. Silently, for years, she'd greeted the Chairman good morning and good night whenever she could remember. This led her to believe that the Chairman knew everything, and when she started touching herself to repair what the teacher had done, she was afraid of incurring the Chairman's displeasure. Nothing happened, and she soon understood that her secrets were her own to keep. Truth be told, life had been a little easier to bear when she'd believed her burdens were shared, but try as she might, she could never go back to that.

She broke a chicken wing in half, the better to eat it.

Hi, she said to the Chairman in her head, how forward her tone was, speaking to the founding father in direct address. Guess what a man once told me in Marseilles, about you. He said you were rejected in your travel application to Europe when you were my age. That must have been a real long time ago, huh? I bet not so many people know that about you. Don't worry, I won't tell a soul. We're good. I mean, if you had gone off and never returned, you wouldn't have become our Great Leader, right?

Listen, could you tell me something?

If you went around the world and ended up back in the same spot you started from, is that the same as never having left in the first place? Chairman, I used to ask my teacher things. I thought he knew everything, because he had more words than I did. How could he be wrong? For an entire year he took me into the shed, and I let him. He told me I was the prettiest in the village and the smartest in class. He told me that even though I was a girl, I was going to go far in life. Yes, I said, as he shook my body, yes. We were lying in the shed after he'd spent himself one day, when he asked me which boy in the village I was going to marry when I was older. Is Bèibèi going to forget her teacher when she is all grown up? Is Bèibèi going to forget who taught her how to feel like a woman?

I told him I did not want to marry a boy in the village, I wanted to go out and see the world.

My precious, he laughed. If wishes were horses, beggars would ride! Know what I said to him?

When I get to the mountain, there will be a way through.

That was pretty quick thinking, right?

I never went into the shed with him again, but it was too late to forgive myself.

Chairman, did you ever make it to Paris? What if there's a way through, but I never get to the mountain?

. . .

THE ORANGY ROOF of the entrance to the Imperial City glinted in the sunlight. It was finished on each end with a dragon. The place was old, but Bèibèi's eyes were new. On each side of the Chairman's face were four red flags and four red lanterns, lucky eight of each in total.

The Chairman's had not been the only portrait at Tiananmen.

There had been five other portraits erected in the square in the same style, but in 1980, Karl Marx, Friedrich Engels, Vladimir Lenin, Joseph Stalin, and Sun Yat-sen were suddenly removed. Now the Chairman was all that remained.

There was just one more thing Bèibèi wanted to know.

But that, she did not dare to ask the Chairman's portrait directly, not even in her head. She wondered what it had really been like back in June, at that protest for democracy. How had so many people believed in the same thing at the same time? Was that bravery or stupidity? Had the client been telling her the truth in Marseilles, or was it all just embellished lies, to paint an ugly picture of China for the rest of the world to point their fingers at? How could anyone shoot their own people, if they were unarmed civilians asking for a good thing? If a massacre had happened at Tiananmen in June, how could anyone be enjoying fried chicken across the street at KFC in November?

Nothing so dreadful could have taken place at Tiananmen.

It was the People's Square, and everything looked so clean.

The sky was so blue. There was hardly a cloud. The Chairman's face was round and benevolent. When your portrait was that large, it was hard to do any wrong. The Great Leader was smiling down on her. He would not take his eyes off her. What could she do, other than smile back at him, too? There are mountains beyond mountains, and people beyond people. She was nobody. He was greatness. Bèibèi finished the last of her chicken. She licked the chicken grease off her fingers, wiping them down on a fresh napkin. All she wanted now was to keep her hands clean.

20

Cameramen slept under satellite dishes in two-hour shifts. Soldiers exchanged hats, as a passerby asked if there were bullets in their rifles. No, they said, grinning. A ring of waitresses working in a bar proximate to Checkpoint Charlie threw their shoes off to dance in their hosiery, moving to the rhythm of a street-side minstrel's accordion. A corner café's proprietor was handing out free cola. Another had filled up a squirt gun with beer, spiking everyone in sight with hops and barley. Boxy single-door Trabants crawled through jammed streets. There were foreign license plates aplenty, cars driven in from Kraków, Prague, Antwerp, all on tenterhook rumors of *revolutie, revoluce, rewolucja* simulcasted on European radio, power to the people! Men and women chipped away at the Wall with drills, hammers, ice picks. Those who could not get close enough were setting off firecrackers, blowing alpine horns, singing patriotic anthems. West Germans gifted East Germans bananas, flowers, sugar wrapped in newspaper cones, inviting them into their homes for coffee and brandy, crying and laughing like family.

THE TV WAS not a hollow glass tube.

It was a window, and it opened onto Berlin.

With the volume turned all the way up, Marlene had been glued to the screen for more than eight hours straight, without eating or drinking. As long as she kept still and focused on the hypnotic images, she could be part of a huge party that would never come to an end. She was dizzy and her ears were buzzing, but she refused to take her eyes off the TV, following with bated breath the crawl of a small construction crane that was inching forward to clear the rubble where a whole part of the Wall had come down. Watching the debris being removed, Marlene was unable to recall why it had been erected in the first place.

People were ecstatic. Their arms were raised, and their eyes were bright as they came through.

Farther down, where the Wall was still intact, they helped each other climb over with bended knee and clasped palm. A man put his hand through a fist-sized hole to light a cigarette for a woman in a yellow coat on the other side. Other than the cigarette and her mouth, the woman's face was not visible at this angle. She had beautiful lips, unrouged. Her cheeks hollowed attractively as she inhaled. Digging through a small drawer in one of her tables, Marlene unearthed an old cigarette butt, a vestige from before she kicked the habit a few years back after a near-fire in bed. Lighting up what was left of the stub, Marlene stared intently into the pixels. After a few false starts, she was able to time her exhale to the woman's, and then she was breathing Berlin in, too.

But all of a sudden it came to Marlene.

If she could see them—they could see her. To think she had been so careful, to think she had not seen a single sunbeam in years, but all this while it had not occurred to her that the TV would be their way in. Anytime now she would hear the zip of film whirling through its canister, as they pointed and started to shoot. They were out to get her, to make a picture. The TV had to go off before they found her. Panicking, she scrabbled around her sheets, but the remote control was not to be found in bed.

The power socket must not be as far away as it looked.

Marlene had walked over before with the help of the Chinese maid; now she had to be able to do it again. Clambering out of bed, she tried to keep herself steady in a standing position, but after taking three steps she knew she would not be able to go on. She thrust out a hand toward the table to support herself, upsetting her postal stamps and fan mail. She looked back at the bed but was unwilling to give up quite so soon. The TV was still blaring. Looking at the anonymous crowd celebrating onscreen, Marlene felt her marrow freeze. All their faces would be forgotten—why should hers be remembered? She felt sick, guilty, fatigued. This was not a party. It was a parody of a cycle she could not explain. Whatever will be has already been. Carefully, she lowered herself down to the ground into a leopard crawl, panting hard as she stabbed one elbow, then the other, to drag her body across the room. She was almost on the other side. The plastic snake of the TV's electrical cord dangled within reach. Her fingers clawed forward.

Everything went dark, and Marlene could not see or hear a thing other than the strain of her own breathing. She could have been anywhere as she backed her body toward the safety of the wall, pulling her knees in and hugging them to her chest. Catching her breath, she tried for the nearest surface. Something snagged on her fingers. She pulled, and the blackout blinds came tumbling down.

Bright light flooded the room.

Pure starkness forced Marlene low to the ground as she shielded her face by reflex, forehead on carpet. Her eyes stung. Adjusting by degrees, she reopened them very slowly, afraid of what might happen next. Nothing moved. Everything that had been in the dark now looked incredibly precious in this light. A bright room. This was what she would like to remember. She made a fist, crushing sun rays like broken straws between her knuckles.

Her skin was tingling.

Marlene pressed both palms onto the floor as firmly as she could to push her body up. From a half-kneeling squat, she forced her weight onto her own two feet. Her shins were hurting so fiercely she thought they would snap, but before her legs could crumple, she locked her knees. Exhaling in a big, jubilant whoosh, she turned around to face the room, holding her arms out as wide as they would go to brace herself in position.

Choupette, she called out, excited. Look!

No one came, but she thought she heard a violin playing, many doors down. Bewildered, Marlene's voice wavered as she tried: Papi? She craned her neck to peer past the hallway. Still there was no one. Growing angry, she screamed so hoarsely it made her knees shake: Look at me! Marlene dug her fingers into the grooved windowsill, scrambling to maintain her balance. Even if there was no one here to see it, she was not about to back down. She turned to the window. Rusty and disused, the catch gave easily in her hands.

Marlene nudged the window open, just a crack.

A trillion light particles strike our skin at every second outside on a sunny day. Eight and a half minutes ago they left the surface of the sun, but they had first to wander blind and torrid for ten thousand years inside that massive star before they could escape to its exterior for emission. Marlene stuck her tongue out. With her eyes closed, the light tasted white and chalky. When she opened her eyes and looked up, she saw the sun burning itself out in the sky. Now was as good a time as any to finish what she'd started.

Taking a deep breath, Marlene began to stare the sun down.

Her eyes watered, but there was no way she was going to let anyone catch her blinking, not now. Steadying her weight, she threw the window wide open, exposing her body to the light.

Acknowledgments

Here I should like to acknowledge an aesthetic debt to my favorite actresses: Liv Ullmann, Setsuko Hara, Gena Rowlands, Monica Vitti, Hanna Schygulla, and the films of theirs I like best, respectively: *Cries & Whispers, The Idiot, Love Streams, Red Desert* (which made me laugh), *The Bitter Tears of Petra von Kant* (which made me cry).

Further, my thanks are due to Jackie Ko, Dan Meyer, Tash Aw, Ben Metcalf, KJ Lee, Nancy Koe, Kirsten Tan, and the Strand bookstore, whereupon in the fine-art photography aisle, searching for Nan Goldin's "Heart-Shaped Bruise," I was waylaid instead by one faithful Alfred Eisenstaedt monograph containing the curious picture (and its kinetic twin) that would begin (and end) this all.

To consort in closing with the sentimental studium of Barthes in *Camera Lucida:*

> The photograph is literally an emanation of the referent. From a real body, which was there, proceed radiations which ultimately touch me, who am here; the duration of the transmission is insignificant; the photograph of the missing being, as Sontag says, will touch me like the delayed rays of a star.

A Note About the Author

Amanda Lee Koe was the fiction editor of *Esquire Singapore,* an honorary fellow of the International Writing Program at the University of Iowa, and the youngest winner of the Singapore Literature Prize for the story collection *Ministry of Moral Panic.* Her working manuscript for *Delayed Rays of a Star* won the Henfield Prize, awarded to the best work of fiction by a graduating MFA candidate at Columbia University. Born in Singapore, she lives in New York. This is her first novel.

A Note About the Type

This book was set in Albertina, the best known of the typefaces designed by Chris Brand (b. 1921 in Utrecht, The Netherlands). Issued by the Monotype Corporation in 1965, Albertina was one of the first text fonts made solely for photocomposition. It was first used to catalog the work of Stanley Morison and was exhibited in Brussels at the Albertina Library in 1966.